Hopelessly Devoted

The Rocker's Legacy Wedding Collection

USA TODAY & WSJ BESTSELLING AUTHOR

TERRI ANNE BROWNING

Hopelessly Devoted to MIA

BOOK 1

CHAPTER 1

MIA

Stomach tossing, I looked at the selection of beautiful wedding dresses. Instead of trying to decide which one I thought would look perfect to get married in, I was doing my damnedest not to puke on everything.

Pressing a hand to my stomach, I tried to breathe through my nose, hoping to calm the urge to vomit Exorcist-style.

Morning sickness was bullshit.

More like all-day sickness.

A soft hand touched my back, rubbing in soothing circles, while her other hand pushed a can of lemon-lime soda into both of mine. "Sip slowly," my mom urged. "It really does help."

The fizzy drink tasted good in my parched mouth, but I only took a tiny drink, scared it wouldn't stay down. The nausea had been so bad initially that I'd ended up in the emergency room on multiple occasions just for fluids. Thankfully, I'd made it through the holiday season at home without it becoming that bad again, which for sure would have given my secret away to Dad. But he was still upset with me after what had happened with Nevaeh at the hospital while Uncle Drake had his liver transplant.

It appeared we were both unhappy with each other.

I still hadn't completely gotten over what he'd pulled by hiring Barrick to babysit me and keep it a secret. Everyone thought it was a double standard that I'd forgiven not only my fiancé but his cousins for lying to me for weeks about their roles in my life, yet I couldn't get past my dad's part in it all.

They didn't understand that I'd tried. For three years, I'd been trying, but I had a permanently sore spot that he'd caused in my heart I feared would never fully heal. I couldn't help the way I felt about what had happened, or that I couldn't get over Dad breaking my heart in a way that could only come from being shattered by one of the two people who were supposed to love me most.

Barrick, Braxton, and Lyla may have kept the fact that they were my personal protection—and my dad's security blanket—from me, but they hadn't even known me when they'd taken the assignment. Barrick's stepfather had forced him to take the job, and since Braxton and Lyla were part of his team, they'd also become part of my secret detail. But Dad had known what I'd wanted, and he'd gone behind my back, giving me the illusion of the normalcy I'd craved. My trust in him had broken right along with my heart.

After a few more small sips, the urge to puke slowly started to fade. At least for the moment.

Giving my mom a weak smile, I handed back the can of soda and pointed to the one dress that stood out among the others. She'd set up a private appointment with the designer. It was just her and me since both my bridesmaids were back in Virginia. Lyla lived there and was planning her own wedding, while Nevaeh was getting ready to start her final semester of college.

If I was honest, I was glad it was just the two of us—with the exception of the two bodyguards standing outside the front doors of the dress shop. I remembered dress shopping with everyone when Lucy was planning her big day, and she'd left the fitting in tears. Eventually, she'd returned, but not before Uncle Jesse, Uncle Devlin, and Dad had arrived to scold Aunt Layla, Aunt Natalie, and Momma for taking things too far with the crazy, circus-like wedding. It should have been a fun day, but Aunt Layla had kind of ruined it for Lucy and made me dread what should be my own magical day.

"That one is beautiful, a little bit sexy, and will hopefully hide this slight bump that is already popping up." Barrick had urged me not to get anything "too sexy." I didn't want to cause him a heart attack on our wedding day, so I'd opted to give his suggestion some consideration.

It ticked all the boxes I was going for—especially hiding the small baby bump that was quickly making itself known, even though I was only in the last weeks of my first trimester. Then again, as a dancer, I had always had a flat stomach. But even on my periods, I would get a little bit of a pooch from being bloated. With my uterus expanding to accommodate the baby, I was likely going to show quickly.

Momma glanced down at the black leggings and sweatshirt I'd chosen to wear that morning. The sweatshirt was bulky, hiding the little bump, but her green eyes still softened when her gaze landed on my belly. "I think you're right. Paul?" she called out to the designer. "Let's try this one first."

"Perfect," he said as he took the dress and carried it toward one of the changing rooms. "I just designed this one. You ladies will be the first to see it and try it on."

"And if we want it to stay one of a kind?" Momma asked casually, but it was a moot question. If Emmie Armstrong wanted something, it typically happened. Which meant, if she wanted my wedding dress to stay mine and mine alone, keeping hundreds if not thousands of other brides from wearing the same style to their own weddings, then she would make it happen.

I couldn't have cared less, but Momma was particular about certain things. And when it came to both my brother and me, those things only intensified.

"I'm sure we can arrange something," Paul told her with a wink as he stepped out of the dressing room. "There is a hidden zipper and clasp at the back, but if you can't figure it out, just give me a shout and I'll assist."

Typically, any number of assistants would be running around the dress shop, but because I was keeping my pregnancy a secret from most of my family—at least the ones who hadn't already guessed—Momma had requested it just be Paul during our appointment...and then made him sign an NDA before the appointment itself. Otherwise, my impending motherhood would have been all over the tabloids before dinnertime.

The woman covered all her bases—and everyone else's in the process. If she wanted something kept quiet, it stayed quiet. Or else.

Once the door was closed, Momma carefully took the dress off the hanger while I undressed down to the white strapless bra and matching panties she'd told me to wear that morning. The dress was a strapless white gown with woven fabric that was intricately embroidered and hand-beaded with seed beads and crystals. It had a sweetheart neckline with a bone-supported bodice and a sheer mesh panel at the center. The high-waist top sat on an overlapping skirt that had a thigh-high slit and a draping train at the back. The skirt's layers of tulle gave it a dramatic effect that screamed it was made for me.

As I stepped into it, I helped keep it over my breasts while Momma zipped it into place. Once she was done, she stepped back, and we both turned to look in the tri-fold mirror in the corner of the dressing room.

Before I could even take in the full effect of the dress, I caught sight of the tears in my mom's green eyes, and they instantly began to flood out of my own. I wasn't sure if it was the pregnancy hormones or just the intense, emotional moment a mother and daughter experienced during such huge, life-changing moments. We weren't just dress shopping. We'd done that plenty of times in the past for proms and red-carpet events. This time, it was different, because it meant that when I wore this dress on my wedding day, I would no longer be her little girl, but Barrick's wife.

"You look breathtaking," Momma whispered.

Blinking in an attempt to contain my tears so I could see, I finally looked back at the mirrors and gasped. The dress would need a few alterations, but otherwise, it was perfect. Not only would it hide the growing baby bump, but it made me feel beautiful. The longer I looked at myself, the more I loved the dress. I began to imagine how Barrick would react when he saw me walking down the aisle to him in a few short weeks.

Barrick had proposed to me on Christmas Eve three years before, and between school, work, and life in general, it had taken us forever to decide on a wedding date. Then I'd gotten pregnant out of the blue, and we'd decided that a quick, intimate wedding was a better option than the huge, gala-style wedding we'd originally planned for the next summer. Most of the plans had already been made, so all Momma needed to do was trim the guest list, move up the date, and dial back the event a bit.

My future husband was adamant I have his last name before the world found out we were going to be parents. To me, that wasn't an issue. My own parents hadn't gotten married until I was nearly two years old. I'd been their flower girl in the wedding that had taken place in a huge tent on the beach outside their house in Malibu. Barrick's Neanderthal personality, however, refused to let his child be born without us sharing the same last name. The caveman I was about to marry needed a wedding band on my hand to go with the engagement ring.

Once my pregnancy truly began to show, I figured he'd pound on his hard chest and roar to the world, "I put that baby in my wife's belly!"

It was enough to make me roll my eyes at his antics, but damn did it cause my panties to become uncomfortably damp just thinking about how much he loved and wanted me.

CHAPTER 2

BARRICK

Agitatedly, I flicked my pen between my thumb and index fingers as I sat at the conference table. Seller was droning on and on about all the private clients the company currently had on its roster, filling everyone in on all the boring details of the latest antics of entitled, spoiled billionaires who needed a little extra personal security. I'd already read all the reports, so nothing he said was news to me.

The fucker knew I didn't want to be there, and he was dragging out the meeting longer than it needed to be. I could barely stand to be in the same room with him on a good day.

It wasn't a good day.

He had been my godfather before my biological dad passed away. It wasn't long afterward that the man I'd once called uncle, the man my father had thought of as his brother, was shacked up and then married to my mom. I lost respect for him then. For both him and my mom.

All I'd been able to wonder was if they'd been sneaking around behind my dad's back while he was still alive. Had they even cared when he'd died? Did they have something to do with his death?

Growing up, I was taught to question anything that didn't feel right. It was what gave me better instincts when I was in the Marines. Then when I went into the family business, that background made me suspicious of everything that went on around me. Maybe that was why I was so paranoid about my stepfather and my mom. But I'd never been able to shake the notion that Seller hated my guts. He was obsessed with my mom—something I understood once I met Mia— but even after falling in love, I couldn't help wondering...

Did Charles Seller kill my dad so he could be with my mom?

Before Charles Barrick Sr.'s passing, Seller and I were close. But as soon as we put my dad in the ground, things changed. I could see the wildness in his eyes when he was around my mom. His need to always have her close.

Part of me understood that to a certain degree now that I had Mia, but what he felt for my mom was...off.

My gaze stayed on my phone, waiting for Mia or her mom or one of the bodyguards to check in.

Someone.

Anyone.

Fuck.

They were dress shopping, which shouldn't have been a cause to worry; nevertheless, I did. Whenever my little firecracker was out of my sight, all I could do was worry. Her father's concern for her safety hadn't been unfounded. She drew attention anywhere she went, and the majority of it was unwanted.

The woman was too beautiful for her own good. Too sassy. Too fucking sexy.

I doubted any of those were the reasons Nik Armstrong worried whenever his daughter left the house. His anxiety was related to Mia having been kidnapped not once, but twice by the same psychotic bitch when she was a child. The first time, a family friend had nearly lost her life. The second, Mia, along with the family friend and one of her honorary aunts, had been taken. Mia had nearly overdosed on whatever drug she'd been shot up with to knock her out for the drive to the farmhouse where she and the others were kept locked in barn stalls—a barn that had then been set on fire.

Both incidents had been traumatic for her parents, which had led to Nik having an almost PTSD kind of reaction whenever Mia wasn't with him or under the watchful eye of a security detail. At first, when the job was forced on me by my stepfather, I hadn't understood her father's reasons for putting a secret detail on Mia.

And then I met Mia, and it hit me like an anvil.

Too many men looked at her, greedy intent in their eyes whenever they let their gazes travel over her.

Over what was mine.

That was just my immediate gut reaction.

Once she personally told me more of her backstory, giving me the details that weren't in the dossier I'd been handed along with what I'd considered another babysitting assignment, her dad's borderline obsession over her safety made sense on an entirely new level.

His need to protect his baby girl became my own. The itch just beneath my skin that I couldn't satisfyingly scratch whenever she wasn't within reach had only gotten stronger, more agonizing, as time passed.

Now there wasn't just her security to consider.

She was pregnant.

And I was beginning to feel what Nik felt.

Keep them close.

Don't let them out of my sight.

Protect.

Protect.

Protect!

The word echoed inside my head like a bell tolling, making it impossible to hear anything else, not even the blood rushing through my ears.

My breath came faster and faster as each minute ticked away with no word from anyone, until it became too much. With a growl, I pushed my chair back from the table while Seller was still in the middle of some ambassador visiting DC who needed extra security. He called after me, complaining that I needed to know all of what he was going over.

It was something Braxton needed to know about, not me. He was the one on the East Coast. He was only a short drive from DC. He could and would handle the ambassador and his wife's visit. My top priority was Mia, and she was driving me fucking crazy. I needed to hear her voice before I threw a chair out the fucking window—or at Seller's head.

Either option might have relieved some of the aggression building inside me, but I knew the satisfaction would just be momentary. The only thing that would ease the beast inside me was Mia. Her voice. Her scent. Her touch. Only then would the calmness come and I could breathe easier again.

As soon as I crossed the threshold out of the room, my phone was to my ear. It rang six times before she answered, sounding out of breath. "Hey!"

"How are things going?" I asked, trying my hardest to keep my voice steady.

"Found my dress," she informed me, still breathing heavily. "Now I'm trying not to ruin it by puking all over it."

"They can make another one if you do," I assured her. "Do you need anything? Crackers? Maybe some toast? I knew I should have brought you some in bed before I left this morning."

"Momma brought me some right after you went to your meeting. It helped for a little while, but I've been feeling nauseated on and off all morning." I heard her swallow and then sigh in relief. "That tastes good."

"What does?" I demanded, mentally taking notes on anything that could help her through the morning sickness. Anything to avoid more time in emergency rooms with her stuck with needles so they could pump her full of fluids because she was so dehydrated from being unable to keep anything down.

"Lemon-lime soda. The fizziness eases the nausea for a little while."

I would stop and buy a trunk full on my way home. Or rather, on my way to Mia's parents' house in Malibu. We were still looking for our own place. Her parents wanted us to find something in their neighborhood. Mia wasn't a fan of that idea. We had a few listings we were considering. Mia was the one on the fence about them. I would have lived with her in a shack somewhere in the middle of the woods if that was what she wanted. It didn't matter to me where we lived or what the place looked like. I just wanted us in our own house.

Not even when we lived in Virginia while going to college had we been on our own. Braxton and Nevaeh were there too. It hadn't been a bad thing. We'd both liked having them around, but with a baby on the way, it was time for it to be just us.

"Are you going back to the house to rest?" I asked, collecting the rest of my stuff from my office. Pocketing my keys, I grabbed the files I needed to review later that evening and hurried outside.

"We actually have a few more errands to run before we can head back to Malibu. It's just small things that Momma needs my opinion on for the wedding." I heard a door shut and then her sigh of relief as she shifted around, getting comfortable.

"Put your seat belt on."

Her little huff would never not be sexy. "I was doing that, Beast. Relax."

"What kinds of things for the wedding?" I asked, unlocking the door to my SUV. The thing was built like a tank. It had the best safety features on the market, which I needed not only for Mia's sake, but for the little one who would be in a car seat for the next several years. "I'll meet you there."

"I'll have Momma text you the address," she said, sounding tired again. "I'm going to nap on the ride to wherever we're going. Love you, Beast."

"Love you, firecracker," I rasped as I started the SUV, waiting impatiently for Emmie to text me.

CHAPTER 3

MIA

Exhausted after another eventful morning of puking, I hobbled to the sink to rinse out my mouth and then reached for my toothbrush. Behind me, where Barrick had taken up residence, holding my hair and rubbing my back while I had my head in the toilet, he watched me with concerned dark eyes.

"We have to tell him," he said quietly.

I stiffened for a moment before going back to scrubbing the taste of bile from my mouth. Using that as an excuse not to answer, I avoided looking in the mirror, so I didn't have to look at him.

"He's going to find out soon. The morning sickness is getting worse, and you can't help whimpering when the stomach cramps start. He's going to hear you in here eventually, firecracker. Then things are going to become more tense between the two of you."

I hunched my shoulders, because in my head, I knew he was right, but my heart didn't want to listen.

"Nik loves you, Mia. This standoff between the two of you will only get worse, and then you're going to be upset on the day of our wedding. You'll be grumpy as he walks you down the aisle. I don't want to start off our marriage like that."

I lowered my head, knowing he was right. I didn't want to start our journey as husband and wife with anything but joy. "Maybe..." I shrugged. "Maybe I won't let him walk me down the aisle."

Behind me, I felt Barrick's tension fill the room. "Mia," he growled in a low voice. "Stop talking nonsense. You want him to give you away. I know you do. Stop punishing yourself as well as him."

Spitting out the toothpaste, I cupped my hand under the faucet to scoop up enough water to rinse my mouth. It gave me a moment to gather myself before I turned accusing eyes on the man I loved. "Stop being on his side!" I whisper-shouted. "Stop feeling sorry for him."

He scrubbed his fingers through his beard as he got to his feet.

The man towered over me, making me feel small, dainty—protected. I'd felt it from the first night I'd set eyes on him. Oddly protected mixed with a hell of a lot of lust for a complete stranger. It was a new experience for me, but not necessarily unwanted. The only thing that had changed since then was that I loved him now. Maybe I'd loved him a little that night too, but it had only grown the more I'd gotten to know him.

It made forgiving him for his part in everything easier. I couldn't live without this man.

The problem was, I couldn't live without my dad either, but I had to keep my heart blocked off from him. The hurt he'd caused was too much, and I shied away from it and him whenever the urge to let it all go began to twist at that painful spot in my chest.

Grasping me by the waist with one hand, Barrick smoothed his other hand over my bare midriff where my sleep cami had ridden up. My bump felt even bigger at this point and kind of squishy. We only had a week left until the wedding, and I didn't even know if I would still fit in my wedding dress by then.

He caressed his fingers over where our baby was growing, his eyes intense as he stared down into mine. "I hate that his choices hurt you, Mia. I hate that I was part of it. But you forgave me. You blessed me with another chance. Can't you find it in that huge heart of yours to forgive him too?"

Tears blurred my vision. "You don't understand. No one understands! He's my dad. Dads aren't supposed to break their kids' hearts. But he broke mine, Beast. He broke it, and I can't put the pieces back together, no matter how hard I try. And I've tried. Over and over again, I try. But it hurts too much."

Sighing heavily, he lowered his head to press his forehead to mine. "He never intended to break anything. All he wanted was to protect what he loves most in the world. You."

"Lies. He loves my mom most."

"Maybe in a different way, but his love for you is something that overpowers any other emotion he's ever felt." Barrick skimmed his fingers over my belly button. "Listen to me, firecracker. His need to protect you was something I understood from the moment I admitted how much I love you. But when we found out you were expecting, I understood that need on an entirely new level. This baby is a part of us, just like you are equal parts of your parents. His love for Emmie created you, and that means his heart is doubly invested. He doesn't have to hypothesize the bad things that could happen to you because he lived through nearly losing you. Twice. Just thinking about those things happening to our little one is enough to drive me insane. He went through it, Mia. He spent hours thinking the worst, and it nearly happened."

"But nothing has happened since then," I argued. "I was only a child then. I'm an adult now."

"Because you were always guarded. There's no way of knowing if another crazy person would have attempted to harm you over the years."

Frustrated, I stepped away from him. "He wasn't like that with Jagger. He didn't have him under lock and key twenty-four seven. My brother got to leave the house without a bodyguard shadowing his every move. He got to be normal."

His husky laugh filled the bathroom. "Trust me, firecracker. There is nothing normal about your brother. And if someone tried to take Jagger, they would pay your parents to take him back."

"This is not funny, Barrick. I'm being serious. All I wanted was a normal college experience. Just once, I needed a balance that was somewhere between the shadows of bodyguards and the spotlight that is always on my parents."

He caged me in against the sink with his arms. "Whether your dad facilitated our meeting or not, we would have eventually found each other, Mia. We are soul mates. It was meant for us to love each other. And once I set my eyes on you, there was no way in hell you would have gotten that normal college experience. Because I would have been all over you, protecting what is mine. Once fate stepped in and gave you to me, your chance at a life free of an overbearing bodyguard shadowing your every step was over."

A tiny smile teased at my lips. I knew every word out of his mouth was true. He was too possessive not to have taken over every aspect of my life—my security—once we'd met.

But he still didn't get it.

"Consider how much you love our baby already," he urged when I didn't respond. "However strong it may be, multiply that by a million. That's how much your dad loves you. Making sure you're safe is the only way he knows to show you how much he cares now that you're grown up."

Huffing, I gave in—a little. "Fine, Beast. We'll tell him."

"You'll tell him," he corrected. "I've already arranged everything. You just have to show up."

I narrowed my eyes on him. "You jerk! You played me."

He pressed a kiss to my forehead, which never failed to make me shiver and melt into him. "Nah, I would never do something like that."

"Liar," I grumbled as he walked into the bedroom. "You'll pay for this."

Laughing, he tossed a wink over his shoulder. "Looking forward to it, firecracker."

CHAPTER 4

Nik

Rodger pulled to a stop outside the building Mia had bought only months before to start her dance school. The stubborn girl had refused to take so much as a dime from me or her mother. She wouldn't even allow Barrick to help her with the purchase. Instead, she'd taken out a business loan.

My daughter had a good head on her shoulders. She'd found the right location, the perfect building, and then a reputable construction company to make all the alterations she needed done before she could open the doors to students. Like her mother, Mia had the brains for business without really trying.

With the list of parents already signing up their kids to be taught under her, she would be able to pay back the loan long before she even gained access to the trust fund I'd started for her when she was born.

It was a kick to the chest that she was so grown up and independent. She shouldn't be old enough to be a college graduate. I wanted to rewind time and go back to when she was a little girl, to when she idolized me.

Before our entire lives were turned upside down, our foundation forever and irrevocably shifted.

Pride filled me that Mia had done everything on her own, that she was already kicking ass in the new career she'd chosen for herself. But my gut remained unsettled, just as it had been since she'd found out about my role in her meeting Barrick. She was never going to forgive me. No matter how hard I tried to make it up to her, how many times I told her how sorry I was, there was still a distance between us that never shrank, no matter how close I attempted to get.

Emmie shifted beside me, her phone back in her hand. "Damn it," she groaned. "Babe, I have to deal with this really quick."

I lifted my brows. "We're picking up Mia to take her to the rehearsal dinner," I reminded her.

"It's about the flowers for the wedding tomorrow. I have to deal with it now." She leaned over and kissed my cheek. "You go with Mia, and I'll meet everyone at the restaurant. Marcus is already on his way here to pick you up."

"She's going to be unhappy with this new arrangement," I muttered. "She can't stand to be alone with me. At least with you here, she'll talk to me. Even if it's in stilted, cold monosyllables."

My wife gave me a sympathetic smile. "You'll be fine, I promise. Now, scoot. I have to hurry so I can at least make it to the restaurant in time for dessert." She brushed her lips over mine, and I grasped the back of her head, deepening the kiss.

When she pulled away, her breathing was labored, and her cheeks were pink. I grinned down at her. "I expect this to continue later tonight, baby doll."

"Trust me, it will," she said, licking her lips. Blinking her huge green eyes up at me, she sighed and pushed at my shoulder again. "Go. I'll see you soon."

"Fine." Opening the door, I stepped out, but I reached back in for one more kiss. "I love you."

"Show me tonight," she challenged. "I love you too."

Winking, I shut the door and walked toward the building. The door was locked, but one of Barrick's guards was waiting just inside. Seeing me, he flipped the lock and opened the door. Stiffly, he nodded toward one of the classrooms to his left. "Miss Armstrong is expecting you."

Of course she was fucking expecting me. We were supposed to pick her up for her rehearsal dinner with the rest of the family. I bit my tongue to keep from snapping the answer at my kid's new personal bodyguard. My frustration with the situation between her and me wasn't his fault, but I found it hard not to take it out on others, especially when I was nervous.

Fucking hell, I was nervous to be alone with my little girl.

"How the mighty have fallen," I breathed to myself as I walked down the wide corridor toward many of the reconstructed dance classrooms.

The sound of music playing caught my attention, and I paused outside one door. Surprised at the song, I turned the knob and stuck my head inside the darkened room. It had been years since I'd performed the lullaby I'd written for Mia. That she was willingly listening to it made my heart squeeze.

A light appeared on the wall that wasn't mirrored, and I stepped fully into the room just as images began to play from a projector

14

hooked up to a laptop. As the door quietly closed behind me, I was treated to Mia's childhood playing out all over again through pictures and video clips.

No.

Not just of her childhood.

Of our relationship from the moment she was placed in my arms after she was born until...I'd broken her heart.

Her first steps and her walking into my open arms. That first birthday party that Emmie had cried over because she'd wanted it to be perfect, but it seemed like everything went wrong. Until the cake was placed in front of Mia, and I sang her "Happy Birthday." She'd clapped her chubby hands and then thrust them into the sugary pink confection and started rubbing it all over her mouth, licking and smacking her lips before offering me a bite from her fingers.

The first time she'd run out onstage at a Demon's Wings concert, her little ears covered in protective, noise-canceling headphones. Her first day of school. Her first trip to the zoo. Her first dance class, the pink leotard and matching glittery tutu she'd picked out specifically for the moment. Her hair had been put up in the tight bun that would become her signature style from that day forward.

A picture of her making her first leap floated across the wall, as effortless and perfect as always. Her dance teacher had made it into a poster and placed it at the entrance to the school, where it still remained. Photos of her in Paris, Italy, Ireland, even India—all the summer programs we traveled to as a family for her so she could learn new dance styles. A video clip of her right before her first recital, nervously looking up at me. With a hard kiss to my cheek, she'd fearlessly walked out onstage with her class, where she'd been flawless.

All eyes had been on her from the auditorium, while I'd stood in the shadows with Emmie, trying not to cry.

My vision blurred as I watched clips of her dancing with me in the kitchen on Saturday mornings. Pictures of her with her head on my shoulder as we cuddled on the couch in the family room for movie nights when she was a preteen. Her and her mother on either side of me the night of her prom and then her graduation from high school.

Everything played out while my lullaby for her echoed through the room.

As the final photo of us together faded—the last one taken before she began to hate me—a different kind of picture filled the wall. My heart lifted into my already tight throat, and I read the information on the ultrasound photo as a message slowly appeared across the wall in a cursive script.

Papa's first grandbaby arriving in July!

A soft hand touched my arm, and I glanced down at Mia with tears still glittering in my eyes. "Surprise," she whispered in an emotionally raspy voice.

"Mia?" I choked. "Are you really pregnant?"

With a trembling smile, she nodded. "Are you happy?"

I didn't even hesitate, just wrapped my arms around her. When she hugged me back without a pause, more tears spilled from my eyes. "My baby girl is having a baby. I'm going to be a grandpa. Of course I'm happy."

Pulling back slightly, she looked at the wall and the pictures that were playing all over again to her lullaby. As her green gaze drifted over them, I could feel her shoulders becoming less tense. She relaxed into me, almost as easily as she'd done in the last photo of us together.

Sighing, she swiped her fingers over her damp cheeks and looked up at me. In the glow of the light coming from the images still floating across the wall, a replay of small snippets from our life, our gazes locked. "I'm going to be honest with you, Daddy. Barrick set all this up. Please don't be upset, but Momma already knows."

I snorted. "Your mom probably knew before you did."

Her soft laugh reached my ears, the sound one of the most beautiful I'd ever heard. "Yeah, she probably did. But the truth is, I didn't want to tell you yet. Barrick thought it was better to let you know now before you found me with my head in the toilet and became upset that we hadn't told you yet."

Her confession stung, but it wasn't anything I shouldn't have expected. "I see."

"No," she said, shaking her head adamantly. "You don't see. I came here not even really knowing what to expect. Barrick and Momma must have worked together, because some of those pictures and videos only she would have had access to. But as I watched them... As I watched you watch them, I began to see it all over again. The good days. How much I adore you. How big a part of my life you are. Even though I've tried to throw up walls and lock you out as much as I could, that was kind of impossible."

"Mia, honey, I'm sorry about how overbearing I was while you were growing up. Nearly losing you, it fucked up something inside me. Your mom went to therapy to help her because she couldn't sleep at times. Maybe I should have gone with her. It was unhealthy the way I worried about your safety." It wasn't easy admitting my faults, especially to the girl who had once considered me her hero, but I knew

I had to say it for us both to heal. Even if only a little. "Going behind your back and arranging for Seller to put a secret security detail on you was wrong, and I regret it now. But at the time, I felt helpless. The idea of you being away from home, without protection, gave me nightmares. I spent a lot of sleepless nights imagining what might happen to you."

"I think I'm starting to truly understand." She touched a hand to her abdomen and rubbed in a loving circle. "A few days ago, Barrick told me to think about how much I love this baby, then multiply it by a million. He said then I would understand how much you love me. I kind of scoffed at the idea, because how can anyone come close to loving anything or anyone as much as I love this baby?"

"Mia—"

"But then I watched that presentation they put together, and I realized he was right. The way you look at me in those pictures and videos... I saw it, Daddy. I see it now. What you did, it still hurts a bit, but not nearly as badly as it did before I came in here a little while ago." She hugged me again, standing on tiptoe to bury her face in my neck. "I love you, Daddy. So much. I'm sorry for all the pain I've put you through over the last few years. I'm sorry...I'm sorry I forgot how much you love me."

A choked sob was torn from me, and I held on to my baby girl a little tighter. "I'm sorry too, sweetheart. I'm sorry I couldn't let you go when...when you needed me to."

"It's okay. I understand now." She gave me a smile while tears streamed down her beautiful face. She looked so much like Emmie that any time she cried, it broke my heart twice as much. "Besides, if you hadn't hired Barrick, we might not have met. And then I wouldn't be living my best life now."

"That's all I have ever wanted for you, Mia. To be happy, but safe."

"Well, you definitely helped me accomplish that." She laid her head on my shoulder, and we both looked at the projector playing on repeat yet again. "You found me a beast to protect me, and he's made me happier than I ever thought was possible."

CHAPTER 5

BARRICK

I mpatiently, I waited for my mom to finish getting ready. It wasn't even a fancy dinner that we were having. Just the majority of Mia's family and friends together with a few of my own, at some restaurant Emmie had rented out for the night. Mia had been specific about everyone being casually dressed because the wedding was formal. She didn't like having to dress up more than once in a row.

If possible, she most likely would have chosen a wedding dress made of Lycra because that was what the majority of her clothes were made of. Anyone who knew her wouldn't have blinked if she'd actually walked down the aisle dressed like the ballerina she was meant to be. But from the vague description she'd given me, the dress was more of a ball gown to hide the little bitty baby bump I loved to fall asleep rubbing every night.

My mother wasn't one to show up to anything in less than designer dresses and dripping in diamonds. She always swore she wasn't vain, but she had to show the world she was rich with how she dressed. The woman donated to plenty of charities, no one could have ever faulted her for that, but she was a snob. The kicker was, Mia and her family—especially her mom—were worth five times more than my mother would ever hope to claim to her name.

When I was growing up, she'd never seemed that way to me. At least, not while my father was still alive. And then he was gone, and Seller was there, spoiling her to the point that it changed her. Now she wouldn't leave the house without one of her five-thousand-dollar handbags or her two-thousand-dollar heels. She hadn't worn jeans or slacks in at least a decade. It was all exclusive dresses from Paris and Milan, handmade, just for her.

At times, I wondered if she used Seller for his money, profiting off his obsession for her. But then I would see the way she looked up at him, and I knew that whatever sickness my stepfather had, she'd caught.

Muttering a curse, I glanced down at my watch. Even with Mia having a little time with her dad before the dinner, we were still going to arrive after them at this rate. Tapping my foot, I glared over at Seller as he patiently took a swallow of the amber liquor in his tumbler.

"Relax. Your mother is always keeping me waiting. She likes to doll herself up for me. I'm sure you know how it is. Mia must constantly keep you waiting."

I gritted my teeth, not answering him. He didn't need to know that Mia rarely kept me waiting unless it was work-related. She didn't spend hours in front of a mirror; she didn't have to. All she did was throw a sweatshirt over whatever dance clothes she'd tossed on that morning after her shower, pulled on a pair of yoga pants if it was chilly out, and then swept her hair up into a knot on top of her head. On occasion, she would put on a little makeup if we were going on a date or she had something important to do regarding PR for the dance school.

Heeled footsteps on the Italian tiled floor had me stepping out of the library where I'd been shown when I'd arrived to pick them up. My mother walked toward me in a knee-length dress that would have only looked casual on a New York City catwalk. Her mahogany hair was pulled up into some fancy French twist, and her makeup looked as if it had taken hours to perfect.

I glanced down at my jeans and T-shirt. Mia had picked it out for me to wear, because she'd been adamant about not seeing me in anything resembling a suit or tux until the following day. Even Seller had been smart enough to dress in black slacks and a polo rather than a suit as he normally would have worn. Too many years of working with Emmie Armstrong had taught him to follow instructions when she threw them his way. No doubt, she had emailed him a reminder that her daughter wanted things low-key.

"You have five minutes to at least change your clothes," I informed my mother. "Or I'm leaving without you."

She huffed. "This dress is the only casual thing I own, Charlie. Your Mia will have to accept me as is, or..." She shrugged, giving me a tight smile.

"'Or' it is, then," I told her with a shrug of my own. "This is her time. What she wants, she's going to get. If that means you aren't there, honestly, I couldn't care less. In fact, it will make this dinner easier on everyone, especially me." Pulling my keys out of my pocket, I swung them around my index finger. "See you tomorrow, Mother."

"Charlie!" she cried behind me. "All right, fine. I think I have an old pair of jeans from..." Her eyes drifted to my stepfather, and a flash of guilt crossed her face. "Before."

"Then you should hurry," I told her. "Because I'm leaving in four minutes and twenty-eight seconds."

Cursing under her breath, she stormed back up the stairs, and I returned to tapping my foot impatiently. I wanted to get to the restaurant to see how things had gone with Mia and Nik. I'd been anxious, hoping this plan Emmie and I had orchestrated together would finally heal the rift between father and daughter.

"I dislike the way you speak to your mother," Seller gritted out behind me.

"She knew what she was doing when she came down here dressed like that. This isn't about her, but she was attempting to put the spotlight on herself. I won't allow her to ruin this. And even if I were stupid enough to allow her to try, she wouldn't have gotten two feet into the restaurant before Emmie would have been all over her." I cocked my head at the man, daring him to argue.

All I got in response was the older man clenching his jaw.

I pocketed my keys again. "Do us both a favor and make sure she doesn't try to show up at the wedding tomorrow dressed in white. Because I can promise you, if she does, my new mother-in-law will ensure the dress doesn't stay white for long. If you're lucky, she won't dye it red with Mother's own blood."

We arrived at the restaurant twenty minutes later than expected, but when I entered the building behind my stepfather, I quickly saw that Mia and her father had yet to arrive. Grimacing, I walked around introducing my mother and Seller to Mia's honorary aunts, uncles, and cousins whom they hadn't already met in the past three years.

Another thirty minutes passed, and then I spotted Emmie as she walked in, leaving her bodyguard at the entrance. Without a word to anyone, I moved toward her.

"Are they here yet?" she asked as soon as I was close enough to hear her.

I shook my head. "And I haven't heard from either of them. You?"

"Not a word." She threaded her arm through mine, a smile on her face. "This is a good thing. I can feel it in my bones."

Wanting to believe her, I escorted her over to where I'd left my mother and stepfather still speaking to Mia's grandfather. Eddie saw his daughter, and his green eyes lit up with love. "There's my Emmie girl," he greeted, pulling her in for a hug. "Where's my grandbaby at? She and Nik run into traffic?"

"Something like that," she said, stepping back but keeping an arm around him as she faced the other couple. "Seller," she said with a nod, then held out her free hand to my mother. "Good to see you again, Meredith," she said in a tone that was only slightly frosty.

"Ember," Mother returned, clutching her husband's arm, holding it in a possessive way while staring Emmie down. My mother was just as jealous of Seller as he was over her. It irritated the fuck out of me that she would think Emmie, of all people, would want a prick like Charles Seller.

"Emmie!"

We turned our heads to find Drake Stevenson walking toward us with his wife, Lana. We all felt a sense of relief at the sight of him looking so healthy. It had only been a few short months since he'd nearly died from cirrhosis of the liver. His scheduled transplant surgery had turned into an unexpected emergency one. Thankfully, his younger brother, Shane, had been a perfect match for him. Drake had been in the hospital throughout the holiday season, and he'd only been released in the last few weeks.

"Where's Mia?" the rock legend asked as he and Lana reached us.

"She and Nik had something to do," Emmie explained as she hugged one of the men who had been like a brother to her growing up. "Are you feeling okay? I don't want you to exhaust yourself. Mia will be upset if you get overtired tonight and don't dance with her tomorrow."

"I promise, the moment I sense he's drained, I'm taking him home and tucking him into bed," Lana assured her as she stepped forward to hug Emmie as well. Her brown gaze barely skimmed Seller. She wasn't a fan of my mom any more than Emmie was.

If Meredith was jealous of Emmie, it was nothing to how she felt toward Lana Stevenson. The woman was at least a decade younger than her husband and looked closer to her eighteen-year-old daughter's age. Mother's hold tightened even more on Seller, staking her claim. Lana didn't even bother to hide her eye roll as she stepped back and linked the fingers of her left hand with her husband's right.

Lana's eyes softened when they landed on me, and she gave me a one-armed hug. "Hey, sweetie."

I bent to kiss her cheek before shaking Drake's hand. "Good to see you, sir."

"You look so much better than I did the night before my wedding," the rocker said with a laugh. "I was scared out of my mind Angel was going to realize she could do so much better and run off."

"Never," Lana said reverently. "You can't get rid of me, babe."

"Thank fuck," he muttered, pulling her closer. Turning his gaze back to me, he nodded toward where his eldest daughter was standing with a group. One of them was my cousin Braxton. "You boys aren't going to be getting into trouble tonight are you?"

"Hadn't planned on it, sir," I told him. "Mia would kill me if I showed up hungover."

"Mia?" Drake laughed, then quickly sobered as he gave me a hard glare. "No, son. You won't have to worry about Mia killing you. Don't be doing anything either my niece or my daughter will get upset over. I might not be at full strength yet, but I won't hesitate to cut off your balls if you do anything to make my girls cry."

"Yes, sir," I promised without hesitation.

"Actually," Emmie interrupted, touching her hand to my back reassuringly. "Nik has plans with the guys. He's taking Barrick, Braxton, and Howler back to our house while I take Mia, Nevaeh, Lyla, and Josie to the hotel for the night. A little innocent girl fun while the guys have some very innocent fun at my place."

"Great idea," Lana agreed and pulled Emmie's dad into the conversation since he'd been standing quietly beside his daughter. "Eddie, will you be joining them?"

"Jagger and I are going to cruise around for babes," Eddie said with a grin, causing Lana to laugh. "Just kidding. Jags and I will be hanging out with Nik and the boys. Drake, you're welcome to join us, son."

"Sorry to spoil the fun," Lana said. "But my husband isn't allowed to sleep anywhere without me. And I plan on going home and getting plenty of beauty sleep before tomorrow's wedding."

"Sorry, Eddie," Drake murmured, staring adoringly down at his wife. "My angel doesn't need the beauty sleep when she's already the most breathtaking woman in the room, but I can't sleep without her and don't plan on trying."

CHAPTER 6

MIA

We arrived at the restaurant much later than I'd anticipated, but Dad and I were all smiles as we walked into the beautiful chaos of our family's happy chatter. My eyes still felt a little swollen from all the tears we'd cried together, but it had been cathartic for both of us.

The moment we crossed the threshold into the building, we were swarmed by family members. I laughingly accepted hugs and well-wishes for the next day, but the entire time, my gaze was scanning farther into the interior, trying to find my groom. He wasn't usually hard to spot. He was one of only a few men who stood well above the others, his shoulders twice as wide as the majority of everyone else's. But it was his beard that made him stand out the most.

I had a love-hate relationship with that beard. It was sexy as fuck, but it hid his dimples, and I loved those damned things so much.

Finally, I caught sight of him. He dwarfed my mom and even my grandfather. Uncle Drake and Aunt Lana stood with the group...along with Seller and Meredith.

I grimaced at the sight of the woman who would be my mother-in-law in less than twenty-four hours' time. It wasn't that I hated the woman; I simply disliked her attitude. Toward my parents, my family, and especially toward Barrick. With my family, she seemed to think she was better than them, which was laughable, because no matter the differences in their backgrounds, my family was miles away from Meredith. Whether she wanted to admit it or not, she knew it deep down, and it ate at her.

But the way she treated Barrick made me want to scratch up her pretty face. Perhaps I'd been spoiled by watching my mom and aunts with their own sons. The way they showed their affection. How my brother and male cousins never doubted their mothers' love.

Barrick had told me that things were different when he was

younger, before the death of his dad. She'd been around more. Then Charles Barrick Sr. had passed, and almost overnight, Charles Seller took his place. As Barrick's father figure. As the head of the security company the two best friends had started together. And then, in Meredith's bed. In a matter of months, Seller's ring was on her finger and they were married, but before that, they had been sleeping together.

After getting to know them a little, I saw that there was true love between the two, even if they had an unnatural obsession mixed into their relationship. Obsession, I got. It struck me the moment I set eyes on Barrick. And I'd witnessed it plenty of times with not only my parents but my uncles as well—especially Uncle Drake and Aunt Lana. But whatever Meredith and Seller had bordered on unhealthy, maybe even crossed the line into something darker.

"You're late," Uncle Jesse accused with a grin as he swung me up into a hug. "I hope this doesn't set the vibe for tomorrow."

"Nah, man," Dad told his best friend. "My baby girl and I had a little father-daughter time."

Understanding filled my uncle's ever-changing brown eyes. "Good. I'm glad you two had your moment. Now maybe things will get back to normal around here."

I released a laugh. "When have things ever been normal?"

"Normal is boring," Dad said with a smirk. "I learned that a long time ago."

We made slow progress through the crowd to where Barrick and Momma still stood. A few times, he'd lifted his head and caught my gaze, his dark eyes asking questions. But I didn't let him see what I was thinking, taking my time to say hello to my family members as Dad and I inched our way toward him and Momma. Each new time I glanced Barrick's way, I could almost feel his frustration, his anticipation.

His need to touch me.

The closer I got to him, the more labored my breathing became until I couldn't stand it any longer. Leaving Dad still talking to Uncle Zander, I shot through the final twenty or so people and torpedoed myself into Beast's arms. He caught me around the waist just as my legs folded around his hips. I wasn't sure who kissed whom first, but suddenly our lips were attacking each other's.

Everyone else in the room disappeared. There was just the taste of his tongue as it skimmed over mine. The feel of his scruff on my cheek. His hands squeezing my ass. My fingers combing through his thick locks. And my hidden baby bump beneath the simple baggy sweatshirt I wore, pressed into his hard abdomen.

The sound of several people clearing their throats loudly finally pulled me back to my surroundings, and I reluctantly lifted my head. Ignoring Seller and Meredith, both of whom had been some of the ones to attempt to make noises to separate us, I licked my kiss-swollen lips and looked at Barrick through hooded eyes. "Hi."

Still holding me in place with one hand on my ass, he stroked the other over my cheek. "Hey, firecracker."

"Ugh, get a room already," Lyla said from right behind me.

Without looking at my best friend, I flipped her the finger over my shoulder. "I'm hungry. And thirsty. Can we eat now?"

Barrick tilted his head slightly, surprise lighting his eyes. "You're hungry?"

"Starving."

Relief filled his face. "Maybe making up with Nik was all you really needed," he murmured for my ears only. "Perhaps our little dancer didn't like the discord between you and her papa. Or his. I'm okay if we have a son and he wants to be a dancer as well."

"Maybe you should shut up and feed me," I groused. "Your bride is hungry, Beast."

"I think we have about ten minutes before Mia becomes a different person," Momma said loudly, causing everyone in the room to chuckle in agreement. "If everyone wants to take their seats, the waitstaff will start bringing out the appetizers."

While everyone around us started moving to their assigned seats, Barrick carried me toward our own table.

"She's a grown woman, Charlie," Meredith complained behind us. "She can walk on her own."

"I don't bitch at you for clutching Seller like he's going to disappear if another woman speaks to him. So don't bitch at me when I want to carry Mia."

When we reached our table, he used his foot to pull out a chair. Twisting my head, I saw that Braxton, Nevaeh, Lyla, and Howler were already seated at our table for six. I grinned at our bridal party and nearly clapped my hands with happiness. That meant Momma had put Meredith and her husband with someone else, most likely her and my dad to avoid the mother of the groom getting all pissy for feeling slighted. Not that it would stop her from being pissy anyway, but at least I didn't have to deal with that while I was eating.

For the first time in months, I felt hungry, and I wasn't going to waste it by getting indigestion from my soon-to-be mother-in-law.

Barrick sat and rearranged me on his lap. "Where's Josie?" I asked when I didn't see Lyla's precious stepdaughter and my junior bridesmaid. Hayat and Evan would be my flower girl and ring bearer the next day. I was so excited to see all three kids in their adorable outfits.

"Aunt Emmie set up a table just for the kids, closer to Lucy's table," Nevaeh answered. "Josie has already made new friends with Hayat and Abi."

"How are you feeling?" Lyla asked, leaning forward so she could drop her voice as much as possible with the crowd still loudly searching for their own seats.

Without thinking, I glanced around for my dad. Seeing him already seated at a table close by with Seller and Meredith, as well as my grandfather, I couldn't help smiling. "Better," I answered honestly. "So much better."

A waiter appeared beside our table with three platters of my favorite appetizers and placed them in the center. Barrick still had me on his lap, but I didn't bother to move to my own chair. Instead, I snatched a loaded potato skin and scooped up a little sour cream before stuffing the entire thing into my mouth.

"Everyone be careful," Howler said with a hearty laugh as he watched me grab a chicken wing drenched in Truff sauce. "You might lose a finger now that Mia's appetite has returned."

I flipped him off and tore the wing apart before skinning the bone in one swipe of my teeth.

"Slow down before you choke," Braxton urged.

I licked the Truff sauce off my thumb and chewed carefully so my friend wouldn't worry, but I didn't pause before picking up a fried pickle with my fork. "We're going to need more of everything," I whined, already sad that the food was quickly disappearing—and I was the one making it vanish.

But no sooner had the platters emptied, than they were replaced by more. By the time everyone was finally seated, I'd eaten the majority of six appetizer platters and was still hungry. So were the other five people at the table since I'd greedily gobbled down so much food.

"Damn, Mia," Howler said, staring down at the empty plates in awe. "We need to enter you into some eating competitions. How many hot dogs do you think you could eat?"

"How much Truff sauce will they have?" I said with a grin.

"I'm not a fan of the smell," Nevaeh commented. "But I wouldn't mind a few more of those potato skins and the pickles."

"I'll be happy with the main course," Lyla said, crunching into a piece of the celery, all that was left on the platters. "What did you decide on? Steak, chicken, pork? Something for the vegans?"

"Fajitas," I said with a shrug as the sound of sizzling pans filled the air along with the scent of onions and peppers mixed with steak, chicken, and, for some people, shrimp. For the few vegans in the room, we had tofu and black bean options. Everyone was already digging in.

"This is the best rehearsal dinner I've ever been to," Howler informed me, already creating his first fajita.

Everyone seemed to agree with him, because they were making pleased sounds over the food choices. Out of the corner of my eye, I saw Meredith poke at a fried pickle that was still on her plate, ignoring the main course completely. Apparently this wasn't to her liking. The fancy-dress, five-course meal, regal reception would happen after our wedding the next day. For this, I'd wanted everything low-key to put our guests at ease—especially me.

The fajitas were a nod to the first meal I'd shared with Barrick—and Braxton, by default. We'd gotten takeout from the best Mexican restaurant in Northern Virginia. I'd had tacos, but the guys had both gotten fajitas. When Momma had asked me what I wanted served at this dinner, I hadn't hesitated when I'd seen that fajitas were an option.

That night, after that first forehead kiss, I'd known I was falling. For the first time since my second knee injury, I hadn't been frightened someone wouldn't be there to catch me.

For the next few minutes, I was too busy stuffing my face to care about everyone else. Maybe Barrick was right, and I'd had such bad morning sickness because the baby hadn't liked the discord between Dad and me. Now that the ache in my chest was nearly nonexistent, my appetite had returned with a vengeance, and I couldn't get enough to eat.

Someone called for quiet, and all eyes turned toward my dad as he and Momma stood. I snuggled into Barrick, already knowing what was coming. I felt Barrick kiss the top of my head, and everything felt perfect.

"Emmie and I want to thank everyone for joining us tonight," Dad began, glancing around at all the members of our crazy family. "Each of you has been there with us for every major step in Mia's life, and we appreciate you being here for her magical day."

He cleared his throat as it grew rough with emotion, and I shot him an encouraging smile when he glanced my way. "My little girl isn't a baby any longer. Tomorrow, she will take another man's last name.

As she was growing up, I always feared this day. I worried that the man she chose wouldn't be strong enough, worthy enough, for her. But then I met Barrick, and I knew that he was different. He loves Mia, maybe as much as I love my own wife. And I know that when Mia is with him, I don't have to worry. She's safe with him—not just her heart, but in every way."

Dad lifted his glass of iced tea in our direction. "Thank you, Barrick. For being the man Mia loves, but also for saving my sanity along the way."

"No thanks necessary, sir," Barrick called over to him.

"I disagree, but we won't argue over it here." Dad took a drink from his glass. "Tomorrow is one of the biggest days of Mia's and Barrick's lives. Emmie and I might not be quite ready to let her go, but we've found we aren't losing a daughter. We've added another son to our family..." He looked down at Momma, who gave him a warm smile, her green eyes glittering with tears. "And in July, we will be expanding our family even more as we welcome our first grandbaby!"

The response to his announcement nearly deafened me as everyone roared with excitement and congratulations. I'd already consulted Barrick while we were eating the appetizers, and I'd texted my dad that Beast was fine with him announcing our pregnancy. If anything, Barrick thought it was perfect because we'd waited so long to tell Dad, and he felt bad for keeping the secret. Giving Dad the glory of telling our loved ones—at least the ones who hadn't already guessed—that we were going to be parents put a smile on my groom's face as he sat back and cradled my head to his chest.

"She's what?" I heard Meredith shriek, quieting the room effortlessly.

"Pregnant," Momma repeated with measured patience. "Mia is due in July."

Barrick's mother looked over at us with an expression on her face that suggested we'd betrayed her. "And when were you going to tell me, Charlie?"

"You found out along with everyone else, Mother," he told her with a shrug. "Mia wanted to wait until after her first trimester passed before making the announcement."

"Mia wanted," she sneered, and the entire room seemed to tense.

The snide way she looked at me wasn't something I was unused to from her. Meredith had made it plain from the day we met that she wasn't thrilled I was with her son. In her eyes, I wasn't good enough. Although my parents were richer, held more esteem and power throughout the music and business worlds, it wasn't the right kind of money and power. Both my parents had come from nothing, living in a trailer park in a small Ohio town until Dad's band got noticed. Later, Momma had become the band's manager, and she'd only made their popularity skyrocket.

Emmie Armstrong had the Midas touch. Any band she took on as a client always got a huge contract with the best record labels. If she decided she wanted to venture into other aspects of the music business, it didn't take long before she was doubling her investment. Considering the childhood she'd had, it had to be Karma making up for what her own mother had put her through for so many years.

"It's all about what Mia wants, right?" Meredith went on, making the room thick with tension and anticipation. I went stiff in Barrick's arms, readying my body for whatever verbal blow my soon-to-be mother-in-law directed at me—but also waiting to see what my mom would do to the other woman. "This pathetic excuse for a rehearsal dinner. Where you live. When you get married, have kids, or even tell the important people in your life that you're expecting. It all comes down to Mia, what Mia wants. What about me? Don't my feelings on any of this matter?"

"No," Barrick told her point-blank, his voice hard and full of warning for her to shut her mouth. "This isn't about you. You should have learned that by now, Mother. Your feelings regarding my life with my wife mean nothing to me. Unless you're happy for us, try to keep your mouth shut and stop playing the part of the toxic mother-in-law. It's unflattering on you."

She made a high-pitched sound that I was surprised didn't break glass.

"Consider it like the color puce," Barrick continued as if she hadn't just nearly burst everyone's eardrums. "As you've commented so many times, it doesn't look good with your skin tone. Your unwanted criticism is just as ugly on you as puce, Mother."

Lyla lifted her water glass in agreement. "Hear hear, cousin," she said, toasting him. "Aunt Meredith, you should either keep your mouth shut or leave before someone shuts it for you."

"I'll second that." Momma agreed in a voice that made many of the people in the room shiver. "This is a special occasion. Don't ruin it for our children."

"Ruin it?" She shrieked. "It's already ruined. He shouldn't even be marrying that piece of trash—"

The verbal blow struck me, but I tried not to flinch. Meredith wasn't lucky enough to hide her reaction to the physical blow she took when Momma grabbed her by the back of the hair and rammed her head into the tabletop. Seller jumped to his feet, but around the room, my grandfather, dad, brother, and all of my uncles, along with my male cousins, were doing the same. More than half the men in the room were on their feet, ready to rip Seller apart if he so much as lifted a finger in my mom's direction.

As if out of thin air, Rodger, and Marcus both appeared. They used to work for Seller, but now they had a contract exclusively with Mom. They were her bodyguards, my father's safety net to keep his sanity when she went to work or had to travel without him. They were family, and they respected Momma. Their job might be to protect her, but they would have done so even if they weren't paid to do it.

While the many rock legends and their offspring had a stare-off with the security expert, Momma was busy holding Meredith in place. "I suggest you apologize to the children," Momma said through gritted teeth. "And if Barrick still decides he wants you to be at his wedding tomorrow, I suggest you keep your mouth shut the entire time."

"I don't," Barrick announced. Gently, he turned my head and pressed his lips to the center of my brow before carefully placing me in the empty chair beside his. Jerking to his feet, he crossed to our moms. "If you'll excuse me, Emmie, I'll show these two out."

I sat there, fighting the knot of emotions trying to choke me. I had no doubt that Barrick always put me first, even with his parents, but that didn't stop it from hurting when his mother took jabs at me. Normally I had tougher skin, but where she was concerned—the woman who had given birth to the man I loved—the arrows didn't bounce off like they would with anyone else.

CHAPTER 7

BARRICK

I could feel the top of my head ready to explode as I firmly grasped my mother's arm and carefully pulled her to her feet. She had a bruise forming on her forehead from where Emmie had smashed her face into the table. Honestly, I was surprised that was all she'd done to my mother. Emmie had shown true restraint; that was for fucking sure.

As I led my mother out of the restaurant and onto the sidewalk, I knew Seller was behind me. Wherever Meredith went, he followed, but he was oddly quiet.

It wasn't until we were down the street a few yards that I finally released my hold on my mother's arm. She'd kept her mouth shut the entire time, but as soon as I let her go, she turned to me with fury on her face. "How could you—"

"Enough!" I roared. "From the moment I first introduced you to Mia, you've been nothing but a heinous bitch to her. You are the thing in-law nightmares are made of. Well, I'm not going to sit back like some husbands and allow you to treat my wife like shit. That kind of toxicity won't touch my family."

"If anyone is toxic, it's that girl and her entire family!" she cried. "Drug addicts and drunks. Violent pieces of filth who think it's okay to put their hands on anyone. Look at my face." She hissed as she touched the growing bruise on her forehead.

"The only filth I saw in there was you and your disgusting attitude. Tonight and tomorrow have nothing to do with you, Mother. This is Mia's and my time. We're celebrating our wedding. The two of us are making a family, one I refuse to let you be a part of if you can't stop being such a toxic bitch."

She balled her hands into fists at her sides, but she turned tear-filled eyes on Seller. "Charles, say something! He's being unreasonable."

My stepfather surprised me when he looked down at his wife in disappointment. "You went too far tonight, Meredith. The way you acted in there is beneath you."

Hurt filled her eyes, but she quickly switched gears. "We shouldn't have even been in there. That girl is all wrong for Charlie. He deserves someone like Darcy Hamilton, who Braxton is going to marry."

"He's not marrying her, Mother. That was just Belinda and Miles trying to control Brax. And I sure as fuck won't let you do the same to me." I stepped back from her and shifted my gaze to Seller. "She's not welcome at the wedding tomorrow. Until she's ready to sincerely apologize to Mia, I won't allow her in our life. Keep in mind that Mia is pregnant with our first child, your first grandchild. If you can't respect my wife, then you sure as hell won't respect our baby. Until you change your attitude, don't expect to see them or me again."

"What about the company?" Seller tossed at me out of the blue.

A tired laugh escaped me. "That's all you're worried about?" He shrugged, and I stepped into his space. "The company is mine. It was always going to be mine. My father owned more shares of it than you. Those shares came to me upon his death. You were just in charge until I came of age. Fuck, you even changed the name from Barrick & Seller to just Seller. When I get back from my honeymoon, you're going to be gone. I'm finally going to use my extra pull and kick you off the board."

Turning to go, I called over my shoulder, "I suggest you speak to Braxton while I'm gone. Get him to buy you out while you still can. Because if you're still part of my company when I return, I'll make sure you're left with nothing." I paused with my hand on the door to the restaurant and glanced back at them. "I've always wondered about something, Seller. Did you start fucking my mother before my dad died, or did you wait until he was in the ground before you started screwing your supposed best friend's wife?"

"Charlie!" Mother shouted in outrage.

"I'm sure you can call for a town car if you don't want to take a taxi home." I opened the door and stepped inside.

I didn't expect an answer to the question, but it sure as fuck felt good to finally ask it.

As the door closed behind me, I noticed the others had gone back to enjoying the evening. Laughter echoed off the walls while everyone ate their dinner. My gaze zeroed in on Mia, who was sitting where I'd placed her, picking at the food on her plate with a fork. The joy that had been on her face earlier was gone, and my rage tried to rear its head again, but I pushed it down. My mother wouldn't hurt her anymore. I'd make fucking sure of that.

I made my way through the tables, and as soon as I reached her, I scooped her up. With a squeak, she wrapped her arms around my neck. "Emmie, I'll bring Mia to the hotel later," I announced without looking away from Mia's green eyes.

"Before midnight!" Lyla and Nevaeh said in unison.

"Just be careful on the road," Emmie told me as I carried Mia out a side door.

I didn't even glance to see if my mother and stepfather were on the street as I walked toward my SUV. Keeping Mia tucked against me, I opened the door and placed her in the passenger seat. Snapping her seat belt into place, I kissed her forehead before finally stepping back. "Your smile is gone."

"Give me a few more minutes," she said with a slight tilt of her lips. "It will make a comeback soon."

"Sit tight. I'll get that sassy mouth happy again in no time."

Her eyes began to glitter. "Will it be because it's wrapped around your cock?"

"That can definitely be arranged, firecracker."

****

I pulled up in front of the house in Beverly Hills. Mia had given the go-ahead to put in an offer on the place the week before, and after a little haggling with the owners, we'd finally agreed on a price. A little piece of information I'd been holding on to for the next day, but my little firecracker looked as if she needed the good news.

When I turned off the vehicle, Mia seemed to pull herself from her inner musings. Frowning, she glanced up at the house. The place was big enough for us, the baby, and as many more as she wanted to add to our family. With the pool in the backyard and the many, many sets of stairs, the place was going to be a royal bitch to babyproof, but I'd find someone to come in and get it done before our little one arrived.

"I thought we were going back to Malibu," she mumbled, sounding tired. But then she seemed to realize exactly where I'd brought her, and her green eyes grew huge. "Beast?"

I turned to face her, leaning my back against the driver's door. "Welcome home, firecracker."

Instead of the happiness coming back to her eyes as I'd hoped, they filled with tears. "R-really? Th-they finally accepted the o-offer?"

"Baby, don't cry," I pleaded, cupping her face so I could wipe away her tears with my thumbs. "Don't you want this place? I-I can find us a different house. It might take a little more time, but I'll find us a home before the baby gets here. Just..." I swallowed hard when she only began to sob. "J-just tell me what you want, Mia. Whatever you want, name it, and I'll make it happen. All I care about is your happiness."

She released a choked laugh, tears dripping from her cheeks, chin, and the tip of her nose. "You are my happiness, Beast. Just you. Nothing else matters."

"But you're crying like your heart is broken." With a groan, I pressed my forehead to hers. "I don't have any PTSD from deployment, but baby, I sure as fuck get twitchy when you cry. It reminds me of—"

Tipping her head back, she gave me a trembling, understanding smile when I broke off. "There's no need for that, Barrick. I've forgiven you for the secrets you kept, and I'm not going to hold the past against you." Sniffling, she glanced over my shoulder at the huge house. "Today has been...rough. I didn't want to meet with Dad earlier, but then I was so glad I did. I've been aching to tell you all about it. We watched that little presentation over and over again, and each time unlocked something inside me. My dad cried so much, it's a wonder we didn't flood the classroom."

"I was nervous about the meeting," I confessed. "But your mom appeared to know it would go well."

"Yeah, she seems to know the outcome of things before anyone else. Maybe she's psychic."

I snorted a laugh. "It wouldn't surprise me if she were."

"Same." She climbed over the console and cuddled into my lap. "Dinner was great...until it wasn't."

Stroking my fingers through her hair, I promised, "You won't have to deal with her shit again. Even if she comes to you on her hands and knees and apologizes, if you don't want to forgive her, then you don't have to. She made her choices, and now she has to live with the consequences."

"I'm sorry," Mia whispered.

"What the fuck are you sorry for?" I demanded.

"She's your mom. If it weren't for me, you two might have a better relationship."

"The way things are between us isn't your fault, baby. That's all on her." I grimaced. "Okay, maybe it's a little on me too. But it's mostly her and Seller. They were so obsessed with each other that they pushed me out of their lives a long time ago. All I've gotten from her since my dad died are scraps. It wasn't until I met your family that I understood what it was like to have two amazing parents who loved and supported their kids."

"At least we know what to do and what not to do," she murmured, sounding sleepy. She did that a lot. The baby drained her, and she napped often. There were times she'd nodded off without even realizing it. After the emotional events of the day, I wasn't surprised she was so tired.

Tucking her head under my chin, I rubbed my hand up and down her arm, enjoying her falling asleep in my arms. "Yeah, firecracker," I whispered so as not to wake her, enjoying the moment alone with her before the chaos of our wedding began. "Now we know."

CHAPTER 8

MIA

Gentle fingers combing soothingly through my hair had me snuggling deeper into my pillow. I didn't need to open my eyes to know Momma was lying beside me in bed. I could feel her aura, the power mixed with the love that always emitted from her whenever she was near my brother and me.

Her tender strokes across my scalp only made me want to hit the pause button and enjoy the moment a little longer, but reality began to set in. I was getting married. That morning, I woke up as Mia Armstrong, but by the time I fell asleep again that night, I would be Mia Barrick.

Excitement began to thrum through my veins, and I rolled onto my back, peeking through my lashes at my mom. "How did I get here?" The last thing I remembered was sitting in Barrick's lap in front of the house that was going to be our new home.

Momma's smile was a little sad as she stared down at me. "Barrick brought you back as promised. You were knocked out. Didn't even wake up when I changed you out of your clothes into your pajamas."

Hearing the quaver in her voice, I snapped my eyes open fully, and I saw the tears. They were just below the surface, her reins on them strong, but at a guess, I doubted even she was powerful enough to keep them at bay for much longer. I threw my arms around her and rolled her onto her back, using her as a pillow like I used to as a kid.

Laughing, she squeezed me back, but I still heard the shuddery little breath she exhaled. "You know this doesn't change anything, right?" I told her as I buried my face in her neck. "Things won't be any different from when I was in college. Only I'll be in the same state. We'll see each other so much more often. And then there's the baby to plan for. We're going to be so busy, you're going to get sick of having to deal with me every day."

"Never," she whispered, kissing the top of my head.

I tightened my arms around her. We were both very slender women, but Momma was considerably shorter than me. Our height difference didn't matter while we were lying down. She cradled me against her, and I was the one who had difficulty fighting tears as she hummed the lullaby Dad had written for me all those years ago. It was a little off-key and raspy—exactly as she'd done whenever she'd tried to hum the song—but it was perfect.

Like always.

We stayed there for a long while before I heard a soft knock on the bedroom door. "Aunt Emmie?" Nevaeh called out before sticking her head inside the room. Her hair was in a messy ponytail, and her glasses had slipped down her nose a little.

Seeing her, I waved her in.

With a giggle, she sprinted across the room and slid into the bed on the other side. She cuddled up to us, and Momma wrapped her other arm around my cousin. "At times, I wish I'd had another girl," Momma commented. "But then I remember how much being pregnant sucked for me, and I realize I got lucky with one of each."

I lifted my head, surprised I didn't feel the least bit queasy. That was new. For three full months, it seemed as if I couldn't go more than a few hours at a time without needing to puke.

"Second trimesters are a little easier," Momma affirmed, reading my mind. "Hopefully you won't have any more issues for the next six months."

"I'm just relieved I won't be puking my way down the aisle today."

"Same," Momma and Nevaeh said in unison, making the three of us laugh.

Cuddle time only lasted a few more minutes before my mom's phone started going crazy with messages and incoming calls. Groaning, I rolled away and slowly sat up before getting to my feet. When the world didn't spin and the urge to vomit didn't overwhelm me, I almost did a happy dance, but I decided not to tempt fate when she was already being kind enough to ease the morning sickness.

From there, things only got hectic. And every time something had to be rushed or Momma got grumpy with someone on the phone, I closed my eyes and remembered our private moment snuggled up together in bed earlier that morning. The peacefulness would float over me once again, and I was able to smile and continue on.

Josie, Lyla, and Nevaeh had their hair and makeup done first. During that time, Lucy showed up with Aunt Layla and Aunt Lana. Hayat was calmly sorted with her hair and dress, while it took all three Daniels sisters to get Evan into his suit. I watched them with wide eyes as they struggled to get his shirt and pants on, and I silently prayed that the baby in my belly was a girl.

Once Evan was dressed, he pretended like he hadn't just screamed the entire hotel down by settling in front of the TV in the sitting room and eating a snack that wouldn't potentially stain his white shirt.

"Are all boys like that?" I asked, a little terrified of the answer in case I was going to birth a tiny demon.

Momma and the three sisters looked at me with pity in their eyes. "It gets better," everyone but Lucy promised. "Look at your brother and the twins."

I cringed. "That doesn't help, Momma."

"Lyric is fine when he's on his own," she amended. "And Damien is a little angel."

That wasn't a lie. Damien was only a few weeks older than Hayat, and he really was a sweet little boy. I put that down to Uncle Drake having nothing but angels as Karma repaying him for his shitty childhood, just like Momma had been repaid with her Midas touch. But given that the chance of having a son who was more like my brother, or the twins was highly probable, I touched my hands to my little bump and prayed a little harder for a girl.

Finally, it was my turn to sit in the stylist's chair. After a few appointments with the stylist in the previous weeks, I'd finally decided on a low updo with loose curls. Instead of a veil, my mom had given me a diamond tiara to place in my hair. As for my makeup, I'd decided to go for the natural look with dewy skin and neutral eye shadow. A little blush, light liner along my eyes, and a nude lip. I looked like me with a simple emphasis on my facial features.

When it came time to step into my dress, I held my breath, scared that my bump had grown too much since my final fitting. It was a bit of a squeeze, but after a small alteration by the seamstress who was there just in case of an emergency, the dress fit perfectly without cutting into my flesh.

No one was surprised when I pulled on a pair of white ballet slippers that tied up my calves.

As I straightened, Nevaeh and Lyla fluffed my dress while the women behind us gasped. I looked at myself in the mirror, checking to make sure my baby bump wasn't showing, that everything was in place, and I didn't have a stain or something wrong with my dress or hair. But everything appeared perfect to me.

"She's so beautiful," Lucy breathed just as my mom burst into tears.

"No, no, no," she chanted, waving her hand in front of her eyes. "I can't cry now, godsdamn it. There are still pictures t-t-to take and so much to do."

Turning away from the mirror, I grasped her hands in both of mine. I would have pulled her into my arms, but she would have gotten pissed if her makeup smeared onto my dress. Through the haze of my own tears, I took in her high updo, her rocker-glam makeup, and the green mother-of-the-bride dress that hugged her slight curves. She was my mirror image except for the difference in our heights, so I knew I was going to be just as beautiful as her when I got older.

"Makeup can be fixed. We'll keep the stylist around for touch-ups all night if we need to," I soothed. "Cry all you want, Momma. You got me to this day. Without you, none of this would even be possible. If anyone is allowed to cry today of all days, it's you."

Someone handed her a tissue, and she dabbed at her eyes, sniffling so her nose wouldn't run. "You are not supposed to be the voice of reason today, kid," she mumbled with a weak smile. "Brides are supposed to be evil on their wedding day, not beautiful angels."

"Maybe you'll get that when Jagger decides to get married," I told her with a wink.

"Shut up," she commanded, pointing a finger in my face. "You'll jinx us all, and that wedding will be a total disaster."

"Momma, it's Jags. Of course it will be a disaster." Laughing, I quickly kissed her cheek. "We should probably head downstairs. Everyone will be in place by now, and I think I heard Uncle Drake outside complaining about Daddy and the others getting restless."

"She's right," Aunt Lana agreed. "Dray was peeking in a little while ago, and he said the guys are getting anxious. Nik, especially."

"Right. Okay." Gulping in deep breaths, Momma dabbed at her eyes one more time before lifting her chin. "Fuck, you're getting married. How are you this old? Weren't you a baby yesterday?"

"Oops, guess you blinked, and it passed you by," I teased.

"You're trying to be a smartass, but you're right. Time did go by too quickly." Sighing, she started herding everyone toward the door. "I think the biggest hurdles we have to face now are getting Evan down the aisle with the rings still actually on the pillow, and your dad down the aisle without the man completely losing it."

"I have my money on Evan," Aunt Layla murmured to the others as they stepped out of the penthouse suite ahead of us.

"Double or nothing, Evan has to be bribed," Aunt Lana laughed.

"I'm already ahead of you," Lucy told her sister. "Braxton and

Howler both have candy in their pockets to show him. If that doesn't get him moving, I told Harris to stand behind the officiant and give him 'the look.' That's all it takes when he's being naughty."

"The hell?" Lana complained. "Your son nearly broke my back putting his pants on. Why wasn't Harris around for that?"

"Aunt Emmie had a strict no-men-allowed policy in the suite. It was all girls except for my hellion."

"He gets it from his Poppy," Aunt Layla said as we all somehow got into the elevator together. Everyone stayed back against the walls so as not to scrunch up my dress. "Jesse spoils him way too much."

Everyone in the metal box except for the kids and Lyla snorted. "Sure, Layla. It's Jesse's fault," Momma said with a roll of her eyes. "Just like it's Jesse's fault the twins are spoiled."

"Hey, it's not all my doing that Luca is still a brat. Violet enables him too much."

"She's not wrong," Nevaeh whispered to me. "Vi kind of does give in to him way too easily."

The elevator doors opened on the second floor where the event space had been set up for the wedding, and everyone went silent.

Uncle Jesse, Uncle Drake, Uncle Shane, and my dad all stood there waiting. Four pairs of eyes went straight to me before I could even move, and they all instantly filled with tears. "Baby girl," Daddy choked out as he stepped forward and offered me his arm. "You're more beautiful than I ever imagined."

I tried not to let my tears blur my vision as I walked out of the elevator. Everyone was afraid to ruin my dress, hair, or makeup, but they bent to give me air kisses before rushing to take their seats. Howler, Braxton, and my brother came out of a room close by as the music began to play inside.

Momma lined everyone up in front of the double doors, with Jagger leading the way to escort her down the aisle, followed by Josie, then Lyla and Howler. Nevaeh and Braxton would be next, followed by Hayat and Evan, leaving Daddy to walk me down the aisle last. Momma took my brother's arm, and the doors opened while Daddy and I stayed out of the line of sight. I bit my lip to keep myself from sneaking a peek in at Barrick.

For the next few moments, I concentrated on the doors opening and closing. First on my mom and brother, then on the three bridesmaids and the two groomsmen. They closed one more time, and I was thankful Hayat took her little brother's hand.

"If you mess this up for Auntie Mia, I will hide every one of your dinosaurs where you'll never find them," she hissed. "And when you go to Mommy and Daddy, crying about what I did, I'll tell them the truth. I won't even get in trouble. Remember that when you want to be a bad boy, Evan. Remember that Poppy and PopPop will take my side, because they love Auntie Mia too. Don't be a butthead for the rest of the day, or I swear you'll regret it."

Dad's blue gaze met mine, and both our eyes widened. Sweet little Hayat was coming into her own, protecting those she loved, and I honestly couldn't have been prouder of her. Normally, she was the one who jumped in to keep Evan out of trouble, but even she was fed up with her brother's antics of the day.

Her warning seemed to do the trick more than any bribes or "look," because when the doors opened again and the two children started their trek down the aisle, Evan stood up as straight as a little soldier, holding on to the pillow which held the wedding bands. I heard "aww"s and "how adorable"s from many of the guests before the doors closed once again.

Which meant it was almost my turn. Anticipation made my palms sweat. After my years of dancing onstage for tens of thousands of people, stage fright was the least of my worries. But what I felt had nothing to do with anxiety and everything to do with the exhilaration of becoming Barrick's wife.

Sucking in a steading breath, I glanced up at Daddy as we took our places right in front of the double doors this time. "You okay?" he asked in a shaky voice.

"I'm great," I assured him. "Best day ever."

His throat worked, but he nodded. "It is a good day. I'm so proud of you. You've turned into an amazing woman. And I'm so honored that I get to be a part of this day with you. For a little while, I thought you wouldn't let me walk you down the aisle."

"That wouldn't have happened," I promised. "Even when I was so angry I couldn't see straight, I knew this day wouldn't be complete without you at my side."

Dad's chin began to tremble, and I inhaled deeply again, fighting the sting of tears. "Daddy, please don't cry. Nothing's changing today except my last name."

"Doesn't matter," he rasped. "You're my little girl. This might be the best day of your life, but it's one of the hardest of mine." He dropped his blue gaze to my stomach. "One day, you'll understand this feeling."

Before I could answer, the music changed, and the doors swung open again. I tucked my arm through Dad's. "No matter what," I whispered as we took the first step down the aisle. "I loved you first."

My words sent him over the edge, and he was sobbing unashamedly before we even took two more steps. In an attempt to hold on to my own composure, I looked at Barrick. Dressed in an all-black tux that was stretched tight over his shoulders, with his mahogany hair hanging below his chin, he looked delicious. Then our gazes locked, and any hope I had of not bawling my eyes out vanished when I saw he was crying just as openly as Dad was.

I barely remembered the walk to the end of the aisle. Everyone on either side was a blur of colors. When we reached the others, the officiant asked who gave the bride away, but instead of placing my hand in Barrick's, Dad slowly released me and stepped forward. The two men I loved the most hugged hard, slapping each other on the back.

"Welcome to the family, son," I heard Dad tell my groom.

"Th-thank you, sir," Barrick choked out.

As they pulled apart, Dad picked up my hand again and placed it in Barrick's. "I'm not giving this girl away," he announced in a voice that only slightly quavered, reminding me a little of when Uncle Jesse has done the same with Lucy. "She will always be mine and her mother's. But now, we take Barrick into our family—with open arms. We welcome him as one of our own. Now and always."

Somehow, we made it through the vows while still crying. If it weren't for the smiles on our faces, a stranger might have thought we were being tortured from how hard we sobbed at times. But then the officiant pronounced us husband and wife, and Barrick tilted my chin up just enough so he could place a kiss in the center of my forehead.

The breath became trapped in my throat, and I closed my eyes, savoring the feeling of his lips on my flesh, his fingertips on my face, the goose bumps that began to pop up and spread along my entire body, making the entire moment almost euphoric. My tears stopped, and all I could do was be thankful that Dad had gone overboard and brought this man into my life.

EPILOGUE

MK

I took the pan of lasagna out of the oven, the scents of garlic and herbs filling the entire house. It was one of Emmie's favorite meals, but she'd called me earlier to say that she had to fly to New York at the last minute for something she couldn't talk about yet. Whatever it was, she'd taken Rodger with her, as well as Barrick.

She'd promised it wouldn't take more than a day, two tops, and then she would be home. Whatever was going on, I pitied whoever was on the receiving end of my wife's ire. With Mia's due date only a few weeks away, having both Emmie and Barrick traveling was only going to make my baby doll agitated as fuck.

But this was Mia's first baby, and they tended to come later than expected. She had a full birthing plan, just as Lana had done with every one of her five pregnancies. Mia was having the baby at the best birthing center, with the most competent staff. I knew because Barrick had done a background check on every person who would potentially come into contact with his wife and child.

Unlike Emmie, Mia wasn't expected to have a C-section. Her hips were a little wider than her mother's, and the baby wasn't measuring as big as I would expect, making us all think that Mia was having a girl, not that we could be one hundred percent sure of that. They hadn't done a gender reveal, wanting to be surprised, and we'd respected that. For her baby shower, everyone had bought gender-neutral items, and the expectant parents had decorated the nursery in the same way.

My phone pinged with a text. Picking it up, I expected it to be Jagger telling me he was spending the weekend with Cannon in Santa Monica, like every other weekend. Instead, I saw Mia's name on the screen.

Mia: Daddy!

I didn't immediately tense when I saw the exclamation mark. Mia got a little overexcited with her punctuation all the time.

> *Me: What's wrong, baby girl?*
> *Mia: Barrick had to go with Momma to New York.*
> *Me: I know. She called me about an hour ago.*
> *Mia: They're already in the air. Barrick's phone is off.*

My muscles slowly began to tense, just a little. She wasn't jumping straight to the point, but instead was rambling. In text. That told me she was nervous.

> *Me: Is everything okay?*

There wasn't an immediate reply, so I sent another.

> *Me: You seem upset.*
> *Mia: My water just broke.*
> *Me: Fu...ck.*

I didn't realize my finger hit the voice-to-text option until the message was already sent. Sighing, I started typing, hoping not to freak her out—even though I was already beginning to panic.
A lot.

> *Me: Okay. Don't worry. Daddy is here. Where are you?*
> *Mia: Home.*

Anxiety and nausea lifted into the back of my throat. This wasn't good. She wasn't supposed to have the baby for another three weeks, at the least. If anything, we'd expected her to go longer since the baby wasn't so big that she was too terribly miserable yet. Emmie and Barrick were supposed to be home when this happened.

My wife was supposed to be here, damn it.

She was the voice of reason, the one who would keep everyone sane. Instead, it was just me, and Mia was all the way in Beverly Hills. She had a guard who stayed on-site whenever Barrick had to travel. Sometimes she came to stay with us, but mostly, she stayed at her place so she could be closer to the dance school. I tried not to panic, but that didn't stop my hands from trembling as I sent another reply.

> *Me: I'll be there ASAP!*
> *Mia: I'm scared, Daddy. My due date is still three weeks away.*
> *Me: Don't worry, sweetheart. I won't let anything happen to you or my grandbaby.*

As soon as I hit send on the last message, I brought up the only other person I could think of on my phone and started typing. By then, my entire body was shaking with nerves, and it was a wonder I didn't drop the damn phone.

Me: Jesse! Mia's water broke, and I can't fucking drive. My hands won't stop shaking, man. HELP!
Jesse: On my way, bro.

My best friend only lived down the street, so he was there to pick me up in less than a minute.

"Where's Layla?" I asked, trying to distract myself.

"Lucy's," he said, weaving through traffic, driving like he did it for a paycheck. "I texted her. She's calling Emmie's assistant. Hopefully she can find a way to reach Em's pilot and get them turned around."

"Yeah," I panted, the panic pushing the air out of my lungs at a faster rate than normal. "Let's hope."

By the time we got to Mia's house, she was already sitting on the front steps. Her bodyguard stood beside her with two overnight bags in his hands. The man's face was pale, but at least Mia seemed calm enough. Seeing that she didn't appear scared put me at ease—a little.

Jesse hit the brakes, and I jumped out.

"Here," she said, handing me a plastic trash bag and several thick towels. I stared down at them in confusion. "So I don't leak all over the seat, Daddy."

"Yeah, okay." I put the trash bag down first and then the towels before lifting her into the SUV, while the bodyguard placed the bags in the back. He took the front passenger seat, and I slid in beside Mia from the other side. As soon as everyone's seat belts were fastened, Jesse burned rubber again as he pulled away from the house.

"The birthing center is expecting me," Mia said, rubbing her belly.

"Good. Good." I raked my hands through my hair. "Good."

My daughter made a little sound in the back of her throat and began breathing deeply. In. Hold. Out. Slow and steady. I watched her with terror in my eyes as she breathed through what must have been a contraction. But surprisingly, my own breathing mimicked hers, and I was able to fight off a panic attack.

In no time, we were at the birthing center and in a huge private room. The staff moved quickly to get Mia set up according to her birthing plan, which meant *no epidural.* Which seemed like something she was fine with...

Until the contractions started getting closer together and more powerful.

"Are you sure about the no epidural, sweetheart?" I asked, wiping the sweat from my brow while she slowly rocked in an antique-like chair while breathing through the latest horrible contraction.

"I'm. Sure," she gritted out. "Was Rachel able to reach Momma or Barrick?"

"They're on their way back now," I told her, reading the last text I'd gotten from Emmie. It had been time stamped an hour before. Their Wi-Fi had been out for a few hours, but once Barrick had sorted it out, their phones had gotten hit with all the voice mails and texts about what was going on. They had been halfway to New York by that time, but at least they were turned around now.

The hope was that the labor would last long enough for them to arrive in time for the baby to be born, but as the contractions kept getting closer and closer, that hope dwindled.

Because of strict protocols, Mia was only allowed the people she'd listed on her birthing plan to be present for the delivery. Barrick's parents were still out of his life, so that only left him, Emmie, and, to my surprise, Mia had put me on the list as well.

It made me happy that she'd thought enough of me to place me on that list, but I'd never thought I would actually be there for the entire laboring process. She'd even laughed at the baby shower and said she figured I would leave when she started pushing. I would have happily switched places with any of her aunts who were in the waiting room. All of them had experience with giving birth. They would have known how to help her through the pain, how to make this all easier on her. Instead, the staff refused even to contemplate letting anyone but the names listed on the birthing plan past the labor and delivery doors.

Mia didn't seem nearly as concerned with having me there as opposed to someone more qualified—like Dallas, who was in the waiting room with Axton. Or Lana, who'd had five babies with no drugs. The woman was a fucking superhero if she'd gone through even half of what I'd witnessed Mia experiencing with every one of her own deliveries. It gave me a new respect for her, that was for damn sure.

Emmie had had C-sections with both her pregnancies, so this was all new territory for me. She'd been strapped to a table, and all I'd had to do was talk to her while the doctors worked their magic on the other side of a tent that separated us from her lower half. There hadn't been any walking around the room or bouncing on an exercise ball. No rocking in a chair or a nurse asking if she wanted them to run her a bath. The most excitement from either of my children being born was when Emmie's water had broken and she'd had to have an emergency C-section rather than her scheduled one.

For hours, I'd been at Mia's side. Wiping her brow, rubbing her back, scratching my fingers through her hair to try to relax her. Feeding her ice chips, singing her lullaby when she grew tense and begged me to sing it. For the baby, she'd claimed, but something told me it was just as much for her as my grandbaby.

"I can't sit here anymore," Mia groused, and before I could help her, she pushed up from the rocking chair where she'd been for the last hour.

As she did, her hands went around her stomach, and she released a mixture of a scream and a groan that echoed off the walls and nearly burst my eardrums. "Fuuuuck!" she sobbed, making the sound again. "Daddy, help. The baby, it's...coming!"

I barely had time to drop to my knees before she pulled up her gown, and I saw a head. Just sticking out from between her spread legs. There was no time for embarrassment, no time to think about the fact that I was seeing a part of my daughter I was never meant to see now that she was an adult. Fuck, I'd changed her diaper a million times when she was a baby. All I could think was that I had to help her, that my grandbaby was going to fall if I didn't catch them.

"Someone get in here!" I bellowed while Mia made that horrible noise again. The baby's shoulders pushed free, making the baby fall right into my waiting arms.

We were both breathing hard as I looked down at the goo-covered little angel in my arms. She was red, coated in blood and other things I didn't want to think about. But there was a little patch of matted hair that, even though she was smeared in gunk, I could tell had an auburn tint to it. She was the tiniest thing I'd ever seen, even smaller than Jesse's twins when they were born—or so it seemed to my befuddled brain. Her arms and legs kicked, her fingers balling into fists as she angrily screeched at her sudden entrance into the world.

Behind me, the doors flew open, and all the nurses, a midwife, and a doctor came running. The baby was taken from me, the nurses helped Mia sit on the edge of the bed, and the midwife assisted her to deliver the afterbirth. Meanwhile, the doctor took the baby, cut the cord, and then took her over to the station that had been set up not long after our arrival in preparation for this very moment.

My gaze was everywhere. On Mia, who was still panting and groaning as the afterbirth was pushed free. On the baby, who was now crying even louder and getting cleaned up. On the blood and whatever else that was on my hands, arms, and shirt.

"Daddy, are you okay?" Mia asked when she could finally catch her breath.

A half-hysterical laugh escaped me. "I should be asking you that, baby girl."

On jelly-filled legs, I got to my feet and stumbled over to her. Dropping a kiss on top of her head, I took stock of my child. "How are you feeling, sweetheart?"

"Exhausted, but good now that the baby is out." She leaned back against the pillows, her gaze going to where the doctor handed a swaddled baby back to a nurse, who then brought her over to us.

"What an exciting entrance your little girl made," the nurse said with a laugh, placing the baby in Mia's arms.

"Girl?" Mia echoed, looking down at the still-crying bundle, continuing to struggle to catch her breath. Her body had gone through a lot in a very short amount of time, and I couldn't be sure she wasn't in shock, which was why her breathing was still labored.

"Surprise." The nurse winked. "Is there a name?"

"Emerson," Mia panted, and the midwife instructed another nurse to put oxygen in Mia's nose. Instantly, she was able to breathe easier, and she relaxed against the pillows. "After my mom and grandfather. Emerson Nikole." She looked up at me. "If the baby was a boy, it would have been Emerson Nikolas."

The tears that had already been close to the surface spilled over. "Beautiful name, Mia. Just like this little one." I leaned down, getting a better look at my granddaughter. Seeing her was like turning back the hands on a clock and setting eyes on Mia for the first time.

Another replica of Emmie.

The best gift anyone could have ever given me.

My heart turned to mush, and I fell head over heels for another redheaded little beauty for the third time in my life.

Emerson kept squealing, and I leaned in closer. "Hey there, Little Em," I greeted, stroking my finger—that had surprisingly stopped shaking—down her soft cheek. "Welcome to the world, baby girl." Her cries began to quiet at my voice, and I kissed the baby's brow. "Hi, sweetheart. I'm your Papa."

What sounded like a huff was pushed from the baby, making her mother and me laugh. "Already like your MiMi," I said with a shake of my head. "Fuck, but I love you, little one."

Mia laid her head back on the pillow. "Did that really just happen?" she asked in a drowsy voice. "Did you really catch the baby as she fell out of me?"

"Something like that," I said softly, taking the baby from her arms. I could see the exhaustion was taking hold of her as the adrenaline from everything began to fade, and I didn't want her to drop the baby.

"Sleep now, baby girl. Daddy's here. You and our Little Em are safe."

"I knew we would be," she said, closing her eyes with a weak smile. "I have the best dad in the world."

BARRICK

"Get out of the fucking way!" I roared, slamming my hand down on the horn as a car cut us off.

Beside me, Emmie was furiously typing away, her green eyes bigger than I'd ever seen them in all the years I'd known her as she tried to get information on Mia. "No one knows anything, and Nik isn't answering my texts. Fuck, fuck, fuck!" Pushing her hair out of her face, she slapped her hand on the dash to steady herself when I made a hairpin turn to pass the asshole who'd cut in front of me. "Godsdamn it! This is all my fault. I should have just sent Annabelle to deal with the New York issue."

"Annabelle could have handled it, but not as easily as you would have," I tried to excuse. "I should have sent Braxton with you instead of going. Then at least one of us would have been here."

"No, I needed you with me," she argued. "If I was there, then you had to be too. The baby wasn't supposed to be here for another three weeks. We had time. There should have been enough time."

Eyes still on the road in front of me, I reached over and squeezed her arm. Her hand covered mine, and she held on for a few moments, the two of us giving and accepting comfort. She was right. The baby wasn't supposed to be here yet. Neither of us had known this would happen when we'd gotten on that plane.

Knowing that didn't stop the guilt from choking me. And then there was the fear. Fucking hell, I'd never been so afraid in my life. I didn't have my eyes on my pregnant wife who had gone into early labor, and it was causing sweat to pour down my face and soak through my shirt.

As soon as the plane had touched down, we'd grabbed the first available vehicle. Rodger had insisted on driving because I was already shaking, but he drove like an old woman who needed glasses. At least, that was how it seemed in my head when I'd considered him getting us to the birthing center as quickly as possible. Subconsciously, I knew he was a great driver. I'd trusted him to get Mia and her mom from point A to point B many times. But at the moment, he was in the back seat while I drove like the freeway was a Formula 1 racetrack.

Finally, the birthing center came into view, and I braked hard at the front entrance. As I did, Jesse and Drake came out of the sliding double doors, which told me they had been waiting on us. Drake got behind the wheel to park the SUV for me, while Jesse gave us a recounting of everything he knew so far—which was nothing we didn't already know.

Emmie pushed her anxiety down and switched from worried mom to total boss in an instant. In no time, the two of us were led back to the private birthing rooms. As we passed a nurses station, we were given warm smiles, but I was focused on trying to listen for any sound of Mia.

I hadn't liked aspects of her birthing plan. The idea of her being in pain had made my stomach churn, but she'd been adamant about no drugs, no epidural. Everything would be as natural as possible unless something went wrong. My biggest fear was that we would arrive and hear her screaming in agony from the contractions.

The nurse who was showing us to Mia's room paused and then knocked softly before opening the closed door. As we followed her inside, I noticed the lights were turned down low. The only sound I heard was Nik quietly singing Mia's lullaby.

In the dim lighting, my eyes traveled around the room in search of my wife. I found her sound asleep, lying in the bed with oxygen tubes in her nose. On the other side of the bed, in a reclining chair, Nik sat with a little bundle in his arms. Even when his gaze met mine and then Emmie's, he never stopped singing.

Realization hit me, and my knees nearly buckled. The baby had already been born. I'd missed the birth of my first child. Guilt mixed with disappointment tried to choke me again, but I pushed that aside as I quietly crossed to my father-in-law. The singing turned to soft humming as he stood and gently shifted the baby, who was wrapped in a yellow blanket.

"How did it go?" Emmie whispered as she reached her husband. "Is Mia okay?"

"We had an adventure," Nik said with a grim smile. "But Mia handled it just like I would have expected her momma to. Like a superhero." He lowered his arms a little so she could get her first look at her grandchild. "Say hello to Emerson."

The name didn't tell me if I had a son or daughter. Emerson was a gender-neutral name that Mia had come up with. I'd seen the glitter in her eyes, knew how much the name meant to her, and I'd agreed without hesitation that it was the perfect name for our child.

"Emerson," Emmie repeated, her voice full of awe as she touched the baby's cheek.

"Emerson Nikole," Nik said, and I felt light-headed.

A girl.

I had a daughter.

Sucking in a deep breath, I watched my mother-in-law through tear-filled eyes as she swallowed roughly and continued speaking to the baby. "Hello, sweet girl. I'm your MiMi."

"Beast?" The sound of Mia's voice nearly knocked me on my ass, but I found the strength to cross to the bed. Bending, I kissed her forehead, scared to touch her for fear that I might hurt her in some way.

She smiled up at me, but I could see she was exhausted. "You made it," she whispered.

"I missed it," I choked out. "I'm so sorry, firecracker. If I had known, I never would have—"

"Shh," she soothed, stroking her fingers through my beard. "There's no reason to apologize. You left me in good hands."

"But I should have been beside you."

"Next time," she murmured with a smile. "I promise, you'll be beside me every second of the next delivery."

"Next time?" Nik nearly whimpered. "I don't like this 'next time' shit."

"Was it bad?" Emmie asked, glancing from her daughter to her husband and back again, her shoulders tensing. Her green eyes got even bigger, if that was possible. "You two aren't telling me something. What happened?"

Mia snickered. "I had a baby. What else could have happened, Momma?"

"How many times did you have to push?" her mom grilled.

"Twice," Nik answered. "Two big pushes and our granddaughter was in my arms."

"Two pushes?" Emmie said with a mixture of awe and disbelief. "That's unheard of for a first-time mother."

"Yeah, it was definitely crazy," Mia said with a yawn. "But I'm glad you two are here now. Have you met Emerson yet?"

"She's beautiful," Emmie whispered, lowering her gaze back to the yellow-wrapped bundle.

I could only stand beside my wife's bed, watching them. My baby girl was right there, waiting in her grandfather's arms, and all I could do was stand like a statue, watching. I ached to reach for her, but my arms wouldn't move. The adrenaline that had been coursing through my veins since we'd gotten the messages that Mia was in labor was finally starting to recede, and I felt just as exhausted as my beautiful wife looked.

"Beast?" Mia said softly, her hand grasping my arm.

Swallowing with difficulty, I tore my gaze away from the baby to shift to her.

"It's time to hold our daughter, Barrick."

"Wh-what if I break her?" I rasped, voicing my fear. "She looks so tiny. I might hurt her."

"Momma," Mia said without taking her eyes off me.

Suddenly, a chair was beside me, and Nik was pushing me into it. I hadn't even realized he'd transferred the baby to his wife until she was standing beside me, rocking the little bundle like an expert. Watching her, I began to sweat again. My hands swung up, ready to catch the baby in case Emmie dropped her.

"Take a deep breath, son," Nik instructed. "The first time is always scary as hell, but you'll become a pro in no time, I promise."

Emmie slowly lowered her arms, ready to place the baby in my hands, and a whimper escaped me. "W-wait," I pleaded, but she was already extracting her hands out from under mine. Awkwardly, I shifted, trying not to jostle the baby.

What if I held her too tight and broke her in half?

I couldn't do this.

I was too big, too destructive, to hold something as precious as this baby, and then Emerson made a cooing noise and yawned. Her eyes opened—eyes that took up most of her face. Just like her momma's. The rest of the world slipped away, and all I saw were those eyes. They pulled me in, and I felt myself drowning in them. Love squeezed at my chest, choking me.

"Hello, Little Em," I murmured, adjusting my hold without realizing it. The fear was there, just beneath the surface, but it was hard to focus on something as trivial as that when I was looking into the face of the most beautiful creature I'd ever set eyes on in my life. "I'm your daddy."

She yawned again and slowly closed her eyes, but the damage was done. I was already hooked, my entire being wrapped around this little girl's finger so tight that nothing could ever untangle me.

The world as I knew it was never going to be the same again.

~THE END~

Book 2

CHAPTER 1

NEVAEH

I tugged nervously at the hem of my skirt while Braxton opened the restaurant door. I'd been to plenty of charity and red-carpet events, had had far too many cameras and microphones shoved in my face to count. A lifetime exposed to the elements that came with being a celebrity's offspring made it close to impossible to experience the feeling of nervousness in front of a crowd.

Yet there I was, so nervous I couldn't keep from trembling as we entered the noisy 3-star Michelin restaurant in downtown DC. I'd graduated from college the previous weekend, and Braxton had proposed right after the ceremony. We were only in the area for a few more days, finishing up with packing and getting everything else sorted. But since Mom was already in wedding planning mode with Aunt Emmie, we still had one major thing that we needed to do before we made the move to California.

In all the years I'd known Brax, and the months since we'd started dating, not a single time had I met either of his parents. Mostly because he was estranged from them. They hadn't condoned his enlisting in the Marines and were even more upset when he'd lost his leg while on deployment. Then there had been the whole diabolical incident of the Collinses announcing their son was marrying Darcy Hamilton, his high school girlfriend.

That shit had nearly cost us our relationship, but thankfully, my dad had made me see things from a different perspective and give Braxton another chance. It was only later that we found out Darcy really was pregnant, and Braxton's father was the baby's daddy. That the older Collins had attempted to push his child with his mistress off on his son was beyond mind-blowing.

After it was confirmed from the tail Brax had put on Darcy, he'd allowed his cousin Lyla to do whatever she wanted with the information and pictures. She had yet to do anything with them, however, and Braxton seemed to have forgotten all about it.

At least until Mom and Daddy had mentioned all of us having dinner together so that we could officially be introduced. What with Braxton and me getting married in August, it seemed only right for the two sets of parents to meet. I'd wanted to argue—not only did I not want to put my fiancé through having to see his parents again, but I wasn't all too thrilled to meet them either. The last I'd heard about the supposed wedding plans Mrs. Collins and Mrs. Hamilton had been arranging for their children, they had both been enraged.

According to Lyla, who got the details from a rare phone call from her own mother, her sister—Braxton's mother—was furious. To them, I was the other woman and the sole reason why Braxton had "turned his back on Darcy and their unborn child." Not only had I ruined a wedding, but apparently I was keeping a father from his own child.

My parents knew a little about what had happened before my dad's life-saving liver transplant, but I hadn't told them the full extent of the Collinses' dislike of me. I was hoping Belinda Collins would have seen reason in the months since Braxton had called and told her straight up that there wasn't going to be a wedding between him and Darcy. As for Miles Collins, I had little doubt he knew that we were aware of his secret life and his impending second fatherhood.

As far as I knew, there hadn't been any announcements in the society pages regarding the canceled wedding plans. Which made me think everyone was simply waiting for Braxton to come to his senses and dump me before moving forward with the wedding.

The news that Braxton and I were not only getting married, but he was also moving to California with me, was probably not going to go over well at all.

My parents had texted to let me know they were already seated, so we bypassed the hostess stand. Braxton kept his hand at the small of my back, guiding me past full tables and busy waitstaff. It wasn't hard to miss which table was intended for us, especially when nearly every eye in the place was on the man kissing his wife like his life depended on it.

Groaning, I stopped beside the table. My embarrassed sound didn't deter the make-out session between the older couple. Sighing, I looked up at Braxton imploringly. Grinning, he cleared his throat, loudly. That only had Daddy gently grasping the back of Mom's head and deepening the kiss.

"For the sake of my ability to keep my dinner down, can you please stop the face-sucking?" I scolded.

Slowly, my dad lifted his head and blinked his blue-gray eyes a few times. "I don't say anything when the boy kisses you in front of me," he reminded us.

"'The boy' has never kissed me like that in front of you," I returned, sitting in the chair beside him after Braxton pulled it out. "You two were putting on a free show for everyone."

Mom waved her hand in front of her face, her brown eyes glazed with—ugh, I didn't want to think about why her eyes were so glittery. Her lips were swollen, and her cheeks had a pretty glow to them that burned through her makeup, making her look overheated. Shaking my head at the both of them, I smiled despite the flutter of nervousness still making me uneasy. Drake and Lana Stevenson were the embodiment of soul mates. I was used to very public shows of affection between them, and as a kid, I'd secretly coveted the same kind of relationship with someone when I grew up.

Feeling Braxton's fingers caress my exposed neck caused by my hair falling over my shoulder, I leaned into his touch. When I'd met Braxton, I'd met my own soul mate. He'd given me the fairy-tale relationship I'd always dreamed of, just as I knew he'd give me the fairy-tale forever we both deserved.

Daddy shifted in his chair before running his fingers through his long hair, untangling it from where Mom had knotted her fingers in the thick locks only moments before. As he pushed the strands back from his face, I couldn't help noticing how healthy he looked. He was leaner than he'd been before the transplant, but in a good way. His skin had a glow to it instead of that jaundiced yellow color from his heavily scarred liver caused by all his years of drinking when he was younger.

Catching me looking at him, he leaned over and touched his lips to the side of my head. As he pulled back, he lifted his phone from where it had been facedown on the table. "Emmie sent more listings. Two of them are in the same neighborhood as us. There's one closer to Shane, but I'm partial to this one myself."

I shifted my chair closer to him so we could look at the pictures of the house he professed to like so much. All it took was a glance at the address to realize why he was so partial to it above the others. It was just a few houses down from the home I'd grown up in.

Laughing, I poked him in the arm. "I told you already, Daddy. I want to do an actual walk-through of any house we consider. We're looking for our forever home, so it has to tick all my boxes or it's a no."

"I'm just saying, it's a great location, and according to the real estate agent, it fits the criteria for all the things you want." He rested his arm along the back of my chair and lowered his voice. "And it will make your mom really happy if you're that close, Nev."

Mom would be happy. Sure. I totally bought that it was she who would be the happiest if we picked a house so close to my parents.

I wrapped my arms around his neck and pressed a hard kiss to his cheek. "I'll give it extra consideration when we do the walk-through," I promised.

That spread a goofy grin across his face. It made me happy to see it and be the one to put it there.

A foot wrapped around the leg of my chair, and I suddenly found myself only inches from Braxton's chair. It was adorable that he couldn't go even a few minutes without me close enough to touch. From across the table, Mom laughed. "That house just happened to get listed a week ago."

"Angel," Daddy grumbled warningly.

"What?" she murmured, blinking at him in faux innocence. "I'm just making conversation about our neighbors, babe."

"Seems like they aren't your neighbors any longer," Braxton commented with a smirk.

"I'm surprised he didn't try to pull his antics on the couple directly next door," my mom said, taking a drink of her water.

"Nevaeh wouldn't have liked that house," Daddy told her with a shrug. "Besides, that house only has three bedrooms. This one has five. That gives them plenty of room if they want to start having babies soon."

"Pregnancy and grad school at the same time?" I shot all three of them a glare. "Not happening."

"Soon doesn't have to mean right away," Mom amended. "It's an unspecified time frame."

I folded my arms over my chest and cocked a brow at her. "I'm not having a baby while I'm in grad school."

"That doesn't really mean anything time-wise," she argued with another laugh. "You're an eighteen-year-old college graduate. You'll have your doctorate in no time."

"I could take the job offer from NASA after all." I didn't realize the words had even slipped out of my mouth until I saw my parents stiffen.

"You were offered a job with NASA?" they both exclaimed at the same time, each with a different emotion in their voices.

Mom's was full of wonder and awe, whereas Daddy's was sharp and filled with dread.

"She didn't take the offer," Braxton rushed to answer for me while I fought an overwhelming feeling of guilt for my moment of word-vomit. I hated that I did stuff like that. There were too many pieces of data in my head all at once, and random comments just slipped out. Usually they were things that embarrassed me, but there were times—like in that moment—when they were words that caused those I loved pain.

"I didn't take the offer, Daddy," I reaffirmed and was rewarded by the tension fading from his handsome face. "Actually, I turned it down before they even finished their pitch. I don't want a job to distract me while I'm getting my PhD."

"Smart thinking," he said then grimaced. "But if NASA will make you happy, then you should take the job."

"Living in Santa Monica near you and Mom, married to Braxton, that's what will make me happy. The job doesn't matter."

CHAPTER 2

BRAXTON

I was thankful Nevaeh was distracted by her parents and talking about her turning down the job offer some headhunter had been sent to hire her for. The guy had shown up on campus one afternoon. Her adviser had asked her to come in for a meeting to talk about her future goals. Neveah'd called me, and I'd shown up just in time for the man to introduce himself.

In the doorway of the adviser's office, he'd gotten out his name and who he worked for before she'd told him point-blank that she wasn't interested and turned to leave. While she'd been walking toward me, I'd kept my gaze on the NASA representative and nearly split my gut open trying to contain my laughter.

He'd been slack-jawed, with a mixture of confusion and irritation in his eyes as my kitten walked away from him.

The man most likely had been about to offer her a job most nerds would have given their firstborn for. But Nevaeh knew what she wanted from her future, and working in Houston wasn't in her plans.

While she reassured her father again that she didn't want to live in Texas, I caught sight of my own parents making their way through the crowded restaurant. They kept as much distance between themselves as was possible, given the busy waitstaff moving around, delivering food and drinks to the other patrons. My father's face was tight, displeasure clear in his expression. Meanwhile, my mother looked as if she'd been sucking on lemons all day. Pursed lips, clenched jaw, narrowed eyes.

Neither of them was happy about being present for this little get-together that Lana had insisted on. She wanted to meet the people who had raised me, get to know her daughter's future in-laws a little before the big move. I'd warned her it wasn't going to go as she hoped, and from the looks on my parents' faces, I knew my prediction was going to be more accurate than I'd expected.

I attempted to keep myself from tensing so that Nevaeh wouldn't grow nervous once again since her dad had already distracted her enough to put the reason for this meal out of her mind. When I alerted Lana to the couple that was slowly making their way toward us, she barely shifted her eyes to see them. Putting on one of her smiles that could light up a room just like her daughter's, she pushed back her chair and walked over to meet my mom before she could reach the table.

"You must be Belinda," Lana said, offering her hand. "I'm Lana Stevenson, Nevaeh's mom."

My mother glanced down at Lana's hand as if it were covered in filth, but all eyes were on the two women. She had no choice but to lightly put her hand in Lana's and shake. Before the women dropped their arms, Drake was at his wife's side, greeting my dad with a handshake.

Beside me, Neveah began to fidget with her dress again. Leaning in, I kissed her forehead. "Relax, Kitten. It's one dinner, and then we will probably never have to see them again."

Sadness filled her eyes when they met mine. "But they're your family, Brax."

"Barrick and Lyla are my family. Judge and Howler are my family. You," I rasped against her ear, "you are my everything. Those two people over there? They mean very little to me in comparison. Especially my father."

"I'm sorry," she whispered. "I tried to talk Mom out of this."

"She has every right to want to meet the people who brought me into the world. I only hope she understands that just because I was raised by them, doesn't mean I'm like them."

Nevaeh cupped the side of my face, her engagement ring catching the lights and glittering like a beacon. "No one would ever think that you are anything like them." She pressed her lips to mine for a kiss that was over far too soon. "If random thoughts come out of my mouth, start shoving things in it to keep me quiet, okay?"

I brushed my nose against hers. "But Kitten, I'll get arrested if I shove what I want to in that pretty mouth."

With a snicker, she playfully slapped my chest. "Food, dummy. Not your dick."

"Charming." My mother's snide voice made Nevaeh jump.

Taking hold of her left hand, I lifted it to my lips for a slow kiss before finally turning my gaze on the woman who'd given birth to me. "Mother, nice of you to join us." Forcing myself to stand, I ignored the pain in my leg as I turned to face my parents. "Father," I gritted out.

"Good to see you again, son," Miles Collins said in his monotone voice that grated down my spine. Then his gaze fell on Nevaeh, who was still seated at the table, her face blood red from my mother embarrassing her. I shifted, blocking her from his view. I didn't like him in the same room as my kitten, let alone close enough to touch her.

He wasn't good enough to breathe the same air as Nevaeh.

"Nevi," Lana said softly. "Don't be shy. These people are going to be part of your family soon."

With a heavy sigh, she stood and forced herself to meet my mother's eyes. "Hello, Mrs. Collins. It's a pleasure to meet you and your husband."

"We can't say the same," the other woman commented.

The air around us changed in a heartbeat. I put my arm around Nevaeh's waist, protectively tucking her close as her parents came up on either side of my mother.

"We invited you here to get to know one another a little better," Lana said in a cool tone. "But I'll have the waiter show you out if you speak to my daughter like that again."

"Your daughter is nothing but a home-wrecking little whore." Mom's gaze traveled up and down Lana's slender body. With her hair free from gray and only a few lines on her face, she didn't look like she should have an eighteen-year-old daughter. Hell, she looked more like Nevaeh's older sister than her mom, but Lana had been in her twenties when they'd had their first of five children. "And I'm sure the apple doesn't fall far from the tree."

"Ah, fuck," Nevaeh whispered. "Things are about to get crazy."

The words hadn't fully left her mouth when her mom swung back and delivered a punch direct center to my mother's face. My mom screamed in pain, while the entire restaurant seemed to gasp in shock as one. Blood poured out from around her fingers and splattered on her designer dress.

"If you ever call my child a whore again, a broken nose will be the least of your worries, bitch," Lana seethed, shaking out her hand.

Drake grasped her hand, inspecting it for any damage she may have caused herself. Briefly, he lifted his head and snapped his fingers at a waiter. "Get my angel a bag of ice for her hand," he commanded before turning his focus back on his wife's already-bruising knuckles.

"You need to have a better rein on your wife, Stevenson," my father grumbled.

Slowly, as if he were a predator capturing his prey in his sights, Drake turned his head and looked at Miles. I heard him gulp at the feral look in the rock legend's blue-gray eyes. "I suggest you take your bitch wife and go, dickhead. Before I start spilling your dirty secrets here in this packed restaurant with people who know you."

"Belinda," Miles snapped. "Let's go."

Even holding her still-bleeding nose, my mother was able to toss her hair back and hmph as she walked past Lana. With a little growl, Lana started to grab for her, but Drake stepped into her path, lightly tightening his grip on her injured hand. "Easy, Angel. You already made your point."

The waiter returned with the bag of ice—and the manager. "Sir, I'm afraid you and your party will have to leave, or I will be forced to call the police."

"Gladly," Drake gritted out. "If you allow trash like that in here, then I'm sure the food isn't nearly as good as your accolades claim."

"Sir," the manager began again, a look of outrage on his face. "Please don't make more of a scene."

Carefully releasing Lana's hand, Drake pulled out his wallet and extracted several bills. Tossing them on the table, he lifted his chin at the waiter who had brought the bag of ice. "For you, kid."

CHAPTER 3

NEVAEH

Pushing my glasses up my nose, I went through my emails, trying to decide which ones I could knock out before I went to bed. Summer grad school classes were no joke, and I was thankful that my mom and Aunt Emmie were the ones handling the intimate little wedding I'd asked for.

If it were up to me, Braxton and I would have had a quickie wedding in Vegas and been done with it. But Mom had pleaded for the whole shebang, and a few kisses from my groom had tempted me into agreeing. At least Mom wasn't all psychotic over the details like Aunt Layla had been for Lucy's wedding. I'd told them something simple; the rest was up to them. All I'd had to do was find a dress, and that had taken several different trips to the designer before I'd finally decided on one.

I wasn't picky about what I wore. Give me some comfy sweats and a pair of fuzzy socks, and I was ready to go. Whether I was working on schoolwork at home, shopping, or going to classes, it didn't really matter. Comfort was everything. Choosing a wedding dress had been a difficult feat for me, but I'd finally picked one I thought looked nice on me.

Halfway through the tedious list of things my professors had assigned for the week, I noticed that Braxton had left his own emails open when he got a notice. Ugh. I fucking hated when notifications popped up. That little red circle always annoyed me, and I couldn't concentrate on anything else.

Clicking on the email icon, I was just going to mark the message as read, but the heading caught my eye, and I paused with the cursor over the X. After I blinked a few times, the words finally penetrated through the numbers and formulas I'd been working on for homework, and I reached for my phone without giving it a second thought. My laughter was a mixture of dry humor—because this had to be a joke—and hysteria—because if it wasn't a joke, someone was going to lose a set of balls.

Me: You're my matron of honor. You better make my bachelorette party worth it.

Since Mia was a new mother, I expected her to take longer to reply, but instead, it was only a matter of moments before I saw those three little dots pop up.

Mia: Brax is letting you have one????

I read over the message again and gritted my teeth.

Me: What Brax doesn't know won't hurt him...
Mia: You're going to get us in SO much trouble, but I'm in.

She was right. Any parties Mia planned for me had to meet Braxton's approval. I hadn't been nearly as OCD about it since Barrick was the best man and anything he did would have to pass Mia's approval. I hadn't really cared—then.

Now, I fucking cared.

Me: Nothing TOOOOO wild. But I'm thinking a stripper would be fun.
Mia: Oh gods, you're going to get someone killed.

Again, she wasn't wrong. Someone was going to die, and if what I'd just read actually happened, then it was going to be the motherfucking groom.

Mia: You do actually want to marry Braxton, right? Not send him to prison. Because that's exactly where he will end up if he kills a fucking stripper.
Me: Of course I want to marry him.

I also wanted to put his balls on a chopping board and cleave them off with a dull, rusty butcher knife.

Me: I'm just a little miffed with him at the moment.
Mia: What did he do?
Me: He's having a bachelor party.
Mia: I'm aware. My husband is the best man.

I rolled my eyes at how condescending she came across in the text. Ugh. Sometimes it was like I had another sister, and I had plenty of experience with what bitches they could be. Lucky for Mia, I loved her. Plus, she was only a few weeks postpartum, so I would excuse her bitchiness.

Me: *Are you also aware that YOUR HUSBAND is getting some chick to jump out of a cake?*
Mia: *...*

Another half-dry, half-hysterical laugh pushed free while I watched those three dots hover in the bubble.

Me: *Oh, did I forget to mention—a topless chick?*
Mia: *Say what now?!*

There was the reaction I was waiting for. The one that would possibly get Barrick's junk chopped off even before I could get the cleaver and find my fiancé.

Me: *I just saw the email with the instructions from the event planner.*
Me: *I guess they sent them to the shared work email instead of Barrick's personal one.*
Mia: *Hold on a sec. I gotta go kill my husband.*
Mia: *And then we're planning a weekend in Vegas.*
Mia: *No men allowed. I'll make sure of it. Just let me call my mom.*

Dropping my phone back on the couch, I went back to doing my homework. Luckily, I could do these formulas in my sleep, because I couldn't stop the anger from rising from a simmer to a full-on boil. He was in his home office on a call with a client who was two hours behind us, so I couldn't burst into the room and demand to know who the fuck he thought he was.

But I sure as fuck wasn't going to just sit there and let the little details he'd been adamant about me not having at my own party be a huge feature at his own.

I didn't even want to go to some strip club. Not really. And Vegas was blah. Especially in freaking August. Dry heat, my ass. Plus, I was only eighteen. Wasn't like I would get to gamble or drink or anything else fun that Mia and Lyla could do.

Realizing that a Vegas weekend wasn't what I wanted at all, I quickly texted Mia to get her to come up with something else, because none of that sounded fun.

Mia: *As soon as I called my mom, I realized that Vegas isn't exactly doable. One, you aren't old enough. Two, I'm breastfeeding and don't want to leave my baby overnight. And three, I'm not any more thrilled about seeing some stranger swing his junk in my face than you are.*

Dejectedly, I texted her back simply.

Me: Yeah.
Mia: Plus, I just logged in to Barrick's work emails and saw the one you were talking about. This is fishy.

I didn't like that word. "Fishy" just sounded wrong in my head. Like "moist" did to other people.

It felt wrong.

Gross.

Grumbling, I hit connect on my friend's name and lifted the phone to my ear. "What do you mean?" I asked as soon as she answered.

"I forwarded the email to Momma and she's going to look into it, but the event planner isn't the one Barrick has been using to put together the bachelor party. I would know, because I am the one who set him up with the small business that runs it. I think we both need to take deep breaths and not think the worst until Momma tells me more."

"Are you sure?"

"Positive. Don't worry about this, Nev. I'll figure it out—or rather, Momma will. No way Barrick would plan some crazy shit like this, and if Braxton knew about something like this, he would make his cousin cancel it immediately."

Her reassuring answer made me realize how ridiculously I'd reacted over something as simple as an email. Grunting at my own idiocy—because Braxton wouldn't do something like that to me, damn it—I began to relax. But then the guilt for even thinking such things about the man I loved began to eat at me.

"I need to go," I muttered, fighting tears. "I'm going to talk to Braxton about this."

"Nev...it's going to be okay," she said soothingly. "I would have responded the exact same way."

"I-I know," I whispered so she wouldn't hear the emotions thickening my voice. "I just... Ugh. I'll talk to you later. Love you. Bye."

Hanging up, I slapped my laptop closed and shoved it onto the couch beside me. After what had happened right before Christmas the previous year, I'd promised myself I'd always give Braxton the benefit of the doubt. Yet I'd jumped to conclusions as soon as I'd seen an email. One that I should have realized was shady as soon as I saw the words "cake" and "topless dancer" together in the same sentence.

That man didn't even think about other women. I was the center of his world—and I fucking knew it. Which was why I was pissed as hell at myself.

Pushing to my feet, I turned toward the back office. The house my parents had bought us—the one just two doors down from their own—was spacious. Mom had even brought in a decorator and selected all the furniture for every room. They'd taken the stress of moving and wedding planning completely off my shoulders so I could concentrate on school as much as possible.

Not two steps from the couch, my phone pinged with a new text, and I scooped it up.

Mia: Momma already spoke to the event planner. The person who requested the topless cake dancer is Belinda Collins! She gave them the work email as a second form of contact so that the guys would see it. If Barrick had seen it before you, he would have been scrambling to stop everything.

I clenched my fingers around the device. In the months since we'd moved to California, Belinda had called Braxton daily, trying to guilt him into leaving me, until he'd blocked her number. Then he'd had to block her on all social media as well as her email. Now it looked like she'd switched gears. Instead of trying to get into Braxton's head about leaving me, she was trying to cause chaos between the two of us. With the wedding only a few short weeks away, she was no doubt scrambling to find a way to drive a wedge between us in a hurry.

That bitch wanted to play?

"Game on."

CHAPTER 4

BRAXTON

As soon as I saw Nevaeh's face, I ended the call with barely a clipped "Call ya back," before I was on my feet and around the desk.

"Kitten?" I cupped her face in both hands, already wiping away her tears. "What's wrong? Did something happen? Drake—"

"I'm sorry," she whispered. "I'm so sorry, Brax."

"There's nothing to be sorry about, baby," I assured her. "Whatever is wrong, we can fix it. I'll take care of everything. Just tell me."

Gulping back a sob, she shook her head, causing her dark hair to float around her shoulders. "I was doing homework, and your work email was open. Th-the one you and...Barrick share."

"Okay."

"There was an email from what I-I thought was the event planner Barrick is using to plan the bachelor party." She sniffled, making her adorable nose twitch. "I thought...he was planning...planning..." She started crying harder, and I couldn't make out anything she said.

Hating how upset she was, I scooped her up and carried her over to my chair behind the desk. Sitting, I cuddled her close. She buried her face in my neck, crying so hard it broke my heart. A lump filled my throat, but I swallowed it down, rubbing her back in an attempt to soothe her.

"I-I-I'm so s-s-s-s-orry," she finished, clinging to my neck.

Leaning back, I tipped up her chin so I could look down into her flushed, swollen, tear-drenched face. Her glasses were fogged so I couldn't see her blue-gray eyes, but the regret and guilt I saw on her beautiful face was difficult to witness. "Whatever you did, I forgive you, Kitten."

"Y-you promise?" she whispered.

"Swear on my life." Wiping away a few more tears, I kissed the tip of her damp nose.

"I didn't mean to doubt you," she said in a rush. "I was doing equations when I read the email, and everything got jumbled in my brain and I think it short-circuited for a minute because I was so angry, I texted Mia and told her to set up a bachelorette party with a stripper and—"

I tensed. "You what?"

"We're not doing it," she quickly assured me. "I saw the words topless dancer and—"

"What do you mean, 'topless dancer'?"

"I'm trying to explain, but you keep interrupting," she huffed, then sniffled again. "The email was from who I thought was the event planner Barrick was using for your party. It upset me, and I got mad. Mia and I texted back and forth, and then I realized I didn't want to go to Vegas, even if it was as payback for you breaking your promise that the bachelor party wasn't going to be wild."

"I would never break a promise to you," I gritted out.

"I know that!" she cried, getting upset again. "It just took me a few minutes to calm down. Mia opened Barrick's emails. She saw the one from the event planner and said it wasn't the company he was using for the party. She sent everything to Aunt Emmie and...and—"

"And?" I urged when she broke off, her chin trembling.

She took off her glasses, tossing them carelessly on my desk, and looked up at me with sad eyes. "Your mom set it up."

I sucked in a deep breath, feeling the blow even though I'd cut both my parents out of my life. I would expect something like that from my father. He was a disgusting asshole who wouldn't think twice about trying to ruin my life for his own gain. But my mother?

Not that I should have been completely surprised. She'd tried everything but actually showing up and locking herself to my side to keep me from marrying Nevaeh. These kinds of antics were beneath her. Something so unsavory as a stripper—or whatever the fuck she'd had planned—wasn't something I expected her to come up with on her own.

"Darcy," I growled my ex's name, only to feel Nevaeh flinch.

"What about her?"

Lifting her from my lap, I placed her on the desk in front of me before standing. Leaning down, I pressed a kiss to the center of her forehead. "Ordering a topless dancer isn't something I would expect my mother to know how to do, Kitten. She's too much of a...a..."

"A snotty bitch?" Nevaeh supplied when I struggled for the right description.

I gave her a grim smile. "Exactly. But Darcy, on the other hand?" I shrugged. "Mother thinks that by me being with you, I'm turning my back on Darcy and her baby. She still assumes the kid is mine. Since I did nothing with the information my tail on Darcy collected, and Lyla has yet to use that dossier, no one knows what we know. Darcy and my father both think their dirty secrets are hidden."

"True," she muttered, nibbling on her bottom lip. "So you're saying she's collaborating with Darcy to come between us?"

"That's my theory, yes."

"Which means Darcy is the one playing games, not your mother." She contemplated that for a moment before hopping down off my desk. "I thought it was just Belinda. But if Darcy is pulling her strings, then it's she who will have to pay. That bitch should have gotten what was coming to her when she showed up at our house back in Virginia."

As she walked around my desk, I frowned. "Where are you going?"

"I have three sisters, Brax. Playing these kinds of games is something I'm not only used to, but very good at." She turned at the door and blew me a kiss. "Don't wait up for me."

"Kitten, wait!" I called after her, but she was already skipping out of the house before I even got to the living room. "Nevaeh!" I called after her as I watched her happily make her way down the street to her parents' house. "Fuck."

I didn't know if I should follow her or let her have her fun. What I did know was that whatever she dished out to Darcy—and anyone else who tried to ruin what we had—would be well deserved. After making sure she went inside her parents' house, I stepped back into our own home and shut the door.

Walking into my office, I grabbed my phone and tried to call Lyla. Even though it was on the later side for the East Coast, I knew she would be awake.

"Sup, cuz," she greeted.

"Ly," I grumbled into the phone. "Why haven't you used any of that information on my dad and Darcy?"

"Ugh, really? I was trying to forget about those images. Now they're back in my head."

"Lyla," I gritted out.

"You seemed to be in a bad place when we talked about those pictures and other...things," she explained. "Then a few days later, you were in a considerably better mental state. I didn't want to fuck with that."

"Thank you for considering my mental health," I told her softly. I loved my cousin like a sister. She and Barrick were all the family I really had. Judge, as well, but he was so busy with everything, he barely had time for anyone else. It was Barrick and Lyla who'd always had my back, no matter what.

"What's going on?" Lyla asked. "I just got a text from Nevaeh to call her."

"Shit. She's going to pull you into the games as well. Look, I'm not sure how it happened, but my mother set up a topless dancer for the bachelor party."

"Bullshit!" she exclaimed then burst out laughing. "No way Aunt Belinda could do that kind of thing. Seriously, Braxton. She wouldn't even know who to call about something like that."

"Exactly. But Darcy would."

"Uh-huh. Okeydokey, then. I'm going to go. Nevaeh needs help making sure everything goes smoothly. See you in a few weeks, cuz. Love you. Bye."

"Wait! Ly...la—" I broke off when I heard nothing but silence.

Blowing out a heavy sigh, I sat back down in my chair and picked up the landline. Whatever Lyla and Nevaeh did to Darcy would be justified, so I wasn't going to worry about that bitch. Instead, I needed to call my client back to arrange a new security system for their mansion in Hawaii.

I kind of pitied whoever got in my kitten's way as she finished the game that Darcy had started.

Smirking, I got back to work. I would step in if Nevaeh needed me to, but considering all the badass women who always had her back, I figured she wouldn't need me to lift a finger to get anything done.

Darcy and my parents wouldn't see it coming.

I almost felt sorry for them.

Almost.

CHAPTER 5

NEVAEH

D arcy Hamilton's baby was only two months old. I felt sorry for the adorable boy who looked so much like his father—and a tiny bit like his big brother. According to Darcy's social media, the little boy's name was Jonah Collins. Despite Braxton not having signed the birth certificate, she'd still given him the Collins last name.

Of course, baby Jonah was a Collins, so it made sense. But what his doting "grandmother" didn't know was that the incredibly adorable little boy she thought was her grandson was really her stepson. I didn't want to hurt the baby; that was the last thing I would ever try to do.

Getting back at Darcy and figuratively slapping some sense into Belinda Collins was a different story. My mom had done plenty of physical damage already, so it would have been overkill to get violent with anyone.

At least, that was what I tried to remind myself. My future mother-in-law wasn't the one I wanted to rip apart, though. No, my fury was directed solely at Darcy.

With the two women having wanted to ruin one of our parties, it was only fitting to play along and destroy one of their own.

Lyla had been invited to her aunt Belinda's birthday party, which was our in. The event planner for the huge black-tie event was easily bought off, and everything was already in place before my grandfather's plane even touched down. I probably should have been back in California preparing for my wedding that was only two weeks away, but this needed to be taken care of so I could not only get Darcy out of Braxton's life once and for all—as well as maybe, hopefully, convincing Belinda to come to our wedding for her son's sake.

By the time the jet taxied onto the tarmac, I was dressed, my makeup perfect. I'd even put in my contacts, which I rarely wore, but this required I look stunning in every way. With my glasses on, I looked underage, and I didn't need the gossip reporters who would be in attendance to think Braxton was about to marry jailbait—even if my age was posted all over the internet, given who my father was. That didn't mean much to the high society of Northern Virginia. They only knew me as the home-wrecker who had ruined poor Darcy's life.

Before the end of the night, I would have the last laugh, and "poor Darcy" would be the outcast in her precious social circle.

A town car was waiting for me as I descended the plane's stairs. Behind me, my bodyguard was dressed in the usual dark suit with his earpiece in place. I would rather have come alone, but Barrick refused to let me step foot on PopPop's jet without Braxton knowing unless I took some muscle with me.

Damn Mia and her telling her husband everything.

I refused to feel even a smidge of guilt for not having told Brax what I was doing. We weren't supposed to keep secrets, but this wasn't exactly a secret. He was in Hawaii on business and wouldn't be home until the following evening, so I'd been able to "sneak" over to Virginia for a quick trip. I planned on telling him everything as soon as he got home.

By midnight, the entire East Coast would know all about Darcy's affair with Miles Collins. The entire country would be talking about it by morning.

Aunt Emmie had already made sure of that.

I just wanted to be there to talk to Belinda when the proverbial shit hit the fan and ask her to reconsider supporting her son when he got married.

If he'd known I was going to speak directly to his mother, he would have tried to stop me, and I couldn't let that happen. He'd said he was fine with cutting his parents out of his life. I believed him when it came to Miles, but Brax deserved to have at least one parent sitting on his side of the church when we said our vows. And not just that, damn it. His mother should be present for every huge moment in his life. Our wedding. The birth of our children. The list was endless, and even if the woman never came to care about me, it didn't matter.

All I wanted was for her to be a part of her son's life for his sake. To have the woman who had felt him grow beneath her heart, kick her from the inside for months, then spent hours laboring over bringing him into the world—I wanted her to fucking care about him now. She should be a part of his present and his future. For his sake...and her own.

The back door of the town car opened, and Lyla stepped out. Dressed similarly to me in an evening gown with her hair in a loose updo and sultry, glamorous makeup, Lyla was drop-dead gorgeous. How she'd left her house without Howler having a stroke because he wasn't going with her, I didn't have a clue. It wouldn't have surprised me if the man gate-crashed the party and carried her off caveman-style.

It wouldn't have been the first time I'd witnessed the architect and underground MMA fighter turn into a raging Neanderthal where Lyla was concerned. There must have been something in the water in Northern Virginia because Braxton was just like him when it came to me, exactly as Barrick was with Mia.

Then there was Judge...

Ugh, Judge.

I didn't want to think about that alphahole. There was Neanderthal...and then there was Zachary Bennett, but no one was allowed to call him anything but Judge. Because he was a total narcissistic jerk, high on his own power as not only an actual judge, but the equivalent of a god when it came to the Sons of the Underground.

Lyla wolf-whistled as her gaze traveled up and down my body. Growing up in the spotlight as not only Drake Stevenson's daughter but also Cole Steel's granddaughter, I knew how to clean up when the occasion called for it. It was rare that I wanted to, however, and I tended to avoid it as often as possible.

But sometimes, sacrifices had to be made.

"Is this a preview of your wedding?" my friend asked as she air-kissed my cheek so as not to smudge either of us. "Because if this is what my cousin is going to get in two weeks, I'm going to place my bet now that he doesn't make it through you walking all the way down the aisle before he's carrying you to the officiant and rushing the poor man along with grunts and chest-pounding instead of actual vows."

Laughing, I linked my arm through hers as we walked the few yards back to the town car, where my guard was already waiting. He held the door while I took my place in the back seat beside Lyla before climbing into the front passenger seat.

"We're arriving about forty-five minutes late," Lyla said as we drove through the typical Friday-night traffic I'd grown accustomed to when I'd lived there. "By then, all the fashionably late idiots will have made their entrance. The party will be getting started. No one will be expecting anything." She heaved a sigh. "My mom will be there, by the way. And I think my brother also mentioned dropping by."

I scrunched up my nose. I'd only met Lyla's mom a few times, and they had been short visits. Lyla's brother, on the other hand, I'd seen at least once a month while attending college. It was hard not to see him when Judge was not only Lyla's older brother, but Howler's best friend. And then there was the not-so-secret fact that he ran the Underground, so anytime we'd gone to a fight, he'd usually been there.

Technically, Judge was going to be my cousin by marriage, just like Lyla, but I wasn't a fan. Something I might have randomly said to him—more than once. And I couldn't say I was all that embarrassed to have let that thought slip out like the word-vomit that usually spilled out to make room in my head for more important things.

The town car pulled to a stop in front of a huge mansion. I lifted my brows at Lyla. "Is this where Braxton grew up?"

"No," she said with a grimace. "This place is considerably smaller than his parents' house. It's actually Darcy's parents'. She and Aunt Belinda have become super close since the birth of Jonah." Her eyes began to glitter. "That's about to change."

CHAPTER 6

NEVAEH

Our entrance wasn't dramatic, which was what I'd wanted. Lyla knew her way around fairly well. Having grown up with Darcy, she'd spent plenty of time at the other woman's parents' house over the years. Lyla confessed that the two of them had even been close friends until Darcy had broken up with Braxton following his losing his leg.

Family loyalty was a huge thing with Lyla. She loved Barrick and Braxton just as much as she loved Judge—although how anyone could love that jerk, I wasn't sure. I'd met Ellianna; she'd even been one of the teaching assistants in one of my classes. The way Judge treated her was nothing less than bullying, and I'd wanted to stab him in the eye more than once when he talked down to her.

With our black dresses, our sparkling jewelry, and our hair immaculately styled, we blended in with the other women. Lyla grabbed two glasses of wine from a passing waiter, but neither of us took a drink as we stayed under the radar for as long as possible. People greeted Lyla left and right, but she didn't bother to introduce me, even when she got curious glances.

Lyla didn't pause long enough to say hello to most of the people who spoke to her. If she didn't want to talk, she didn't. That was something everyone who knew her understood. Lyla was kind to those she loved, but she had zero time for fake bullshit from people who didn't matter in her eyes. There was nothing fake about her, which was why I'd gotten along with her so well over the years.

"There you are," a voice I only vaguely recognized gushed.

Lyla rolled her eyes at me before turning to face her mother. Brenda looked very similar to her sister, Belinda. Having seen pictures of their brother—Barrick's father—I could see the three siblings had shared similar features, especially the brown eyes. It was easy to tell that Braxton, Barrick, Lyla, and Judge were all related.

"Mother," she greeted, air-kissing the older woman's cheeks.

"I saw your brother briefly when I first arrived, but he was grousing about something and left soon after telling your auntie happy birthday." Brenda glanced at me, took a sip from her nearly empty wine glass, then did a double take once recognition hit her. "Lyla!" she gasped. "What are you doing with this girl?"

"Oh hush, Mother. Be quiet, and you'll learn something important in about five minutes." Lyla exchanged her still-full glass with her mother's now-empty one. "Here. Sip this, and keep your mouth shut."

Brenda took another drink. "Fine," she mumbled. "This party was becoming stale already anyway."

"I'm sure it will liven up shortly," Lyla said with another roll of her eyes.

"I trust you're right," her mother said with a huff as she walked away.

I tipped my own still-full wine glass at the empty one in my friend's hand. "You normally toss those back like water."

"Yeah, well...I'm not much for alcohol lately." She touched her free hand to her belly. "Thankfully, your wedding is soon, or I might not still fit into the dress I bought for the occasion."

For a moment, I forgot about my reasons for being there and nearly squealed. "I'm so happy for you, Lyla. How are you feeling? How far along are you? Is Josie excited about being a big sister, or haven't you told her yet?"

Lyla grinned. "I'm feeling fine. I was worried at first since Mia had such horrible morning sickness, but apparently both the baby and I are doing great. I just hit the second trimester, and we took Josie to the ultrasound appointment last week. It's killing her because I swore her to secrecy, but she's overjoyed to be a big sister." She leaned in, whispering, "I haven't told anyone but Mia and my brother. I was waiting until after the wedding to tell Brax. We found out it's a boy. Howler is relieved, because he says he can only take so much estrogen in the house with Josie and me."

"I really am happy for you both. And I promise not to mention anything to Brax until you're ready to tell him."

"No, it's fine. You can tell him if you want. I know how hard it is to keep secrets from Howler, and I wouldn't ask you to do the same with Braxton." Lifting her empty glass, she pointed to where someone was setting up a projector. "Looks like the party is really about to start. Darcy's plan was to do a montage of pictures with Aunt Belinda over the years. After I did a little greasing of the planner's hands, she switched the last half of the presentation with all the pictures of Darcy and Miles. I've added a couple extra ones that my own intel was able to catch in action over the last few days."

My eyes widened in surprise. "I didn't know you had a tail on her."

"Not her," she said. "Miles. That was...interesting."

I wasn't sure I wanted to know what that meant. Just from the description I'd been given of the pictures taken the previous December, I knew it wasn't going to be pleasant. Braxton thought his cousin had been overly dramatic about what she'd seen in the dossier she'd been given, but I wasn't so sure.

The lights were dimmed, and the cellist who had been part of the live orchestra began to play a pretty solo as pictures of Belinda as a young girl with her siblings and other family members played out on a screen set up for the occasion. Her youth, teens, and high school graduation. Pictures of her with a very young Miles Collins. Their wedding day, and then several with Belinda noticeably pregnant with Braxton.

My heart squeezed when I saw the way she looked at her son in the pictures after his birth, as a toddler and then as a preteen. The pictures of her with her husband became fewer and farther between, but the ones of her with Brax continued to hurt my heart. I saw so much love, and I hated there was a divide between the two of them.

After Braxton enlisted in the Marines, his parents hadn't been happy, but then when he'd lost his leg, they—mostly his mother—had become unbearably clingy, and he'd moved in with Barrick. Gradually, he'd reduced contact with his parents more and more, until it completely stopped. At least, until they'd tried to force him into marrying Darcy.

The photos began to change from those with Belinda in them, to Miles, and then Darcy. Separately. Together. At parties or just sitting together in a restaurant. Nothing about it seemed unusual...

Except for the way Miles touched Darcy.

The interval between pictures sped up, and suddenly there was nothing that could suggest innocence in the photos. There were pictures of Miles, nude—except for the ball gag in his mouth and the harness he was strapped into that hung from a ceiling. Darcy in all leather, her hair pulled into a high ponytail that hung down her back. It was hard to look at, yet impossible to tear my gaze away from as I watched their relationship play out with whips and chains on the screen. I didn't even realize when the music stopped, but the pictures kept going.

The sexually explicit scenes passed and blended into photos of Darcy heavily pregnant, Miles touching her stomach with adoration.

Then came the photo of Jonah, a side-by-side comparison of the two, with Miles at around the same age. A small clip of Miles and Darcy walking through the park that ended with Miles kissing his son on the head before backing Darcy against her car and kissing her passionately.

Finally, a copy of DNA test results was the last picture to appear on the screen and stayed frozen for everyone to read. The document stated clearly that Miles Collins was Jonah Collins's biological father—not his grandfather.

The entire room was deathly quiet as the lights were turned back up, and a very pale Darcy stared at Belinda, who was still gaping at the screen. Miles stood off to the side, his skin a sickly gray. I was sure I would have felt ill, too, if my naked ass had been on full display for everyone to see. There had even been a brief glimpse of Miles and his erection, and I could honestly say that the older Collins wasn't nearly as well-endowed as his eldest son. But even as that thought had filtered through my brain, I'd been grossed out.

"B-Belinda...?" Darcy squeaked. "I... Um, I can explain. This was all... It was a-a setup. Yes, a setup."

Slowly, Belinda canted her head to look at the blonde. "A setup?" she repeated with banked fury in her eyes. I knew that look all too well. It happened all the time when Braxton was pissed and didn't want to scare me. "Which part? Where you dominated my husband and turned his ass red with a flogger?"

"Yuck, she knows what a flogger is," Lyla whispered, and I wasn't sure if she was talking to me or herself.

My eyes traveled around everyone near the three people closest to the screen. I'd seen a few pictures of Darcy's parents, so I knew who they were, and they were trying to blend into the crowd surrounding them as discreetly as possible. Obviously, they were making their feelings clear without words, turning their backs on their only child and avoiding the confrontation that was already unfolding in their home.

"A-all of it?" Darcy stuttered.

"Are you telling me or asking me?" Belinda asked between clenched teeth.

"I... Um. Yes."

"Jonah isn't Braxton's son," Belinda said, taking a stumbling step back from Darcy. Then her eyes landed on Miles, who had been trying to back through the crowd similarly to how the Hamiltons had done, but without the same success. As soon as his wife's gaze caught him, he froze. "You fucked her. Jonah is your child. Braxton tried to tell me.

He said he hadn't even seen Darcy in years, but I believed you when you said he was lying to be with that scandalous rocker's daughter."

I nearly laughed at her description of me. Rumor had it that my dad had been overzealous with scandal before meeting my mom, but once they were together, he became an entirely different person. For the better.

"Remind me not to let you plan any of my parties," Brenda hissed as she came up beside Lyla. "I don't want any of my skeletons coming out of the closet like this."

Lyla lifted a brow at her mother. "What secrets are you keeping that could possibly be worse than this?"

Brenda drained her fresh glass of wine. "Don't ask questions you don't want the answers to, darling." Placing her glass on a side table, she dusted her hands together as if they were covered in imaginary filth. "And on that note, I'm going to make myself scarce so I'm not a witness to my sister bludgeoning her husband to death."

My gaze jumped back to Belinda in time to see she was, indeed, about to do physical harm to Miles. She had an iron statue in her hands, lifting it over her head.

"Wait!" I cried, rushing through the crowd to stop her from committing murder. Everyone else seemed frozen in shock by what they'd watched. Those who were finally coming around were already whispering about the size of Miles's cock.

Gross.

Reaching Belinda, I grabbed for the statue, surprised by how heavy it was. I had no idea how she'd lifted the thing on her own, other than she must have been running off pure adrenaline.

Recognition filled her eyes when she realized who was trying to take her weapon away. "You!" she cried. "You set this up?"

"I had help," I said with a shrug, not bothering to deny it. Lyla had followed me, and from the squeaks of other partygoers, I figured my bodyguard was pushing his way through the masses to get to me. I ignored them and everyone else to focus on Belinda. "But you started this creepy game by trying to make me doubt Braxton."

That alone would have gotten someone a pencil to the eyeball. But this was Braxton's mother. I'd refrained from violence and opted to open her eyes to the ugly truth those she assumed were her nearest and dearest had been keeping from her. It wasn't pleasant, especially with all her supposed friends witnessing the horrible scene. In the end, Belinda probably would have preferred I kick her old ass, over the public humiliation of finding out her husband had been cheating on her with her son's high school girlfriend and fathered a child with her—then subsequently attempted to play off the baby as her grandson.

"You!" Darcy screeched at the top of her lungs, and I imagined the crystal champagne flutes cracking from the high frequency. "You took Brax from me, and now you're trying to destroy the rest of my life!"

I felt a puff of air behind me and tilted my head a fraction to see Lyla grab the other woman by the arm, twist it behind her, and bend her in half.

"No touchy-touchy," Lyla tutted, pushing Darcy in the direction of Miles, who barely caught her. When her weight hit him, he was unprepared for it, and they both fell. A thud echoed through the mostly quiet room as his ass hit the floor, with Darcy's head in his lap. A few snickers followed, and if I hadn't been busy wrestling the heavy statue from Belinda, I might have giggled at the sight of Darcy with her face in Miles's crotch.

Also, gross!

I didn't need another visual reminder that those two had a kinky-as-fuck relationship.

Belinda finally relinquished her hold when she saw her husband and his mistress on the floor. Out of breath, I placed the statue on the floor once she released it. More like I dropped it, but it wasn't Belinda's or my own house, so I didn't really care if the hardwood was damaged. Huffing from exertion, I grasped both of her hands. "I'm sorry if what you saw upset you, but you needed to open your eyes. You've been trying to hurt Braxton with how you've treated me. Honestly, I don't care how you feel about me—I'm not all that keen on you either. But when you start hurting the man I love, I won't just sit back and take it."

"I just wanted him to be with his son," she said in a weak voice. "I wanted our family to be together. My grandchild..." Tears filled her eyes. "But he's not my grandson, is he?"

"No, he's not." Still grasping her wrists in one hand, I wrapped my free arm around her shoulders in a half hug, attempting to comfort her. "I'm sorry that disappoints you. I've seen pictures of the little guy. He's adorable. Looks a tiny bit like Braxton. But just think, one day, you will have grandbabies who look more like your son than Jonah."

I bit my tongue when that word-vomit left my mouth, but instead of getting angry at me, Belinda only sighed. "You're not a home-wrecking whore."

"Again, sorry to disappoint you."

Her lips twitched with a ghost of a smile. "You're an odd girl."

"Gee, no one's ever said that to me before," I replied dryly. Voices around us got louder as the shock began to fade from more and more people. "Would you like to get out of here?"

Her dark eyes shot venom over my shoulder, and I was glad not to be a victim of it. "Please."

CHAPTER 7

BRAXTON

My driver pulled up outside the house in Santa Monica, and I scribbled my name across the slip before giving it and a tip to the man in the front seat. Driving was one of those tasks I could do with a prosthetic, but it wasn't something I did well. I knew my limits, which meant using a car service or getting one of the men on our payroll to drive me where I needed to go. We had an SUV, which Nevaeh used to drive herself to classes most days, but she still had a team member watching over her.

She huffed and complained at times, but I knew she only did it to bust my balls. My kitten knew I needed eyes on her at all times or I couldn't do my job—or function in society, period. Meeting her was the best thing to ever happen to me, and the thought of something taking her away from me left me with a hollow pit in my gut.

Grabbing my overnight bag, I slowly got out of the car. I felt stiff and sore from the flight to Hawaii, being cooped up in an office for two days, and then another plane ride home before spending over an hour in the back of a car. I wasn't a small man, so that meant even my fake leg was long, which left me cramped up despite being in the back of a town car.

After punching in my code, I used my thumbprint to unlock the front door. Stepping into the house, I dropped my bag by the door to take upstairs later, and I quickly moved through the house. It was dinnertime, and Nevaeh loved cooking. I could already smell garlic and herbs, which never failed to make my stomach growl. With all the amazing foods she filled me up with day and night, I would have been triple my size if I didn't work out every day.

"Kitten," I called out before I reached the kitchen door so as not to startle her. "Are you making spaghetti or those meatball sandwiches I love so much?"

She didn't answer, and when I pushed open the door, I realized why. She was sitting at the kitchen island with a mug of coffee in front of her. Seeing me, she gave me a grim smile then turned her gaze back to the woman seated across from her.

With her face washed clean of all traces of makeup and her hair in a messy ponytail—both things I'd never seen the woman do a day in my life—my mother was nearly unrecognizable at first glance. But then she smiled, and I saw myself in some of her facial features. "What the fuck are you doing here, Mother?"

"Brax," Nevaeh scolded when my mother flinched. "She's our guest. Don't speak so harshly."

I blinked at the love of my life. With her hair twisted into a knot at the back of her head, her glasses sitting low on her nose and giving her an adorably owlish look as she blinked her blue-gray eyes at me, she looked like the same woman I'd left with a kiss goodbye only days before. But she sure as fuck wasn't acting like the same person.

"What is she doing here, Kitten?"

"I invited her to stay with us for a little while. Until the divorce is finalized." She lifted her mug to her lips and took a sip before continuing, as if she didn't need to go into more detail about the bomb she'd just dropped. "Belinda is going to house-sit for us while we're on our honeymoon. But she has a real estate agent looking into finding her either a small house or an apartment as close by as possible so she can be a part of your life. And the lives of our babies when we decide to start having kids."

Scrubbing a hand over the stubble on my jaw in frustration, I used my other hand to make a rewind motion. "Back up, would you? Maybe start from the beginning."

Some of what she liked to call word-vomit would have been great right then. It happened mostly when she was stressed. Random thoughts simply spilled out. I kind of needed that at the moment. But she didn't seem stressed in the least. If anything, she actually appeared to be comfortable in the same room with the woman her mother had punched in the face only a few short months previously.

I glanced back at my mother, trying to determine whether she'd had a nose job since then, but other than a slight new curve to her nose, I didn't see any difference. Then again, she'd spent so much time in perfectly contoured makeup that the subtle curve to her nose could have always been there, just well hidden behind artistically applied foundation and bronzer—or whatever the fuck women used to hide their supposed imperfections.

"Yesterday was your mom's birthday," Nevaeh reminded me.

"Happy belated birthday, Mother," I gritted through clenched teeth. "More context, Kitten. Now."

"I flew to Virginia and went to her birthday party with Lyla. Your mother is now aware that Darcy was having an affair with Miles, and that baby Jonah is his son, not yours. She knows that I'm not the home-wrecker she accused me of being, and we made up. With the gossip a little out of hand—what with pictures of Miles and Darcy all over the local papers back in Virginia, especially the ones of his ass and little bits all over the front pages of some of the less-reputable trash mags—she needed a place to decompress. I offered her sanctuary with us so that she could spend a little time with you before the wedding. The two of you can get to know each other again before the big day. You can walk her down the aisle before the wedding or something. Or my brother can walk both my mom and yours down the aisle. Whatever works best. We still haven't figured out that little detail about the wedding yet. Anyway, Belinda is relocating to California to be closer to us."

It all came out in a rush, and I quickly rethought wanting her to do the cute word-vomit thing.

"Did I fall asleep on the flight home and just haven't woken up yet?" I muttered. "Because this feels like a really weird dream, baby."

"What Nevi means is, she and Lyla got their rightful payback for my attempt at hiring a rather unsavory surprise for your bachelor party," Mother explained with a weak lift of her lips. "She very graciously offered me a place to stay so that I didn't have to deal with the press after the evidence of your father's infidelity hit the papers. The good news is that my divorce attorney says I've got a great claim to get half of everything without a battle. Not that I need his money. I have plenty of my own, as you know. But I want to hit him where it hurts the most, and that's his bank account. Taking half of his assets, including stock in the business, will be the ultimate revenge."

Sighing, I replayed everything in my head before pointing at Nevaeh. "You and Lyla used the dossier pictures from December to publicly embarrass my father and Darcy. Now his ass is literally all over the society pages back in Virginia."

"Yes," she confirmed.

"There was a confrontation between you and my mother, but no bodily harm was done?"

"Not between us, no," Nevaeh said with a casual shrug. "There was a near miss between Belinda, Miles, and an extremely heavy iron statue. But I wrestled that out of her hands before she could bludgeon anyone with it. Darcy did try to attack me, but Lyla used her Jedi fighting powers and twisted Darcy into this weird human pretzel before basically tossing her into Miles, who fell on his ass hard enough that rumors are spreading that he fractured his tailbone. But Lyla says there isn't much weight to that gossip because, as far as she knows, he didn't even go to the doctor or hospital. Other than that, there were no physical altercations."

"Did you take security with you?" I demanded, suddenly feeling sick to my stomach at what could have happened if my cousin hadn't been with Nevaeh. "Other than Lyla?"

"Barrick refused to let me step on to PopPop's plane without one of the bodyguards on the payroll."

I angrily slapped my hands on the island's surface, causing my mother to jump. "Barrick knew about this and didn't tell me anything?" I roared.

Nevaeh didn't even flinch. Instead, she calmly lifted her mug and took another sip before replying with a pout in her voice. "Stupid Mia narced on me, and he insisted on the muscle. It's not like I couldn't have gone on my own. I'm getting my doctorate, for fuck's sake." She glanced at my mother. "Tell him, Belinda. I'm about to have a freaking PhD to my name. I can handle a ride on a plane and going to a party on my own. Obviously, I'm capable of making logical decisions."

"But you're a little bitty thing." Mother surprised me by arguing in my favor. "And so beautiful, darling. I would be worried for your safety too."

I gaped at the woman who'd birthed me for a long moment before snapping my mouth shut and giving my fiancée a glare. "See? Even she thinks I'm not being overbearing where your safety is concerned."

"Oh, hush up, you." She wagged a finger in my direction. "All I can say is that I hope we have only boys when we do decide to have kids. Daughters will be too overwhelmed with all your high-testosterone protectiveness bullshit."

I leaned in until I could taste the coffee on her breath. "Are you going to make me worry about you when I have to go on business trips, Kitten?" I murmured softly.

"Of course not." She erased the last of the distance between our mouths and kissed me, not giving a damn that my mother was sitting right across from her. "I'll be a good girl from now on, Brax."

"You better," I growled, brushing another soft kiss over her lips. "Or I'll tell Drake."

"Narc!" she exclaimed, stabbing me in the chest with her long, elegant index finger. "That's playing dirty, mister."

"I know," I said with a grin before turning my head to find my mother glancing around, looking at anything but Nevaeh or me.

Public displays of affection weren't something she was used to. Watching the ease with which Nevaeh initiated it made her uncomfortable. "Speaking of Drake, how does he feel about our guest?"

"He and Mom were displeased when we first got back. Daddy might not have known I'd gone to Virginia. He maybe...sort of...thought I'd gone with you. When he found out PopPop loaned me his plane, there might have been an angry phone conversation between the two of them that Mom had to calm down." Nevaeh looked over at Mother and rolled her pretty eyes. "All men think that the 'poor little woman' can't take care of herself."

"All a real man thinks is that the woman he loves is too precious to risk losing, so he has to protect her at all costs," I corrected her. "And that doesn't answer my question. Drake and Lana weren't happy about this new arrangement?"

"Not at first. But then Belinda apologized to Mom, who graciously accepted. After that, Daddy thought it was a great idea to have her stay with us so that she can not only be here for the wedding, but spend time with you, getting to know you again after the long years you've spent apart."

I pushed back from the island, realization hitting me square in the chest as love poured through my veins for the little kitten who fucking owned me. "That's why you did this," I whispered, in total awe of her. "It wasn't about revenge for the bachelor party or playing games. Your huge, generous heart couldn't stand that my mother and I were at odds, and she wasn't going to be at the wedding. You went to Virginia hell-bent on mending the rift."

"You definitely picked a woman worthy of your love, darling," Mother murmured quietly, and I dragged my gaze away from Nevaeh to look at the woman who had given birth to me. Respect filled her eyes as she looked at my woman with a small, appreciative smile on her face. "In the little time that we've spent together, I've gotten to know more about her than it took years for me to discover about Darcy. Nevi has a soft heart, but a backbone made of steel. Her family may be a little unorthodox, but they are good people who raised an amazing child. I'm so glad you two found each other."

"That's really sweet of you to say, Belinda," Nevaeh told her with a smile.

"I mean it, dear," she said with a sincerity that rang true to my ears, and I was finally able to relax around the woman who had raised me. "I think the two of us may have made a few mistakes the last few months, but the end result was worth the angst that I went through. I want to apologize for any distress I may have caused either of you."

"I'm just glad that you and Braxton have a chance to be a part of each other's lives now." Nevaeh grasped my mother's hand across the island. "It wouldn't have mattered to me if you hadn't wanted to get to know me. All I care about is Brax's happiness."

"My happiness revolves around you, Kitten," I reminded her. "If she can't accept you, then I don't want to harm our relationship."

"Well, we don't have to worry about that," she said before draining her mug. "I'm going to go take a shower while the meatballs finish simmering in the sauce. You two take that time to find common ground so we don't get indigestion from dinner. I don't want any tension when I return."

I caught her around the waist before she could move away. For a long moment, I just stared down into her eyes, trying to tell her how much she meant to me without words. Her smile was full of warmth and happiness when she cupped my stubbly jaw. "I love you too," she whispered.

CHAPTER 8

NEVAEH

"Something's got to give."

My eyes widened as PopPop muttered the song lyrics to "Bodies," while everyone bustled around in an attempt to get ready for the wedding.

"Dad! You're only singing that to make Dray more anxious."

"Something's got to give," PopPop continued, and I could see the steam practically billowing out of Mom's ears.

"Something is about to give," Arella hissed close to my ear. "And I think it's going to be Mom's patience. Daddy is already trying not to cry. I think PopPop has a death wish today if he's going around singing shit about bodies hitting the floor."

"I don't think he's doing it to upset Daddy." Heavenleigh joined our whispered conversation. "It's more to do with how Braxton is reacting. He's all twitchy. PopPop saw him being grumpy a little while ago, and I think that's the song that came to mind. We need to get Nev down the aisle ASAP to chill out the groom and get PopPop to STFU."

"Heavenleigh!" Mom snapped, overhearing her choice of acronyms. "What did I say not twenty minutes ago?"

"She said STCU, Mom," I lied for my sister. "You must have heard her wrong. Please calm down. Everything is going exactly as it should. I don't know why everyone is so anxious."

Mom paused and gave me her full attention. When she saw me in my wedding dress, tears filled her brown eyes. The lace-embroidered mesh and dotted tulle layered together overtop a nude lining to form a plunging sweetheart neckline with a princess-seamed bodice; the high waist sat atop a figure-skimming fit that ended in a trumpet silhouette that flared at the bottom. It had taken me forever to decide on the dress, but once I'd put it on, I'd fallen in love with it.

For my hair, I'd opted for a tousled fishtail braid with diamonds and pearls accessorized throughout. My glasses had been replaced by my contacts again so my makeup could be seen to its full effect. I'd had the stylist emphasize my eyes and lips—both of which were the features I knew Braxton liked the most about my face because he was always staring into my eyes or thinking about my mouth.

"You're so beautiful," Mom said in a trembling voice. "I can't believe my baby is getting married. That's why everyone is so off the wall. I want everything to be perfect for you, and it feels like nothing is going right."

I glanced around at my sisters. The three of them were my bridesmaids, and Mia was my matron of honor as my best friend. Arella, Heavenleigh, and Bliss were ready to go, looking beautiful in their dresses with their hair perfectly styled and their makeup only lightly glammed up. Mia stood off to the side, not looking like a new mother at all with her body already back to slender. The only exception might have been her huge boobs, but she was nursing, and the seamstress had made alterations so as not to risk her flashing everyone and causing a riot from Barrick.

My baby brother looked so cute in his tux, a replica of my dad, who had spent the morning coming and going from the bridal suite at the church where we'd all been getting ready for the ceremony. Even rushing around, Mom should have looked harried and flushed. Instead, her hair was perfectly in place, tucked into a low updo with a few locks cupping either side of her gorgeous face. Her dress was sexy as hell, and I wasn't sure how Daddy was keeping his head on straight with her walking around in what could only be described as mother of the bride meets Jessica Rabbit, with the slit of her blue-gray dress going all the way up to her hip.

Seeing just how hot she was, I realized maybe it wasn't just Braxton who was having issues waiting for the wedding to begin. PopPop really was fucking with my dad's head because anyone who looked twice at my mom would be another body that dropped to the floor.

My gaze met and locked with Mia's. She must have read my thoughts because she rushed everyone along, getting my sisters lined up and ready to walk down the aisle. My brother took Mom's arm just as Daddy came out of the groom's suite. His gaze zeroed in on Mom and me as PopPop sang another verse of "Bodies."

"Dad!" Mom hissed.

"Not my fault, darlin'," he called to her. "You're the one who decided to dress like that and drive the poor boy mental."

"Boy," Bliss snickered at our grandfather's description of our father, who was well into his fifties. "Does that make Braxton an

NEVAEH

infant?"

"You always did have a smart mouth, pretty girl," PopPop said with a grin. "I love that about you."

"He says that about all of us," Arella said with a huff.

"That's because you're all just like your momma," the old rock legend said before stopping long enough to give me a quick kiss on the cheek, and then he made himself scarce by joining the rest of the guests inside the church.

Daddy took my hand and gently placed it through his arm, seeming to force himself to focus on me rather than Mom. As I stood there, waiting for the music to start so the others could make their way down the aisle, I looked up at the first man who ever loved me. Outwardly, he appeared cool and calm. But I felt the slight tremble in his arm that told me he was struggling to hold on to his emotions.

Upsetting this man was the last thing I ever wanted to do, but on this day, it was unavoidable. I was sure that was why Mom had chosen such a sexy dress, to distract him as much as possible. If he was being all growly and possessive over her, he didn't have time to think about what was about to happen.

He had to walk me down the aisle, hand me over into Braxton's safekeeping for the rest of eternity. My dad loved Brax like a son, that had never been in question, but even though he approved of my choice in husband, actually letting me go was destroying him.

"You look beautiful," Daddy murmured as the others started down the aisle as they were supposed to. "I told Braxton how amazing you looked earlier, and he nearly climbed out a window to sneak a peek. Barrick and Howler had to basically bear-hug the poor bastard until it was time for them to take their places."

My soft giggle filled the corridor outside the gallery. "I can definitely picture how that played out."

"He's a good man. I wish I'd been more like him at his age. More deserving."

I tightened my hand around his arm. As far as I was aware, I was the only one he'd told about what had happened before he'd married Mom. When he'd shared a few details about his past with me, it had bonded us even more than we'd always been. "Daddy, whether you realize it or not, you were a good person all your life. Mom didn't change you, she just brought out the best part of you. Because people don't change that dramatically, no matter how much they want to think they can. You made mistakes, that's true, but you were always the amazing man in front of me."

His throat worked hard, and he opened his mouth to speak but quickly snapped it shut. After clearing his throat, he gave me a smile that trembled around the edges. "If it were anyone else who tried to say that to me, I wouldn't have believed them, Nevi. But you're the smartest person I know, so I have to believe you... Right?"

"Absolutely."

Jaw clenched, he glanced along the aisle we were supposed to walk down in a matter of minutes. I followed his gaze and saw Mom take her seat beside my grandfather. "Does that mean I'm still a good man even if I end up killing a bunch of motherfuckers for eyeballing your mom in that dress?"

"She's technically an angel," I reminded him. "I don't think it's frowned upon to murder in the name of protecting angels."

He popped his jaw left and right, causing his long hair to fall over his shoulders. "I'll keep that in mind for the reception."

I was still giggling when the music started. I watched as his throat worked roughly again. "I guess we should do this thing, huh?"

My gaze flickered to the aisle then back to him. "Yeah, I think it's time."

"Fuck," he rasped. "Are you one hundred percent sure?"

"Closer to a thousand percent," I teased, before growing serious. "It's okay, Daddy. I know this is difficult. Just remember, you were the first man I loved, and you'll be the last one too."

His sharp inhale made my eyes sting, but he bravely gave me a nod, and we finally took that first step.

The one that carried me straight to the man who held my heart.

Directly to my future that was so perfect, I couldn't imagine it was possible to get any better.

EPILOGUE

DRAKE

Braxton repositioned a sleeping Carver in his arms so he could open the door, while I lifted Conrad onto my shoulders and grabbed the packed diaper bag.

"G-Pop are we goin'a your house?" my eldest grandchild asked excitedly. There was nothing Conrad liked more than spending the night with G-Pop and G-Mom.

With nothing left but my teenagers, who were gone with their friends more often than home, I enjoyed my time with the grandbabies just as much as they seemed to like being with us. But after seeing the way Angel was dressed for her girls' night out with my sisters-in-law and Nevaeh, I wouldn't be able to indulge my grandson.

"Sorry, bud," I said as we followed his dad out the door for the short walk down the block to where Braxton's mom had bought a house.

At first, I hadn't been all that pleased that Belinda Collins had moved so close. After that first meeting with her and her now ex-husband, the woman calling my baby a home-wrecking whore, I'd wanted to throw a few punches her way, too. Angel had taken care of her and ended up with a bruised hand for weeks. But after Nevaeh cleared everything up and we'd gotten to know our daughter's new mother-in-law, we'd come to appreciate her.

Especially on nights like this.

With the boys wanting to hang out with me so much, Belinda didn't get as much one-on-one time with the grandkids as I did, so she jumped at any chance to babysit. Something I was extremely thankful for because I needed to go find my wife and daughter before my son-in-law and I had to bury a fucking body.

"But I like your house bettah," Conrad complained as we walked up the front steps to his grandmother's home.

"Tell ya what," I bargained. "Tomorrow, G-Mom and I will come over and pick you up. We'll eat breakfast at my house, and then we'll work on a new song together."

"Yay!" he cheered. "And then we can take the car apart and put it back togethah?"

"You bet, buddy," I promised. "But only if Grandma says you were a good boy."

"I'll be good, G-Pop," he assured me as I placed him on his feet. He wrapped his little arms around my leg, giving me a tight hug before running up to Belinda. "Hi, Grandma. Daddy and G-Pop are going to go kill a mf-er, and then I get to eat bacon at his house in the morning."

Belinda gaped at him for a moment before shaking her graying head with a laugh. "All right, then. I guess you'll need a good night's sleep so you can eat that bacon with G-Pop." Her brown eyes traveled to her son, her brows arching. "Kill a mf-er?" she mouthed, and he shrugged.

"Nevaeh is having a girls' night. Her mom and the aunts went too. Some pictures were posted to social media, and their bodyguards aren't telling me anything about what they're doing. With the way they were all dressed tonight, they were asking for spankings." He kissed her cheek. "Thanks for watching the boys at the last minute. I appreciate it, Mom."

She gave him a quick hug, lovingly adjusting Carver's sleeping body in her arms. The boy was huge for his age, just like his older brother, but she seemed to be able to manage his weight without issue. "I'm always here for you, darling. Have fun, and please don't kill anyone unless you know you can get away with it."

He smirked. "I'll do my best."

Once we said our goodbyes, I pulled my keys from my pocket, and we both practically sprinted back to my driveway. Braxton jumped in shotgun, and I revved the engine of the classic car my wife had given me as a present years before. I'd rebuilt the entire thing while Conrad watched, occasionally helping. Now I had a new vintage car that we played with on the weekends. The kid wasn't even three yet and was even smarter than his mom, because he already knew the different parts of the engine and could walk me through putting it back together like it was nothing.

It took over half an hour to find the club where Angel had gone with the girls. It had started out as just her, Emmie, Layla, Lucy, and Harper. But then Mia decided to join them, which meant Nevaeh and Arella were invited. Jordan hadn't let my second-eldest child out of the house. I didn't know what he'd done to convince her to stay in for the night, but I wished I'd done a little convincing of my own, because Angel had had my blood pressure up the minute I'd seen the outfit she'd chosen for the night out.

Black skirt that barely covered her ass. Crimson cold-shoulder with a plunging neckline and a pushup bra that had made her tits more mouthwatering than ever. Chunky black and platinum belt. And of course, a pair of her killer heels that made her legs look a hundred miles long. She'd styled her hair in a messy, just-fucked way and dolled up that face that was already so beautiful I never got tired of looking at her. Even when she had dark circles under her eyes, her hair was a mess, and she was in nothing but baggy pajamas and a robe, she was the sexiest thing I'd ever seen.

With her dressed up, and all those motherfuckers out there just waiting to have a reason to get close, my angel became a sinful little demon who was going to end up on her hands and knees with my dick in her all night long.

Pulling up in front of the club, I tossed my keys to the valet. "Don't go far," I told him, handing him a hundred-dollar bill. "I won't be long."

"Yes, sir," the kid said with wide eyes.

Braxton was waiting for me beside the bouncer. The guy was in charge of who got in and when. He looked like he got off on the power he wielded with his clipboard, velvet rope, and headset. I pulled a roll of bills from my pocket. "Drake Stevenson," I dropped my name and slid the guy a hundred when we shook hands.

"Got your name right here, sir," he said without even glancing down at the clipboard. "Enjoy your night, sir."

A few flashing cameras were already going off, but I ignored them as Brax, and I entered the club. If the girls had just gone to First Bass, none of this would have mattered. Harris had a full team of security who would kill a motherfucker if they messed with Lucy or anyone else in the family. I should have insisted they go there and not to some new place that had just opened up.

The music was shit when we entered. The DJ, who was on his little platform, didn't know how to spin, and it was already giving me a headache before we'd even reached the VIP. But before I could hand the second line of security another bill, I caught sight of the girls. And they sure as fuck weren't in the VIP.

All of them were on the dance floor. Nevaeh, Mia, and Emmie's bodyguards were basically standing as a barrier between them and a line of salivating dickheads who were all watching my wife's tits bounce as she moved to the beat of the music.

"Glad you're picking my kids up in the morning," Braxton grumbled loud enough for me to hear. "Because I'm taking my wife home and not letting her out of the house again for a damn week."

I grimaced, not wanting to think about what he was going to be doing with my daughter. But then I saw Angel lift her hands above her head and sway her hips, singing along to the song playing, while her sisters and the other girls laughed and joined in. Her skirt had hiked up a little, and I got the barest glimpse of her red panties. All thoughts of any other person on the planet vanished, and I charged through the crowd, practically throwing motherfuckers out of my way to get to Angel.

The instant my arms wrapped around Angel from behind, I felt her melt into me. "I win!" she yelled. "My husband showed up first!"

"Tie!" Nevaeh squealed as Braxton tossed her over his shoulder and barked at her bodyguard to get the car. "Mine arrived at the same time."

"Playing games with me, Angel?" I husked against her ear. She shivered and began to dance again, rubbing her sweet ass along my already-aching cock. "You're going to get yourself in trouble, baby."

Turning, she wrapped her arms around my neck and kissed me. She tasted as good as the first time I'd kissed her. Every good thing in the world was tied to the brush of her lips over mine. Hungrily, I deepened the kiss until someone bumped into me.

My head snapped up to find my brother grabbing Harper and dragging her toward the bathrooms. His gaze briefly locked with mine, but the raging emotions I saw simmering there told me all I needed to know. I was going to take Angel home and fuck her until neither one of us could walk. Shane wasn't the waiting type. He'd find a bathroom stall and mark his wife so no one could be in doubt who she belonged to.

Hand on Angel's ass, I turned her toward the nearest exit in time to see Jesse and Nik coming through the door together. Frowning, I glanced back at Lucy and Mia, and I wasn't surprised to see Kin with them. But a glance to the side showed Harris, Jace, and Barrick had already arrived; they were just letting the three of them have their fun. For now.

I didn't have the same ability to allow a club full of unworthy bastards to look upon what I held holy for another minute.

Outside, I waved at the valet, and he pulled my car up. I slipped him another bill as he handed me the keys. Once he was gone, I opened Angel's door and helped her inside before jogging around to the driver's side.

"You're not going to get any sleep tonight, Angel," I warned.

"That was the plan," she said breathlessly, squirming on the seat.

"Just don't be complaining when we have to pick up the grandbabies from Belinda's in the morning. I promised Conrad."

She released a happy laugh. "Best weekend ever!"

I reached across the console and took her left hand. Lifting it to my lips, I kissed her knuckles. "Best life ever, Angel."

"Yeah," she said with a contented sigh, leaning her head back against the seat and staring at me through her lashes. When she looked at me like that, my entire body ached with need for her. "Best life ever."

~THE END~

Hopelessly Devoted to ARELLA

Book 3

CHAPTER 1

ARELLA

I startled awake, my heart pounding violently in my chest as I tried to catch my breath. A hand stroked over my hair, and I screamed, before Jordan's deep voice penetrated my sleep-fogged brain. Slowly, the panic began to ease, and I dropped my head back onto the pillow as tears spilled through my clenched-closed eyes.

Jordan turned me into him, tucking my head under his chin, and I clung to him as the memories from the nightmare tried to linger. "It's okay. I've got you, love."

Sniffling, I nodded against his chest, unable to speak yet. All I could think about was the feel of the knife against my abdomen, making me fear for my unborn baby's life. Then against my neck when my bodyguard, Samuel, lifted his gun, demanding that Garon release me. The color of his eyes. The madness in those honey-brown depths.

The same as PopPop's had been, minus the evil.

The same shade as my mom's.

Eyes I'd once loved seeing light up with laughter now made me sick to my stomach if I looked into them for too long. It was hard to even look at Mom these days. To see the sadness and anger that still brewed in her just below the surface. She and her brother had never been close, and to find out he'd been the one who'd stalked me, sent me horrible things, even tried to put a video of me with Jordan on revenge porn sites. All of that made her hate the man she'd shared DNA with that much more.

She couldn't possibly have hated him more than I did.

Garon Steel was dead, but the fear he'd instilled in me that day lingered, even if I tried to pretend it didn't. If I kept busy, then I didn't have to think about it, so I tried to keep moving as much as possible. With wedding plans, moving into a new house, and dealing with all the ups and downs of being pregnant, I had plenty to keep my mind occupied during my waking hours.

But when I closed my eyes to sleep, he came back to haunt me. There was no escaping him and the terror he'd inflicted in my dreams.

Jordan kissed the top of my head, his voice trying to soothe me. Normally it did, but for some reason, my panic still lingered. My heart rate didn't completely go back to normal, staying slightly faster than usual as we lay in our bed while the sun slowly lifted into the sky. He tried to tell me it was okay, that there was nothing to fear. My own personal boogeyman was dead. Braxton had shot him. Garon's brains had been in my hair, for fuck's sake. There was no surviving having part of your head blown off.

But I still had the mark that would leave a scar on my abdomen and would always remain, just like the memories. Maybe if I was lucky, one day the nightmares would cease. But this wasn't that day.

Eventually, our alarms went off, and I was almost relieved. I didn't want to leave the safety of Jordan's arms. His warmth was the only thing that kept me from trembling at times. But getting out of bed meant turning off the nightmares and focusing on the endless tasks of the day.

With a groan, Jordan rolled over to grab his phone and turn off his alarm. "I have a meeting with Winston Cline. Taylor will be here soon. Do you need anything?"

I sat up slowly, knowing that if I moved too quickly I would either vomit all over the bed or pass out. The joys of first trimester pregnancy were still new to me, but I was quickly learning how to manage the morning sickness and the occasional blood pressure changes. "Nah. Elliot is bringing me breakfast before we meet up with our moms and aunts. We all have our final dress fittings today."

His eyes brightened. "Only one more week and I get to call you my wife."

My laugh pushed away most of the lingering fear of the nightmare. "How is that any different from every other day?"

"You haven't been paying attention," he chided. "Right now, you are my bride. Your last name is still Stevenson. Very, very soon, you will have my last name. That's a gigantic difference. Huge, actually."

"Actually," I reminded him, biting the inside of my cheek to keep from grinning. "I will still be Arella Stevenson when it comes to work."

He stiffened over me. "You're not changing your Screen Actors Guild name?"

"Nope."

"Arella," he growled, lowering his head until our noses barely grazed against each other. "You're going to be my wife."

"Jordan," I mocked in the same tone. "You're going to be

producing my next movie. How much crap do you think I'm going to get in the press if I change my name and then suddenly show up as the lead in your new project?"

"Fuck the press."

My own alarm went off, and he jerked to his feet. This was going to be a problem. I'd known it the moment I'd made the decision not to change my name for work. Jordan wanted me marked in every way as his, which I understood. My possessiveness of him knew no bounds. But on this, I had to remain firm. It wasn't about him and me, but my career, something I'd worked my ass off to get to this point without help from my dad or anyone else in my family. It was mine and mine alone. My accomplishments. My success. Behind the scenes, I wanted to be Mrs. Jordan Moreitti. But in front of the camera, I needed to be Arella Stevenson.

Turning off my alarm, he stomped his way to the bathroom. As he did, I caught sight of his left hand and the tattooed ring on his finger. My name looked good on his skin. Biting my lip, I considered following him into the bathroom, maybe dropping to my knees beneath the spray and making him forget why he was pouting. But before I could get to my feet, my phone rang and I reluctantly picked it up.

"Why can't I wear a tux like the guys?" Palmer asked as soon as I lifted the phone to my ear. "You know I hate dresses. As your maid of honor, I should get a choice."

"We've already had this argument, Palms." I slowly stood and walked over to the closet. Most of my clothes were already at the new house, but we couldn't move in until after the wedding. I only had a few selections to choose from at the apartment, so it didn't take long before I'd picked what I would wear to the final fitting.

She'd had the same complaint from the moment I'd asked her to be my maid of honor. It went without saying that my three sisters would be bridesmaids, but I needed Palmer as my number one. I had a visual in my head of what I wanted all four of them to look like, and I couldn't give my bestie what she wanted and let her wear a tuxedo. Something she knew, but that didn't stop her from complaining. Or trying to change my mind. But so close to the wedding, it wouldn't have even been possible at this point.

"Fine," she huffed. "But only because I love you. At least the dress isn't ugly like the one they made me wear to my cousin's wedding last year. That damn thing is any bridesmaid's worst nightmare."

I shuddered as the memories of my own nightmare flashed on fast-forward through my head again. Gulping, I tried to laugh it off.

"You know I wouldn't do that to you, bestie."

"Uh-oh," she muttered. "What's wrong?"

"What?" I pretended not to understand. But there was no getting out of it. Palmer knew me better than anyone else in the world, probably even more than my own parents. We'd been to hell and back together. From the moment I'd set eyes on her, she was my best friend, and no one else would ever fill that all too important role.

"Your voice is off. Again. Did you and Moreitti argue?"

"No, of course not." After putting the phone on speaker and placing it on a shelf, I pulled on fresh panties and then the white strapless bra I had to wear to the fittings.

"Then what's with the voice?" she demanded.

Sighing, I told her the truth. I didn't have to pretend with Palmer the way I did with the rest of my family. "More nightmares."

"Fuck, babe. I'm sorry. Listen, you need to speak to a therapist. This is going to turn into some scary PTSD if you don't take it seriously. I know someone who can get you in as soon as you give me the green light to set up the appointment."

"Ugh. I don't want to talk about my feelings with a stranger," I complained, pulling a dress over my head.

"You want to talk to your parents? Your sisters? Your aunts? Cousins?" She kept going, and I cringed more and more.

"Okay, okay," I grumbled, zipping myself up before slipping my feet into a pair of flats. "I get it. And no, I don't want to talk about any of this with them. Give me the number. I'll set the appointment up myself."

"Yeah, that's a big hell no," Palmer said with a dry laugh. "You'll forget about it or keep putting it off. Those nightmares you've been having every night will start playing out in the middle of the day. And then you'll be spending the rest of your pregnancy locked in some asylum or in a special care rehab. Your career will go down the drain, your kid will be fucked up, and your husband will be driving the rest of us insane because he can't reach you mentally."

I blinked at my reflection in the mirror in the walk-in closet. Part of me wanted to think she was being overly dramatic, but the sad truth was, I could foresee all of what she was predicting actually happening.

"Set it up," I told her after a pause. "Then text Elliot so he can add it to my calendar."

CHAPTER 2

JORDAN

I shook Winston's hand across his desk, and we both stood. Taylor, who had been taking notes on her phone during our meeting, stood as well but didn't offer her hand. Instead, she continued typing, but I didn't pay her much attention as the movie producer kept going on.

And on.

And on.

The man was an endless bag of air. If Arella hadn't asked me to accept the offer to continue with the villainess movie, with Winston instead of that dead bastard Garon, then I wouldn't have taken the first meeting with the man, let alone gotten to the point that we were now looking at audition clips for some of the minor parts that still needed to be filled.

"Sir, you have a lunch appointment," Taylor said in a quiet yet firm voice. I liked it when she used that tone. It told whoever I was in a conversation with that I needed to take her words seriously, and they never gave me shit about ending a meeting. She more than earned the salary I paid her. If anything, I was thinking about giving her another raise.

As we got into the back of my SUV with my driver—one of Barrick's men—at the wheel, Taylor finally placed her phone facedown on her lap with a barely there sigh. "Palmer was able to convince her to see the therapist," she informed me. "And the first appointment is tomorrow morning."

"They couldn't get her in today?" I asked with a grunt as I shifted to face my personal assistant a little better. Without thinking, I rubbed my thumb over my left ring finger, caressing the tattoo of Arella's name her cousin had inked into my skin. When I got edgy, needing to see her but couldn't, I found comfort in touching the black writing. Some days, I rubbed it more often than not. In the beginning, while it was healing, I'd had to stop myself from touching it so much so as not to ruin it.

Fuck, but I needed to see her. Now. Hear her voice. Touch her. Kiss that mouth that drove me crazy.

"They could, but she had a packed schedule for the day, and she told Elliot today wasn't possible. After some convincing, Palmer got her to agree to tomorrow's appointment, and Elliot was able to rearrange tomorrow's meetings and other appointments."

A surge of relief filled me. It wasn't as soon as I'd hoped, but at least she was finally going to talk to a specialist about her trauma. It was slowly killing me to watch her fake it through the day or work herself into exhaustion so she could fall asleep each night. But no matter how tired she made herself, Arella always had nightmares. Sometimes she simply jolted awake. Others, she woke up swinging, struggling to get away from me. Or screaming her head off, the terror in her voice sending chills down my spine even though I knew the threat to her no longer existed.

"Should I clear your morning meetings so you can attend with her?" Taylor asked after a beat.

My instant reaction was, fuck yeah, I was going to be there, but in my gut, I knew this was something Arella needed to do on her own. "Rearrange my meetings. I want to ride with her to the appointment."

"Yes, sir." Picking up her phone again, she started typing away. She was going to get arthritis in her fingers with all the typing she had to do for me all day long, but she never complained. She'd been a godsend since my mother hired her for me once I'd officially come back from Italy.

That she was in a serious, committed relationship with my future wife's best friend made it even better. I could steer Arella in a particular direction—that she was too stubborn to accept on her own—with their help in situations like this. Arella didn't want to talk about what happened with her uncle to me or anyone else. Not even Palmer. Part of me understood why she stayed quiet about it. I'd freaked out big-time after nearly losing her to that psychopath. She thought she had to protect me and everyone else from her mental state. As if she thought we would all fall apart because she was having issues from something that would have traumatized a grown man.

Her parents had already told me that Braxton was in therapy after killing Garon. Nevaeh hadn't been pleased when she learned her husband and parents had kept something important about her sister from her, but she'd insisted that Braxton speak to a counselor about what he'd had to do in order to save Arella. She'd gotten him in for an appointment the same week everything happened, so he didn't appear to be suffering from the aftereffects.

Maybe I should have insisted as well, instead of taking Arella's word that she was fine. That had only lasted for about a week before the nightmares began, and neither of us had gotten a full night's sleep since.

I'd dropped the ball, and now the love of my life was struggling with her mental health.

But hopefully this therapist would help. I'd already vetted the woman before letting Palmer make the suggestion to Arella about seeing her. If anyone could talk sense into my bride, it was her best friend. Palmer didn't hold back, gave zero fucks about pissing people off—including Arella. And Arella didn't take offense because she knew that was simply how Palmer was, and she loved her anyway.

Perhaps I was scared that Arella wouldn't feel the same if it were me making the suggestions. I might have loved her since she was sixteen, but our relationship was fairly new. I didn't want to risk rocking the boat, even if we were about to get married. After all the mistakes I'd made in the past, I wasn't ready to chance making more now.

What if it pissed her off and she decided she didn't love me enough?

What if I pushed her too hard and she no longer wanted to become my wife?

That was why I hadn't pushed her about not changing her name for work. She kept saying it was because of the blowup from the press. After the field day they'd had following Garon's death, and it had come out that he'd had an unhealthy obsession with his niece, she wasn't ready for more publicity. But I fucking wanted her to have my last name in every aspect of our lives, especially work. When dickheads saw her name on the big screen, I wanted them to know who she belonged to—me, god damn it!

For the moment, I wouldn't push. But once her mental health was on the right track, I was going to go for broke and tell her exactly what I wanted.

Even if my palms were already sweating at the idea that she would laugh in my face and tell me to go fuck myself, I eventually had to let her know that I wasn't okay with her not having my last name associated with every part of her life. That meant personal as well as her career.

The entire world needed to know who she belonged to.

CHAPTER 3

ARELLA

After a full day, I was exhausted as I waited for Samuel to open the back door to the bulletproof SUV. I'd more than learned my lesson about waiting for my bodyguard and his associates to clear the area of any dangers before stepping out of the vehicle.

I touched the still-tender spot on my abdomen. The stitches had long since been taken out, and all I was left with was a scar. But I felt a phantom-like pain there from time to time. Usually whenever I thought about Garon pushing that deadly knife into my flesh.

Shaking my head at myself, I stepped down from the SUV and kept my focus on the elevator ahead, not daring to look at the spot where my uncle's blood and brains had once stained the cement of the garage. The ride up to the apartment, I couldn't help but tremble. Palmer might have been right when she said that the nightmares would eventually bleed over into my waking hours.

The appointment with the therapist the following morning couldn't come fast enough.

Once I was safely behind the closed and locked door of the apartment, I was able to relax—a little. Kicking off my shoes, I walked into the kitchen to get a bottle of water. Deciding on a shower before Jordan got home so we could go out for dinner, I turned in the direction of our bedroom when the landline rang.

I hated that damned thing, but I picked it up when I saw it was the concierge from downstairs.

"Miss Stevenson," Tim greeted, his tone respectful as always. "A package was delivered for you about ten minutes ago. Would you like for me to bring it up?"

I frowned. "My personal assistant normally takes care of all my mail."

"When I signed for the package, I was told it was a wedding gift for you and Mr. Moreitti. It's very heavy, ma'am, so I suspect it's an appliance for your kitchen."

My bridal shower had been the weekend before, and I'd gotten nearly everything on the registry that I'd created with Mom and Alexis. The moms had put a lot of time and effort into the shower. Everything we'd received was already set up in the new house. But there had been one or two people who couldn't make the event at the last minute.

"Okay, Tim," I told him, pasting on a smile with energy I honestly didn't have to expend. "Please bring it on up."

"Yes, ma'am."

I drank half the bottle of water before the doorbell rang, announcing Tim's arrival. I opened the door and waved him in. "What in the world could that be?" I muttered to myself as I watched him struggle to carry the huge box into the living room and deposit it on the floor.

"No clue, ma'am," he said, out of breath. "But whatever it is, I hope you get some use out of it." Tipping his head, he said goodnight and closed the door behind him on his way out.

I barely watched the door shut before dropping down onto my knees beside the box, my curiosity taking precedence over my need to shower. The return address said it was from the same store where I'd registered, but nothing that was left on my list could have been that big, especially not a kitchen appliance, and nothing else could have been so heavy that Tim would have struggled so much with the box.

Opening the drawer of the end table beside the couch, I grabbed the letter opener I'd placed in there to go through the work mail Elliot occasionally left for me to open myself. Using it, I cut along the taped seams of the box and lifted the flaps.

Only to discover a different box inside. My brows lifted when I saw this was a plain box that just barely fit inside the larger one with the store logo on it. It was more like a moving box, taped up almost erratically. Annoyed at the unprofessional way the item had been packaged, I started tearing through the thick layers of tape with the letter opener again.

Once it was undone and I could open the flaps of the second box, I came to a Styrofoam box that was also overly taped closed. Irritated, I grabbed my phone. As it rang, I started cutting away the tape yet again.

"Hey, sweetheart," Mom greeted. "How was the rest of your day?"

"Tiring," I told her distractedly as I kept cutting. "I got a last-minute wedding gift. The concierge had a hard time carrying it up because it was so heavy. I'm sitting on the floor in the living room, and

I think you should call the store we registered at to complain about the way they ship items. The outer box was perfectly taped, but the second box was pure insanity, and now I've reached a Styrofoam one that is even more unevenly taped."

"Well, what is it?" she asked, sounding perplexed.

I finally got the last of the tape undone and tried to pull off the top. It was stuck, so I used the letter opener to help open each side, which was made even more difficult because I didn't dare try to lift the heavy box out. Jordan would freak if he found out I tried to pick up anything that weighed more than my handbag.

It was frustrating, and I huffed and puffed and cursed at the damned thing while Mom laughed through the receiver.

The instant the lid was off, the smell had me gagging. The scent was so overpowering that I began to retch before I could even look into the box.

"Arella?" Mom frantically yelled my name. "What's going on?"

Wiping my hand across the back of my mouth, I peeked inside the box and puked again. "Help," I squeaked as memories of dead birds flashed through my mind.

Only this wasn't a dead bird.

It was a dead cat. Huge, thick blocks of dry ice surrounded it, which was probably why it had been so heavy, but the scent of death and decay had now been unleashed, and it was permeating the air. I didn't doubt it would soak into the furniture, if not the paint on the walls.

The poor kitty had been decapitated, its head lying separately from the rest of its body. Its insides spilled out of its belly. Vaguely, I saw the note stapled to the intestines, and I knew.

Garon's reign of terror wasn't over after all.

CHAPTER 4

JORDAN

"**S**ir?"

Something in Taylor's voice had my head snapping up from my phone where I'd been going through my emails. The driver was trying to pull up in front of the apartment building, but it was hard to get close with all the police cars parked haphazardly in front of it.

Their lights were on, flashing from blue to red in the darkness. No police tape had been put up, but it was obvious that something had happened. People were standing on the street, barricades and several men in uniforms holding back the growing crowd as they tried to see what was going on.

A knot began to form in my gut. Instinctively, I knew whatever was going on involved Arella.

"Stop here!" I shouted at the driver. The door was open, and I was already out before he completely came to a stop. Running like my life depended on it, I zigzagged through the police cars and shoved a uniformed cop out of my way when he tried to block me from getting into the building. In the lobby, things were chaotic. At least a dozen policemen were standing around, talking to other tenants. Tim stood at the bank of elevators, his face ghostly pale as he nodded to whatever the man in a cheap suit said to him.

"What happened?" I demanded as I made my way toward the concierge.

"Mr. Moreitti," he said, and I watched his throat work as he gulped. "I didn't know what was in the box, sir. If I'd known, I wouldn't have carried it up. But the package said it was from the same shop Miss Stevenson registered, and—"

"What. The. Fuck. Happened?" I gritted out, stopping him from going on and on with no real information.

My heart was already pounding hard, causing the blood rushing through my ears to make everything else sound like I was in a tunnel.

"Mr. Moreitti."

My eyes shifted from the concierge to a man I was all too familiar with. Detective Kirtner stood inside one of the now-open elevator doors, an expression on his face that made me want to puke. "Is she okay?" I choked out, knowing if this man was present then something had definitely happened to Arella.

"Come up to your apartment with me, sir," he said instead of answering my question.

"Is she okay?" I bellowed, raking my trembling fingers through my hair.

"Physically, yes." That didn't really tell me anything. With her mental health currently in question, his answer only made me quake. "But she needs you."

The ride up in the elevator seemed to take an eternity but truly lasted less than thirty seconds. As soon as the doors opened on my floor, I stepped off. More cops stood along the corridor, speaking to my neighbors, who all held tissues or clothes to their noses.

That was when the smell hit me. Caught off guard, I couldn't help the gagging noise that left me reflexively. A glance at Kirtner showed me he didn't seem affected by the terrible stench. I pulled the pocket square from my suit jacket and lifted it to my nose, smelling the cologne Arella had spritzed on it after getting it back from the dry cleaners.

"What the fuck is that smell?"

"Death," Kirtner responded deadpan. "Miss Stevenson received another...gift."

"I need more context than that," I told him as we continued walking toward the open door of my apartment.

Inside, it was pure insanity. The smell was more prominent here, so strong it nearly knocked me back a step when I entered the living room. Four people were in head-to-toe protective gear. Not hazmat, but it wouldn't have surprised me if they'd had that gear on too. These outfits were all white, like an adult onesie with a hood and booties. They wore medical masks over their mouths and clear shields that covered their faces from forehead to chin.

"Forensics," Kirtner commented when he saw my gaze land on them.

Mentally shaking my head, I glanced around for Arella but didn't immediately see her. "Where is she?"

"Bathroom," someone answered me without shifting their attention from the box the four forensic professionals were examining so thoroughly.

Unable to stop myself, I paused beside the box to get a look at what they were so interested in. Only to be thankful I'd skipped lunch earlier.

"Is that a cat?" I asked shakily.

"It was," Kirtner said with a shrug. "There was a note with it. Luckily Miss Stevenson didn't get any bile on it when she threw up earlier."

"Luckily," I replied dryly. Fuck, she'd been ill after smelling this. I needed to get to her. My skin felt too tight, just as it did whenever I went too long without seeing her. Yet all I could do was look inside the box at the hideous remains of a defenseless little animal. "What did the note say?"

One of the forensic guys lifted a plastic bag, which held a piece of paper inside. "Little birds get eaten by the big, bad kitty," he read.

"Little birds," I repeated, taking a step back from the box and turning to glare at Kirtner. "That's what Garon called her. His little bird."

"Yes," he agreed with a nod. "But that bastard is good and dead. Either he had someone helping him we didn't know about, or this person is working on their own to terrorize Miss Stevenson."

"Jordan?"

At the sound of Arella calling my name, I took off running. I could hear the fear in her voice, and I needed to wrap my arms around her, take her away from the disgusting sight in the living room and as far away from the danger that had come back to try to steal her from me.

In the bedroom, a female officer was with her. Arella had on a robe, and her hair was damp. Steam still filtered out of the bathroom. Pushing her damp locks back from her face, she looked up at me with blank blue-gray eyes. "I'm sorry," she cried. "I meant to call you. But I couldn't stop puking. Mom called Kirtner, and he arrived with an army of cops. That was only like half an hour ago."

Instead of worrying about why no one else had bothered to call me, I did the only thing I could right then and wrapped my arms around her. If Lana had called Kirtner, then she was probably a nervous wreck. No doubt she and Drake were already on their way to check on their daughter.

Arella shivered then turned her face into my chest before letting go of a shuddery sigh. "Did you see?" she whispered. "That poor little kitty."

"Don't think about it, baby." I kissed the top of her hair. It smelled sweet as usual, a dramatic contrast to what the apartment—fuck, the entire floor—smelled like now. "Get dressed, and we'll get out here."

"Okay," she muttered, her voice emotionless. "I won't be long."

Leaning back, I looked down into her face. She looked exhausted with the dark circles beneath her eyes from lack of sleep for so long. Her skin had a paleness to it that was unnatural. She looked unhealthy, fragile...and empty.

After struggling with her mental health for weeks, had this irreparably broken something in her?

CHAPTER 5

ARELLA

There was noise all around me. I knew it. Could see people's mouths moving. But I heard nothing.

My stomach cramped from puking until nothing was left. It was completely empty, and I didn't even want to try to drink water for fear it would set off my gag reflex again. The smell of death seemed permanently burned into my nose, making my sinuses sting, and if I opened my mouth, I could actually taste it on my tongue.

No matter how many times I'd washed my hair, or how hard I'd scrubbed my body, I couldn't get away from the scent. Everything smelled like it, even Jordan's jacket and skin. My favorite smells in the word were associated with him, yet he was part of the scents that were causing me pain now.

The items Garon had sent me—the pictures of him touching himself and dead birds—were nothing compared to the horrible things I'd seen in the newest box. I couldn't get the sight out of my head. Not when I closed my eyes or looked at Jordan, or my parents wrapped me in what should have been comforting hugs.

I wasn't safe.

That meant the baby wasn't safe.

How was I going to protect the one person who depended solely on me when I couldn't even protect myself?

Garon was dead. I should have been safe. But now there was a new boogeyman out there, waiting, ready to kill "the little bird." Why had he called me that? Why would this new stalker refer to me as one? I'd never really liked birds, although they were kind of cute from a distance. There was just something about them that made me...sad? Not just the ones people kept as pets, always caged up, but the ones in the wild as well. Even in their flocks, I felt a sense of sadness every time I looked at them.

It was crazy to think that birds were lonely even in a huge flock, yet I was unable not to feel empathy for them. How could anyone or anything feel completely alone in the world when they were surrounded by everyone they loved?

Holding my breath, I tried to push those thoughts away. Although they were a million miles away from the horrible ones that flooded in when they disappeared. Broken kitty. Entrails. Creepy note stapled to delicate intestines.

Broken kitty.

Broken...

Me.

"Arie, breathe!" Daddy's deep voice commanded as his hands cupped my face. I blinked, and his eyes came into focus, the same shade as my own.

Gasping, I sucked in a deep lungful of oxygen as tears blurred my vision. His eyes were so beautiful. Years before, the whites had been a sickly yellow shade. I'd thought I was going to lose him. If not for his brother, my uncle Shane, he would have died.

"Da-Daddy!" I sobbed, lowering my head until I could press my forehead against his chest. Even he smelled like the putridness that was back in the apartment. My parents had arrived just as I'd finished getting dressed, and they'd insisted on taking us back to their house. I'd wanted to argue. If I wasn't safe, then they wouldn't be safe either. Very few things were more important to me than protecting my dad. He'd been through so much in his life already, and I wasn't sure if I could survive if something happened to him. Even more so if it was because of me.

But Braxton lived just a few houses away. He was going to come over with my other bodyguards, plus several more that he'd called Barrick to send over. I was supposed to be safe there, which meant everyone else would be safe.

But I didn't believe them.

I didn't believe anyone anymore when they said I was safe.

"I-I'm scared."

And so very tired.

I didn't speak the last part aloud, but it echoed through my mind.

More than that, I was angry. I was pissed that I couldn't do anything about this fear that had taken over my life. I was losing energy that the baby growing in my belly needed. Would all the stress from everything harm my child's development as he or she grew inside me? Was I harming them by not getting enough sleep, by constantly being scared of my own shadow?

Fuck that.

And fuck whoever wanted to harm me.

I was done with this shit.

"I know, sweetheart," Daddy soothed, stroking one hand over my hair. "But we'll figure it all out. Daddy won't let anyone hurt you, I promise."

Everyone kept saying that. Him. Braxton. Mom. The bodyguards. Jordan. Over and over, one after another, all evening. But no matter how badly I wanted to believe them, I couldn't. Someone out there wanted to cause me harm. Just like Garon. And the worst part was that I didn't know why.

What was so special about me?

What had I done for them to target me?

"You're mine." I flinched at the memory of Garon's words as they played through my head. "She got everything when the old man died. Everything. If I take you, one of her precious children, and make you mine, it will destroy her."

The knife had touched my cheek tenderly, as if he were actually caressing me lovingly with the deadly blade. My skin had felt raw for a day or so from how sharp the knife had been.

Shivering, I glanced up and met Daddy's gaze. "Mom," I breathed. "Garon wanted to hurt Mom by hurting me. He was so pissed that she got everything from PopPop. The money, the acknowledgment. Everything. He was obsessed with me because it would have driven Mom crazy."

His brows pulled together, his eyes darkening with anger and lingering fear for both Mom and me. "I remember."

"The note." My stomach cramped, wanting to rebel again, but I swallowed the saliva that filled my mouth. "It said, 'Little birds get eaten by the big, bad kitty.'"

"Creepy, but I'm not catching on to where this is going, honey."

"Claudia!" I shouted, then quickly pressed my lips together when every eye in the living room turned to us. Swallowing roughly, I tried to control the volume of my voice when I spoke again. "PopPop once said something about his first wife in passing that was weird at the time. He was joking around, telling Damien not to get married because kittens have long claws that will shred a man apart. He brought it up again when Braxton kept calling Nevaeh 'kitten.' He said Claudia was the baddest kitty of them all. She attempted to destroy him after the divorce, but he made it back to the top even though she tried to bury him."

"Arie, Claudia is harmless. All talk and no bite," Mom said with a dry laugh, lovingly tucking a lock of my hair behind my ear.

I shifted my gaze to her. "That's what we thought about Garon too."

She paled and jerked to her feet. "I'm going to call Detective Kirtner."

Daddy pressed a kiss to my forehead before straightening. "No, Angel, I'll make the call," he said in a voice that had Mom rolling her brown eyes at him. "Maybe it's nothing, but at least it's somewhere to start, even if it's by simply eliminating her as a suspect."

Phone in hand, he walked out of the living room, and Jordan quickly moved to sit beside me. From the time we'd arrived, my parents had surrounded me, making it nearly impossible for my fiancé to get close. I'd been so out of it, I hadn't really noticed.

The moment his arm slid around my back and his thigh pressed against mine, I felt as if I was actually thawing. I didn't think I would ever feel safe again but having him beside me was as close to feeling safe as I would get.

And for the moment, that was enough.

Closing my eyes, I leaned my head against his shoulder and let my exhaustion pull me under. But even as I drifted off, the frustrated anger began to simmer into a consuming fury that threatened to overtake the fear. And I wasn't sure whether that was better than being afraid all the time or not.

CHAPTER 6

ARELLA

My anger only burned brighter when Detective Kirtner couldn't confidently say whether Claudia had been a party to the poor kitty I'd been sent as a wedding present. Mom continued to say the bitch was harmless, but I didn't remind her again that her stupid brother had supposedly been harmless too. Barrick and Braxton seemed to agree with her. Everything they could find out about the woman, from their own investigation, pointed to her being too old and frail to do anything remotely threatening.

I didn't agree.

She had too many reasons for it not to be her.

The woman had thought her son would inherit at least a part of his father's fortune. When that didn't happen, Garon had tipped over the edge of reality, developed a sick obsession with me, and then started stalking me to the point he'd actually hidden a camera in my dressing room at the studio where we'd both worked. All because of his hate for my mom. Claudia might be old as dirt, but she was also an angry, no doubt unhinged, mother who had lost not only the chance at more money from a man she hated, but she had lost her son as well.

Her hate for Lana Daniels Stevenson was always there beneath the surface. No one could ever deny that. It was the birth of my mom that had proven Cole Steel had cheated on her and given her the evidence she needed to take him to the cleaners when she divorced him. The way I saw it, the hate she felt for Mom would only double where I was concerned if she blamed me for her son's death.

Which, technically, I was.

The bastard had held a knife to my throat, threatening not only my life, but that of my unborn baby, and Braxton had taken the first chance he was given to save me. The result had been Garon's brains being blown all over the parking garage.

After another night of nothing but terror-filled dreams, I woke up the next morning determined that I wasn't going to sit by and let someone try to scare me until I went crazy or even potentially had a miscarriage from all the fucking stress. Messing with me was one thing. Maybe I would have let the fear take complete control of my life and allowed Claudia to win. But it wasn't just me, damn it. I had the safety of my baby to consider.

Like my mother, I was already a protective mama bear where my child was concerned.

And nothing was more dangerous than a mama bear fearing for her cub's safety.

"How are you feeling today, Arella?"

I blinked back my thoughts and gave the woman sitting across from me a grim smile. "If I told you I was more angry than scared, would you think I was insane?"

Jerrica Burke was a woman in her mid to late thirties. She had this calming aura to her that, during the previous two sessions I'd had with her over the last few days, had put me instantly at ease. The morning following the unwanted wedding present, Jordan had insisted that I keep my appointment, and I was glad he'd been so persistent in urging me to attend.

Talking to Jerrica had helped in a way I didn't think anything other than a few weeks in a rehab facility could have done. Considering my dad's past, no one would have believed I was in rehab for anything other than alcohol—even if it was to get mentally healthy rather than fight an addiction. She'd taken the strain of talking to a stranger out of the equation, and I'd found myself unloading so much baggage.

Some of which I hadn't realized I'd carried.

Like feeling lonely even in a crowd. My empathy for birds had been my own manifestation of often feeling all alone even when surrounded by my nearest and dearest, something I'd hidden from myself for my entire life. Apparently my acting abilities were better than I'd ever dreamed if I could pretend enough to convince myself I hadn't been fighting a mild form of depression for years.

Maybe it had started when Daddy got sick, the fear of losing him. Or when things hadn't gone as I had foreseen them on my eighteenth birthday with Jordan. Perhaps it was losing my grandfather, a man who had seemed immortal with his gigantic presence and his unwavering love for my mom, my siblings, and me.

Or it could have been long before any of that. It was possible nothing could have triggered my depression and it had everything to do with my brain chemistry. All I knew was that talking to Jerrica made me feel better. I'd gotten more restful sleep over the past two nights, although I'd still had a few nightmares. At least they hadn't been nearly as frightening as the ones I'd had over the previous weeks.

Jerrica gave me an understanding smile. "It is completely natural to be angry over feeling as if you don't hold the control in your life. With what happened with your uncle, and now this unfortunate incident with the wedding present, I think you have every right to think everything is out of your control." She lifted her left hand, which held her pen that she took occasional notes with. I liked that she did that, expressing herself with hand movements. It made her more human to me, rather than just the medical professional Jordan was paying in hopes of fixing me. "But the truth of the matter is, you hold all the power, Arella. It may not seem like it, but you do, in fact, control every aspect of your life."

I chewed on the inside of my cheek, considering her words for a moment before responding. "How?" I choked on the pressing question. "I really need to know how I have all the power when I don't feel like I have any right now."

"You control how you respond," she said confidently. "If something scares you, it's okay to show it. In fact, you need to react to every emotion you experience. By acknowledging that you are scared or angry or even sad, you control the outcome of how it affects you. But when you bottle it up, internalizing it, those emotions build and can manifest in unhealthy ways. Having discussed your parents' history as well as your own, you can see that your father let his emotions manifest into alcoholism that eventually caused him a physical illness, as well as the mental health challenges he struggled with up to and after meeting your mother. In my opinion, his addiction actually transferred from drinking to your mother." She laughed softly. "I'm not saying that's a bad thing. I've observed your parents together, and their relationship is something incredibly special. Every woman deserves to have a man love her the way your father does your mother."

"Addictions and obsessions are both toxic," I mused aloud. "But that doesn't mean they are always unhealthy."

"I both agree and disagree," she said with a grimace. "Any addiction is unhealthy. No matter what form it takes. Obsessions are very unhealthy as well, but what may seem like obsession can actually be something different. It could just be that someone's love of that person, place, even an object, is so overwhelming that it seems like obsession."

Again, I considered her response for a moment before speaking.

"As you've said, you've observed my parents together. You have also seen how Jordan and I are. What would you label each relationship?"

She was quiet for a long moment, and I mentally braced myself as I waited for her answer. "In both cases, I can see that, to an outsider, it would appear as if both Mr. Stevenson and Mr. Moreitti are borderline unhinged where your mother and you are concerned. Both men seem unreasonably jealous, even twitchy at times when you aren't within Jordan's sight. The same can be said for your father. But it's my honest opinion that where Mr. Stevenson is concerned, it is solely because he loves Mrs. Stevenson so much that he can't rationally think past being with her."

I held my breath, waiting for her to give me her opinion on Jordan's feelings for me.

She paused again, gathering her thoughts. "Jordan doesn't have a past trauma that would make him stress over losing you the way your father would your mother. However, the time the two of you spent avoiding the issues of your relationship in the past has made him lack confidence in himself and your feelings where he is concerned. It's not obsession that drives him, but the need to constantly reassure himself that you are now his."

Her answer nearly caused me to snort. "Jordan? Lacking confidence?" I shook my head at the woman in total disbelief. "That seems preposterous. He's never been anything but fully confident a day in his life."

"Maybe in other aspects of his life," she agreed. "But after speaking to him privately before our first session together, I concluded that he actually does have self-confidence issues where your relationship is concerned. Why else would he ask your best friend to convince you to meet with me rather than broach the subject himself?"

"Wait," I whispered, leaning forward. My hands grew damp, and I didn't understand why. "You spoke to Jordan before our first session?"

"Yes."

"And he was the one who wanted me to see you, but instead of telling me this himself, he went behind my back and had Palmer do the dirty work?"

Jerrica's eyes scanned my face for a moment. "Does that make you angry?"

"A little bit, yes," I admitted, wiping my hands on my dress-covered thighs. "But..."

She smiled as she crossed one leg over the other. "But, what?"

"But it's kind of sweet, if a little insane." I tossed my hair over my shoulder as I leaned back on the comfortable sofa again. It was oddly sweet, but I needed to focus on why it made me angry. "I mean, how could he ever think that he can't talk to me about something important like this? Why would he be afraid to bring up anything, but especially something like this?"

"You would need to ask him about that," she said with a slight lift of one shoulder. "But if I had to take a guess? He's scared of rocking the boat so early in your relationship."

"But we're getting married in a few days!" I cried in exasperation.

Should we be going into that level of a committed relationship with doubts between us?

I didn't voice that question aloud, because it wasn't something I thought she should be the one to answer. It was something only Jordan and I could figure out for ourselves.

"After dating for how long?" she tossed at me.

I twisted the huge engagement ring on my finger, suddenly nervous. Were we rushing into things? Just because I was pregnant didn't mean we had to get married right away. We could have waited. There was nothing wrong with taking time to build our relationship before taking such a gigantic step.

But even as the thought filled my mind, my stomach roiled in protest.

"I wouldn't say we actually dated," I admitted to her. "It was more lots of sex, admitting our feelings for each other, him getting me pregnant, and then putting a ring on it."

Her light laughter filled the room. "Sounds like a desperate man trying to lock you down. If what you're worried about is if Mr. Moreitti loves you, or if what he's feeling is an unhealthy obsession, then I can honestly say, in my professional opinion, he is one hundred percent in love with you. It's just an extremely overwhelming feeling for him. I doubt he's ever experienced this kind of love for anyone else."

CHAPTER 7

JORDAN

Too restless to sit, I paced the waiting room while Samuel stood
in front of the door that led into Jerrica Burke's office, and the
other two guards flanked either side of the main entrance. This
was the third appointment Arella had attended in just as many days.
Each time I kissed her before she went into the therapist's office, I got
a gnawing ache in my stomach that didn't go away until after she
walked out again.

There was no need for the anxiousness I felt. She was safe in there
with Jerrica. Yet I couldn't stop the overwhelming nervousness that
Arella might suddenly have an epiphany and decide that I wasn't who
she wanted to spend the rest of her life with. What if she finally
opened her eyes to the fact that I wasn't worthy of her or her love?

Trying not to comb my fingers through my hair, I stuffed my
hands into my slacks pockets and paced the length of the room. There
was no receptionist at the desk since the appointments were arranged
for after Jerrica's normal hours. Evening had descended since Arella
had gone in for her session. I'd watched the streetlights flicker on
when I'd passed the bank of windows. The darkness only escalated my
already erratic heart rate.

I didn't like Arella being out at night, even if the guards and I were
with her. Not knowing who had sent the disgusting box rattled me.
They had no leads except for the person Arella insisted was the only
culprit who could be behind the vile incident. After personally seeing
Claudia Steel from a distance the day after Arella had reached the
conclusion that Garon's mother was the only possible answer, I found
it hard to believe, just as Lana and the others did.

Claudia was barely able to lift her legs to walk, using a cane to
assist her as she'd made her way from a town car to the simple, one-
story home that was all she was able to afford now. Her son's will had
left everything to Arella. She'd rejected the money and told the

lawyers to donate to an advocacy group for victims of stalking and abuse. As for his share of Strive, I now owned that.

Arella had assumed that by gifting it to me, I wouldn't have to deal with Winston Cline or any of the other producers at the company. But it was such a huge project that I needed at least one of the other partners to back it to ensure the others wouldn't try to pull the plug should the studio lose money from the endeavor.

Not that it would. As soon as Arella recovered from having our baby, production would begin. Her pregnancy and maternity leave would give us enough time to secure every position, including director, special effects, and the music for the movie. I predicted that it would be a hit, and that we would get at least two additional movies out of the franchise.

The success wouldn't be possible without Arella as the lead. No one else would fit the character better than her.

Just as no one would fit me like she did.

Agitated, I couldn't stop myself from running my fingers through my hair. As I did, the door opened, and Jerrica stepped through before turning to allow Arella to exit. I stopped my pacing and let my eyes eat up the sight of my fiancée as the two women stopped to speak to each other.

"I think we've made some great progress," Jerrica told her confidently. "I've got you scheduled for another session the day after you return from your honeymoon, but if you need to speak to me before then, I have my cell on me at all times. Day or night, if you're struggling mentally, I want you to at least text me."

Arella's smile didn't completely reach her eyes when she gave the doctor a nod. "Thank you. I guess I'll see you in a few weeks, then."

"I mean it, Arella," Jerrica reiterated. "Day or night."

"Okay, thanks." Her blue-gray gaze shifted, instantly connecting with mine. I felt the breath leave my body in a whoosh when her shoulders squared. The softness I'd grown accustomed to—was fucking addicted to—when she looked at me wasn't there.

Clearing my throat of the sudden emotion clogging it, I stepped toward her. "Ready, love?"

She gave me a small nod before waving to Jerrica. The two new guards took point, leading us out of the office and toward the SUV that was parked nearby, while Samuel stayed directly behind Arella for the brief walk.

As we exited the building, I placed my hand at the small of her back and felt her tense, but she didn't shy away from my touch. My heart began to pound violently against my ribs, making it impossible to take a deep enough breath. By the time we reached the SUV, I felt like I'd just run five miles.

Once we were in the back with the doors shut, Samuel climbed behind the wheel, and the other two got into the other SUV to follow us. Arella remained quiet the entire time, and I waited until Samuel had pulled into traffic before raising the partition. The silence was making me twitchy. All I wanted was to pull her onto my lap and kiss her until whatever was bothering her escaped her mind, but from the tilt of her chin and the tense way she held herself, I knew that wasn't a good idea.

Swallowing roughly, I opened my mouth. "How did—"

"You're an idiot, do you know that?" she snapped as she finally turned to look up at me, her eyes flashing nearly blue-white with fury.

"Baby." Her rage only seemed to grow at how weak my voice came out.

"If you doubt my feelings for you—if you truly think there is anything you can't say to me without me wanting to leave you—then maybe we should rethink getting married. Because obviously, this relationship isn't strong enough to move forward."

Her words hit me with the force of an uppercut, knocking me out of my stupor and some sense back into my brain.

A pain-filled howl left me as I grabbed her and turned her so that she was straddling my lap. I hit the overhead light before I clutched her hair in one hand and twisted it until I was cupping the back of her head. I gripped her chin with my other hand, just in case she tried to break our locked gazes.

"There is nothing stronger in my world than our relationship," I growled.

"Really?" Shaking her head, she lifted her brows. "Because it sure as fuck doesn't appear that way. You didn't talk to me about seeing Jerrica. Instead, you put it off on Palmer to 'convince' me." She made air quotes, while her tone grew mocking. "I didn't notice it before, but now the blinders are off. You tiptoe around certain subjects, like you think you're going to set off a land mine. If you have so little faith in how much I love you, then we should just—"

I released her chin to cover her mouth with my palm. "Don't you fucking say it, Arella!"

Her eyes narrowed, but she didn't try to finish the sentence.

Breathing hard, I tightened my grip on her hair. "I don't doubt your love for me. I know you love me. What I'm scared of is that you'll open your eyes and realize that I'm not worthy of that love."

Her teeth sinking into the fleshy part of my palm startled me enough to drop my hand from her mouth. "Idiot," she snapped. "I swear to god, Jordan. If you ever say such a stupid thing to me again, I'll...I'll..."

"What?" I demanded, my heart beating so fast I actually worried I might have a heart attack. "Leave me?"

"No!" she shouted. "Fuck, you are such a dumbass. Why is the first thing that comes to your mind that I will leave you?"

"Because you should," I whispered, closing my eyes. "Because I don't deserve you."

"Jordan." Her voice had softened, but I couldn't find the courage to open my eyes. "Jordan, please look at me."

Gulping around the lump in my throat, I slowly lifted my lids. The sight of tears in her eyes made my stomach bottom out. "Baby, don't cry. I'm sorry."

"Don't be sorry," she rasped. "I love you so much, Jordan. I've loved you since I was sixteen, and not once has that love lessened. Not even when I thought we would only ever be friends. Every inch of my heart belongs to you. There is nothing you can say or do that will make me stop loving you." She cupped both sides of my face in her hands and leaned in until our lips skimmed each other. "The only way I will leave you is if you cheat on me, and I trust you to never do that. Because I know you love me. Because...." She pressed her core down on my already throbbing erection.

Even in the midst of my panic over her leaving me, I couldn't control the intensity of how much I wanted her.

Arella licked my bottom lip before pulling back just enough to whisper against my mouth, "Because I know every part of you belongs to me, just as every part of me is yours."

"It does. I belong to you, love," I agreed with a groan as she rubbed her center along my cock, working herself toward an orgasm that only I'd ever given her. I grabbed her ass beneath her dress, my fingers slipping under her itty-bitty panties covering her already drenched pussy. "And you absolutely belong to me."

"And that's why you're going to start telling me everything." She whined when I thrust a finger into her from behind while grinding her down on my hardness. "Right, baby?"

"Right," I vowed. "I swear to you, I'll always say what's on my mind. Even if I think it might make you upset with me, I'll tell you."

"Good," she breathed, tossing her head back. "Jordan, I'm close."

I loved watching her get off. Every time she used my body for pleasure, it brought me gratification even if I didn't get to find my own release. "Arella, I want you to change your name in the Screen Actors

Guild. It bothers me that you keep refusing to add my last name."

"You know why," she said, licking her lips as her orgasm quickly approached.

"I don't give a fuck. The press is going to talk, regardless. The moment you become my wife, the world will know. Let them speculate and come to the wrong conclusions. You and I know the truth." I curled my finger inside her, rubbing her G-spot. "And that is all that matters, isn't it, love?"

"Yes," she whimpered. "Only us. No one else."

"You'll change your name in SAG?" I persisted.

Her teeth bit into her bottom lip for a second before she nodded. "If it means you'll stop doubting that you can tell me anything, then yes. I'll be Arella Stevenson-Moreitti."

It was a compromise I was all too happy to accept. Reaching between us, I quickly pulled out my cock and sat her down on it. Her scream bounced off the soundproof walls of the SUV, sealing our new deal.

CHAPTER 8

JORDAN

Mia had been my best friend since we were both toddlers. There was no one else I wanted to stand beside me while I said my vows to Arella. Dressed in an all-black tux that was similar to my own, she adjusted her jacket over her growing baby bump and eyed me up and down critically.

"I guess you'll do," she said with a sigh.

Grinning, I stepped out of the little room where we'd been waiting and found my parents already in the corridor. My father shook my hand before giving me a hug while slapping a hand on my back. We'd never been all that close, but after Arella finally became mine, we'd started seeing things on the same level for the first time.

Mom shooed Dad out of her way and wrapped me in a hug that belied her slight stature. Dad held on to her cane and stood behind her, braced in case he needed to catch her if she stumbled. But there was no reason to worry, because I held on to her so tight there was no way she would fall.

"I'm so happy for you," she whispered emotionally. "I can't believe this day is finally here. Of course, I always knew it would arrive, and that it would be Arella you married, but it seems like no time since I realized you loved her and now this. I'm getting a daughter and a grandchild. The last time I was this happy was the day they placed you in my arms, Jordan."

"Mom, don't cry," I pleaded. "You'll make Mia cry too."

Mia slapped me in the back of the head. "Will not. Shut up, jerk." But I heard her sniffling, and I smirked at my dad over Mom's shoulder.

After a few more moments, I kissed Mom's cheek and straightened, being careful so she didn't lose her balance. It had been decades since the accident that had nearly taken her life. She'd struggled to learn to walk again and still struggled with pain from it

131

every day. But she was here, and other than the occasional migraine, she didn't have many health issues.

"Let's take our places," Mia suggested, taking my father's arm. "You look handsome in your suit, Mr. Moreitti."

"Thank you, Mia," he murmured, sparing her a glance before turning his attention back to where it always stayed—on my mom. "You look beautiful."

The two of them walked down the aisle while Mom and I were slower to make the journey. I didn't want to rush her, especially when she'd requested that I walk with her without her having to use her cane. Sometimes she wanted to pretend like she wasn't disabled, and if I could give her that small thing, I would every time.

Mia took her place at the altar, while Dad stood at the front waiting for us. Mom took her time, smiling both at members of our own family as well as some of Arella's whom she'd grown close with over the years, through my friendship with Mia. Once we reached my father, Mom hugged me again, lingering a little longer this time.

When she finally released me, it was just in time for the doors to close, and I felt my heart begin to pound. As if sensing my switch in emotions, she cupped one of my cheeks. "You're going to be a great husband and father, honey. I'm so proud of you. Be happy."

My throat clogged with emotion, making it impossible to do anything except nod. Seeing the tears in my eyes, she kissed my cheek and then took her seat.

Jaw clenched in an attempt to hold myself together, I stepped up beside my best friend and turned just as the double doors opened. Damien walked his mother down the aisle, his head held high as he escorted her as I'd done with my mom. Each of Arella's sisters walked down the aisle alone, starting with Bliss, then Heavenleigh, and finally Nevaeh. Palmer followed as the maid of honor before the doors closed again.

As she took her place, she flipped me off, but I only winked at her and we both shared a grin.

The music changed, and my breath seemed to catch in my throat as I waited for the doors to open once more.

Moments later, Drake stepped through the doors with his second-eldest daughter on his arm. The sight of my beautiful bride nearly knocked me on my ass. The vision of her in her wedding dress would remain with me until my dying day. Her dress had a plunging V-neck, a figure-hugging skirt beneath the many layers of crisscrossing organza, which was ruffled and double-layered, with hidden tulle beneath to make it extra poofy. Arella's hair was in a low, textured side bun with the same diamond and pearl pieces her sister had worn in her hair at her own wedding just a few years before. Her makeup was done with a soft, smoky eye, and her lips looked succulent with whatever lipstick she was wearing.

Mia had provided me with every last detail of the look Arella was going for as her honorary cousin was getting ready earlier. My best friend had stayed with the others as the bride was turned into the breathtaking woman who walked toward me.

The building could have caught on fire, but I wouldn't have been able to look away from her. This moment would last for eternity, but the closer she got, the blurrier she became. I couldn't hold on to my tears any longer.

When I saw her chin trembling and the tears threatening to spill from those eyes I loved so much, I took a step forward. Needing to erase her tears, I met Arella and her father at the bottom of the steps. The priest didn't have time to ask about who was giving her away, because I had already lifted her off her feet and carried her up the few steps before he could open his mouth.

Behind me, I vaguely heard Drake chuckle and then Lana teasingly telling him to take his seat beside her.

"Jordan," Arella whispered. "You need to put me down."

"Can't," I whispered back as I turned us to face the priest, her feet dangling over the floor by several inches. Not that anyone would know. With as long as her skirt was, it hid the fact that her feet didn't touch the floor. "Be thankful I can find the willpower to let the man do his part without demanding he jump to the end to declare us husband and wife."

Her lips tilted up in a ghost of a grin. "I love you so much."

The priest started speaking, but I didn't hear a word he said. My eyes, still blurry with happy tears, were glued to Arella's mouth. I wanted to destroy her lipstick and kiss her for the entire ceremony, but I knew it would embarrass my mom. I was wondering if I really cared or not when Arella nudged me.

"Jordan," she hissed. "Repeat the vows."

Without having heard a single word the man wanted me to speak, I said what was in my heart instead. "I, Jordan Moreitti, take you, Arella Stevenson, to be my wife. My partner in life, and as the other half of my soul. You own me, but I declare here and now, before everyone we both care about, that I am yours. Through good times and bad. In sickness and in health. I will be by your side until I take my last breath."

Tears poured down her face, yet her makeup remained perfectly in place. She swallowed with difficulty, and it took her a few tries before she could speak. "I-I, Arella Stevenson, take you, Jordan Moreitti, as my husband. My partner in life, and as the other half of my soul. You own me, but I declare here and now, before everyone we both care about, that I am yours. Through good times and bad. In sickness and in health. I will be by your side until I take my last breath."

The priest cleared his throat loudly before pronouncing us husband and wife. "I present you, for the first time, Mr. and Mrs. Jordan and Arella Moreitti."

"Mr. and Mrs. Jordan and Arella Stevenson-Moreitti," I corrected, without looking at the man. Arella's mouth gaped open at my declaration. "I am yours as much as you are mine. Right, love?"

"Right," she whispered before grabbing my face and pulling me in for a kiss that sent the world spinning.

EPILOGUE

LANA

I smiled down at the latest series of pictures Arella had posted to her social media. She and Jordan were having a great time on their honeymoon from the looks of it. The incident with the unwanted wedding present was out of their minds as they baked in the sun on the beach in a country Jordan had refused to disclose.

Not that I could blame him. With the identity of who had sent the disgusting "present" still unknown, keeping their location a secret was better for everyone. Especially my own sanity, as well as Drake's. Knowing our precious angel was safe with not only Jordan to watch over her, but five bodyguards as well, had made letting her go off on this mysterious honeymoon easier.

"She's happy?" Emmie asked quietly from beside me in the back of the unmarked SUV.

I nodded, turning the phone so she could see the screen that was filled with my beautiful daughter in a bikini with her husband wrapped around her. The smiles on both their faces, the joy in their eyes, were all I needed to see to know I was doing the right thing.

Emmie's eyes softened at the sight of the pictures, and then she nodded to the two women in the front seat. "We're ready."

The blonde in the driver's seat glanced at me for a long moment before reaching back to pat my leg. "You know in your heart that she did this to your child," Raven Reid said, further strengthening my conviction. "Getting rid of the threat to your baby is the only way you'll ever be at peace."

Clenching my jaw, I nodded.

Across from her in the passenger seat, Anya Vitucci was busy checking the chamber of her gun before shifting her gaze to me as well. "We are all family now," she said with a grim smile. "We take care of our family. Right?"

"Right," I whispered, not afraid to admit that the woman scared the fuck out of me. Something about her was so chilling, yet at Lyric's wedding, I'd seen the way she treated her children. I'd seen the softness in her then—and only then—but when she called us all family, I caught a flicker of that same gentleness I'd seen before.

Emmie didn't seem intimidated by either woman, and as long as she wasn't scared, then I wouldn't be either. And even if I was, it didn't matter, because the threat to my baby would be gone once and for all after this night.

It had taken every bit of acting skill I possessed to pretend like I didn't believe Claudia had something to do with sending Arella the decapitated cat. As soon as the suggestion left my daughter's mouth, I'd gotten an oddly calm feeling after all the chaos I'd felt for hours. Hearing Arella scream and then being sick from opening the "present" had sent me spiraling down the same path I'd been on when she and I had both received notes and packages from her original stalker.

That it had been my own brother had left me physically ill for days. I'd been unable to eat for over a week because of the nausea from knowing the bastard had tried to harm someone I loved. Our dad had loved her too, and those facts had driven his weak mind over the edge until he'd snapped and started stalking her.

I didn't think Claudia was as weak-minded as her son had been, but I did know she was an evil cunt. One who wouldn't get the chance to so much as scare my child again.

When Detective Kirtner had said he couldn't prove her involvement one way or the other, that only pressed the truth home for me. Barrick and Braxton ran surveillance on her for a few days, but I'd asked Emmie to keep it short. As far as they could tell, she was a weak old lady who could barely walk, let alone harm an animal.

That didn't change my mind. I knew it was her, and I didn't need proof of it. But I'd kept that to myself. Until yesterday, when I'd confided in Emmie that I knew it was Claudia and I needed her to help me eliminate the danger to Arella.

She'd made a few phone calls, and right after dinner, she'd picked me up at my house. I'd told Drake it was just Emmie and me getting together to plan a birthday party. With as big as our family was, there was always a birthday party to arrange. When I'd climbed into the back seat, I hadn't been completely surprised to find Raven there, but I'd been unable to hide my apprehension when I'd spotted Anya.

On the drive to Claudia's house, the Russian woman had told me about her childhood, and how she was still in the "business" when the work was something worthy of her time. Since we were family now, and one of her family had been threatened, she felt it was her duty to help take out the threat.

Ten minutes later, I watched the life fade from Claudia's eyes after she'd admitted to me that she'd been the one. She'd tried to put up a fight at first, showing that the cunning bitch wasn't nearly as frail as she wanted everyone to believe.

Despite the hole in her head, there wasn't much mess to clean up. Apparently Anya knew what she was doing when it came to this kind of thing. Not only did she erase any visible trace of DNA, but she had Raven run a light over everything to ensure there were no invisible signs left behind either.

It took several more hours before Emmie dropped me off at my house. I felt lighter. The fear of anything happening to Arella was gone. I harbored no guilt for what I'd asked others to do for me. Just a sense of relief that the danger was gone once and for all.

As Raven pulled to a stop at the end of my driveway, they all turned to me with bright smiles. "This was fun," Raven said with a laugh. "Best time I've had in a while."

"Agreed," Anya said with a wink at me. "Let's do this again sometime."

"It's a maybe from me, ladies," I said with a snicker. "But I did have a surprisingly good time. Learned a few new things too."

"It was definitely educational," Emmie agreed with a smirk.

I leaned forward and grasped Raven's and Anya's hands. "Thank you," I whispered. "For everything."

"Don't mention it," Raven said.

"No, really. Don't mention it," Anya urged, her blue eyes sparkling with not just amusement but something dangerous.

"Never," I vowed. Turning to Emmie, I hugged her, hard. "Thank you."

"It's what I do," she said, hugging me back. "Now go snuggle with your husband. I bet he's getting twitchy without you home."

"Oh, I know he is." Waving, I jumped out of the back and was halfway up to the house when the door opened, and Drake stepped out onto the porch.

Seeing him, I took off running and threw myself into his arms. He caught me around the waist as I circled his hips with my legs. "Take me upstairs," I purred against his lips. "I need you to fuck me. Hard. Right now."

I felt his growl rumbling in his chest before it reached my ears. "Fucking missed you tonight, Angel."

The next morning, the news hit the papers that Claudia had killed herself. She'd left behind a note saying she couldn't take the pain of losing her son anymore—or the guilt of trying to scare Arella. I texted Jordan the link to the article and then sat back to enjoy the breakfast my husband made for us.

After the breaking news, Drake had nearly fallen into his chair at the table as the stress finally left him. I'd wanted to take away the fear for Arella, but I'd wanted to ease the load on Drake's shoulders too. If that had meant adding to my own, then I would have been okay with that. Neither of them suffering was all I'd wanted.

But oddly, I hadn't added to my own stress.

It was all gone.

Leaving behind only peace, along with love for the man who would always be at my side and our children.

Hopelessly Devoted to SHAW

BOOK 4

CHAPTER 1

SHAW

Jenner stopped outside the posh boutique but didn't try to get out of the front seat right away. Beside me, Violet huffed, her purple gaze on the vultures who were already flashing their cameras at the SUV.

"This is nuts. You would think your engagement to Jags was announced yesterday, instead of months ago. Why do they even care that you're picking up your dress today?"

I gathered my hair and put it in a quick, extra-messy knot on top of my head before stretching my neck left and right. If we were going to need to make a run to and from Riley's store, then I needed to loosen up more than I already was.

"It's because everything about the wedding is top secret," I informed my best friend as I tried to limber up. I really shouldn't have eaten a heavy breakfast, but I'd been so excited about picking up my dress that I'd completely forgotten about the paps that had been stalking me since a photographer had spotted me going in for my first fitting.

Riley didn't even do wedding dresses, but she was like family. When I'd been inundated by offers from wedding gown designers, all of them begging me to wear one of their creations at my wedding, I'd been so overwhelmed that I'd thought about just walking down the aisle naked. But then Riley had offered to create one for me and sweetened the deal by allowing me to help her design it. I'd found I liked that side of the fashion business more than I'd ever thought I would.

My life had revolved around modeling clothes for the hottest designers—Riley included—but I'd never once thought about trying my hand at actually creating clothes. Riley was so impressed by my ideas that she'd asked me to collaborate with her on her spring line for the following year. My name would be on anything she liked of the designs I came up with. So far, I'd already gotten ten pages of outfits drawn, and I worked on more every night before bed.

Maybe one day I'd have my own line, but for the moment, I was content just to play around with Riley and continue my career as a model.

But I still needed to pick up my dress after trying it on one more time to ensure it fit as perfectly as it was supposed to. The wedding was in two days, and Riley would be at the wedding, so if there were any last-minute issues, she would be available to fix them, but I wanted the dress with me until then.

"Are you up to running?" I asked Violet as the paps tried to get closer. But as I watched, two more bodyguards appeared and pushed the vultures back so that Jenner could finally get out. He stood outside Vi's door, waiting for her to give the okay to open it. "I can go in and get the dress on my own."

"I need to do a final of my own dress," she reminded me, running her fingers through her hair. Since the death of her husband, she'd tried to shy away from the public eye as much as possible. But now that she was officially Luca Thornton's girlfriend, she couldn't hide away from the press any longer.

They had a field day when it was made public that Love Bug's birth certificate had Luca listed as her father. But that was months ago, and they'd quickly moved on to invade other celebrities' personal lives. Like mine, and the secret wedding Jags and I were having.

I'd wanted something small and intimate. But the world thought it should be a three-ring circus. Every client I'd ever worked with wanted me to wear their products. Wedding dress. Lingerie. Makeup. Perfume. I even had one client who thought I should wear their sunglasses during my wedding reception. They went through my agent, who thought every one of the offers was a great idea.

I'd told her to go fuck herself and leave me alone until I returned from my honeymoon.

Thankfully, my soon-to-be mother-in-law was handling all the details for the wedding, including security. Every aspect of the wedding was so secret that the guests had no idea where it was being held—and wouldn't until they arrived by private plane. Between Emmie's, Barrick and Braxton's, and Violet's jets, there was just enough room for everyone to make one trip to the small island in Hawaii the morning of the ceremony.

The plan was for me to be on one plane with all the girls, have a little bit of a party in the sky before we landed, and we would then get ready for the sunset beach event. Jags would do the same with the guys on one of the others', while anyone who didn't want to participate in the parties would be on the third plane with the younger kids.

"This sucks," Violet grumbled as she seemed to mentally prepare herself to step out of the vehicle. "I wish Luca were here."

I grasped her hand and gave it a gentle squeeze. "I'm just glad his coach is letting him out of the game this week so he can come to the wedding."

She chewed on her bottom lip while she nodded. "Yeah. It's just a preseason game, and when Luca tossed out Remington's name, the man didn't hesitate to give him the week off. I guess my husband arranged to have Luca's every need met when it comes to Love Bug or me before he...died."

"Hey." Grasping her chin, I turned her to look at me instead of the flashing of the cameras outside the blacked-out SUV. Sadness darkened her pretty eyes, and I felt my stomach clench. The memory from high school, when she'd been so lost in a dark place only she could wade through, always came back to haunt me whenever I saw the light was faded from her eyes. I never wanted to lose anyone, but if I lost Violet or Jagger, it would destroy me. They were the two halves that made me whole. Maybe in different ways and for different reasons, but my life was worthless without either of them.

"It's okay to be happy right now, Vi," I assured her. "It's what he wanted. Fuck, it's probably what he expected. He didn't want you to get lost in your depression over missing him. That's why he sent Luca to you when he died. All he cares about is that you and his baby girl are happy." She swallowed roughly, and I lowered my head, taking a deeper look at her face. "You are happy, aren't you?"

"Yes," she whispered. "But—"

"There are no buts. You're either happy or you aren't. Which is it?" My eyes narrowed when she hesitated. "Violet Hope Stevenson Sawyer."

Her lips twitched when I used the same tone her mom would have spoken in during a moment like this. "I'm happy. I just feel guilty."

"For being happy?" I asked quietly, and she gave a slight shrug. "Ugh. If I didn't love you so damn much, I'd slap some sense into your beautiful head. There is no reason to feel guilty for being happy. I just told you, Vi. Remington wanted your happiness. If you aren't happy, then he's going to come back and haunt you."

"Maybe he already is," she mumbled, turning her head, breaking our gaze.

"No, you are haunting yourself. Look, no one is saying you can't miss Remington. Or that you shouldn't think about him. But if all you do is think about the things he's not here for, or that you shouldn't do something because it would disrespect his memory, then all you'll end up doing is getting in your own way. You won't have time to enjoy the really good moments."

"I hate when you're smarter than me," Violet complained, but when she glanced at me again, she was grinning. The sadness that had been in her eyes was thankfully replaced by the bright light of life that I was always relieved to see. "All right. Let's get this shit over with."

"Let me go first," I told her, climbing over her to get to the door.

"Get your ass out of my face," she cried. "I don't know what kinky things you allow Jags to do to it."

"Probably the same kink you let Luca do to yours," I countered, tossing a smirk over my shoulder and watching as pink filled her cheeks.

"Luca's too big for butt action," she sassed, despite the heat in her face.

"Didn't need to know that."

"Like you haven't told me how big Jagger is. And you said you saw Lyric's once."

"By accident. When we were like fourteen," I argued. "He was wearing really loose swim trunks at Jagger's house, and the water kind of turned them into floaties. It's not my fault I looked. No one can catch a glimpse of that Pringles can and not get hypnotized."

"Lyric and Luca are identical twins. That means they are the same in every way." She waggled her brows at me, making me laugh.

"Then you are definitely not having butt fun with him. You're too tiny for that." I paused with my hand on the door handle, still leaning over Violet, my ass right in her face. "I wonder if Mila can take Lyric."

"Gross. I don't want to think about the guy who is my best friend, second only to you, having sex with anyone."

"But he's basically Luca's clone."

"No, he is not!" She covered her ears. "No, no, no. He is completely different in all the ways that count."

"Apparently his dick size counts if you're comparing it to his brother's," I said more to myself than to her since she was still covering her ears in denial.

Even when we were younger and there had been no ink to differentiate which twin was which, Violet had been able to tell who was who. Their own mother couldn't do that at times when they were kids. But there had always been an invisible connection between Vi and Luca. It was as if she didn't even see Lyric, at least not with the same eyes she looked at his twin with. Which was weird to me, because even with the different ink on their arms now, the only way I could tell the two of them apart was because Luca had about thirty more pounds of muscle from playing football.

Grabbing hold of her wrist, I opened the door and pulled her out behind me. Jenner and the two other guards jumped into action, keeping anyone from actually touching us, even though I could practically feel their body heat from how close they were. At the door, one of the guards moved to open it, leaving a brief opening, which one of the photographers took advantage of and got close to Violet.

She jumped aside, her back hitting the other guard before Jenner could get between her and the man with the camera. Seeing the fear in her eyes, I didn't even think about what I was doing. Drawing back, I punched the guy in the jaw, making him shout in pain and drop his camera.

"Assault!" he cried. "She assaulted me."

"You're the one invading personal space," I argued, shaking out my throbbing hand. "But keep crying assault. I'm sure you'll get your moment in the spotlight for getting punched by a woman."

A few of the other paps snickered, but that didn't stop them from click-click-clicking away on their own cameras.

Fucking assholes.

CHAPTER 2

JAGGER

I was sitting on the couch in my living room, eating a bowl of cereal, when the smell hit me. Love Bug made a pitiful little whining noise and then squirmed in the travel swing thing Luca had set up as soon as they'd arrived the day before. A loud fart left the tiny little human, and I dropped my spoon into the half-full bowl as another wave of stench hit my nostrils.

The baby began to cry, and I panicked. "Luca!"

He came out of the kitchen with a slice of toast sticking out of his mouth, a mug of coffee in his other hand. The instant his eyes fell on his daughter, his entire face changed. Placing the mug on the coffee table, he crouched down so he was as level with the swing as his huge body would allow. "What's wrong, princess?" he cooed. "Do you have a tummy ache?"

She only cried louder, and he sniffed. He didn't make a face at the smell, but he stuffed the toast into his mouth and wiped his hands on his basketball shorts before picking her up. "Let's get my love bug a clean diaper," he said in a voice I'd never heard him use except with Love Bug.

The baby was average size, maybe a little smaller, but she looked like a baby doll when the huge defensive line footballer lifted her into his arms. Cradling her close, he walked over to where a baby blanket was spread out on the carpet. All the items needed for changing a diaper were already arranged, and he carefully got on his knees before placing the baby on the floor.

If the smell trapped in her diaper was harsh to the senses, then when Luca unsnapped the messy thing, it was enough to burn a person's nose hairs. I quickly pulled my T-shirt up over my nose, inhaling the fabric softener, my body wash, and deodorant. Luca wasn't even fazed as he cleaned up the mushy mess. I couldn't watch for long, because the sight was enough to make me gag, but I couldn't help looking back every few seconds, enthralled by how efficient the most irresponsible guy I'd ever known was with the itty-bitty baby.

My honorary cousin had always been a dumbass, too caught up in his own wants and needs to care about anyone—except for maybe Violet. And even she had suffered the aftereffects of Luca's tantrums over the years. Yet the moment Love Bug was placed in his arms, it was like a switch flipped inside him. He became a different man, on a mission to show Violet that she could trust him to take care of her and the tiny baby he'd been tasked with protecting by Violet's husband.

Shaw and I both had our doubts at first, but after witnessing how amazing of a dad Luca was, we'd begun to relax. Our worry hadn't just been for Love Bug's sake, but for Violet's mental state. The dark place she'd gone to when she broke up with Luca back in high school was something we'd feared happening again with the death of Remington. Maybe he'd feared it too, and that was why he'd turned to Luca to ensure she didn't fall down that dangerous rabbit hole when he passed on.

Once Love Bug had on a fresh diaper—as well as a new onesie—he cleaned the smear of baby shit off his thumb with a wipe. Standing, he reached down and lifted her into his arms. "Is my princess happy again?" he murmured with a smile, making the baby gurgle at him. He kissed the top of her head, and she laid her ear against his chest.

He stood there, rocking back and forth, rubbing the baby's back until her eyes drifted shut. It didn't take more than a few minutes, and then he was placing her on a different blanket spread on the carpet, this one surrounded by pillows and the gigantic midnight-black pit bull.

"Crush, be good," Luca commanded, and the dog turned so his head was closer to the baby, his eyes hyperfocused on the sleeping infant.

Luca went back to the diaper-changing blanket and started gathering the messy items. That he cleaned up after himself was almost as surprising as it was watching him take care of the baby.

"You can drop the mask now," he said with a smirk as he came out of the kitchen, drying his hands on a dish towel.

Cautiously, I pulled down my T-shirt a little and took a tiny sniff before inhaling deeper. Smelling nothing but coffee in the air, I blew out a sigh. "Fuck—"

"Language!" Luca growled in a quiet voice.

"Crap," I amended and was surprised I didn't roll my eyes. The baby probably didn't even understand words yet, but Luca wouldn't allow anyone to use curse words around her—not even Vi. "How do you deal with that smell all day long? I hope Shaw doesn't want kids right away, because I don't think I could handle changing diapers."

He shrugged before picking up his mug of coffee and draining the contents. "It's different when it's your kid, man. It was hard at first. I cried because I thought I was hurting her. But after my dad and Uncle Shane showed me a few tricks, it was a heck of a lot easier." He tipped his empty mug at me. "I'm getting a fresh cup. You want some?"

"Nah, but thanks." My eyes widened when he picked up my bowl of soggy cereal and took it into the kitchen. From my place on the couch, I heard him rinse and then place the dishes in the dishwasher.

Holy shit. Luca Thornton was domestic as fuck.

I nearly laughed at the change in him, but honestly, it was good to see him finally being mature.

A smile still lingered on my face when my phone rang. I quickly answered it before it could disturb the sleeping baby.

"This is Jagger," I said quietly since I didn't look at the screen before lifting the phone to my ear.

"Jags, don't freak out."

I leaned my head back against the couch, trying not to do just that. Violet's voice was calm enough, but I heard something underlying in it that told me whatever she was going to say was going to upset me.

"Did you two pick up your dresses?" I asked instead of demanding she tell me what was going on.

"Yes," she said after a slight pause. "They are safely locked in the back of the SUV right now. I... Ugh, okay, I'm just going to say it. Shaw kind of fractured two knuckles."

I tensed. "How did she fracture anything while trying on her wedding dress?"

"We were ambushed in front of Riley's beforehand," she explained. "One of the photographers got too close to me, and Shaw punched him in the face. It was one little punch, and he was such a crybaby about it." She huffed loudly. "But anyway, the cops are questioning her while we wait for the doctor to get her discharge papers."

"For fuck's sake!" I snapped, jerking to my feet.

"Language!" Luca called from the kitchen.

Ignoring him, I practically jogged into my bedroom. "Are they going to arrest her? Do I need to call Ma?"

"No, the cops are just taking her statement. The photographer tried to press charges, but Riley turned over the CCTV footage from in front of her shop, and they aren't taking the douchebag seriously. If anything, they asked us if we wanted to press charges against the photog."

"What about Aunt D?" I asked, grabbing jeans and then a different T-shirt. "Does she know about Shaw's hand? Do we need to talk to a specialist?"

My own hand continued to throb a little from where I'd broken it months before. I was still working my way through all the hours of community service I had been sentenced to rather than spending time in jail. Even if I'd been locked up, I would have gladly accepted the punishment after that fucker had taken pictures of my fiancée.

"She knows, Jags. Please relax. This is why Shaw asked me to call you last." She blew out a heavy sigh. "We'll be on our way back to your place soon. She has a soft cast on, and we need to see the orthopedic specialist in the morning, but the doctor assured us that it's just two small fractures. Her fingers are a little swollen, but nothing is purple, and she claims she's not in any major pain."

"You're not calling to tell me this because of Shaw, are you?" I mused aloud, as what she'd said really began to click in my brain. One of the paparazzi got close enough to Violet that Shaw reacted by punching him in the face. That told me she'd been scared—not for herself, but for Vi. Luca was going to lose his shit, for sure. "Fucking hell, Violet. He's going to go berserk on someone."

"No, he won't," she said with confidence. "Not with Love Bug there. This is probably going to hit all the social media platforms soon. I thought you should be prepared."

"Gee, thanks," I snarked, then grimaced at my tone. Shaw would kick my ass if I talked to her best friend like that, and I wasn't exactly pleased with my own actions either. "Fuck, I'm sorry. I'm just... She's hurt. And I'm here. And she's so damn excited about the wedding. And she's not going to be happy about wearing a cast in the pictures. And—"

"Whoa," she cut me off. "That's a whole lot of 'ands.'"

"The press has been hounding her since that first dress fitting," I gritted out. "Now they're fucking up the wedding."

I wanted everything to be perfect for Shaw on our wedding day, but those damn pricks were already ruining it for us.

"I'm sorry," Vi whispered.

"This isn't your fault, sweetheart," I assured her, blowing out a long breath. "Listen, you take care of Shaw. Stay close to the guards. We don't need anyone being charged with murder before the wedding." I wasn't sure who would be the one committing homicide if anything happened to Violet—Shaw or Luca. "I need to get dressed and take care of a few things."

"All right," she murmured. "But make sure you take your own advice, Jags. We don't need any murder charges."

"I'll do my best, honey," I said with a dry laugh. As soon as I hung up with her, I hit the contact that was only two down on my recents list. The first ring didn't finish before it was answered.

"I already know about Shaw's hand," Ma said in a light voice.

"Not surprised. I was the last to know," I grumbled unhappily.

"Of course you were. It makes things easier if you're the last to be informed. You aren't Mr. Subtle, baby boy."

I raked my free hand through my hair. "Make it stop, Ma," I pleaded, feeling like a helpless little kid again, begging my mom to make the bad things go away. But I wasn't above turning to the only person who I knew could make that happen. "They're ruining everything before we even get a chance to enjoy the day. I want... No, Ma. I fucking need Saturday to be perfect."

"Ah, my sweet boy," she whispered. "I'll do whatever I have to in order to ensure that your wedding is perfect. I promise."

"Ma..." I closed my eyes, fighting the frustration of feeling out of control. "She deserves this."

"So do you, Jagger."

CHAPTER 3

SHAW

"I don't see a necessity for a hard cast at the moment," the doctor said as he examined the X-rays the hospital had emailed him the day before. "Just be sure to wear the soft cast as much as possible, and we'll do another X-ray in four to six weeks to ensure everything is healing."

Flexing my fingers, I silently listened to his instructions about ice and heat therapy for the pain and taking NSAIDs for any discomfort and swelling. I knew all the dos and don'ts by heart at this point. After Jagger had broken his hand—ironically enough, on another photographer's face—I'd spent weeks making sure his injury didn't get inflamed so he would be ready for his summer tour.

That tour had only recently ended, and he hadn't had too many issues with a hard cast while playing. I wouldn't say it had been comfortable for him, but he'd at least been able to get the job done during his sets with my brother.

Leaving the doctor's office, I slipped on my sunglasses and made sure my baseball cap was pulled down low. The guard I had to take with me every time I left the house without Jagger, or my parents was already waiting in the lobby. There wasn't much use in trying to hide my identity when the press had already figured out, where the hulk in a suit went, I was nearby.

Which was why I wasn't the least bit surprised when he opened the door and flash after flash flickered from a dozen different cameras. Questions were randomly tossed at me—how long would my community service last compared to Jagger's, was the photographer suing me since the police hadn't taken him seriously when he'd tried to file charges against me for assault, and countless other questions about the incident from the day before. It was mundane bullshit that everyone knew I wouldn't respond to, but I begrudgingly gave them props for continuing to ask the same nonsense every time they ambushed me.

I ignored them all as my bodyguard, whom I referred to only as Hulk, pushed our way toward where he'd parked the car earlier. I was used to cameras being in my face, not only because of the harassment from the press wanting to know every detail about my private wedding, but also standing in front of one regularly for my career. I could zone them out, pretend they weren't even there...

And then someone opened their mouth and said the wrong thing.

"Is Remi really Luca Thornton's biological daughter?"

Hulk didn't realize I'd stopped walking, and he kept going, while the paps moved in closer. Slowly, I turned my head to look at the guy who'd asked that very personal question. With measured movements, I took off my sunglasses so he could get the full effect of my glare. A number of the other photographers took several steps back, but the idiot who'd caused me to pause just stood there, looking smug as fuck. He seemed hell-bent on pissing me off, and he'd accomplished just that by speaking Love Bug's name.

"You already know the answer to your question, motherfucker," I said in a quiet voice just as Hulk pushed his way back to my side. "My goddaughter's paternity isn't anyone's business. The fact that you are trying to make a quick buck off an innocent baby's DNA says more about you and your morals than any of these other vultures."

I shrugged off Hulk's hold on my arm and stepped into the photographer's personal space. The smugness on his face disappeared when I looked down my nose at him. I was tall in flats, but the six-inch heels I wore put me well above the man, causing him to have to tilt his head back if he wanted to hold my stormy gaze. "You're a sick bastard with no soul. I'll be keeping my eye on you, douchebag. And if I ever hear you ask another question that even hints about my goddaughter, I'll make it my mission to ensure you never get a picture published again." Leaning closer so I could lower my voice even further, I promised, "Harper Stevenson will be speaking to your editor. I don't think she will be any happier than I am that you're even speaking her grandchild's name, do you? She knows every newspaper and magazine editor from here to Paris. One word from her and your career will be over."

"Freedom o-of speech," he stuttered.

He gulped when I grinned down at him, prey caught in my predatory gaze. "You're right. You do have the right to free speech. Just as I have the freedom to sue your ass for defamation." I leaned even closer so that my mouth was only inches for his ear. "Spread the word to your little friends. If the name Remi Sawyer Thornton so much as shows up in a hashtag that questions her paternity, my lawyer will bleed you dry. I look forward to facing you in court."

Slipping my sunglasses back on, I patted him on the cheek. "It's been a pleasure speaking to you, but let's never do this again. 'Kay?"

Pushing all thoughts of the paps out of my mind, I concentrated on the positives in my life. We had an intimate party scheduled at Jagger's parents' house that evening as a casual kind of pre-wedding dinner. Everyone who was going to be flying out with us the next morning had already arrived. Only our closest family members were invited, which meant the party was going to be a smaller version of Emmie's Christmas Eve get-togethers.

As I walked into my apartment, the first thing I heard was laughter, and I paused with my hand on the closed door. Turning my head, I saw Luca standing by the window, looking out at the view below as he swayed back and forth with Love Bug in his arms. While he watched the day pass beyond the window, she watched her daddy, her unique eyes glued to his face in awe.

Jagger sat on the couch with Violet, the two of them huddled close as they watched something on Jagger's phone, their laughter like music to my ears. Dropping my stuff on the table by the door, I walked behind the couch so I could bend over and see what they were looking at.

It was an old video of Violet and me sitting in her bedroom. We were younger, and I suspected it was after Vi began her therapy to help her come back from the dark side of her depression. Jagger's voice hit my ears, and I knew he had been the one recording us. My heart squeezed. Back then, the three of us had hung out a lot. I wasn't sure if it was because he'd been just as worried about Vi as I had, or if he'd used it as an excuse to be closer to me. Either way, I'd cherished those times with the three of us together.

"Come on, Dimples. Tell the truth. Did you really kick Tyler Vance in the balls, or is Vi just bullshitting?"

Younger me rolled her eyes at the camera. "He asked if Violet was my girlfriend, then when I didn't answer, he asked if he could watch."

Jagger's laughter dried up offscreen. "Watch what?"

"Us," younger me responded with a shrug. "Vi and me having sex."

Luca turned, drawing my gaze, and I watched him tuck Love Bug's head under his chin as his ever-changing brown eyes glittered with growing fury. "What happened to Tyler Vance?"

Violet snorted. "Shaw really did kick him in the balls. It was hilarious to watch at the time, especially because he'd been condescending about the entire thing. Every word out of his mouth was meant as an insult because he had a thing for Shaw, and she couldn't be bothered to give him the time of day. But afterward, it wasn't so funny." She turned on the couch, so she was facing me, but I saw a glitter of lingering amusement in her purple gaze. "Tyler had to have surgery because the kick burst one of his testicles. Rumor was they had to replace it with a prosthetic, but his body rejected that, and they had to do emergency surgery to extract it because he became septic."

I laughed at the memory. "Tyler tried to sue me when he found out he was infertile. But after our lawyer got his medical records, it was determined that he didn't have any healthy swimmers to begin with. The judge threw out the civil case before the press could get word of it."

"What she means is that my dad, Uncle Shane, and Uncle Ax paid Tyler's father a visit and convinced him that letting the world know his son was shooting blanks would only make the Vance family subject to public ridicule."

Gasping, I looked down at Jagger. "They did not."

"Dimples, I was there." Reaching up, he caressed his thumb over my right dimple. "My dad also threatened to unleash Ma on Vance if his kid didn't leave you and Vi alone."

I propped my chin on my hand as I looked down at my fiancé adoringly. "You loved me so much you ganged up on a bully's father and threatened him with public humiliation?"

"Absolutely."

I grasped his face in both hands. "That's kind of sexy."

Silver-blue eyes darkened. "If that gets you wet, then wait until I tell you about—"

Violet pushed her face closer. "Did you forget you're not alone?"

"Nope." I kissed Jagger then smirked at my bestie. "Since when have we ever cared if someone watches us or not?"

"At least let me put the baby to bed before you two go at it," Luca grumbled. "Her innocent eyes don't need to witness Jagger's naked bottom."

His choice of words made me burst out laughing. Luca Thornton saying "bottom" instead of "ass" was one of the most hilarious things I'd ever heard in my life. While I wiped tears of mirth from my eyes, Jagger grabbed me and pulled me over the back of the couch onto his lap.

"You're still wearing the soft cast, so I'm going to assume you won't have to wear anything during the ceremony tomorrow." He gently grasped my injured hand and rubbed his thumb over my fingertips. "Are you in any pain?"

"I'm good." Snuggling deeper into his arms, I laid my head on his chest. "And no, I don't have to wear the soft cast during the ceremony or for pictures, but that's the only exception." It sucked that I would be spending my honeymoon in a cast, but I wasn't going to pout about it—much. I'd known there might be consequences when I'd punched the photographer the day before, and I'd accepted them even as my fist had connected with his face.

Kissing my hand, Jagger tucked it against his chest. "I'm glad that won't throw off the wedding for you."

Lifting my head, I frowned at him. "It's our wedding, Jags. Not just mine."

"It's the bride's day," he argued.

I grasped his face in my uninjured hand. "Our day." He opened his mouth to argue, but I covered his mouth with my fingers. "Our. Day. Understand?"

He hesitated, but then he nodded.

"Good." Kissing him one more time, I jumped to my feet. "Now, you two boys have a nice afternoon with Love Bug. Violet and I are going to go get our hair done."

Violet hopped up behind me, and I pointed a finger at Luca. "He spends the rest of the day relaxing."

"Yes, ma'am," he agreed.

"And if my stupid brother shows up, don't let them pull any sh—" I cut myself off when Luca's eyes narrowed. "Crap. Don't let them pull any crap. Fun is fine. Trouble, not so much."

"Got it." With the baby still in his arms, he crossed to Violet. Bending his knees, he kissed her forehead. "Have fun. Love you, Vi."

Her hand touched the baby's back, but her gaze stayed on Luca's. "I love you too."

CHAPTER 4

JAGGER

"Second thoughts?"

I gritted my teeth as I glanced at Cannon before turning my gaze back to the others gathered around my parents' living room. Everyone seemed to be having a good time. People were laughing in small groups, drinking sparkling grape juice or cider, playing with the kids, or just reminiscing. I should have been having the time of my life right along with them, but all I could feel was the ever-growing knot of anxiety in the pit of my stomach. "No."

"Then why do you look like you're about to make a run for it?" My ex-best friend, soon-to-be brother-in-law, and now kinda my best friend again, asked. He was going to be my best man at the wedding the next day, so I had to admit he was still one of my favorite people—even if I wanted to murder him at times. There was a tone in his voice that I recognized, a mixture of humor and seriousness that set my teeth on edge because he wasn't one hundred percent wrong.

I was thinking of making a run for it, but not in the way he assumed. I wanted to grab Shaw, yell at Luca to get Vi, and make the five-hour drive to Vegas. Just be done with the whole farce of a wedding—because that was what the fucking press was turning it into. The world didn't need to know every detail of our ceremony and reception. There was no reason for the press to be stalking Shaw like she held the secrets to some holy grail that didn't exist.

That they had ambushed her again outside the salon that afternoon had only ratcheted up my anxiety over the wedding. In my gut, I knew someone would find a way to spill the beans on where we were going the next day. It wouldn't surprise me if they were waiting for us when the planes landed on the private Hawaiian island. There was a leak somewhere within the few people who knew the details, and I needed them found before they ruined what should be the best day of my bride's life.

Without consciously realizing what I was doing, my eyes sought out Shaw. She was standing in a group of our honorary cousins, holding a champagne glass full of sparkling white grape juice since we never had any actual alcohol at family functions out of respect for Uncle Drake. Not that anyone drank much to begin with. His kids all steered clear of anything remotely alcoholic, and the rest of us rarely indulged as well. The few times I'd gotten drunk, I'd lived to regret it.

Shaw didn't seem the least bit concerned about the events of the day, but I'd had a red haze around my vision since she'd called to let me know that not only had the paps been waiting on her and Violet at the salon, but one had actually been inside. They'd pretended to be a customer and had used their cell to get most of the pictures. It wasn't until Shaw began to get hashtag notifications of her trending on Twitter that she'd realized what was going on.

The salon manager had kicked out the pap and apologized profusely. Shaw hadn't sounded too upset about the incident, but I'd been unable to contain my anger ever since.

Once the wedding was over, we'd be yesterday's news. I understood that.

What I didn't understand was why they targeted Shaw every time she so much as left the apartment, yet I hadn't been bothered once. Anytime she was out without me, they harassed her endlessly, but if I happened to be with her, they never showed their faces. That meant someone was purposely targeting her, trying to ruin the pre-wedding rituals for her. Which meant they would try their damnedest to ruin the ceremony as well.

Ma already knew my suspicions, and she'd asked Barrick to look into it. But there wasn't anyone on her small team whom she didn't trust one hundred percent. She was very careful who she allowed within her inner sanctum, and she wouldn't permit just anyone to assist with something as important as one of her children's weddings. Not to mention, everyone who worked for her signed NDAs that prohibited them from speaking a single word about the inner workings of her personal and professional life.

Shaw threw back her head, causing her glossy blond hair to cascade over her shoulders like a waterfall of pure sunshine. Her dimples were on full display, and all I could do was watch while she drained her glass then threw her arm around Violet's shoulders as the two of them began dancing to the quietly playing music.

All eyes turned to the two of them, everyone amused by the best friends as they played around like we were back in high school again rather than adults with families of our own. Shaw and Violet were like sisters. From the moment Vi could walk, they'd been inseparable. They were each other's biggest cheerleader. All their lives, where one went, the other followed, both of them leaving a trail of destruction behind them.

Seeing them together always soothed something in me. Where Vi was concerned, it was because watching her laugh and dance told me she was okay mentally. With Shaw, just seeing her dimples flash gave me a kind of peace no one else had ever been able to produce for me—not even Ma.

Cannon laughed at his sister's antics, but his eyes remained glued to Violet, his blue gaze full of torment. I elbowed him in the side. "Kill the misery, man. Luca sees you looking at Vi like that, and you're gonna end up in the emergency room again. Not so sure it will be a simple concussion this time."

With a grunt, he shifted his gaze to where Luca was standing with his twin. Both men held a baby in their arms. Lyric was holding his son, Ian. His set of twins wasn't identical like he and Luca, but I couldn't honestly tell the little demons apart. Like their dad and Luca, the two were already hellions. Like his father, the other twin, Isaac, was much more laid-back. He didn't care who held him. He had a smile and a hug ready for everyone. Whereas Ian was so much like his uncle Luca, it was a bit scary. He was sullen, only allowed a select few people close, and the spark of trouble glimmered in his ever-changing brown eyes.

It was hella amusing, but definitely a little terrifying.

Ian was a few months older than Love Bug, and from what little I'd seen of the baby so far, a living terror. Yet when he reached out to touch Love Bug's back, he was oddly gentle. His mouth moved, gurgling something to her that made her giggle loudly enough that all eyes shifted to them.

"Tell me that's not weird as fuck," Cannon muttered.

"What?" I asked with a frown.

"Love Bug and Ian. That could easily be Violet and Luca two decades ago."

"They're babies, dumbass," I admonished. "And Luca wouldn't let that happen. He's raising Love Bug as his daughter. They're cousins."

"Not by blood," Cannon said with a shrug. "And we were all raised as cousins, more or less. That didn't stop Luca and Vi from being together. Or you and my sister."

"That's because we're soul mates," I growled at him. "We were meant to be together. Like your parents and mine."

He tossed me a smirk before glancing back at the twins. "Exactly."

"I'm not having this conversation, and you should keep your mouth shut too. Luca is just looking for a reason to kick your ass again."

A giggle drew my gaze, and I found Shaw walking toward me. Behind her, Vi was moving toward Luca and Lyric. She took Love Bug from her boyfriend while he pouted down at her. Shaking my head, I shifted back to watch Shaw. She looked beautiful in her blue dress. The blue was closer to my eye shade than her own, something I hadn't missed when she'd slipped into the clingy little thing before asking me to zip her up earlier.

All I'd been able to think about was peeling it off her again later.

Before she reached me, she jumped, wrapping her long legs around my waist. I barely had time to grab and secure her before she kissed me senseless. Vaguely I heard her brother huff, but he didn't move away, and I wasn't going to stop kissing the love of my life because he didn't want to see it.

When Shaw lifted her head, her lips were swollen, and I knew my hair was a mess as she continued to run her fingers through it. "I have a surprise for you," she murmured, licking her lips.

My eyes locked on the movement. "Does it have anything to do with you and me upstairs in my old bedroom?"

"Nope, sorry." Laughing, she gave me another quick kiss. "But I'm hoping you'll enjoy it."

"Maybe you plan on sneaking into the bathroom for a quickie?" I guessed again.

"Brother. Standing right here."

"Shut up, Cannon," Shaw and I both said in unison without sparing him a glance.

Shaw scraped her nails down the back of my neck, and I had to bite back a groan as my muscles started to relax, yet my dick began to pulse. "You're having a guys' night. Starting now." Behind her, a grumbling Luca and Lyric, both sans babies in their arms, were being pulled along by Violet. Their identical gazes locked on Cannon, open disdain in their odd brown eyes. Whatever the plan was, they weren't going to be the best fun because Cannon was going to be a part of the action.

Seeing the tiny woman towing the giant twins behind her was enough to make anyone blink a few times. Yet even though they dragged their feet, Vi didn't have to put much effort into pulling them through the crowd. They might not want to do whatever she'd conned them into, but they wouldn't let her down. Or me. Growing up, the twins were the closest things to brothers I'd had, other than Cannon's stupid ass.

There were a few times I'd gotten into trouble right beside Luca and Lyric, and there may have been a time or two that I'd dragged them into my own shit. But every time, the three of us knew that we wouldn't let one another down. It had never mattered that we weren't related by blood. The twins were my people, and I loved those two assholes wholeheartedly.

After she wiggled her ass in my hands, I reluctantly placed Shaw on her feet so she could turn to face the twins. "Your mission is to take him out and make him have the time of his life." Her blue eyes narrowed. "But if I so much as hear a whisper that strippers were involved, your women will never find your bodies."

Lyric glanced over his shoulder to where Mila was standing with Uncle Jesse, who now held Ian while she rocked Isaac in her arms. Beside them, Uncle Shane had Love Bug in his arms, kissing on her as he rocked her back and forth much like I'd seen Luca do over the past few days.

"I'm more scared of her than I am of you," Lyric told Shaw deadpan as he faced her again.

"I've never been to a strip club and don't plan on checking one out now," Luca assured her. "But where are you two going to be while we're out?"

"Girls' night," she said with a shrug. "Mila and the others will be joining us, while the grandparents take the kids."

"I mean afterward," Luca corrected, draping his arm over Vi's shoulders. "I want to know what bed I'm sleeping in tonight."

"We're going back to the house," Violet told him, sinking her teeth into her bottom lip. "That's where I have a little party set up for the girls."

"What house?" Lyric demanded.

"Remington's old house," she said reluctantly. "My...house."

"Oh. Why didn't you just say that?" Without another word, Lyric walked across the room to kiss his wife before Violet could answer.

Luca grasped Vi's chin and gently worked her bottom lip free of her sharp grip on it. "I'll see you tonight at the house."

I nudged Shaw. "Do I get to see you tonight?"

"And have both our moms freak out because the groom saw the bride before the wedding?" she asked loud enough for everyone in the room to hear her. "No way!" Throwing her arms around my neck, she touched her lips to my cheek and whispered, "I'll be in the room we shared the last time we stayed at her house. Leave me hanging, and you'll be spending our honeymoon with blue balls."

CHAPTER 5

SHAW

The lights were turned down, and the sappy rom-com Violet had chosen to play for our little "girls' night" had already begun. Everyone had their individual bowls of popcorn and Big Gulp-sized soft drinks in hand. The theater room was ginormous, so we were all spread out with our own blankets tucked in while we enjoyed a carefree few hours.

As girls' nights went, it seemed a mixture of boring—and total perfection.

But I had other plans for the evening.

Mila and Violet had exited the darkened room, a few minutes spaced out between them so no one would notice. I was the last to leave, but when I glanced back at everyone, they were more into the movie than I originally expected. Their soft laughter reached my ears, and I smiled as I left them to it.

Vi grasped my wrist in one hand and Mila's in the other, the three of us making a run for it as we rushed toward the door.

"Are you seriously leaving your own girls' night?" a voice demanded as a shadow stepped in front of us, making Vi squeak in surprise. Mila and I stopped, both of us drawing up for a fight until we realized who it was.

"Damn it, Piper!" I whisper-shouted. "I nearly brained up."

"Why are you leaving?" she asked, crossing her arms over her chest.

"We're crashing guys' night," Vi told her with a shrug.

Piper's gaze drifted over the three of us before she huffed. "That sounds less boring than watching that stupid movie."

"Hey," Violet pouted. "I love that movie."

"You have poor taste in movies, Vi." Piper didn't try to sugarcoat anything. "But your heart was in the right place. Now, let's go and crash the boys' fun."

Mila glanced at me over Violet's head, her brows drawn together. Piper was too young to get into the club where the twins had taken Jagger, but I knew her too well. "Her fake ID looks more real than her driver's license."

"Of course it does," Piper said with a roll of her eyes. "I only get the best, bitches."

"Fine." Mila gave in. "It's not like I'm one to judge. I was underage in the club when I met Lyric."

"Lyric said you were with a group of gangsters," Violet tossed out as we climbed into the SUV where Jenner was already waiting.

Mila snickered. "Something like that. Oddly enough, I was crashing a guys' night out then too. It was the night before Theo and Tavia got married. I ended up spending the night with Lyric and got pregnant."

"No one better get pregnant tonight!" Vi said, pointing her finger at each of us, lingering longer on Piper than the rest of us.

"Maybe point the finger at yourself too." Piper waggled her index finger in Vi's face. "I don't plan on hooking up with anyone at this guys' thing. Seriously, the only single one there will be, who? Cannon?" She made a gagging noise. "No, thank you."

"She's right," I agreed. "I don't think we need to worry about Piper. It's the rest of us who need to be careful we aren't taking anything home but the men we love."

"Come on. We have to make sure Cannon gets back safely too," Vi defended. "He's the best man tomorrow."

"Luca can step into that spot instead," I said with a shrug, only half joking. I loved my brother, and I would admit he'd calmed down a lot over the past few years, but part of me couldn't help remembering what a dickhead he'd once been. That Violet was the one to defend him fucked with my head. She should have encouraged us to leave him behind.

The drive to the club took a little time, but with Jenner behind the wheel, no one felt uncomfortable. Once we reached our destination, we didn't go in the front. Instead, Vi made a call, and the head of security at First Bass let us in the back.

I patted Tiny on the arm as the big man held the door open for us. When he spotted Piper, he cocked a brow but didn't say anything. We all knew Harris had let Lucy in starting when she was seventeen, so as long as Tiny didn't see Piper drinking, he didn't have a leg to stand on when it came to letting in anyone underage.

"VIP," Tiny instructed. "Boss made sure they had a quiet corner so no one would bother them."

"Perfect. Thanks, Tiny," Violet gave him a grim smile as we started up the stairs to the second floor.

At the top of the steps, Mila glanced around with a critical eye. "Lyric's never brought me here. It's nice, but I prefer Hannigans'."

"I'm assuming there's a big difference between LA's hottest club and a small-town biker bar," Piper said as she waved at a few people she knew. Mila made a sound in the back of her throat, and I quickly stepped between her and Piper before someone got pushed down the stairs behind us.

"We're trying to sneak up on the guys," I complained, grasping her hand. "If you're being Miss Popular, you'll give us away. And if Uncle Liam finds out we brought you to a club, he's never going to let you hang out with us again."

The little rocker snorted. "I do what I want. And it's not like this is the first time I've been to First Bass. Although I try to be incognito when I do." Her eyes flickered over my hair and down to the tips of my toes. "You stand out like a neon sign in the middle of a moonless night. I'm not knocking it, because you look smoking hot, Shaw. But if you wanted to surprise Jags and the rest of those asshats, you should have put on a baseball cap or a wig."

Violet squished her way between Piper and Mila and hugged me. "No one knows we're here except for Tiny. For now. Let's get closer and see what the guys are doing."

Nodding, I kept my arm around her as we walked away from the other two women. The VIP was so busy with celebrities from every branch of the entertainment industry that we blended into the masses. A few of them shot us glances, but from experience, they knew I wasn't someone to stop and make small talk with. If I wasn't working, and I was with one of my favorite people, I would rip out a person's throat if they tried to interrupt my personal time with them.

A few of them had had to learn that the hard way—and it might not have been just the figurative throat ripped from their body experience they may have expected. Truthfully, I had my enemies, but that was because people didn't know how to mind their own business and leave me the fuck alone while I was having downtime.

It wasn't hard to find the quiet corner where the guys were seated that Tiny had spoken of. Two members of the club's security personnel were standing several feet away, keeping anyone from approaching the four men. I paused by a pillar to take a moment to observe them. Four comfortable leather chairs were set up in a square facing one another. An ice chest of what looked like bottles of beer and soft drinks was on a table between them. Jagger leaned forward, his arms on his knees as he laughed at something Lyric was saying.

Out of the corner of my eye, I saw a group of girls approach, but the security team blocked them before they could get close. The guys didn't even notice when one of the girls started to get rowdy and tried to push her way past the guy in the T-shirt that read SECURITY across the front.

It took me a moment to recognize who the chick was, but as soon as her name clicked in my head, I quickly grabbed Piper and pushed her and Violet toward the balcony that overlooked the lower level so my best friend didn't notice the woman.

"I thought we were going to join the guys," Mila said as she followed. "Not spy on them. I'm not okay with spying on my husband. I trust him, and if he catches me here watching from a distance, he's going to get pissed." Her eyes began to glitter. "Although, I'm not sure if I'm against his punishment or not. My ass is still a little pink from the last spanking he gave me, but the tiny sting feels good when he's..." She broke off when Piper waggled her brows at her.

"Do tell," Piper encouraged. "I always figured Lyric was a Dom. But I didn't figure you for the sub type."

"There's a difference between enjoying the occasional spanking and being a submissive."

"I'm very much aware of that," Piper assured her with a wink. "I like a little Dom/sub play every now and then too. Guess which part I like more."

"How old are you again?" Mila muttered.

"Old enough to know what I like when it comes to sex," she said with a shrug.

"I don't even remember hearing you've dated anyone," Violet commented, glancing out over the crowd below.

Piper sighed heavily. "Dating and I don't go hand in hand. But sex and dating aren't synonymous. I don't have to torture myself with one to get the fulfillment of the other."

"Lyric mentioned you're..." Mila trailed off, pressing her lips together to keep from speaking the words her husband had confided in her. Lyric and Piper used to be as close as siblings, so I didn't doubt the validity of whatever he knew about her.

Piper smirked. "It's fine, Mila. My sexuality isn't a secret. I'm pan. That means I don't see gender. I don't go around announcing it to everyone, because not everyone matters. But the people who matter the most are well aware of my sexual preferences."

I was only half listening to them discuss Piper's sex life, which was weird for me in a way. I considered her a younger cousin and a good friend, but she'd always been a baby in my mind. Even as she'd grown along with Vi and me, I still thought of her as a baby. It didn't bother me who she was having sex with, but what I couldn't get over was the fact that she'd been having sex for fuck knew how long.

My gaze went back to the corner and the security team that had thankfully finally dragged the bitch and her posse away. I didn't need that bullshit, of all things, to blow up the night before my wedding. I had no way of knowing how either Vi or Luca would have reacted if they had seen Megan Hawthorn after so many years had already passed since the bullshit that had gone down with that manipulative slut.

Luca had a restraining order against Megan, as did both of his parents. I wasn't sure, but I thought Lucy had ended up taking one out against her as well when Megan had become so psychotic following her alleged miscarriage. If those orders of protection were still in place, then Megan technically would have been breaking it by showing up at Harris's club.

Making a mental note to mention Megan to Emmie the next morning, I nudged Violet with my hip before walking toward the back corner. The two men saw us coming and tensed, but when they recognized me, they relaxed, and one even gave me a cocky grin. With a wink at him, I slipped past them. "They're with me." Pausing, I leaned closer to the one who'd had to deal with Megan. "The blonde from a few minutes ago?"

"Escorted off the premises," he said in a tone just as quiet as my own. "We made sure the gentlemen weren't disturbed, Miss Cage."

"Thank you," I whispered just as Vi smacked my ass and then jumped around me.

"Vi!" Luca cried happily. "Baby, I was just talking about how much I missed you."

I joined them and slid right into Jagger's lap. "He really was," my fiancé faux-complained. "Thought we were going to have to end the night early to keep him from crying into his Dr Pepper."

"Bullshit," Cannon said, lifting his bottle of Corona to his lips. "All three of you idiots were whining about missing your wives."

"Aww," Mila cooed as she dropped onto the arm of Lyric's chair. "Did you miss me, big guy?"

"So bad, babe." He snaked an arm around her waist and lifted her onto his lap.

"At least they each have a heart that works enough that they can miss their wives," Piper sniped at Cannon as she crouched down by the ice chest and shifted through the contents. "Ugh, beer and Dr

Pepper is all you ordered? What kind of stag party is this?"

"A boring one," Cannon grumbled, ignoring her jab at him for not having a working heart.

I cupped Jagger's face. "You were bored?"

"I was missing you," he corrected. "We were about to call it a night when your sexy ass dropped right into my arms. Which made the evening perfect."

I snuggled deeper into his lap, nearly purring when I felt exactly how happy he was to see me. Things might have nearly taken a turn for the worst, but the blast from the past hadn't gotten her evil way. Which meant I could enjoy the rest of the night with the people who mattered the most.

CHAPTER 6

JAGGER

My eyes were just starting to drift closed when my phone started going off with alerts. Shaw grumbled, half asleep, and turned away, her naked ass capturing my attention from the soft glow of the lamp we'd left on so I could watch her ride my cock. But then I got another alert, and Shaw whined unhappily.

"Make it stop," she mumbled in an adorable, disgruntled voice that was thick with satisfaction and sleep. "We have to be up in a few hours for the flight to Hawaii."

Rolling, I reached across her for my phone on the nightstand. Before I picked it up, I brushed a kiss along her bare shoulder blade and was rewarded with her sensual shiver. "You sure you want to sleep, Dimples?"

"Sleep now, fuck later," she said with a yawn.

Two more alerts, back-to-back, pinged on my device, and I cursed as I snatched it off the nightstand. Rolling back onto my pillow, I looked down at the screen and felt my stomach bottom out. "Shaw, who knew you were going to be at First Bass?"

She huffed and lifted her head to prop it on her hand. "Mila, Vi, and Jenner. Piper tagged along at the last minute."

"No one else?" I asked without looking at her, my gaze glued to my screen as I flipped through the social media feed, with Shaw hashtagged in every damn one of them.

But the subject matter wasn't my fiancée. It was Violet, Luca, and—of all fucking people—Megan Hawthorn.

"No. Not even your mom or my own. I left a group of women watching some rom-com downstairs with snacks and a housekeeper who was supposed to take care of their every need. Seeing as Mia, Nevaeh, and Arella are all pregnant, I figured Mrs. Briggs needed to stay alert in case of random weird cravings."

My theory that Shaw's every move was being watched by someone on Ma's staff didn't seem to hold water any longer, but someone sure as fuck was keeping tabs on her. But what was going to infuriate her even more was that the damn press was more focused on Violet.

Lowering my phone from my face, I turned it to let her see the picture of Megan practically being wrestled by the two security guards who I remembered had blocked us off from the rest of the VIP at First Bass earlier. A few of the pictures were angled just right to show both Luca and Lyric in the background while Megan obviously screamed at the guard.

Apparently I'd been so lost in the conversation, mixed in with the good music that was always playing at First Bass, that I hadn't noticed what was going on outside my group of friends until Shaw and the girls showed up.

"Did you see that crazy bitch Megan at the club?"

Shaw grabbed my phone and sat upright in bed, her hair falling over her tits to hide the lusciousness from me. I nearly pouted. If I had to deal with this shit, I should at least be gifted with the view of her beautiful body as a consolation. "Holy shit," she whispered as she zoomed in on one of the pictures. "That crazy cunt!"

"We already knew that about her," I muttered, reaching out to brush her hair over her shoulder.

She slapped my hand away and snapped her fingers in my face. "Focus, Jags. This entire time, I thought the paps were stalking me because of—well, me. But instead, it was all about Violet!"

I cocked a brow at her assumption. "How do you figure that, babe?"

"Her." She zoomed in again and then shoved the screen in my face. "See that brunette?"

Grasping her wrist, I pulled it back from my face a couple inches so the person on my phone could come into focus. I had to blink a few times before I could really take the woman in, but when I did, I couldn't place her. Although, she did look vaguely familiar.

"What about her?"

"She was one of Megan's posse back in high school. I remember her always being around whenever Megan would try to get Luca's attention at football games. Then when we would wait on him outside the locker rooms, this chick would always be off to the side, waiting with Megan."

"Okay...?" I still didn't understand what the brunette had to do with Shaw being stalked and ambushed.

"She works for one of the gossip magazines in New York," Shaw informed me. "I didn't really pay attention to who was who when they were all flashing their cameras at me, but I did see several familiar faces every time I went out. A few guys who have always followed me in hopes of getting some details on my latest comings and goings, but she was the only woman at every incident."

"You mean one of Megan's minions is stalking you to get shit on Vi?" I gritted out. I was beyond pissed. Not only had this person been harassing Shaw, but she'd been trying to bring down our sweet, precious Violet in the process.

"Probably to stir up shit between Vi and Luca. That's what Megan lived for." She dropped my phone on the bed and reached for her own. "But Megan couldn't get close enough to either of them, because most of the family has an order of protection against her. Although that might not still be valid if Megan dared to get close to Luca tonight at the club."

"Fuck, I need to call Ma."

"Yeah, you do that, and I'll call Mieke. Maybe she can get this shit taken down before Vi sees any of it." She already had her phone to her ear.

Acting quickly, I called Ma. It took a few rings, but she answered. "Jagger?" she demanded, sounding as alert as always, not even a hint of sleep thickening her voice. She was in mom mode, alert and ready to deal with anything I might throw her way.

"Ma, I'm sorry if I woke you up," I apologized. "But something's come up. Do you know if the order of protection everyone has against Megan Hawthorn is still in effect?"

"What?" she growled. "You're getting married in less than twenty-four hours. We're supposed to be at the airport in a matter of hours, but you're asking me about some crazy little brat from years ago?"

"I know, but it's important, Ma."

There was a brief pause on her end before she sighed heavily. "To be honest, I don't know. She faded into the background once we took out the last few restraining orders. I was told that her parents sent her away, to quietly get her some mental health help. I haven't even thought about her in so long, I forgot she existed."

"Unfortunately, she's trying to make a comeback," I said with regret. "I'm sorry, but I think you're going to have to deal with her before we can leave. Otherwise, there might be some serious drama. Megan tried to approach Luca at the club tonight, and now she is trending at number three on social media, right behind Luca. And Vi is number one. Shaw caught sight of one of Megan's friends in a picture and recognized her as one of the paps that has been following her around."

It all made sense, though. I'd gone to the same high school as Luca, Lyric, Megan, and the brunette—whose name still didn't click in my head. She just hadn't been important enough to remember. If Megan hadn't caused so much trouble for Luca and Vi, she wouldn't ever have been on my radar either. But apparently the brunette thought I might recognize her from school, which would explain why the press never bothered Shaw when I was around.

"You're telling me that the bullshit from the paps showing up everywhere for the past few months has been about Violet and not Shaw?" Ma muttered. "How did I not see this one coming?"

"Because you've been so focused on making our wedding perfect that the press turning this into anything to do with anyone other than Shaw or me didn't enter your mind?" I suggested, trying to soothe her. "And it shouldn't have. No one would have imagined Vi was the target of the paps when the ambushes related to our wedding. Plus, there aren't many papers that would accept gossip about Violet with Aunt Harper still in charge of the most popular music and political magazines in the world. They had to do this with stealth, making it look like Violet was just a bystander, when in reality, it was firing up the trolls to drag Vi through the mud."

"It does make sense," she gritted out. "Okay, I need to get off here to take care of a few things. You get some sleep. Tomorrow is a big day for you and Shaw."

"Ma..." I glanced over at Shaw, who was whisper-shouting into her own phone, not paying me the least bit of attention. "I'm sorry I'm adding more stress to your load, but tomorrow has to be perfect."

"Baby boy, have I ever let you down?" she asked softly.

"Never."

"Then don't you worry about anything from here on out. Your wedding is going to go flawlessly," she promised.

CHAPTER 7

SHAW

I didn't know how Mieke did it, but every trace of Megan at First Bass, along with any signs of Vi and Luca trending on social media, was gone by the time I made my way down to the kitchen the next morning. There wasn't a lot of time to waste, so I grabbed one of the muffins Mrs. Briggs had set out and a travel mug of coffee as I flipped through my phone one more time, ensuring that my best friend wasn't anywhere on any of the feeds.

Taking a giant bite of the huge, fluffy muffin, I strode out to where three blacked-out SUVs were already waiting. Jagger, Luca, Lyric, and Cannon were already in one. Mila and Violet were waiting on me in another, with all our luggage in the third.

"Mia texted me earlier to let me know everyone made it back to their houses safely last night," Vi said, fighting back a yawn. "She assumed we just went to bed, and I didn't correct her."

I stuffed another bite into my mouth, noticing Mila already had a half-eaten one in her lap, along with a travel mug of coffee in her hands. "Piper got back to her parents' house safely, according to my brother."

"I have to admit, I had some qualms when he insisted on driving her back to Malibu personally," Vi commented. "I was a bit fearful for his life the way Piper was throwing threats his way all night."

"Meh," I mumbled around the food in my mouth. "It wouldn't have been anything he didn't deserve."

"I can't wrap my head around your dynamic with your brother," Mila said with a frown. "Sometimes Maverick drives me crazy, but I've never actually wanted to kill him. Whereas you always seem ready to help anyone who wants to murder him."

"I have my reasons."

"We're not going to talk about Cannon and your willingness to help Piper bury his body," Violet chided. Grabbing my hand that held my muffin, she took a bite off the top. If it were anyone else—except maybe Jags or Love Bug—I would have pushed them out of the moving vehicle. Instead, I just stuffed the rest of the muffin into my mouth before she could steal another bite.

Laughing, my best friend threw her hands in the air. "You're getting married today!"

After the stress I'd fallen asleep to, the realization of what the day meant only hit me when she squealed so happily. Pushing down the guilt of not telling Vi about what had happened online, I mentally told myself it was for her own well-being. I wouldn't be responsible for Vi having to deal with Megan's bullshit again. With the guilt out of the way, I allowed myself to enjoy the moment, and by the time we reached the airport, I was already laughing and dancing to the music Vi was playing on her phone.

It was a little chaotic getting everyone on the planes, but Emmie had us in the air in no time—and not once did I see a single flashing camera from the paps. Whatever she'd done after getting Jagger's phone call had obviously ensured we wouldn't be bothered any longer. I knew Jags had been worried about the day being perfect for me, but he kept forgetting it wasn't just about me.

This was our day.

Our wedding.

The first day of the rest of our lives started the moment we said, "I do."

Music blasted from the overhead speakers while I played games with my friends and honorary female cousins. The tiredness from my lack of sleep didn't even bother me. I was too amped up from excitement. Honestly, the rest of the world could catch on fire, but as long as I still got to marry Jagger at sunset, I didn't give a single fuck.

We arrived on the island just in time to be shuttled to the private resort, where everyone had a spa treatment before being pushed into a chair for hair and makeup. Every now and then, my mom would shove a bottle of water into my hands and stuff something to eat in my mouth between getting ready herself. When I was younger, that had always been our dynamic on the sets of photo shoots or fashion shows. She hadn't wanted me to follow in her shoes and become a model—something that had been forced on her by her own mother— but when she realized it was my passion, she'd relented and made sure I learned the ins and outs, so I didn't have to worry about being taken advantage of.

Emmie supervised, going between where we were getting ready and where Jagger was with the guys. At one point, she discreetly gave

Violet a document, telling her she just needed a signature. Because it was Emmie, and we all trusted her with our lives, Vi didn't even hesitate to scribble her name where she was told to. Green eyes caught mine, and my soon-to-be mother-in-law gave me a wink before taking the signed documents and rushing out the door.

"I don't like people touching my face," Mila complained when she was done with makeup. "How do you handle a stranger constantly fixing your face on shoots?"

I shrugged. "It's just something I got used to over the years." With my own hair and makeup complete, I stood, checking the time as I did.

Seeing it was close to the moment I was supposed to walk down the aisle, I took one last bite of my sandwich and wiped my fingers on a napkin. "Riley!" I called when I didn't see her.

"Right here," the pocket Venus designer said as she came in, carrying the bag with my dress in it. "I've guarded it with my life from the moment I got on the plane this morning. I swear not even my husband has seen what is beneath this garment bag."

Having spent the majority of my life walking around in front of complete strangers in nothing more than my bra and panties—sometimes less—I walked over to the mirror in my white thong and matching strapless, push-up bra. With my hair in soft curls falling over my left shoulder and a tiara made of sapphires, I anxiously waited for Riley to unzip the bag.

Everyone grew silent as I stepped into the dress, and Riley did up all the buttons on the back. The gown was stunning—strapless, white mesh embroidered with intricate white threading that formed a beautiful lace overlay across a light nude liner. The bodice had hidden support boning that gave it a sexiness I was hoping would knock the air right out of Jagger's lungs the moment he saw me.

The instant the last button was in place, I turned to get everyone's reaction. I saw tears in Mom's eyes as she grasped one of my hands and twirled me around. "You are so damn beautiful. I can't believe I created you."

Laughing, I gave her a light hug, not wanting to wrinkle either of our dresses. "I think Dad would say he helped."

"Nah, you're all mine," she argued. "He can claim Cannon."

"Why are you being mean to Dad?" I teased as I stepped back. "No one wants to claim that asshole."

"He has his moments," Mom defended. Behind her, the door opened, and Dad walked in. "Ax, look at this beautiful creature I made."

"We made," he corrected, his hazel eyes drinking in the sight of me before filling with tears. "I've changed my mind. He can't marry you. No one should be lucky enough to call you their wife. You have to stay my baby girl forever."

"Fight me!" I heard Jagger shout from outside the door.

"Jagger!" his mom scolded. "I told you to stay in the other room. Stop trying to sneak a look."

"Ma, Axton is trying to talk her out of marrying me!"

"He's bullshitting," she attempted to soothe.

"Language!" Luca shouted from somewhere. "Love Bug is right here."

"She's supposed to be with Layla," Emmie snapped. "What are you doing with her? She's going to spit up all over your tux."

"Then I'll have baby puke all over me," he argued with her. "She was crying and wanted her daddy."

"Ma, stop worrying about the baby and focus on the fact that Axton is trying to talk my bride out of marrying me. I'm going to need you to find someone to dig a hole on this freaking island so I can bury him. Wait, have there been any shark sightings? That would be even better."

I pressed my lips together to keep from laughing. It was funny as hell, but the distress in Jagger's voice was too real for me to giggle over—although holding back the urge was almost painful.

Dad opened the door. "Relax, kid," he said with a snort. "Even if I'd been serious, Shaw would have kicked my ass if I tried to get her to back out."

"Language!" Luca growled, sounding closer. "Innocent ears, people."

Violet carefully got out of the stylist's chair and smoothed her hands over her hips, making sure her matron-of-honor dress was perfectly in place before walking toward the door. "Luca, take Love Bug to my dad," she commanded. "The wedding will be starting soon."

"Shane and Dad have Isaac and Ian. Your mom is in there with you, and Love Bug wasn't happy with Mom. I'll just keep her with me."

"The wedding is about to start," Vi argued. "Babe, please. This is Shaw's day."

Suddenly, Luca's hulking body was in the doorway, his arms full of tiny baby, holding my goddaughter as if she were the most precious person in the universe. And he wasn't wrong. I adored Love Bug, much like Aunt Harper adored me. If I was never blessed with children, that would be fine with me because I could spend my life spoiling and loving that beautiful little girl.

"Shaw." Luca's voice and eyes were full of a plea that I'd rarely seen or heard from him. "Please, I'll do anything you want. Just let me hold her during the ceremony. She will be a good girl. I promise. She's always a good little princess for her daddy." He looked down at the baby with so much love on his face, my heart turned to mush. I'd never thought Luca Thornton would ever care about anyone more than himself, yet he'd proved to me over and over again since Remington's death that he would spend his life loving Violet and Love Bug with every fiber of his being.

"Won't you, my beautiful princess?" Love Bug gurgled happily up at her daddy, her little hand waving around in an attempt to touch his face. "Yes, you will, precious baby." He kissed the top of her head while looking at me with pleading, swirling brown eyes. "Please," he whispered.

"Luca—" Vi began, but I cut her off.

"You can keep her with you," I announced. "Besides, she's my goddaughter. She needs to be a part of the ceremony too, right?"

"Of course she does!" Jagger exclaimed, still out of sight of the door. "I can't believe we didn't think of that earlier."

"Thank you," Luca said with true sincerity before raining kisses all over Love Bug's giggling face.

It was such a sweet sound, I nearly teared up. Ugh, he was making me emotional before I even walked down the aisle. I didn't know if I wanted to hug him or slug him.

"All right, people," Emmie called so everyone could hear her. "We have five minutes until go time. Get to where you are supposed to be!"

Luca paused long enough to kiss Violet. "You look beautiful, Vi," he told her in a husky voice before he disappeared in a hurry, almost as if he were scared I might change my mind about the baby at the last second.

"Dimples?" Jagger said my name hesitantly.

"Jags?" I called back, letting him know I was there.

"I'll see you soon."

My heart leaped. Soon, I would be his wife, and life would be complete.

"Jagger?"

"Yeah," he said, sounding reluctant to move away from the door.

"Today has already been perfect," I assured him, knowing it was what he needed to hear. "I can't wait to see you on the beach."

CHAPTER 8

JAGGER

The ceremony passed in a blur. One minute, I was standing by the water with all eyes on me; the next, every gaze was on my breathtaking bride—mine included. I'd seen Shaw with red, swollen eyes, snotty nose, and no makeup while wearing sweats two sizes too big for her. I'd seen her wearing couture dresses with perfect makeup and hair. And everything in between. But no matter what she did or didn't wear, I could honestly say she was always the most beautiful woman I'd ever set eyes on.

Yet right then?

My knees actually went weak. There could never be a more stunning bride in the universe. Tears stung my eyes as her dad walked her down the aisle, which was basically a silky liner that was placed on the sand. Other than the first rows on either side of the aisle that were filled with our parents, my sister, and brother-in-law, everyone had been told to sit wherever they wanted, because it didn't matter whose side they were there on. We were all family, after all.

Axton placed Shaw's hand in mine, and the world disappeared except for the officiant. I didn't remember a single word he said, or even if my voice wobbled when I repeated my vows. All I saw was Shaw's eyes, the tears glazing those baby blues, and her wobbly chin. But the smile on her face, the sight of those damned dimples that always affected me, told me she was fighting happy tears.

She'd said the day was already perfect before she even walked down the aisle, and a weight had been lifted off my shoulders.

The instant our wedding bands were on, it really did become the perfect day. And then the officiant announced us as husband and wife right as the sun seemed to fall into the ocean behind us. Ma had truly made sure to plan everything down to the exact detail that Shaw had foreseen our ceremony.

Grasping my wife around her waist, I pulled her into me before taking her chin between my thumb and index finger. Tipping her head up, I drank in the moment—the fading natural light, the glow of the torches that had been lit around us flickering in her eyes, those dimples when she grinned up at me.

"Kiss your wife, husband," she commanded.

"Shh," I murmured. "Give me a second. I have to memorize how you look right now. When I'm in a nursing home and can't remember my own name, I want to have this memory pop into my head."

"I'll be right there beside you then too, dummy."

"And you'll still be just as beautiful then as you are right now." She rolled her eyes, and I caught her mouth in our first kiss as husband and wife, keeping her from snapping something sassy back at me.

Cannon hooting behind me pulled me back to reality sometime later. Lifting my head, I blinked, and all of our guests came back into focus, but I ignored everyone but Shaw as I brushed another kiss over her lips. This one was softer and over within seconds, but I tried to tell her with each sweep of my mouth over hers how much this day meant to me, how much I loved her, and how happy I was to get to spend the rest of my life as her husband.

When I lifted my head, a tear finally slipped free from her right eye, and she gave me a nod, as if she understood exactly what I'd promised without words.

Linking our fingers together, I turned to face everyone. They were all standing, clapping, most of them openly crying. Luca stood behind Cannon, Love Bug asleep on his shoulder. I didn't understand how she could sleep through the loud volume of everyone cheering, especially when Ian and Isaac were whining from having been seated on Uncle Jesse's and Uncle Shane's laps for so long.

Vi, Piper, and Mila moved in behind Shaw. Violet nudged us, urging us to walk down the aisle together. I swung Shaw up into my arms and carried her down the aisle, garnering even louder cheering from everyone. From there, it was time for pictures, while everyone else moved on to where the tents were set up for the reception.

Like the ceremony, everything passed in a blur, and all I saw was Shaw. Picture after picture was taken until everyone else was complaining that they were hungry and tired. At some point, Love Bug woke up, but she didn't whine once as we took a few photos with our goddaughter.

Seeing Shaw holding the baby stirred something inside me.

I wanted this.

A little replica of her momma in my wife's arms, gazing up at me like I hung the stars in the sky, like Love Bug stared at Luca.

When Shaw looked up at me over that tiny blond head, I knew she was thinking the same thing. I felt a predatory smile tilting my lips and lifted the baby from her arms. Giving Love Bug a kiss on the cheek, I handed her over to a hovering Luca.

"Ma, Shaw and I need a minute to rest before we join the reception," I called out, knowing she was close by. She hadn't been far from my side all day, making sure that nothing went wrong, working her magic to fulfill the promise of giving Shaw the perfect day.

"You can take a breather where you waited before the ceremony earlier. I'll have the DJ entertain the guests until you're ready." She stepped into my peripheral, and I finally shifted my hungry gaze from my bride. "But I'm warning you, baby boy. Whatever damage you do to her appearance better be fixed before you show up at the reception. Or whatever perfection you were hoping for will be mussed up in the extra pictures and the video."

"Ma!" I groaned, embarrassed that she knew exactly what I was going to be doing.

"What?" she grumbled. "I gave birth to you, Jagger. If anyone knows what you're thinking at any given moment, it's me. And I've seen you look at Shaw like that way too many times not to understand what you're about to do to her." She patted me on the arm. "Have fun, but put yourselves back together once you're done."

The urge to devour my wife diminished somewhat. "Um, I think we'll just go into the reception as we planned."

Giggling, Shaw grasped my elbow. That beautiful sound and her firm touch were enough to cause all that hunger to come roaring back to life. But I couldn't bring myself to act on it with my mom standing right in front of us, those big green eyes staring unblinkingly at me in that knowing way that had always urged me to be good.

"I think we're ready for the first dance," Shaw announced. "Maybe a few bites of dinner, and then we can cut the cake. After I've gotten a few tastes of that delicious dessert, then we can go to the honeymoon suite."

Liking the new plan, I looked down at Ma, but the glimmer of amusement in her eyes had heat filling my face. Fuck, she made me feel like I was fifteen again and she'd just caught me with a girl in my room. "Er... What Dimples said."

"I always thought Mia and I understood each other better," she said after a silent, thoughtful moment. "But I've realized that I just have to hear your voice to know what you're thinking. Never change, baby boy."

EPILOGUE

EMME

It was easy to let life speed past. Between all the chaos of work, sometimes it was hard to hit pause and take a breath so I could appreciate the small but most precious things in my world. If it weren't for the phone that always seemed to be attached to my hand—to the point that I felt as if I were missing a limb without it—I probably wouldn't know what day of the week it was more often than not.

Waking up to all three of my grandbabies bouncing on my bed, singing "Happy Birthday," was the only reminder I had that it was, in fact, my birthday.

Time was slipping past too quickly. I was getting older; the proof of that was in how much my grandchildren had grown over the years. I didn't even want to look in the mirror to see the new lines on my face or the gray in my hair. How Nik still found me sexy when I was an old woman, I had no clue, but for some reason, he couldn't keep his hands off me.

Shaking away the weird feeling that with each birthday, I grew closer to the end, I sat up in bed with a happy laugh. Reaching out, I grasped Grier around the waist and pulled her down onto my lap. With Jagger and Shaw spending more and more time at their home in Tennessee, I didn't get to see Grier as much as I did Emerson and Hendrix. I didn't even know they were visiting, so seeing the blond hair floating in the air as she'd bounced with her cousins had been a truly welcome surprise.

Tiny arms wrapped around my neck. "Happy Birthday, MiMi!" she cried, giving me a tight squeeze. "Did I surprise you? I told Daddy I wanted to give you the best gift ever, and he said the only gift you would appreciate was seeing me and my cousins."

I kissed the crown of her sweet-smelling head. "It's the best surprise ever," I assured her. "I love every minute I get to spend with you and Emerson and Hendrix."

She turned on my lap, and I waved Mia's two children over. Emerson smacked a kiss on my cheek before sitting cross-legged on the bed in front of me, while her younger brother sat down in my lap once Grier made extra room for him. My arms were full, but my heart was overflowing with happiness and love.

"We brought you cake and presents," Hendrix informed me. "Momma said I wasn't supposed to tell you that, MiMi, but I can't keep secrets from you. That's not right."

Fighting a laugh, I stroked a hand over his hair. "I'm glad you get it, Hendrix. No one else understands the way you do."

"Surprises are fun!" Emerson said with a huff. "We were supposed to distract you while Momma and Uncle Jags set up all the decorations with Papa. Now Hendrix snitched."

"Yeah, Hendrix, you ruined MiMi's party!" Grier glared at him.

I felt her muscles tensing and knew I had only a matter of seconds before she had him pinned to the bed. And because Hendrix would just roll over and take it like he always did for fear of hurting her, I tightened my arm around my youngest grandchild. "Nothing's been ruined," I promised. "In fact, I appreciate that Hendrix warned me. I don't really like surprises."

Which everyone in my family knew, but apparently my husband and grown children had forgotten that little detail. If I didn't love them so much, I would have strangled them, but at least Hendrix had given me a warning.

"But Daddy and Auntie Mia worked so hard on planning the party with Papa," Grier grumbled, her hands balled into fists as fire sparked out of her blue eyes at my sweet little grandson.

"I swear to you all that I will act very surprised so as not to hurt anyone's feelings," I vowed. "As long as none of you tells your parents Hendrix forewarned me, then no one but the four of us will know."

Grier rolled her eyes and stuck out her tongue at Hendrix, but Emerson gave a firm nod. "Okay. No more snitching on anyone. But you have to pretend to be really, really surprised, MiMi. Otherwise, Papa is going to be sad, and I can't have that."

I bit the inside of my cheek to keep from grinning again. Emerson was more like me than she realized. Her unwavering loyalty and concern for her grandfather's feelings were too adorable at times. The bond between the two of them was more than I could have ever asked for with any of our grandchildren. I tried to spread my attention between all three of my grandbabies, but Grier spent more time with Dallas and Axton than me, which was understandable since they had more time to travel to West Bridge, Tennessee, than I did. Hendrix

180

and I were the closest of the three, and not just because he was the only boy.

There was just something about my grandson that made me pause every time I looked into his green eyes. From the first time I held him, a part of my heart I didn't even realize was unused opened up, and he'd filled the space. Grier and Emerson had their own places within my soul, but this boy was magical.

A firm tap on the bedroom door had our heads turning, and I called out for whoever it was to come in. Seeing Jagger, I nearly jumped off the bed, the only thing stopping me Grier and Hendrix. I hadn't seen my son in months. Although he'd been dividing his time between the two states for several years at this point and I should have been used to not seeing him for long periods of time, I wasn't.

Seeing all of us on my bed, he walked over and lifted his daughter into his arms before bending to kiss my cheek. "Happy birthday, Ma."

"Thanks, baby boy. Getting to see you and the grandbabies has already made today perfect."

His blue eyes, the same shade as his father's, lit up. "That's all I wanted."

"Get up, MiMi," Emerson urged. "Once you're dressed, we can have breakfast. Papa made pancakes and bacon."

"Bacon!" Hendrix cheered.

"But…" Grier's voice wobbled. "Bacon is pigs. Daddy, they're going to eat Wilbur!"

Jagger tried to fight a sigh but couldn't quite contain it as I looked up at him in confusion, unsure why she was so upset. "Grier and Love Bug watched Charlotte's Web a few weeks ago. Since then, neither one of them will eat bacon."

"Not eat bacon?" Emerson whispered with stark horror on her face. "But… But… Why?" she sputtered. "It's the most delicious thing in the world, Uncle Jags. Not eating bacon should be a crime."

"Yeah!" Hendrix shouted, jumping to his feet on my mattress. "Grier, you should be arrested for not eating bacon."

"No," she argued. "You two should be arrested for killing a poor little piggy and eating him! Murderer. Murderer. Murderer!"

"Am not!" Hendrix cried. "I never hurted anything in my whole life. I didn't kill the pig, I just eat him."

"Daddy, put Hendrix in time-out for eating the poor piggy!" Grier commanded her father, who was already squeezing the bridge of his nose.

"What the hell's going on in here?" Nik demanded as he came into the room.

"Papa." Emerson climbed down and went to take his hand. "Grier is calling us murderers for eating bacon, and she's going to ruin MiMi's birthday! Tell her bacon is delicious, and eating it for breakfast, especially on your birthday, is tradition."

"I don't want to eat Wilbur," Grier whispered. "Or Millie. We're not gonna eat Millie, are we, Daddy?"

"Who the hell is Millie?" Nik asked, just as confused as I was.

"Millie is the Miniature Belted Galloway cow that Shaw and Violet bought for the girls to take care of together," Jagger explained. "Lyric and Mila visited a few weeks back, and Ian made the mistake of saying he was going to eat Millie for dinner and..." He shrugged. "I'm sure you saw the pictures Mila posted of Ian with a black eye."

Grier crossed her arms over her chest and lifted her chin, both proud of herself and still upset over the whole bacon—and now apparently beef—issue.

"Sweetheart, does that mean you're a vegetarian now?" I asked as I stood, touching her leg to pull her gaze to me.

"What's that?" she asked with an adorable frown scrunching up her brows.

"It means you don't eat meat," Emerson supplied before I could explain. "Do you eat eggs?"

"I only like the eggs that Henrietta lays," she said with a stubborn tilt of her chin. "They're fresh and taste better than the ones at the store."

"Henrietta. Millie. Do you have an entire farm now, son?" Nik teased.

Jagger grinned. "More or less. We have a couple chickens, the cow, horses, and a few baby goats. All of which Grier and Love Bug take care of together."

"I want a baby goat!" Emerson announced. "MiMi, can we visit Uncle Jags and see their baby goats?"

"You can help me feed them!" Grier exclaimed, wiggling free, her upset over the bacon momentarily forgotten in her excitement over sharing her animals with her cousin. "They're so cute. Love Bug named two of them, and I named the other two. But we can get you one so you can name it. I'll take care of it while you're here, and you can come visit us all the time to check on it."

Taking Emerson's hand, she dragged her out the bedroom door. "Mommy! We have to get Emerson a baby goat!"

"Say what now?" I heard Mia shout.

Nik blew out a heavy exhale. "You know, I'm on the fence about you being all the way across the country ninety percent of the time.

But that other ten percent—like now—I'm kind of glad I don't have to deal with this kind of whiplash every day."

"I'd take the whiplash drama anytime if we got to see our son and granddaughter every day."

"Granddaughters," Jagger corrected. "Shaw had a scan yesterday before we flew out. She's having another girl."

"Yes!" Hendrix shouted. "Still the only boy!" He high-fived me, then Nik, before skipping out of the room. "Hey, I want a baby goat too!"

"To answer your question," Jagger said, throwing an arm around my shoulders. "Yes, both Grier and Love Bug no longer eat meat. They're vegetarians not vegan, because they still enjoy eggs and dairy. No way my girl is going to give up ice cream."

"Is she going to cry if we eat bacon?" Nik asked with concern. "Because I just made two huge platters."

"Just pile extra pancakes on her plate and ignore her evil glare when you eat your bacon," he advised with a smirk. "It's what we've been doing the last few weeks. We're teaching her boundaries. She can decide what she does and doesn't want to eat, but she can't dictate what we eat. Trust me, with Shaw's cravings this pregnancy, it's been a battle I've had to fight almost every day between those two."

"She's more like Shaw than you," I agreed. "But maybe this one will be more of an Armstrong than a Cage."

"I wouldn't bet on it," he said with a shrug. "Sorry, Ma, but Dallas and Axton's DNA is stronger when it comes to my kids."

"Gods help us," I teased. "Another mini Shaw running around will end us all."

Jagger threw back his head, laughing happily, making my heart squeeze with love. "Sounds like perfection to me."

~THE END~

Hopelessly Devoted to DOE

CHAPTER 1

Doe

I stared down at the dress Shaw had pushed into my hands after she'd selected it from the rack. "Okay, this will look killer on you, but I'm too round for this kind of outfit." Even though she was a new mom, her body had snapped back to its flawless shape in no time at all.

Sighing, Shaw didn't argue with me. Instead, she went back to looking at the other racks in the boutique. I didn't even want to go shopping. I never felt comfortable in the designer boutiques in Nashville—or anywhere else, for that matter. But Piper and the other two had shown up at my front door and dragged me out of the apartment over Luca's garage and into the back of Vi's SUV.

My parents were hosting a party for both Pixie and me later that evening. Pixie because she'd been given the *all clear*. She was officially in remission and had remained there for the past six months. If there was anything worth celebrating, it was her continued good health. As for me, they wanted to acknowledge my part in her recovery. We were only a few weeks from the anniversary of when I'd donated my bone marrow to Pixie, which was why she was now cancer-free.

I didn't really want to celebrate my role in it. Honestly, I didn't think it was appropriate. But when Pixie had found out that Mom and Dad wanted to throw a party in her honor, she'd insisted it be a joint celebration. If I refused to be in the spotlight with her, then she didn't want the party. I loved her too much to tell her no—something she knew and had shamelessly exploited—so now I was stuck with having to be front and center. It wasn't my idea of a good time. If anything, it was one of my biggest nightmares, but Pixie was stubborn, and I wanted her to celebrate her victory against cancer.

"Trust Shaw's judgment," Piper urged as she took a few selections from a nearby rack and examined them before slinging them over her shoulder. Grasping my elbow, she walked with me to the back where the changing rooms were and practically pushed me into one before moving to the open room beside mine.

In my head, I could already see the seams splitting as I tried to wiggle the dress over my body, but I stripped down to my bra and panties. To my surprise, the dress went on with ease, and I was even able to zip the back without any issues. Turning around, I examined my reflection in the mirror, enjoying the way the skirt floated around my knees while the top clung to my breasts. It was the perfect mixture of innocence—so my dad wouldn't lose his shit—and sexy, which would ensure Jenner couldn't keep his hands off me.

Then again, Jenner always had his hands on me. He couldn't seem to help himself. If I was within touching distance, then he touched. If I wasn't, then his eyes were constantly glued to me. It was getting to the point that I distracted him even when he was working. His entire focus should be on Violet and Love Bug when they went out, and it was...as long as I wasn't with them too.

Luca had actually hired a second bodyguard directly from Barrick and Braxton. I understood his need to protect his two favorite people, but I'd been upset, thinking they wanted to replace Jenner. But then Jenner had sprung something else on me, which had been the true reason why Luca had hired someone to step in as Violet's personal protection when he wasn't available.

The local police chief was retiring, and while the small town of West Bridge had five other cops on the payroll, none of them was truly qualified to take on such an important role. The mayor had approached my parents, who had arranged a meeting with Jenner— without my knowledge.

Without even discussing it with me, Jenner had accepted the offer to step in for Police Chief Stafford. Unlike the sheriff position, the chief of police position was an appointed one, typically by a city manager, but West Bridge wasn't big enough for a city manager. So Mayor Teller had officially appointed Jenner.

It wasn't until it was a done deal that Jenner had "surprised" me with the news.

He thought I would be happy that meant he was a full-time resident of West Bridge. He wouldn't be working for Vi any longer, which meant no traveling when she decided to visit her parents on the West Coast or followed Luca to whatever city where he had an away game during football season.

But for one, I didn't like surprises. If anything, I hated them. Throughout my school years, I'd learned that surprises were never a good thing, which had carried over into the rest of my life. For another, how could he make such a life-changing decision without consulting me first? Our one-year anniversary was only a few days away. When he spoke of the future, he made me think I was going to be a part of it.

Yet, this was one of the biggest decisions of his life, and he hadn't mentioned it to me once.

Then there was the whole cop thing. It was a dangerous job. Sure, the chief of police position was more of an administrative job, but there would be times he would be on patrol. I knew him too well. Sitting behind a desk all day, every day would drive him crazy, and he'd be out there cruising around town with the other officers. He'd show up to calls; there might even be times when he would have to use his weapon.

If anything happened to him, it would destroy me.

And he'd taken a fucking job that would potentially put him in danger every damn day.

I'd tried to remind myself that we lived in a small-town miles and miles away from the bigger city of Nashville. Not a lot of action went on in West Bridge. Typically, the only law that was broken on a daily basis was that of the speed limit. But there was that time when one of the sheriff's deputies had pulled over a van full of people who were being trafficked. And there was that other time when a simple speeding ticket had turned into a shootout because the driver had been carrying nearly half a million dollars in coke hidden in the dashboard of his truck.

Those two instances had been years apart, and the last one had happened when I was around twelve. But I still remembered it being on the front of the local papers for two weeks straight as the entire town waited with bated breath to see if the officer who'd been involved in the shootout survived the two bullets he'd taken—one to his neck, the other to his hip. Our small town had made national news because it had basically stopped the drug pipeline into Nashville. At least, for a few months, until a new supply had made its way into the city.

"Well?" Piper called from outside my dressing room door, pulling me out of my head.

Shyly, I stepped out. The instant her eyes raked over me, I was even more convinced it was the perfect dress for the party. "Holy shit," she breathed. "How did you get all the good genes? I am so damned jealous that you have all those curves and legs. Why couldn't I have looked more like my dad?"

"You're beautiful," I rushed to assure her. Unless someone knew who our parents were, they never would have guessed that the two of us were actually biologically related. Her dad and my mom were siblings, and then there was the whole thing about my dad and her dad being cousins. My parents weren't related by blood, but that hadn't stopped the bullies in school from whispering that I was inbred. They never said things like that about my brothers, though— even though we were quadruplets and had been born within minutes of one another. No, my brothers were considered gods in West Bridge. The golden three of baseball. "You're small with just the right amount of curves, and you don't look like a bull in a china shop."

Her dark eyes began to glitter with each word out of my mouth, so I pressed my lips together and turned to look at the selection of shoes. None of them were my size. My feet were far too big for any of those dainty shoes.

"Courtney Wilcox better be glad she's gone into hiding from the press right now," my younger cousin seethed between gritted teeth. "Because if I ever see that bitch, I'm going to give her the beating of her life."

Ignoring any mention of my biggest childhood bully, I went to the tri-fold mirrors and shifted from one side to the other, examining the dress from every angle. Luckily, I had a pair of flats at home that would go well with the dress. But I'd have to text Jenner to pick them up for me since the girls and I were going to the spa straight after we found appropriate outfits, to have our hair, nails, and makeup done.

They were in one of the boxes I'd packed earlier in the week in preparation for our move. Jenner had found us a house to rent in town since Vi's new bodyguard needed to be closer to her and would have to live in the apartment above the garage. Luca and Vi hadn't rushed us to move out, but the apartment was no longer home, and I wanted out of there as soon as possible.

But I was dreading moving in to the rental. Our neighbors on either side of the house had been just as horrible to me for my entire life as Courtney and the rest of her tribe. Mrs. Cain was all smiles in front of my parents, but I couldn't count how many times I'd heard her stage-whispering about me when I'd been out on my own. Then there were both Mr. and Mrs. Dotson, who would shake my father's hand and then snicker at me as soon as Dad's back was turned. I didn't know why the adults in town had picked me to target with their meanness. It was as if they took pleasure in hurting my feelings.

I'd learned quickly who to avoid in West Bridge and who was safe. Sadly, the number of people who used words and leers to make me feel like less than I knew I was outweighed the number of people who didn't.

And now the Cains and Dotsons were going to be my next-door neighbors.

Going back into the dressing room, I quickly changed and then went to pay for my dress.

"I got this," Violet said as she nudged me out of the way, placing her outfit on top of mine and pulling out her credit card.

"Violet, that isn't necessary. I'm capable of paying for my own things."

"My treat," she said, the tilt of her chin telling me she wasn't going to relent.

"You are so annoying," I grumbled.

"Found us shoes!" Shaw announced as she came over with several boxes. I leaned back against the counter, not expecting her to have found anything in my size. I usually had to shop in the men's section for work boots, but if I wanted anything pretty, I typically had to special order them.

"Here, Doe," she said, thrusting a box into my hands. "These will make your legs look amazing."

Frowning, I slowly took hold of the box and flipped up the top. Inside was a pair of heels I wasn't confident I would be able to walk in without breaking something—not necessarily myself, but everything around me. The bull in the middle of a china shop scenario popped into my head again, and I set the box on the counter without attempting to try them on.

Blue eyes snapped to me, and Shaw demanded, "Why aren't you trying them on?"

"Because I can already tell you that even if they happen to fit, I'll be too clumsy in them. I'd rather not embarrass myself, thanks."

"You need to have more confidence in your gracefulness," the supermodel chided gently. "The few times I've seen you in heels, you were a natural in them. And they looked fabulous on you. Jenner is going to take one look at you in them and want to fuck you against the nearest hard surface."

Heat filled my cheeks, but I couldn't help imagining my boyfriend doing just that. I wanted him to tear the dress off me and take me against the door as soon as we got home later that night, with me in nothing but the heels my friend had picked out. But I also wanted to get through the party without falling on my face or my ass or into the cake. Flats made better sense. They would keep me from towering over everyone even more than I already would, and they would ensure I didn't make a fool of myself by tripping over anything that had the misfortune to get in the way of my huge feet.

Taking my hands, Shaw bent her head to lock gazes with me. She was the only woman I'd ever met who was taller than me, but where she was super slim and perfect, I was a giant. Shoulders, boobs, ass, thighs. Luckily, Jenner loved all my curves, but I wasn't a fan of my own body. Too many years of being called a freak by the other girls in school had convinced me that I was basically a mutant.

"You're going to wear that dress and these shoes, and not a single person at the party will be able to tear their eyes off you. Because you are going to be the most beautiful person there. Even without the clothes and footwear, you are gorgeous. Inside and out. No one can compare to you, Doe. Not in selflessness or beauty. You are a goddamned angel walking among us, and if I didn't love you so much, I would be jealous of everything you are." Her fingers tightened around mine. "Get out of your head and enjoy this day, or I'm going to have to find that twat who put such stupid thoughts into your head and slit her throat."

"Listen to her," Piper and Violet both said as they stood on either side of her, caging me in against the counter. "I have more money than God now," Violet continued. "I'll use every penny of it to track down that skank and make sure no one ever finds her body."

Violet was the sweetest person I knew, so if she was contemplating getting rid of bodies, then I knew it was time to move on with this shopping adventure before people started popping up unalived.

"Her entire future has already been flushed down the drain. I think she's gotten her karma for how she treated me." I pulled my hands free from Shaw's hold and grabbed one of the heels. Kicking off the sandal I had on, I stepped into the heeled shoe before doing the same with the other.

When I didn't immediately wobble, I accepted that Shaw was right—just like I had to accept everything else that had been thrown at me in recent months—and added the box to the counter for the saleswoman to ring up. "I'm paying for these."

"No way!" Violet was so much smaller than me, but she stepped in my way like a fierce tigress. Damn Luca for teaching her how to look like a scary linebacker about to charge the offense. "Everything is on me today."

"Vi, it's just a party."

"A party that is partially in your honor," she corrected. "I'm paying for everything, and you're going to let me." Her bottom lip pouted out, and she looked up at me with her pretty purple eyes. "Please?"

And damn me for not being able to say no. To anyone, apparently.

"How does Luca put up with you?" I muttered, crossing my arms over my chest.

Her pout turned into a wicked grin, and she looked down at the huge rock on her hand, but it was Piper who answered. "I think the question should be, how does Vi put up with Luca?"

"We both have our moments." Violet scribbled her name across the bottom of the receipt the saleswoman gave her as she returned her card. "But we make up for it in the bedroom."

CHAPTER 2

DOE

We met Mom and Pixie at the spa, where we spent the next few hours being pampered before the party. It wasn't being held at my parents' house, but at a local restaurant, and since Mom had hired a party planner to handle everything, she was able to relax rather than stress over any last-minute hiccups.

As we all sat together getting pedicures, I watched Mom and Pixie whispering and giggling together, and it made me smile. I loved how close they had become over the months since I'd introduced them. Pixie hadn't had a stable parent growing up, just as Jenner hadn't. She'd basically raised herself. But as she'd endured her final battle with cancer, she'd learned to lean on my mom, who'd gone through a similar journey in her teens.

The two of them had bonded, and I was glad the woman I considered an older sister had become a huge part of my family. Mom had basically adopted Pixie, including her in every family function, down to making sure that she came to dinner at least once a week at the farm. Sometimes Pixie brought Dr. Contreras with her, but more often than not he was working, so she came alone. With my brothers away at college, it was typically only my parents, Pixie, Jenner, and me at our family dinners. It made missing my brothers easier to handle when I stepped into my childhood home.

Once everyone was glammed up and dressed, two blacked-out SUVs were waiting on us outside the spa. One of the drivers was Vi's new bodyguard, Brady. He was a quiet man in his forties, but he took great care of Vi and Love Bug when they had to go anywhere without Luca. His eyes were always shifting, looking for possible dangers, making it impossible to feel comfortable saying anything other than a murmured "Hi" to the man.

I was hustled into the back of an SUV with Piper and Vi—minus the car seat Love Bug typically rode in, giving us more space since she was with her daddy for the day—while the other three took the second vehicle. Sending my cousin a disgruntled side-eye, I adjusted my skirt and put on my seat belt before Brady eased into traffic. "I'm kind of getting tired of everyone pushing me around today. I'm capable of getting into a vehicle on my own."

Piper grasped my hand. "Sorry. I'm just ready for this night to be over. Cannon is going to be there."

Violet gave a soft sigh on the other side of Piper. "He still hasn't completely pulled his head out of his ass," she said with regret. "Ignore him, Piper."

"I'm used to it," she muttered before giving me another regretful glance. "I really am sorry if it seemed as if I was pushing you around."

"Yeah," Vi agreed. "We're all sorry, Doe. I swear we didn't mean to treat you like that. We just wanted to spoil you, and you're so dang stubborn. We have to get all bossy if we want to pamper you."

"Is my stubbornness the reason why Jenner went behind my back and took the police chief job?"

She pressed her lips into a hard line. "I can't tell you why he did that without discussing it with you first. When he told us what his plans were, I thought you were on board with the career change."

Every muscle in my body tensed. "He..." I paused, took a deep breath, and tried again. "He told you about it?"

But not me?

The last three words I left unsaid, but they hung between us as if they had been spoken.

Pressing a hand to her forehead, Violet nodded after a slight hesitation. "Yes, he spoke with Luca and me before he accepted the offer. He wanted our opinion and to make sure I would be okay with a replacement before he took the job."

A feeling of betrayal hit me so hard it nearly knocked the breath from my lungs. Folding my hands in my lap, I turned my head so I was staring out the front window, unable to look at anyone for fear they would see the tears stinging my eyes. "Okay, then," I choked out around the lump in my throat. "I guess that really tells me everything I need to know, doesn't it?"

"Doe—"

"Don't," I snapped, then quickly lowered my voice. This wasn't her fault. It wasn't anyone's fault. Finding out I was the last person on my boyfriend's priority list was a hard pill to swallow. Especially after everything else we'd been through. "I'm sorry."

"Why the fuck are you sorry?" Piper demanded. "You have every right to be pissed off right now. How could he not tell you about his decision to become a cop? If he plans on spending the rest of his life with you, then that's a conversation he should have had with you. Not everyone else. Aunt Marissa and Uncle Wroth. Pixie. Even Luca and Vi? For fuck's sake, Doe. I think I even knew about his plans before you did. And I've been in New York. Jackson, Bryant, and LJ told my brother, who then told me."

"Piper." Violet attempted to intervene. "I don't think for a minute that Jenner made the decision without considering Doe's feelings. If anything, I think it was because of her that he took the job in the first place. To show her that he's ready to settle down in one place. For her."

"Are you telling me that if Luca got offered a starting position with, say, the Seahawks or the Patriots or the Texans, and he took it without even bothering to ask your opinion, you would be okay with that?" The blonde opened her mouth, but Piper cut her off before she could answer. "If he took it, and you were just expected to accept it, to pick up and move your home from Tennessee to a different part of the country, without being allowed to speak your mind, you wouldn't have a problem with it?"

"That's different," Vi tried to argue.

"How?" my cousin gritted out.

"For one, Luca would never do that to me. I'm not saying I wouldn't be on board with relocating, because of course I would go wherever he went." Violet ticked off another finger. "For another, Jenner didn't suddenly decide to pick up and move across the country. He made a choice to stay in West Bridge. To make it his home. He knows that Doe loves West Bridge—"

"Does she, though?" Piper tossed out. "Until recently, only a few people knew, but the citizens of that fucked-up town made her life a living hell. If I had to guess, the only reason she lives there is because that's where her parents are. Where the farm she loves so much is. But if given a choice to leave, I bet you an entire summer of tour profits that she would jump at that shit with both hands and never look back."

"Is that true, Doe?" my friend murmured softly.

Not wanting to answer, I shifted my gaze, but I didn't meet her purple eyes. "I don't feel like talking about this right now."

"Doe—"

"Leave her alone, Violet," Piper commanded. "As her friend, you should have told Doe what Jenner was considering. So many people should have spoken up so that she wasn't blindsided by the man she loves taking on a career that could potentially get him shot at."

"He could just as easily have been shot at as my bodyguard," she countered.

Piper snorted. "Keep telling yourself that, princess. There's no one stupid enough to shoot at your pretty little head. Not when they've seen your man rage out on the football field every Sunday. Face it, protecting you is a cushy job that requires little physical effort. The only thing your bodyguard needs is to be vigilant. Luca will take care of the rest by literally tearing any dumbass apart with his bare hands."

"But—"

"We're here," I said with relief when Brady stopped in front of the restaurant where the party was being held. Wiping my damp palms on the skirt of my dress, I nudged Piper, and she quickly opened her door.

As soon as my feet were on the ground, I didn't wait on everyone else. Instead, I walked into the restaurant, intending to find the bathroom and lock myself inside for a few minutes until I could gather my thoughts.

"Doe?" Mom's voice called out from behind me as I grasped the door handle. "Wait for us!"

Pretending like I didn't hear her, I stepped into the restaurant, only to find the place completely dark. Even though no lights were on, I could sense people gathered close by. Frowning, I carefully walked forward. I saw an "Exit" sign, and I figured there would be a bathroom close to it. Inching my way toward it, I fought the growing panic that clutched at me along with the hurt—the heartbreak.

The door behind me opened, and I sensed the others joining me just as the lights were flipped on, blinding me for a moment. I blinked, my brain trying to play catch-up as I took in the scene before me. Everyone I'd expected to be there was, and then some. Like my brothers, who'd told me they had an away game this weekend so they wouldn't be able to make the party—not that I'd expected them to make the time for something as mundane as a party anyway.

Yet there they were, all three of them, plus Aspen. All four of them dressed in suits. As were Dad and my uncle Liam. Aunt Gabs and Asher were right beside him, both of them dressed for a fancy occasion rather than a casual party. Someone could have mistaken this event for a huge gala or a red-carpet experience because every single person in the room was dressed to the nines.

But what had me taking a stumbling step back was Jenner.

Several feet in front of everyone else.

Down on one knee.

A ring box opened and held out in one hand as he grinned up at me like a fool.

My heartbeat violently in my chest, making my palms damp once again. Every fiber of my being screamed at me to step forward, to hold out my left hand, and tell the man I loved "Yes." To shout it at the top of my lungs.

But my brain was also screaming at me to turn, run, get away from him because if I said yes to him, then I was the one who would be a fool.

He'd gone from the man who showed me every day how much he loved me, to making decisions behind my back. If he wouldn't consult me on such a life-changing choice, how would the rest of our life together be? Did he expect me to just sit around and let him decide everything for us and not say a word?

"Doe?" he rasped when I took another step back. His face lost that huge grin, and my heart lurched when his eyes darkened with hurt. But I was hurting too, damn it. I was the one who had just realized our relationship wasn't as strong as I'd spent the past year blissfully thinking it was.

The entire day began to make sense. Why Vi and Shaw had been so bossy and pushy. They'd been in on the surprise proposal—fuck, they all had. But Vi and Shaw had pushed and pushed, getting me to buy a dress I wouldn't normally wear. And the shoes! I hated the shoes I wore, but I'd put them on to avoid conflict.

Because everything had to be perfect.

I had to be perfect.

But I wasn't fucking perfect!

I never would be.

And Jenner had finally made me see that even to him, I would never be good enough.

Not to consult about his career change.

Not to share his life.

If I was enough, why did I have to dress in clothes that made me feel out of place? Like I had to pretend to be someone I wasn't. If I was truly the one he was supposed to spend his entire life with, then why wasn't I worthy of being asked if he should become West Bridge's chief of police?

Why the fuck did I have to sit back and just accept it all, while everyone around me knew beforehand?

It was my life too, damn it.

CHAPTER 3

JENNER

The instant my eyes found Doe, my heart gave a happy lurch. She looked so damned beautiful in her new dress, wearing a pair of heels that made her long legs look like they went on forever. I barely took in all that beauty before I was overcome by the urge to hide her away from every eye in the room as jealousy ate at me.

But then she took a step back, instead of forward as I'd played out in my head for weeks as I'd planned this moment with her parents', Violet's, and Shaw's help. I'd even gotten her brothers there, which had been no small feat, considering they were in the middle of baseball season.

Everyone who didn't know what the party was really for had been informed once they arrived at the restaurant. As soon as the women were a block away, Pixie had texted me, and I'd gotten into position while someone turned off the lights. Nervousness was the last thing I'd felt as the door had opened once, and then again moments later.

But as I watched the emotions flicker across Doe's gorgeous face, I realized that maybe I shouldn't have been so confident in her accepting my proposal.

My stomach churned as she took another step back, away from me, bumping into the women behind her. Piper grasped her elbow to steady her while Vi moved in closer. "Doe, just talk to him."

Why the fuck did we need to talk?

I wanted to shout the question as she backed farther away, inching her way closer toward the door.

"What happened from the time we left the spa until now?" Marissa hissed. "She was all smiles—"

"Aunt Marissa, I love you," Piper bit out. "But if you thought she was all smiles, you seriously need a pair of glasses. She's been upset all day, and it's only gotten worse the closer it came to time for the party."

I jerked to my feet, shoving the ring box into my suit jacket pocket. "Little lamb?" I spoke her nickname softly, as if I were speaking to a spooked animal. She looked like a deer caught in the headlights of an oncoming semi, her skin a sickly color while tears filled her blue eyes. Flinching at the sound of my voice, she took another step backward.

"I-I can't do this," she whispered, the tears glittering like diamonds in her eyes. "I-I-I'm sorry. I just... I can't."

Turning, she made a run for it and was out the door before I could form words.

"The fuck just happened?" Jackson demanded from right behind me. "I thought this would be a wham-bam, yes-ma'am proposal, and then we'd have cake."

"Obviously, Doe is upset," Aspen muttered. "I'll go talk to her."

I didn't give him the chance to follow her because I was already running. Thankfully, she was in heels and couldn't move as quickly as she would have if she were in boots or flats. I saw her get into the back of the second SUV parked in front of the restaurant, and I jogged over to follow her inside. The driver gave me lifted brows from the front seat, but I gave a nod for him to exit. The back door closed behind me before Doe even realized it.

"Go away!" she sobbed, scooting across the back seat. "Leave me alone. I'm sorry, but please. I can't do this."

"Baby," I groaned. "What happened? Why are you crying?"

She scrubbed both hands over her face. "Just get out. I want to go..." Her voice trailed off, and she started crying harder. "I don't even know where I want to go. Not home. Where the hell is home now, huh? I don't want to live in the middle of town!"

Frustrated, I tried to reach for her again, but she flinched away. "Okay," I choked out. "You don't want to live in the house I bought for us, that's fine. We'll buy something else."

"Bought?" she squeaked. "I thought you rented that house."

"I closed on it last week," I admitted. "Your parents thought it would be a nice starter house for us."

Her tears still poured down her face, but the sobs suddenly stopped. "You bought a house without talking to me first? A house you actually expected me to live in with you? Surrounded by people I can't stand?"

I didn't understand. Not even a little bit. What was wrong with the people in the town of West Bridge? Why the fuck couldn't she stand them? Hadn't her brothers and I worked with Mieke to destroy her bullies? Courtney Wilcox was still in hiding because we'd ruined her life so thoroughly in retaliation for the hell she and her minions had put Doe through during high school.

Locking those questions away for later, I tried to explain. "Your parents—"

"You aren't planning on spending your life with my parents!" she shouted, cutting me off. "You were down on one knee with a fucking ring in your hand, Jenner. I'm going to assume you were planning to ask me to marry you. But instead of talking to me about the house you bought, you asked my parents. Just like your damn job."

She practically spat the last word at me, and it was only then that I realized she wasn't happy about my career change. As if my brain hit rewind, I replayed every moment since making the announcement to her that I'd accepted the chief of police position in West Bridge. Recalling her reactions now, I realized her smiles hadn't reached her eyes, her congratulations had been monotone, her arms not quite fully wrapping around me when I'd swung her up into my arms.

Fuck, how had I missed it?

How the hell had I gotten it all wrong?

I'd had help every step of the way to get settled in and then plan the proposal. Marissa and Wroth. Pixie. Violet and Shaw. Everything should have been perfect, but I realized in that moment that I'd gone about everything the wrong way. Swallowing the knot in my throat that threatened to choke me, I tried to explain again.

"The mayor and Chief Stafford know your parents, and both men asked them to speak to me about the job. I only took it because it meant I didn't have to travel, and I didn't have to guess when I would be home or who the fuck knew where with Violet from one week to the next." Anxiety and fear of not knowing how to fix what I didn't even know I'd broken made my voice rise. "I wanted to surprise you, show you how committed I was to settling down in West Bridge to make you happy before I asked you to marry me."

Anger flashed through her eyes as she glared at me across the seat. "You made two life-changing decisions that I should have been consulted on, especially if you were contemplating asking me to marry you. You want to get married, but from where I'm sitting, you don't even know what that means."

My brows pulled together as my heart began to pound harder against my rib cage.

"Marriage is a partnership, damn it!" she cried. "But nothing about what you've done in the past few months suggests you're ready to be anyone's partner in life, especially not mine."

"No," I whispered. "No, I'm ready. I swear to you, I'm more than ready. I...I was just trying to show you—"

"What? That you're going to spend our married life making all the big choices without once asking me about them? That I'm supposed to sit back and allow you to control my life while I have zero say in it?" She turned so she was facing the back of the driver's seat, her arms wrapping around herself as if she was cold. "Thanks, but I think I'll pass."

"Doe." My voice was raspy with emotion, but her gaze didn't so much as flicker in my direction. "Little lamb—"

"I think we should break up."

My heart stopped, causing the blood in my veins to turn to ice. All I could see was the side of her face. A tear spilled down her cheek, but from the set of her chin, I had no doubt that she wasn't playing with me.

"I'm going to move back to the farm. Luckily, everything is already packed, so I'll send a few of the farmhands to pick up my stuff." She tightened her arms around herself, and another tear dripped off the tip of her lashes.

"No, stop it. Talk to me about this." I grasped her elbow and gently pulled until her hand was in mine. Her fingers were cold as ice even though the temperature outside was above average for a spring day in Nashville. "You're going to just walk away without even attempting to work this out?"

Slowly, she shifted her head. "You already have everything worked out, Jenner. You've got your new job and a house right beside two of the most upstanding families of West Bridge, Tennessee. Your future is already laid out, and I'm sure from where you are standing, it looks promising. But from here, I can't see where I could possibly fit into this new life you've chosen for yourself. Not once did you pause and ask me if I was okay with you becoming a cop. You didn't hesitate to buy a house you expected me to live in that was right between two families who've shunned me if they saw me at the grocery store or simply walking down Main Street. Grown women who've whispered about me just loud enough for me to hear the nasty things they were saying as I passed them. Calling me inbred and Godzilla. Cackling like the witches they are about how the Niall farm had so many cows because I probably ate an entire steer for dinner each night. Old men who looked at me like I had two heads whenever I helped load fifty-pound bags of grain from the feed store."

"What?" I had to work hard to keep my voice from rising at this new information. "They were mean to you?"

"Everyone but a very few people in West Bridge has always been horrible to me."

"Baby, why didn't you say something? I know about Courtney and the bullies in school, but—"

"Because it was embarrassing!" She scrubbed her free hand across her cheeks, wiping away tears that were quickly replaced by more as they dropped freely from her pretty eyes. "Who wants to admit that nearly every single person in their hometown seems to take pleasure in making nasty, snide comments about them?" She released a dry, pained laugh. "And they knew I would never say a word about it, because I refused to be the reason my parents suddenly developed feuds with people they had grown up with. Or risk my brothers doing anything to get themselves in trouble with the law and ruining their futures. I put on a smile and pretended that what people said about me behind my back didn't bother me, when the entire time, all I could think about was one day moving out of this stupid hick town."

"You should have told me. I would have—"

"You know, I've had to put up with a lot of people walking over me my entire life. The adults in West Bridge. The bullies at school. Sometimes, even my own family. Although I'm not sure they realized what they were doing." Those glittery, tear-filled eyes looked up at me with so much pain, it pushed the air from my body. "But I never thought you would do it too. It never once entered my mind that you would trample all over my feelings and make me feel like I wasn't worthy of being with you."

"Doe, baby, please listen," I begged. "I didn't mean for any of this to turn out the way it has. Hurting you was the last thing I would ever want to do. If I ever do it again in the future, you have to speak up. To me or anyone else who makes you feel less than you are. Because, little lamb, you are everything. We don't have to live in West Bridge. We can go anywhere you want. I have money saved. I can buy us another house. Anywhere you want, in any state. Fuck, any country you want. Let's go back to the apartment and grab the boxes and just leave. Right now."

A small, pained sound left her. "It doesn't matter anymore. I love being close to my parents. The farm is mine, Jenner. I'm the one who takes care of it now that my dad has basically retired. The foreman answers to me. It's where I've always been the most at ease—except for when I was beside you." She shrugged. "That's why moving away was just a passing thought. I had my parents, the animals, a few honorary family members who lived just a few miles away in either direction. And you. I had you, and life was perfect."

Teas burned my throat, stinging my eyes as they filled them, making it hard to see her. "You still have me."

"No, you stopped being mine the moment you started making decisions about our future without including me."

"I made a mistake. More than one. I'll own that. Give me five minutes, and I'll rectify it all." I grabbed my phone from my slacks pocket with my free hand while still clinging to her with the other. "Just... I just need to make a few phone calls. We can start this entire day over. I'll tell Stafford and Teller they have to find someone else for the job. I'll call a real estate agent and put the house back on the market. We can..."

My fingers shook as I flipped through my contacts, unable to read any of the names. Ah, fuck. I needed to see so I could call the mayor and the ex-police chief and tell them to find someone else. I couldn't lose my little lamb over something as unimportant as a job, damn it. "We'll move wherever you want. Buy a farm of our own. You'll be able to choose everything. Where we live, the house, where I work."

She grabbed my phone out my hand and angrily tossed it into the front seat. "Keep the job and the house you already have. I won't be the reason you give up two things you wanted so badly that you forgot all about me."

"I didn't forget about you!" I exploded in frustration, the tears spilling over, making it hard to breathe. To fucking speak. "You were the reason I wanted the house and the job, damn it. They were for us. For our future."

"There was nothing 'our' about any of it, Jenner. They were your choices." Jerking her hand out of mine, she reached for the door handle, and I struggled to find the words to stop her.

Before she opened it, she paused, causing my heart to lift with hope that she would give me a chance to correct the shit I'd inadvertently fucked up. Taking a deep, steadying breath, she destroyed me when she whispered, "I'll have all my things out of the apartment by tonight."

CHAPTER 4

DOE

After I tripped over a crack in the sidewalk for the third time, I stopped and pulled off the ridiculous heels. Going barefoot on the streets of Nashville was a safer bet than breaking my neck in the shoes I'd been pushed into wearing.

Tears poured down my face as I looked down at the stiletto heels in disgust. I had no idea where I was going, but I knew I couldn't return to the restaurant. I'd already embarrassed myself enough in front of my entire family for one day. How I was going to face any of them now, even my own parents, I didn't have a clue.

Angrily, I tossed the shoes into a trash bin as I passed it. I didn't know who I was more upset with. Jenner, my parents, or myself.

How could my mom and dad just go behind my back and help Jenner like that? It was as if they didn't even know me. They'd helped him find a job and, no doubt, the house he'd bought. But there was no way they could have thought I would be on board with any of it...

Then again, they had been known to run over top of me more than once throughout my life. I didn't know if they realized what they were doing, or if they just thought they were helping. Maybe Dad thought he was protecting me. He could be a little overzealous about that. But this... All of this was too much.

I was an adult, whether they wanted to see it or not. The worst part was, they never did shit like this when it came to my brothers. They never interfered with those three. When the boys decided to go to Arkansas for college so they could play baseball together, my parents had been overjoyed. They were states away, rarely came home even on breaks, but Mom and Dad didn't try to run their lives.

Why the hell were they intent on controlling mine?

If I were truly honest, I was more pissed at myself.

I'd allowed it all to unfold.

When Jenner suddenly announced his career change, I'd forced a grin and gone along with it. Because if he was happy, then I'd find a way to be happy for him. Loving him meant supporting him. Then he'd told me he'd found us a house—and apparently bought it before I could even look inside the damn thing. Maybe it wouldn't have been so bad if it weren't for the neighbors. Although, I wasn't sure if living beside different residents of West Bridge would have been any better. With the exception of Aspen, Aunt Dallas's father and stepmother, Luca, and now Shaw since she and Jagger had bought a house near Violet, no one else in town had ever treated me like anything but a freak.

For most of my life, the farm had been the only thing that had held me to West Bridge. After moving in with Jenner, it had taken a back seat from time to time. But I'd been stupid to think it was safe anywhere off the land I'd grown up on. In the end, Jenner wasn't the safe place I needed.

The farm was my only solace. The one place where I could be myself and not have to worry about anyone whispering and laughing at me behind my back—or to my face. But now, it no longer felt like home. Not when my parents had already proven they couldn't be trusted—just like I couldn't trust Jenner.

I had nowhere to go. I was basically homeless and still needed to figure out what I was going to do with the boxes of my stuff back in the apartment above Luca's garage.

"Doe!"

I stiffened when I heard my name shouted. Hesitantly, I glanced over my shoulder and, through my tears, saw my brothers and Aspen running toward me. I turned slowly, waiting for them to catch up. As they neared, I put up both hands to stop them. "Did you three know about any of this?"

Bryant and LJ bent in half, hands on their knees as they tried to catch their breath. It was only then that I realized how far I'd walked since leaving Jenner in front of the restaurant. Jackson was struggling to catch his breath too, but it was Aspen who, while sweaty and exerted, wrapped his arms around me. "We didn't know anything, sweet pea. The only thing we were told was that Jenner was proposing to you today, so we made sure we were here for it."

Squeezing my eyes closed, I nodded, believing him. After I'd donated my bone marrow to Pixie, Jackson had gotten his head out of his ass—for the most part—and had taken the step to ask Aspen to transfer to Arkansas to be with him. Neither of them had actually come out and announced they were together, but I knew they were in a relationship. Now, if they would just tell our parents. As for Aspen's mom and dad, fuck them. They were homophobic bigots who would rather Aspen be dead than gay.

At this point, I was sure Jackson hadn't said anything to anyone other than our brothers and me because of Aspen. I was just glad they were finally together and happy. That was all that mattered to me.

With my friend hugging me, I was able to let go. A sob ripped its way out of my throat, and I felt myself go weak. "Wh-what am I going to do?" I whispered brokenly as I pressed my face into his chest, my hands balled into fists around the material of his designer dress shirt. "I-I don't h-have any...anywhere to go."

Aspen rubbed his hands up and down my back soothingly. "Shh, don't cry. We'll figure everything out. There's no need to worry."

Suddenly, I was surrounded on all sides, each of my brothers joining the group hug. I felt all of them kiss the top of my head, their warmth and strength trying to chase away the chill I hadn't realized had invaded my body until they were there, holding me up.

"Let's go back to my apartment," Aspen suggested. "It's not far from here. We can sit down and talk."

Unable to speak for the lump in my throat choking me, I nodded.

"Doe, where the fuck are your shoes?" Jackson demanded.

I shrugged, not sure how far back it had been when I'd tossed them into the trash.

Muttering a curse, the eldest of my brothers lifted me into his arms. "LJ, get us a cab."

Turning my head, I buried my face in Jackson's neck and just let the tears flow. It was a long while later before I could bring myself to lift my head. We were sitting in the kitchen of Aspen's apartment. Although he'd transferred to Arkansas for college back in the fall, he'd still kept his apartment. He'd bought it with his own money, so he would always have a place to stay when he was in Tennessee, as if my parents wouldn't let him stay with them if he ever needed a place to sleep.

A hot mug of herbal tea had been pressed into my hands, but I couldn't bring myself to take a sip as I sat there staring into the delicate cup.

"You need to tell us what happened, Doe," Bryant finally urged. "We saw Jenner when we came looking for you, and he looked like he was contemplating swallowing a bullet."

Flinching, I set the cup in the saucer and pushed it away from me, unsure if the liquid would stay down if I did attempt to swallow it. "We broke up," I was able to get out in a hoarse voice.

"What?" all four of them exclaimed at the same time.

"Why?" LJ demanded.

"What did he do?" Bryant followed up.

"Did you fall out of love with him?" Aspen murmured.

"No!" I cried, my eyes widening on my best friend. "Why would you think that?"

"It's the only explanation I could come up with for why you would break up with the man who had been down on his knees, ready to ask you to marry him," he answered with a shrug.

Squeezing the bridge of my nose, I slowly recounted everything that had happened, most of which I'd only found out earlier in the day. Quietly, they listened, not interrupting me, even though I could tell they were itching to ask questions.

"I need to get my boxes out of the apartment," I muttered when I finished. "At least everything is already packed up."

"If you really don't want to live with Jenner, or at the farm with your parents, you can stay here," Aspen offered.

"She's not living here alone!" Jackson growled.

"Why not?" his boyfriend countered. "The security is good, and she doesn't really have another option. Unless she wants to come back to Arkansas with us."

They had a three-bedroom apartment off campus. Something our parents had found for them over the summer before their sophomore year. Everyone knew that Aspen lived with them, but no one ever asked where he slept since there were four of them, but only three beds.

"Yes," Bryant and LJ rushed to agree. "Come back with us, Doe."

"Yeah, sis. Bryant and I will get a set of bunk beds, and you can take my room," LJ enticed. "The four of us will be back together. Where we belong."

I was already shaking my head. "You guys are going into the draft in July. I don't want to be stuck in Arkansas all by myself. I want space from Mom and Dad, but not that much."

"Which is why you should stay here," Aspen said with a decisive nod. "I'll use one of the trucks at the dealership, and we'll go to West Bridge to grab your things."

"I-I don't want to go," I said, drawing my arms around myself. The day's events had exhausted me, and all I wanted to do was curl into a ball and fall asleep.

"You don't need to," my friend said as he got to his feet. "Are all your boxes labeled?"

"Mostly," I confirmed. "There were a few things that we put in the same boxes. Like kitchen and living room supplies. But my toiletries are in their own box. So are my books. And there are two big suitcases full of my clothes, as well as one smaller one. I'm not really worried about anything but my clothes and bathroom supplies."

"Don't worry, sweet pea. We'll get everything you need." Aspen bent to kiss the top of my head. "Come on, you three. We need to get this taken care of tonight since we have an early morning flight tomorrow."

One by one, they stood, kissed my brow, and followed Aspen. As the door shut behind them, my phone rang. Frowning, I pulled it out of the pocket of my skirt. Seeing it was my mom, I sent it to voice mail. But as soon as it stopped ringing, it began again. This time from Dad. I did the same with him, not wanting to speak to either of my parents.

Pixie's name popped up on my screen next, followed by Vi, then Piper. I almost answered my cousin's call, but everything felt too raw. Instead, I texted her.

> Me: I'm safe. Just need a little time to figure out what to do next.
> Piper: Everyone is freaking out. Jenner is a mess, and your parents are beside themselves. I've never seen Aunt Marissa so upset. I told her she only has herself to blame, but my dad told me to keep my mouth shut. Did you really break up with Jenner?

My head was pounding from all the crying and the chaos my life had suddenly turned into, but I still replied.

> Me: Yes. We're over.
> Piper: Tell me where you are. I won't tell anyone, but I don't like that you're alone.

Biting my lip, I contemplated sending her the address, but in the end, I just turned off my phone. On shaking legs, I got to my feet and stumbled through the apartment. There were two bedrooms, the master and a guest. I chose the latter. Not bothering to turn on a light, I crawled into bed and closed my eyes. Sleep took me while the tears still spilled down my cheeks.

CHAPTER 5

JENNER

Scrubbing my hands over my face, I dropped down onto the couch in the living room. Beside me, the cushion shifted, and I glanced over at Pixie.

"You haven't said anything since you came back inside after talking to Doe," she said, staring at me with wide, sad eyes. "I thought this was going to be a great day, but instead, everyone was crying. And not the happy tears I was imagining."

"I fucked up."

Her brows pulled together, the baby-fine hair she'd been able to style into—ironically—a pixie cut, shifting on her forehead. "How?"

Inhaling slowly, I leaned my head back against the couch and glared up at the ceiling. "She thinks I went behind her back and made decisions that we should have made together. In her mind, I excluded her from important things, and she assumes that will be how the rest of our life together will be."

She slapped me across the chest. It was a light tap, but the intent was there, causing me to snap my head up and frown at my sister. "You idiot. Of course she would think that. Fucking hell, Jenn. I thought you asked her about the job and the house. Wait... That is what she's upset over, right? You didn't go and do anything else without telling her, did you?"

"No!" I hadn't really wanted to keep those two things from her, but her parents had insisted they would be great surprises for her. My gut had told me to just go ahead and talk to Doe about everything, but Marissa was so damn convincing at the time. Her blue eyes, so like her daughter's, had stared up at me in a way that had me caving in no time.

"But you didn't talk to her about taking the job? And the house...?" My silence was answer enough, and she jumped to her feet, pacing in front of me. "Okay, the job thing is iffy. That was your choice, but still, you should have at least talked to her about it. But the house? Why would you not include her in something that ginormous? She has to live there too. A woman wants to be a part of choosing her home. The location, the layout, all of those are important factors that anyone would want to have a say in."

"I guess, but she said it was more to do with the neighbors."

She stopped midstep and shot around to face me, her hands going to her tiny hips. "What about the neighbors?"

I gripped the back of my neck and squeezed as hard as I could, my stomach churning. "They were mean to her. Are still mean to her, from what I've put together."

"What?" she whispered, her eyes blazing.

"Apparently almost everyone in this town has been, or still is, cruel to her." I didn't understand that. How could anyone mistreat Doe? She was so sweet. My precious little lamb was the most selfless person I knew. She'd decided to give a piece of herself to Pixie before she even knew her. Without Doe's sacrifice, my sister most likely wouldn't have been standing in front of me right then.

Doe's heart was bigger than the moon, and yet, the citizens of this small town got off on bullying her?

"You told me you took care of her bullies." Pixie went back to pacing. "You said that you and her brothers destroyed them all."

"Obviously, there were more that she didn't tell anyone about." No one in that fucked-up town deserved to breathe the same air as Doe, but I hadn't even realized it. And now I was just as unworthy as those motherfuckers.

"What did they do to her?" Pixie was getting all worked up. A feral older sister, ready to take on anyone and everything that caused harm to someone she loved.

"I don't know all of it," I told her honestly, my own temper rising as I remembered what Doe had told me earlier. "But she said they would call her inbred and Godzilla."

"Marissa and Wroth knew about this?"

"Do you really think if her parents knew about it, they would have talked me into buying a house right between those two evil bitches?" I raked my hands through my short hair. "I have to sell the house. The sooner, the better. Maybe I can find us a place closer to Nashville. Anywhere besides this goddamn town."

"But she's happy here," Pixie said as she chewed on her bottom lip. "I mean, she's always seemed happy here. I never got the impression she was unhappy."

"Because she's an angel," I whispered. "She tries to see the good in everyone, even when they've done nothing but treat her like dirt. And it's not like she would do anything to upset her family. If she even hinted that anyone caused her pain, her brothers would murder everyone in their wake. For their sake, she never said anything, to keep them out of trouble."

"Unacceptable!" Pixie snapped. "I want names. Every single person who ever treated Doe as anything other than the most precious person on this messed-up planet. They will all pay for hurting her."

"I couldn't agree more," a deep voice said from the open doorway, causing us both to turn to find Doe's three brothers and Aspen standing in the doorway. Jackson stepped inside without bothering to wait to be invited. "And I think we'll start with you, dickhead."

Pixie jumped in front of me, using her small, fragile body as a human shield between me and the four angry guys stomping toward me. Grasping her by the waist, I lifted her and set her beside me before facing them again. "Where is she?"

"I think you gave up the chance to be worthy of caring about anything concerning my sister when you stopped including her in your life choices," Bryant answered, while LJ and Aspen walked behind the couch. Each of them grabbed a box that was labeled with Doe's name, and my vision dimmed.

"Wh-what are you doing?" I choked out, ignoring Bryant and Jackson so I could grab the box of books from LJ.

"We told Doe we would get her things," Aspen answered.

"Where is she?" I asked again, my voice rising.

"Not in West Bridge," LJ said with a shrug as he picked up another box with his sister's name labeled on it in her pretty handwriting. "Guys, grab a box. We should only have to make a few trips to the truck."

"She's not at the farm?" Pixie attempted to ask, getting in their way when they would have walked to the door.

Bryant sighed heavily when she kept stepping in his path. "Pixie, we don't have time to play these games. Doe is alone and hurting. The quicker we grab her things, the sooner we can get back to her."

"So, that's a no?" She stubbornly continued to block his way to the door. "Does that mean she's in Nashville?"

"Pixie, I need you to move."

"Which hotel?" she asked, grasping his arm. "She and Jenner need to talk this out."

Bryant shot me a scathing look from across the room. "He had his chance, and he blew it."

"He fucked up!" Pixie stomped her foot. "But he deserves to know if she's okay and where she is. All of this was a misunderstanding that can be sorted out if Doe will just meet him halfway."

"And what is halfway?" Bryant demanded. "Why is it that she has to be the one to compromise on anything to do with her future? Everyone wants her to move in the direction they want her to. Wear the clothes they want her to wear, live where they want her to live, be the person they think she should be. Everyone has done that to her all her life, and sadly, even we have been stupid enough to do it a time or two to get our own ways. But she's a grown-ass woman now, and she can do whatever the fuck she wants. It's her life, and no one is going to make her do anything she doesn't feel comfortable doing."

"I'm selling the house," I broke in. "And I'll tell the mayor first thing tomorrow to find someone else for the job."

"Yeah, she said you already made that offer," Jackson said as he stacked two boxes on top of each other and lifted them with ease. "I doubt she's any more interested in you making that sacrifice now than she was then."

"I'm trying here, guys," I told them, feeling defeat inching its way into my soul. "But I have no idea how to fix any of this."

LJ came back into the living room after having taken his first load of boxes out. "What happened to the guy who told us he foresaw Doe smiling until you two took your last breaths? My sister in a wedding dress. A house with all the horses she wants, and as many babies as she was willing to give you." He cocked his head at me. "Were those just words you spewed to get us to back off and welcome you to the family, or did you mean any of that shit? Because my sister sure as fuck isn't smiling now, and that wedding dress? She doesn't appear to want it anymore."

"And how the fuck did you plan on giving her as many horses as she wanted in a house in the middle of town?" Bryant spoke up.

"Your parents thought it would make a good starter house," I tried to explain. Frustrated, I raked my fingers through the short hairs of my beard. "It wasn't supposed to be our forever home. Just a place to call our own for a little while."

"Until when?" LJ asked, putting his hands on the back of the couch and leaning forward. "A year? Two? Five? When would she have gotten the horses—or the babies?"

"I don't know!" I shouted. "I was only focused on right now. On making her my wife. The rest of the details would come later."

"What he means is that he would give them to her when Mom and Dad decided it was time," Jackson said. "Just like they thought it was time for Jenner to settle down with a local job. In a house within driving distance."

The other three men inhaled sharply. "Of course it fucking was," Bryant and LJ muttered angrily. I hated when they spoke at the same time. They were the identical ones of the quads, and Doe had once jokingly said that they shared the same brain as well as the same face. But when they spoke in unison, it was like a weird movie sound effect. The same, yet not.

"They were losing control," Jackson explained when I just stood there, staring at him in confusion. "No doubt they sensed you were about to propose, and they wanted to control what happened with Doe when that finally happened."

"Your parents are the least controlling people I know," Pixie argued, getting defensive. She and Marissa were close. Doe's mom was the first real parental figure she'd ever had, and she was loyal to everyone in her heart.

"Sure," Jackson agreed. "When it comes to us boys. They couldn't care less. As long as we're happy and staying out of trouble, they don't have a care in the world. But with Doe, it's always been different. Especially with Dad. Doe is our mother's replica. If she's not close by, then he gets twitchy. It isn't as bad as it is with Mom, but still, he has to be in control of certain aspects, or he goes dark."

"That's not how it was..." My voice trailed off, my argument fading as I rethought everything. "Was it?"

"Think about it, man," Jackson said, his anger with me fading. "Who came to you regarding the job?"

"Marissa and Wroth," I answered honestly as the realization of how badly I'd been played fully hit me. "The mayor and the chief of police knew my background in the marines, and—"

"They knew, all right. Probably after Dad talked to them about your credentials. And let's be honest, you probably are a better fit for the police chief position than the rest of those idiots on the payroll. But no way Mayor Teller came up with your name on his own. He's too full of himself to notice anything unless it will get him votes. It was probably the other way around. Mom and Dad went to him and put that little bug in his ear. And because no one wants to say no to my mother—and they're too scared of Dad—the mayor decided you were the best man for the job."

"Makes sense." Bryant nodded. "Jenner wouldn't be traveling so much with Violet, which means Doe wouldn't get the idea in her head to start traveling with him. Something that Vi would be all for, because she adores Doe. And then there's Love Bug. Doe has babysat for her in the past. Even Luca is comfortable with her taking care of his little princess. What's to say she wouldn't become their traveling nanny?"

"Yeah, a stable local job was needed to make Dad feel at ease," LJ put in.

"And the house?" Pixie asked curiously, her voice wobbling ever so slightly with the realization that the brothers were onto something. Marissa and Wroth had used me to control Doe.

Fuck!

"With Jenner no longer Vi's bodyguard, the replacement would need a place to stay, so Doe would be shopping for a new place to live. And if Jenner is right about the fine citizens of West Bridge treating her like shit, then she would want something outside of town. Mom and Dad couldn't risk the happy couple finding a place too far away. My guess is they needed something in a hurry and just picked whatever house was big enough to suit Doe and Jenner's needs for the moment." Jackson cocked his head. "Did they tell you to keep it hush-hush, or was that your idea?"

"I..." It was their suggestion, but I was stumbling, trying to figure out how I'd been stupid enough to listen to them when they had insisted I keep everything quiet.

"Poor idiot doesn't know," LJ said with a sad shake of his head. "That means it was Mom who got into his head. Convinced him it was his own idea."

"She said Doe would be happy for us to have our own place, that it would be the perfect surprise after proposing," I recalled, feeling gut-punched.

"They played you, man." Bryant had already set his boxes down on the floor and slapped me on the back. "Through you, they controlled Doe."

"Ya know, we were going to kick your ass after we got all of Doe's boxes," Jackson informed me, his face completely serious. "But since we see that this mostly wasn't your fault—mostly, not completely, you still went along with all their shit—we're not going to beat on you."

CHAPTER 6

DOE

A door banging open startled me awake. Heart pounding, yet disoriented from sleep, I sat upright, my eyes flickering around in search of danger. Grabbing the blanket, I pulled it up over me just as the bedroom door opened. I had no time to react as someone crossed to me and lifted me as if I weighed no more than a sack of potatoes.

My hands flew out, slapping away whoever held me, but he was already moving back to the open door, the only light coming from the living room. When I saw the outline of Jenner's jaw, I started slapping at his arms harder. "Put me down!"

He grunted as he stomped to the front door and out into the corridor. Seeing my brothers standing in the open elevator, my jaw went slack for a moment before hurt filled my chest. "Traitors!"

Aspen slunk back against the wall, trying to hide behind Jackson and Bryant as LJ hit the button for the lobby.

"I see you, Williams. Don't try to hide behind these assholes."

No one spoke to me as the elevator descended, but they talked among themselves as if I weren't trying to wiggle free of Jenner's arms. "Piper is already at the house," Bryant said as he texted away on his phone. "We need to get there before she goes nuclear on Mom and Dad."

"You're the one who included her in this," Jackson complained. "It would have been easier if it were just us. But you said Piper would be a good ally."

"She and Pixie will be the female support team that Doe needs. If it's just us guys, she'll feel outnumbered and won't listen."

"Then maybe you should have called Violet instead," LJ suggested. "She's the sweet one."

"Vi means Luca, and we all know that he can be unpredictable. When in doubt, you go with the devil you know, not the one who can flip a switch in the blink of his swirling eyes."

"I don't know what you idiots are talking about, but as soon as I'm on my feet, I'm going to kick you all in the balls!" I shouted as the elevator door slid open, and everyone stepped off.

Outside, Jenner carried me to his car, where Bryant opened the back door. Jenner placed me inside, then nudged me over so he could get in next to me, while LJ got behind the wheel. Meanwhile, Aspen and Jackson got into a truck I didn't recognize, and then Bryant took shotgun in the car.

While they were getting settled, I tried to escape through the other back door, but the child locks were engaged. "Motherfuckers!" I screeched, pounding a fist against the window. "LJ, you let me out of this car right now, or I'll tell everyone who set off the fireworks in the library junior year and caused it to catch on fire."

"Bro, that was you?" Bryant asked with a laugh. "I thought it was Jackson."

"Nope," our brother said proudly. "Overheard the librarian running her mouth."

"About?"

Bryant and Jenner asked at almost the same time.

LJ's eyes caught mine in the rearview mirror. "Precious things," he said softly before pulling out into traffic.

Embarrassed, because I could only imagine what the old crone had been saying about me, I shifted my gaze out the side window. Even the teachers at school had been horrible. I didn't know that LJ had known about the librarian, though. I'd thought he'd done it for no other reason than boredom. No one had ever caught him, and as far as I knew, I was the only one who knew it had been him. It wasn't like I would have narced on him, not when it would have meant he would have faced criminal charges for destruction of property and arson.

"She got what she had coming to her," he muttered, and the car grew silent again.

Beside me, Jenner gently urged me to sit back. I smacked his hand away from my shoulder, but he only reached for the seat belt and tried to fasten it around me.

"I'm not a child," I snapped. "I can put on the damned thing if I want it on."

"Please put it on," he said in a hoarse voice. "I can't stand the thought of something hurting you."

"You should have thought about that before—"

"Doe!" Bryant snapped from the front passenger seat, turning to give me the same look our dad tended to give us when someone was misbehaving. "Put on the goddamn seat belt. Stop and just listen! Everyone in this car fucking loves you, and we don't want you to be harmed if we're in an accident."

Stubbornly, I sat there glaring at my brother. "What happened to picking up my stuff? Instead, you guys came back with Jenner, and I don't see any of my boxes. Thanks for proving that I can't even trust the three people who were supposed to always have my back. Just like everyone else in the world who claims to love me. You're like the rest of them, Bryant. Unreliable."

He flinched but didn't argue with me. Jaw clenched, he shifted so he was facing the front window once again.

"Doe—" LJ began, but Bryant cut him off.

"Don't. She doesn't know yet, and now isn't the time. Doe has every right to be upset right now."

"What don't I know?" I demanded angrily. "That even my brothers, the people I shared a womb with, can't put me first? I've done nothing but consider the three of you and your feelings my entire life. I've put all of you before myself. Your happiness was always more important to me than my own. And not a single one of you could even do something as small as getting my stuff back for me." Tears snuck up on me, and two spilled free before I could stop them. "Well, I'm tired of putting everyone else's needs over my own. I'm tired of being the one who gets walked all over. I'm done, period."

"No one asked you to put our needs over your own!" Bryant exploded. "If anything, I'm pissed as fuck that you did that, Doe. How dare you let stupid people hurt your heart for years. You just sat back and took it. You put your mental health at risk for people who don't deserve to walk the same streets as you. For what?" he shouted. "Me? LJ and Jackson? We aren't worth such sacrifice. But you? You are our baby sister and the most precious person in the world, second to no one."

"If I'm so precious to you, then where is my stuff?" I shot back.

"Don't worry about your shit," he growled. "Soon, you're going to know everything, and then you can decide what happens to your things. Until then, you remember something, baby sis." He reached out and took one of my hands. I balled my fingers into a fist, but he gently wrapped his around them. "Remember that we will do anything to ensure your happiness. Even if it means burning West Bridge to the ground to accomplish it."

Unease settled over me. "What does that mean?"

He didn't answer.

"Bryant, what does that mean?"

When he remained silent, and LJ avoided looking in the rearview mirror, I leaned forward. "Bryant? Tell me what you meant."

"It means that no one is going to walk all over your feelings again, Doe," he finally said. "Especially the people of West Bridge, Tennessee."

I jerked back, already fearing what my brothers would do—the impact the results would have on their futures. July was so close, and then they would get drafted and I wouldn't have to worry about them so much. But until then, they had to stay out of trouble.

Scared of what they were planning, and why, I turned to Jenner. "You told them about why I don't want to live in the house." It came out as a statement, because I already knew the answer. The way his jaw clenched was the only reply I expected, but it still felt like a direct blow to my heart. "Will there ever be anything that stays yours and mine? Why does everyone else get to know our secrets? Was I blind this entire time, thinking we were equals in this relationship?"

In the passing lights, I saw his throat bob several times. Even as hurt and angry as I was with him, all I could think was how good he looked. The short beard, the strong jawline. His wide shoulders that took up most of the back seat. We'd made love just that morning before I went shopping with Violet and the others. I'd whimpered how much I loved him as he'd finished inside me. Everything had been right in the world at that moment. There was no thinking about his new job or moving. It was just the two of us, and for a mere moment in time, it was as if the rest of the world didn't exist.

"I know you don't believe me right now, little lamb," Jenner rasped. "But from here on out, it will only be you and me. No outside influences. No making any decisions without talking it out first. You are all that matters to me. I promise, my only goal has been to make you happy. Now I see the mistakes I made, and I'm trying to rectify them."

"By continuing to lock me out?" I countered. "How can I believe anything you say when you just dropped me into the back of this car like a bag of trash? You haven't told me where we're going or why. I trusted you with my heart, Jenner. I gave you a piece of myself I've never trusted anyone else with in my entire life, but all you did was shatter it. I thought..." Swallowing around the lump in my throat, I gave a dry laugh before continuing. "I honestly thought we could make it because we love each other. But the joke was on me all along for believing in such a fairy tale."

The car filled with what could only be described as the howl of a wounded animal. His huge hands cupped the sides of my head, his thumb stroking over my cheeks lovingly, while his fingers tangled in my hair to the point of pain. Jenner's eyes were wild, like a feral beast that had locked eyes with the only person who could truly tame it.

But I was no longer sure that I was the one who was supposed to spend my life taming him.

I wanted to—wanted him and us—but at what cost to myself?

"Doe, Mom, and Dad are the reason Jenner took the job. They convinced him to surprise you with the house," Bryant explained when it appeared that Jenner was unable to form words.

"I know," I replied quietly without looking away from the man who held on to me like the lifeline I'd always wanted to be for him.

"You knew?" my brothers shouted in unison.

"I'm not a complete idiot," I said, speaking more to Jenner than to Bryant or LJ. "I realized they'd had a hand in everything, and why, earlier. When you told me you bought the house instead of renting, it clicked. That doesn't excuse anything. All it did was prove to me that we aren't as strong as I'd hoped, and I felt like a fool."

"No, baby, no!" Jenner groaned, pressing his forehead to mine. "I'm the fool. I didn't suspect they were playing me. Not once. My gut told me to tell you what was going on, to get your opinion on everything, but your mom convinced me that it was better to surprise you."

"I think you let her convince you because you wanted the same things they did," I murmured. "And you didn't consider my opinion on any of this because I allowed you to think stomping on my feelings was okay. I understand because everyone..." I clenched my eyes closed against the pain of the reality that single word caused me. "Everyone has done it my entire life. But I can't do it any longer, Jenner. I can't marry you and let the cycle continue."

"I know I hurt you." His voice came out as little more than a raspy, pain-filled whisper. "I'm so fucking sorry I've caused you even a moment's worth of pain. Punish me all you want, little lamb. I deserve it. But don't leave me. That's not punishment. It's nothing short of torture."

CHAPTER 7

JENNER

The rest of the drive to the farm was accomplished in complete silence. I kept my fingers in Doe's hair, our foreheads pressed together, breathing in her scent—and praying.

Her brothers had given me hope that once she knew I'd been manipulated by her parents, she would magically forgive me. But it seemed she'd already figured out what her mom and dad were up to on her own. That didn't stop her from holding me accountable, as she should. I'd had a gut instinct, but I'd ignored it.

Never again.

I wasn't sure how I was going to win Doe back, but I knew living without her wasn't an option.

First, however, we had to deal with her parents. Marissa and Wroth couldn't be let off the hook for how they had used me to control their daughter's life. They knew I would do anything to make Doe happy, and that's what I'd thought I was doing.

Now, I was at risk of losing her forever.

LJ stopped in his parents' driveway and killed the engine just as Aspen turned off the truck behind us. There were a few other vehicles already parked there, and I realized that more than just Piper had shown up. I glanced at Bryant, but he just shrugged, unsure of what was going on any more than I was.

Jackson opened my door since he'd been smart enough to engage the child safety locks before we'd gone in to pick up Doe at Aspen's apartment. The golden three, as so many people called them, knew their sister well. Otherwise, she probably would have been able to make a break for it back in the parking lot, and it would have taken more than gentle coaxing to get her to come with us to West Bridge.

Still holding her hand, I helped Doe out of the back of my car. Once her feet were on the ground, she tried to pull away, but I interlocked our fingers and guided her to the Nialls' front door.

Without bothering to knock, LJ and his brothers walked in, with Aspen following them. Doe glanced at her friend's back and paused, but none of us could hide from this confrontation; there was no use prolonging the inevitable.

"I can't believe you two would do something like this." Liam Bryant's voice rang out, and we followed the sound into the family room. "Especially you, Rissa. You were playing with your own child's future. Her happiness, for fuck's sake."

He stood at the fireplace, glaring at his sister and brother-in-law. A quick glance around showed me that Liam's wife, Gabriella, was also there, as well as Piper, Pixie, and even the fucking mayor. The sight of Teller caught me off guard, but it would only make things easier since I could tell him to his face to shove the police chief job.

"Jenner makes her happy," Marissa argued. "And I thought that if she had her own home near the farm, she would be even more so. I had no idea that the people of this stupid town were making her miserable. No one ever gave me a hint that she was being bullied by grown adults!"

"That isn't the issue at the moment," her brother countered. "You should have let the boy make his own choices. You shouldn't have stuck your nose in their lives and convinced him it was for Doe's own good. They're together, and that means they're partners. When you conspired to get him to keep this shit from her, you essentially broke their partnership and Doe's trust in him. That's manipulative and beneath you."

"She was getting ready to leave us!" Wroth interjected. "What the hell were we supposed to do, Liam? Doe is too soft for the real world. They will gobble her up and spit her out without a care for her tender heart. I couldn't risk her getting hurt."

Beside me, Doe let out a sharp gasp, and all eyes turned to her. "Is that what you really think of me?" she demanded angrily, jerking her hand from mine to move farther into the living room. "Am I truly so weak in your eyes that you think I can't make it in what you call 'the real world'?"

Wroth squeezed the back of his neck. "You're not like your brothers, Doe. You're sweet and kind to everyone. We've sheltered you from the worst of the bad things in the world. Things that would break your heart. I trust Jenner to keep you safe, but not even he could protect your bright soul from the darkness."

"I know exactly how dark the world is, Dad," she gritted out. "I've been living in a town where everyone—every fucking person—has treated me like a pariah. If none of them could tarnish my soul, I doubt anyone or anything else could."

"You should have told us about that—"

"Really?" She lifted her brows at him. "And become an even bigger outcast because you raged out on anyone who so much as looked down their snotty noses at me? Should I have let their words not only hurt me, but destroy the people I love? I refused to allow anyone to drive me to the point that I came crying to any of you. The farm is here. The boys still had their baseball dreams. Everyone was happy, and I was happy because of that alone."

"They hurt you!" he shouted angrily.

"Yeah, they did," she agreed. "But you hurt me more, Dad."

He blanched and stumbled back a step at her heated words. But she wasn't done. "You played with my life. And it is mine, Dad. I'm the only one who gets to say where I live. To whom and where and when I get married. But you and Mom both manipulated Jenner into thinking everything he did was for my own good, when all along, it was so you could keep me close and control me."

"We just wanted to protect you," he said softly, which was an odd contrast to his harsh voice.

"Stop lying to yourself! You've always treated me differently from the boys. But I can assure you, I'm a hundred times stronger than they are. I can protect myself from the people I know will hurt me. Too bad I didn't see until it was too late that I needed to protect myself from you, Mom, and Jenner."

"Doe, sweetheart," Marissa tried to break in, but Doe turned wounded eyes on her mother.

"I always thought you were the best parents. I've seen how bad it can be for some kids. Aspen is standing right there, and he can give testimony as to exactly how big of a contrast you two are compared to his own. Maybe you never physically hurt me, and you tried not to harm me emotionally, but this thing with Jenner? That's manipulative as fuck. By using him, you hurt me in a way no one else had the power to."

"That wasn't our intention," Marissa whispered.

"Bullshit!" I'd never seen Doe so angry in all the time I'd known her. Not even the rare occasions we'd argued in the past had she exploded like she did then. "You knew what you were doing, Mom. Don't lie to me or yourself and pretend like you didn't. And Jenner trusted you. You are the two people he expected to have only the best of intentions where I'm concerned. Should he have told me what was going on, regardless of how many times you told him your idiotic surprise would make me happy? Yes. But he didn't suspect that you were trying to use him to control me. And now..." She scrubbed her hands over her face, and it was only then I realized she was crying. "Now, I'm lost. I don't know what to do. The people I love and should be able to trust the most have broken something inside me."

"Honey, I'm so sorry." Marissa was openly crying too, and she stepped forward, intent on hugging her daughter, but Doe took two steps back, holding up her hands to warn the older woman away. "Doe, what can we do to make this up to you? How can I fix this, sweetheart?"

"You think this has an easy fix?" Doe shouted. "Do you honestly think you can turn my life upside down, and after a few days, everything will go back to normal?"

"No, but I want to try to fix what we broke!" Marissa cried.

"Well, you fucking can't!"

"Okay," Gabriella said, moving between mother and daughter. She grasped her niece's hand and gave it a gentle squeeze. "Emotions are high right now. You both need to take a deep breath and rein it in."

"Maybe I should give you some privacy," Mayor Teller mumbled, backing toward the door.

"I don't think so, Mayor," Wroth growled, causing the man to turn a sickly shade and gulp. "We aren't done with our discussion. You've been running unopposed for several terms now. My money has helped fund your campaigns. Tell me, did you know your constituents were mistreating my daughter?"

"Of course not!" he answered, but it came too quickly, too nervously. "I would have put a stop to anyone speaking ill of Doe, had I heard it personally."

"Right," Wroth muttered with a disbelieving nod. "I'll be dropping by your office tomorrow. I think a few changes around this fucked-up town are in order if you expect my family to continue to contribute funds."

"Before you go," I said, stepping in the hastily retreating coward's way. "You can consider this my official resignation."

The mayor's eyes nearly bulged out of his head. "Now listen, son. I don't care what anyone else says. You are the best candidate for this town's chief of police. I would gladly put the citizens' safety in your hands."

My eyes drifted to Doe, but she wouldn't even look at me. "Fuck off."

"You want a bigger salary? I can pull funds from other departments to give you a raise. Anything you need, Carling. Just because your in-laws came to me first doesn't mean I wouldn't have offered you the job if you'd applied for it personally. You have what this town needs."

"He said no, dumbass," Piper snapped at him. "Now go before someone has to show you to the door. And if it's me, I promise, you'll be leaving with a few bruises. I'm not nearly as civilized as my cousins."

Blowing out a frustrated sigh, the mayor nodded and started for the exit again.

"Mayor Teller, wait," Doe called before he could reach the door.

He turned so fast he nearly tripped over his feet. "What can I do for you, Miss Doe?"

Squaring her shoulders, she turned to look at me. "How badly do you want the job?"

"I didn't even want the job until your parents approached me about it," I told her honestly. "But once they had my ear, I realized that I did kind of want something different. A steady job that meant settling down, to give me roots and show you how committed I was to being here with you."

"Do you still want it?"

In three steps, I'd erased the distance between us. Grasping her around the waist, I molded her body to my own. "I only want you. The job, that house? None of that matters without you."

"Oh, the house is a big fuck no," she muttered grumpily. "But the job...we can discuss it if you really want it."

"It's a good offer," I told her, feeling hope zinging through my blood. "We'd have great benefits. The money isn't the best, but no law enforcement position pays that well anyway. But it will be enough that I can provide for you and any children we might decide—together—to have in the future."

"Money doesn't concern me." She tipped her head back, her blue eyes shimmering with unshed tears. "I love you, Jenner. And while we obviously have some things to work on, I don't want to break up. If this job will make you happy, then I want you to take it."

"You make me happy, little lamb. Having you is all I care about."

"Jenner," she grumbled frustratedly. "I'm having a serious conversation with you about the damn job. Something we should have had to begin with, instead of you just announcing that you were taking it without including me. Now, I'm making you include me. Do you want the job or not?"

I pulled her closer, wanting to kiss the breath from her lungs, but I knew if I did that with all the emotions running through me in that moment, I wouldn't be able to stop. And I would have to fucking stop, because her brothers, father, and uncle were right there watching. "If I can have you and the job too, then yes. But if taking it means losing you, then fuck no."

"See, was that so hard?" She glanced over at the mayor, who was sweating bullets from how hard Wroth Niall was glaring at him. "Jenner will take the job."

"Right. Then I'll see you on Monday, Police Chief Carling."

I didn't spare him a glance as I watched the first signs of amusement flicker through Doe's eyes as the mayor practically ran out of the house.

"You're sure about this?" I asked, needing to be certain.

"I know you don't like to be idle. You weren't a fan of all the traveling Violet does during football season, and I wasn't either. I would be lying if I said I wasn't a little nervous about you being a cop, but the position is mostly an administrative role." She shrugged. "Plus, I can use you to scare the assholes in this town now. I think everyone who ever called me Godzilla should get at least one speeding ticket."

"They fucking called you Godzilla?" Piper snarled. "Who the fuck did that kind of shit, Doe? I need names."

"A list would be nice," Liam agreed, his jaw popping. "I'd like to pay a few of them a personal visit."

"Lyric married into an actual motorcycle club, or is it a gang?" Gabriella commented. "Maybe they can come with him the next time he visits and scare the piss out of some of those old fuckers."

Doe huffed. "I'm not giving anyone a list. There's no reason why anyone needs to stir up trouble after all these years."

"But what about that house?" Pixie spoke up. "The market isn't exactly booming right now. Jenner put a lot of money down for it."

"It doesn't matter," I assured my sister. "We'll find somewhere else."

"You won't have to," Wroth announced, putting an arm around his wife. "We caused this trouble, we'll fix it." The two of them shared a look before Marissa nodded. "Doe, honey, the farm has been yours from the time you could ride a horse. We always intended for you to inherit it, but we think you should take over fully now. The house, the land, everything, it's yours and Jenner's. Your mom and I, we'll buy the house from Jenner, and it will be our West Bridge residence."

A devilish gleam filled Marissa's eyes. "Yes, I think that's the perfect solution. We've never had close neighbors before. I'm sure it will be fun getting to know the Cains and Dotsons better."

CHAPTER 8

Doe

The idea of my parents living between two of my biggest adult tormentors in town nearly caused me to burst out laughing. The Cains and Dotsons having to deal with Mom and Dad on a daily basis seemed like the perfect visit from the Karma Fairy.

But as amusing as the thought of those two couples getting a dose of hell every morning, noon, and night was, I was far from wanting to laugh.

Their fix didn't feel like it was fixing anything, at least not where my heart was concerned. Maybe I was overreacting, or maybe I'd just had too much, and for once, I couldn't overlook having my heart stomped on, only to then have to go on about my life like everything was perfectly fine.

While Aunt Gabs and Uncle Liam joked with Mom and Dad about torturing their new neighbors, I just stood there, unable to speak for fear of exploding into a million pieces and taking everyone in the house with me. How was I supposed to pick myself up and dust myself off after everything they'd done?

Giving me a house and the farm didn't ease the ache in my chest. It didn't erase the way they'd used the man I loved. It didn't excuse the pain I'd been put through and still felt while they laughed and joked around like nothing had happened.

Angrily, I tore my gaze from my parents and looked up at Jenner. "Do you want to marry me?" I demanded.

I heard Jenner's breath catch in his throat as he looked down at me with emotion swelling in his eyes. I licked my lips, almost afraid of his answer when he didn't immediately speak.

"Give the dude a second to catch his breath before you go giving him a heart attack like that, baby sis," LJ teased, breaking the tension I felt growing in my body.

"Yes," Jenner gasped, the air rushing back into his lungs. "Of course I want to marry you, little lamb. I have the ring right here."

He pulled the box from his pocket, but I snatched it from his fingers before he could open it. "Good. Let's go."

"Wait, time out." Jackson stepped in my way. "Where are you going?"

"To get married," I announced. "Everyone is invited but Mom and Dad."

My mom's anguished cry behind me did nothing to ease the pain she'd caused me. Petty, sure, but I was done caring about everyone else's feelings when they'd been so careless with my own.

"Doe, baby." Jenner grasped my wrist and turned me to face him. "Slow down. This isn't how this should go."

I cocked my head at him. "How should it go, Jenner? You have two options. Come with me now and we fly to Vegas to get married, or you take the ring box back and we never mention marriage again."

"What happened to discussing everything? Making important decisions together?"

"Yeah, not getting included sucks, doesn't it? But this is me giving you the option. It's now or never, and the option of now is quickly ticking away." I glanced around the room, pointedly ignoring both my parents' gazes while landing briefly on everyone else. "Piper, you and Pixie can be my bridesmaids. Bryant and LJ can be groomsmen, and Jackson can give me away. There, everything is settled. If we hurry, we can catch a flight out of Nashville."

"Doe, stop it," Jackson snapped at me. "You have every right to be pissed at Mom and Dad, but you're being cruel. Mom's already crying, and Dad's got tears in his eyes. This isn't you, baby sis. You're not mean."

I turned to confront my brother. "Maybe I've finally had enough. Maybe I've let the last person walk over me for their own gain. My heart is no longer the soft, weak organ that everyone so readily takes advantage of."

"No," Pixie denied vehemently. "That's impossible. The Doe that I know, and love is too selfless to allow that to happen. You're just hurting and want to make them hurt too. But don't do anything you're going to regret tomorrow."

"Marrying Jenner isn't something I'll regret. Allowing anyone who isn't worthy of witnessing our nuptials to attend the wedding, now that is something I will definitely regret." Folding my arms over my chest, I looked up at Jenner. "Last chance. Are we getting married tonight or not?"

He scrubbed his hands over his face, into his hair, and ended by squeezing the back of his neck as if he was in pain. I slowly counted down from ten in my head, telling myself if I got to zero before he gave me an answer, that was it. Game over. We wouldn't break up, but I'd never entertain the thought of being his wife again. This was his only chance; there would never be another one.

"Fuck it," he muttered and scooped me up. "Pixie, I'm getting married. Get your Dr. Contreras and meet us at the airport."

"But Jenner—"

"Or don't," he called over his shoulder as he carried me out of the family room. "It doesn't matter. I'm getting married tonight, regardless of who is or isn't there."

"Doe!" My name was shouted behind us by a handful of people, but Piper and Aspen were already following us toward the car.

"Please don't do this," Mom sobbed from the porch. "Let's plan a nice wedding. Something small. Or big. It doesn't matter. Let's just do all of this the right way."

"Sorry, this is my way," I called back, holding on to Jenner's shoulders for all I was worth. He'd passed the test; he'd chosen me. And with each step closer to his car, the more the hurt he'd caused was healed. "If you meant what you said about the house, then you should move in while we're gone. We'll be back Sunday night."

"Doe."

Jenner stopped at the passenger door, and I slowly looked back at where my dad was standing on the bottom step. All the outside lights were on so I could see him clear as day, and there was no missing the tears streaming down his face. "Please," he begged. "I know we've messed up. And maybe we don't deserve to be at your wedding, but I'll plead on my knees if that's what you want. Please let us see you get married."

My teeth sank into my bottom lip as tears filled my eyes. I looked up at Jenner, silently asking him what he thought I should do.

"I'll do whatever you want, little lamb," he vowed. "Tonight, tomorrow, or even next year. I don't care when or where we get married. The choice is yours who you have there. I won't make the decision for you."

"We're getting married tonight," I said, trying to keep my chin from wobbling. "But…I guess…" My gaze went back to Mom, and then Dad. Both of them were openly crying, and it hacked away at the walls I'd put around my heart all day. "I mean, the mayor could call in a favor with a judge or something. It's not too late, right? Getting married in our new living room isn't a horrible idea."

"I'll call Judge Wilson," Uncle Liam announced. "He's our next-door neighbor and owes me for not telling his wife about the stripper we saw sneaking out of their pool house the last time we were in town."

"You can wear my wedding dress!" Mom offered, her voice catching on another sob. "It might be a little short, and several sizes too big, but we can do a rough alteration."

"C-can I walk you down the aisle?" Dad asked hesitantly, sniffling loudly.

Groaning, I pressed my forehead against Jenner's shoulder. "Okay," I whispered, but everyone must have had supernatural hearing because my parents each gave a small cheer, and Jenner turned, carrying me back to the house.

"Thank fuck," I heard Bryant hiss to LJ as we passed them in the yard. "I wasn't sure how we were going to explain to Coach that we were going to have to miss another game because we had to fly to Vegas for a wedding."

"It wouldn't be the first time," LJ muttered. "We did the whole surprise wedding thing just last month."

"Wait, what?" I yelped just as my parents exclaimed, "Who got married in Vegas?"

"Yo, Jackson, I think that's where you need to do some explaining, bro," LJ said as he calmly walked by our older brother.

"We were drunk. It doesn't count," Aspen hissed.

"Yeah," Jackson was slow to agree. "It doesn't...count."

"It totally counts when you have a marriage certificate," Bryant said nonchalantly as he walked into the house.

"You got married without me?" I whined, my chin wobbling. "I could have been Aspen's best woman or something. You guys are always doing things without me!"

"We were drunk," Jackson snapped. "It doesn't count."

"Then make it count!" I snapped back. "Double wedding right now, or I'm never speaking to you again."

Jackson's jaw popped a few times before he threw his hands up in the air. "Talk to Aspen about that shit. He's the one who wouldn't let me say anything."

I wiggled out of Jenner's arms, but he kept his hand around my waist as I looked over at my best friend. "Well?"

Aspen swallowed hard. "If I do this, then everyone will know. There won't be any going back. If my old man sees me, he'll try to kill me."

"You leave Walter Williams to me," Dad snarled as he came up to us. "If you're ready to be a part of this family, then you don't have anything to worry about, son."

The tears that filled Aspen's eyes in that moment cleared away everything still simmering inside me. A peace I didn't know could exist washed over me, and I was able to give my parents a clean slate with no regrets when Dad hugged my friend and welcomed him to the family.

"I-I guess we're having a double wedding," Aspen choked out.

"Fuck yeah!" Bryant crowed.

"About damn time," LJ hooted.

"For real?" Jackson nearly stumbled as he came back down the porch steps. His eyes wide and full of hope. "Do you mean it, Aspen? You'll marry me?"

"Right here, right now," he said with a nod. "Although, we're technically already married, dumbass."

"Doesn't matter. That one didn't count. This one does." With a loud whoop that they could probably hear all the way over at Violet and Luca's house, Jackson grabbed Aspen by the waist and twirled the two of them around. "Baby, you are my everything. Thank you for letting me finally tell the world."

Fighting happy tears, I walked with Jenner into the house to give the other couple a little privacy. But no sooner did I cross the threshold than Mom was ushering me upstairs. "We'll have to find a belt or something to take in the waist of the dress a little. You're so much thinner than I was when I married your father. Brie, what do you think? A chunky belt, or can we do a quick sew to make some alterations?"

The next hour passed in a whirlwind, but suddenly, I found myself in front of the living room door, my dad standing between Jackson and me.

"This wasn't exactly what I was expecting when Jenner asked for my blessing to marry my baby girl, but I'll take it," Dad said as he held out both his arms. "You look beautiful, sweetheart. That dress survived the test of time." His gaze went to my brother. "And I've never been prouder of you, Jackson. I'm gaining two new sons tonight. You two did well in picking life partners."

Jackson had trouble speaking for a moment, but he was finally able to croak out, "Thanks, Dad."

Clearing his throat roughly, Dad nodded toward the living room. "I guess we should do this thing, huh?"

I offered him a small smile. "Yeah, Daddy. I think it's time."

Swallowing hard, he nodded again. "I love you both. So damn much. I hope neither of you ever doubts that."

"I think you proved that tonight," I assured him. "We're ready. Are you?"

"Just give me another sec, okay, honey?" He inhaled slowly and then squared his shoulders. "Okay. Let's go."

Jackson and I shared a look, both of us fighting back a laugh—as well as tears—and let Dad walk us both down the aisle.

EPILOGUE

WROTH

I heard the siren outside the house and picked up my cup of coffee to watch as my son-in-law pulled over Old Man Dotson just as he left his driveway. Snickering, I watched as Jenner got out of his cruiser and then approached the old fucker with a mean swagger that had my neighbor sweating bullets.

Dotson got pulled over at least once a month, and every time, Jenner wrote him a ticket. Sometimes it was for failure to use a turn signal. Other times, it had been for bigger things—like DWI. Dotson didn't pass a breathalyzer one night after having a couple beers with Mr. Cain at the bar a few blocks over. I might have let the chief of police know to expect the fuckers, and Jenner hadn't let me down.

The boy kept things civil. He never raised his voice to the men who were part of the trash that had made Doe feel like less than she was, and he only messed with the men. Mrs. Dotson and Mrs. Cain were both left to my beautiful wife, who was more dangerous than the man in uniform currently asking to see Dotson's driver's license, registration, and insurance.

Marissa fucked with those two hags every day of the week—and twice on Sundays. She and Pixie didn't give either of them a moment's peace. I was honestly surprised neither of them had moved yet, because Mari and our honorary daughter were terrors to those old ladies.

And then there was Raiden.

"Grandpa, I'm going to play in the yard!"

"Sure thing, kid," I told my grandson as he skipped out of the house. Raiden was four and spent the weekends with us more often than not. It gave his dads a little break from him. After my sons retired from baseball five years ago, Jackson and Aspen had decided to start growing their family. They'd used a surrogate and a donor egg. Raiden was technically Aspen's biological son, but we didn't see any

233

difference between him or Elizabeth, Doe and Jenner's daughter, who was nearly twelve now.

As soon as Raiden was in the yard, he noticed his uncle and called a hello.

Jenner waved back before tearing off the ticket and handing it to Mr. Dotson. "See ya, buddy," Jenner told Raiden as he got back into his cruiser. "Be good."

"Aw, Unc. Where's the fun in that?" he crowed as he picked up a stick and started digging at the same trench he'd been constructing every weekend for the past few months. It made the water run out of our yard and flood Mrs. Cain's flower bed when it rained. I may have talked my grandson into the little demolition of my own backyard to be petty.

Seeing me standing at the window, Jenner saluted me and then went on about his day. Saturdays were a half day for Jenner. At lunchtime, he'd go home and eat with Doe and their daughter before going to dinner at Pixie and her husband's house. Sundays, however, were when all the kids came to us. Marissa made a big meal, and the small house was overfilled with laughter as my grandchildren played in the yard and my grown children—both biological and honorary— told us about their week. When I saw Marissa smiling on Sundays, the love shining so brightly out of her pretty blue eyes, I knew that life couldn't get more perfect.

"Raiden?" Marissa called as she stepped out onto the front porch. "How about we walk down to the ice cream shop and get a treat after lunch?"

"Yay!" Raiden cheered.

"But only if you can get that trench in tip-top shape."

"Sure thing, Grandma!" he promised.

The front door closed behind my wife, and she walked over to lean against me as we both watched our grandson through the window. "It's supposed to pour tonight," she said with venomous glee as we saw Mrs. Cain's curtains flutter. "Ah, and she just planted those petunias. So sad."

"Mari, you're sexy as fuck when you're being evil." I kissed the top of her head. "I love it."

"No one messes with my baby and gets away with it. What does Elizabeth call me?" Her nose scrunched up, reminding me of our granddaughter when she made that exact same face. "Oh yeah. The Karma Fairy."

"Whatever it is, it makes me want to bend you over that kitchen table and fuck you until you can't walk."

"Shush you," she said, playfully slapping at my chest. "Besides, we can't do that until Raiden goes home."

Bending, I touched my lips to the shell of her ear, causing my beautiful wife to shiver deliciously. "It's a date. Tomorrow night."

Her giggles were all the answer I needed as I set down my empty mug and went to help my grandson dig the trench a little bit deeper, making sure Mrs. Cain's petunias met a quick death once it started raining.

~THE END~

Hopelessly Devoted to TRINITY

BOOK 5

CHAPTER 1

TRINITY

"**D**o you have a list for everything?" Banks asked from the back seat, sounding bored. Having spent the last two months on tour with three rockers and all the shenanigans that came with them—especially when it came to Cannon and Piper—returning home with only a week to go before school began again most likely seemed boring as hell to him.

Of course, he'd also spent the last four hours with no one but his dad and me to talk to as we'd driven from the final concert venue of the summer tour. He'd played on his phone for a while, put his earbuds in and listened to some music, but then lost interest in that and started annoying his dad. That had begun about a third of the way into the drive, and I'd decided that getting lost in the endless cycle of work and to-do lists was a safer bet than paying too much attention to Banks throwing barbs at his dad and Jarrett becoming increasingly agitated with each mile closer to home.

"You wound me," I teased, typing away on my current to-do list. "It's like you don't even know me."

"What's this one for?" He leaned forward between the passenger's and driver's seats, his head almost leaning on my shoulder as he tried to read what I was typing.

Lowering my phone, I turned to give him the glower that I'd learned quickly got him to move his ass when he was being particularly stubborn. "Seat belt, mister."

"I'm wider than the space between these two seats," he argued, proving his point by bumping his shoulders against the back of each seat. "Even if Dad did slam on the brakes, I wouldn't go through the windshield."

"Banks. Seat belt." When he just sat there looking at me without blinking, I used the tone that always made him crumple. "Please, Banks. If anything happened to you, I would be lost. Even if you didn't get tossed through the windshield, you could be seriously injured, and I love you too much to want to see that."

His handsome face, a much younger replica of his father's, softened, and he dropped back against the seat before carefully fastening himself in. "There. All strapped in."

I gave him my sweetest smile. "Thank you."

"So what's the current list got on it?" He was back on the to-do list, and I shrugged.

"I'm categorizing everything in my apartment that I plan to keep, donate, or leave behind."

His brow furrowed at the same time I sensed Jarrett tensing in the driver's seat. "Why would you leave anything behind? Will it make the resale value increase or something?"

"Who said I was selling my apartment?" I asked with raised brows. "Just because I'm moving in with you guys doesn't mean I'm going to put my place on the market."

"Why the fuck not?" Jarrett demanded as he braked for a red light. He shifted, putting his arm across the back of my seat, and leaned forward. I could feel the heat of his breath on my cheek and had to press my thighs together to keep from squirming. Damn it, the ban on sex I'd put on our relationship early into the tour was still in effect, and I planned on keeping it that way until we were married. But he did his best to make it hard for me every chance he got. "Your home is with us now. The apartment isn't necessary."

"I bought that apartment with my own money. No one helped me. It's mine, and I'm not selling it just because I'm getting married." He opened his mouth to argue with me, but I cut him off. "The light is green."

With a muttered curse, he eased on the gas and drove for another block before speaking again. "Are you keeping the apartment as a backup?" he demanded, causing his son to suck in a deep breath. The sound hurt my heart, but I slowly, noiselessly inhaled to ease the pain. "Are you anticipating leaving me?"

"No, dumbass," I snapped, irritated with his interrogation. "I'm keeping it for Madalyn."

"What?" he half shouted, but the relief on his face was so apparent that I couldn't really stay upset with him and his stupidity.

"I'm saving it as a graduation present for her," I informed him. "She may have a little more time before she's finished with high school, but she's already been talking about college options. Since she wants to stay local, I figured she would rather have her own place than living on campus. Why waste money when I already have an apartment that is paid for?"

"Oh," he muttered, his fingers easing their death grip on the steering wheel as he continued to drive us to his house in Beverly Hills.

Our house.

Or so he, Banks, and Madalyn had continuously reminded me as we'd planned for my move into their home. According to them, everything that belonged to them was now mine as well. It was sweet of the kids to tell me that—repeatedly—but I wasn't in this for the material things that came with marrying their dad. He might allegedly than God, but I wasn't exactly broke. I had my own money, that I worked hard for, and then there was the trust fund that I'd left untouched from my parents.

But once the press got wind that I was marrying Jarrett, it was going to be a whole PR nightmare. Between our age gap, the fact that his ex-wife had already tried once to sell an exclusive interview to some gossip magazine about how I'd been in a relationship with Jarrett while they were still married—something that Mom and Aunt Emmie had squashed before it had hit the front page and every social media platform—and the differences in our economics, I was going to be labeled a gold digger.

I didn't care what people thought. Everyone who mattered knew the truth, but I didn't want any negative press to impact Banks and Madalyn. They still had to go to school every day, be around asshole kids with even bigger asshole parents who had opinions on shit that wasn't any of their business. I didn't want them to start resenting me because I'd caused them to be bullied or stressed out at school.

"Does that mean I get my own apartment when I graduate from high school too?" Banks spoke up, breaking what remained of the tension in the car.

"Depends on where you go to college," I said, turning my attention back to my phone and the list I was making so I didn't forget anything the following day when we went to pack up my stuff.

"I'm eleven, Trin. Do I really have to decide what college I'm going to right now?"

"Of course not," I assured him. "You don't even have to go to college. There are plenty of trade schools that will teach you important skills for a job that doesn't require a degree. But you can't go into the military like your dad did or become a cop or a firefighter or—"

"You made a list of careers you don't want me to pursue, didn't you?" I could hear the smirk in his voice.

"They're too dangerous," I muttered, typing away so I didn't have to look at him or his father. "I don't want to think about the bad things that could happen to you. I'll never get any sleep because I'll always be worried. And then I won't be able to work, and my company will suffer, and my mom will yell at me and I'll cry, and then you'll feel bad. So, in the long run, I'm saving us both a lot of turmoil, bud."

He snorted a laugh. "You are seriously insane. I fucking love it."

"Banks," Jarrett bit out. "How many times have we discussed you cursing?"

"About ten thousand, Dad," he said deadpan. "And we'll probably discuss it another twenty times before bed tonight."

"I'm not raising a smartass," Jarrett snapped. "Watch your language. Be respectful."

"You curse all the time. I'm just following your example, sir."

"He's got you there," I whispered, hiding my smile by lifting my phone closer to my face.

"You're always going to take his side, aren't you?" my fiancé grumbled.

"Probably." There was no reason to pretend otherwise. I loved my two amazing stepchildren, and I'd fight the hounds of hell for them—or their own father, which was potentially more dangerous.

"Military school sounds really appealing right now."

Not liking the threat to my child, I slowly lowered my phone and tilted my head until I was glaring at my future husband. "So does staying at my apartment until the wedding."

"It was a joke," he quickly excused.

"I didn't find it amusing. Did you, Banks?"

"Not particularly," he said sullenly.

"Apologize," I told Jarrett.

"Baby, I'm sorry," he said imploringly.

"Not to me. To our son."

His hazel eyes darkened when I called Banks "ours." Stopping for traffic, Jarrett shifted in his seat to look at the boy in the back. "I'm sorry, buddy. It was a poor attempt at a joke. I apologize if I scared you or hurt your feelings."

"Yeah, I guess it's okay." Banks sat up straighter. "You were jealous she chose me over you. Not sure I can say I've ever been in the position of someone being jealous of me before. For as long as I've known her, Trin has always picked me. Which is nice, since Mayra sure as fuck never did."

"Banks," I said softly. "Can you watch the language? People are going to think I'm a bad stepmom if you are always using words like that."

His eyes widened, and he slouched down in his seat. "I didn't think about it that way. I don't want people to think you aren't good to us. You're the best stepmom. No, I take that back. You're the best mom. Is it all right if I start calling you 'Mom,' like Maddie does?"

My heart was back to contracting painfully, and I quickly nodded, trying not to be too enthusiastic about it. I didn't want to embarrass him—or myself. Banks thought I was cool, and doing a happy dance in the front seat of his dad's car while in the middle of traffic would lose me cool points for sure. "Absolutely. Call me whatever you want. I already told you that, remember?"

"Yeah, but I didn't really consider it. You were like fifteen when I was born. It was kind of weird. Now, though, I don't really give a fu...dge. I don't give a fudge, yeah. The age thing doesn't matter because you are a great mom, and I want you to be mine."

Emotion clogged my throat, and I had to swallow a few times before I could so much as draw in another breath of air. "You are a great son, Banks, and I want you to be mine. Just like I want Madalyn to be my daughter."

"It's a good thing she went back early with Nana and PopPop so she could start dance classes on time," Banks said with a grimace. "Otherwise, she'd be all happy tears and get me soggy back here."

During the tour, he had quickly fallen into calling my parents Nana and PopPop. Banks and my dad spent so much time together that they had bonded. Dad had started teaching Banks a few things on the drums, which had only gotten Hayat involved. Between Dad and Uncle Jesse, two of the world's best drummers, my niece had been playing drums since she was able to grasp a stick in her fist. She and Dad had begun teaching Banks all the basics, and now he was talking about joining the school band's percussion line.

When my parents left the tour, I'd asked them to help me with a little surprise for my stepson. I didn't want to drive Jarrett crazy, so I'd asked Dad to turn one of the spare rooms in my new home into a place for Banks to practice by soundproofing it and setting up everything needed for the newest drummer in our family.

Jarrett had agreed—well, he'd basically just said, "Whatever you want, sweet angel," before I could fully explain what I had in mind. It wasn't my fault if he hadn't been paying attention to what I was saying. Especially when he'd been more focused on tasting the sensitive spot on my neck just above my shoulder.

Not that he could complain. With the room soundproof, it wasn't like he would be able to hear the ruckus that Banks was going to make.

And if he did have an issue with it, I would just have to find a way to distract him until he got on board with the changes to his house.

Maybe I'd remind him that it was our house now.

And then I'd let him go a tiny bit further than simply kissing his favorite parts of my body.

CHAPTER 2

JARRETT

I sliced into my stack of pancakes as soon as Mrs. Hoffman placed them in front of me on her way out of the kitchen with a basket of freshly folded towels under her arm. Months of being on the road for the summer tour had made home-cooked meals few and far between. A man could only live off cold cereal and instant oatmeal for so long when it came to the most important meal of the day. All those years of eating MREs had prepared me for long spurts of dissatisfying food, but if I didn't have to tough it out, I sure as fuck wasn't going to.

The housekeeper had loaded us all up with a breakfast of champions for our second morning home. She most likely would have done it the day before as well, but we'd been up and out the door before the sun was fully risen to get Trinity's apartment packed and ready for the movers to either bring the boxes back to the house or to a storage unit to await Madalyn when she was old enough to live in the apartment herself. The rest went to a local charity that helped abused women find new housing and assisted with donated furnishings.

Platters of eggs, bacon, flaky biscuits, and an endless stack of pancakes were set on the table, making my mouth water. The scent of perfectly brewed freshly ground coffee filled the air along with the saltiness of the bacon. Fuck, it was good to be home. Banks had already devoured one entire plate before I'd even made it downstairs, barely breathing as he chewed or talked with his mouth full, while he and Trinity discussed everyone's plans for the day.

"Sundays shouldn't be so busy," Banks grumbled as he picked up his glass of milk to wash down his last bite of pancake, scrambled eggs, and bacon. "While we were on tour, sure, I got that. There were concerts on Sundays sometimes, and there was always maintenance of some kind to do on the equipment or instruments. But we're home now, Mom. We should be relaxing."

Smiling, Trinity placed her mug of coffee on the table. "You are more than welcome to remain home, bud. But I have a wedding to plan. That means dress shopping and talking to vendors. There are caterers to meet and discuss menus with. And then there is the most important part of all, which your dad and I just happen to be taking care of this afternoon."

"What's that?" Banks asked, his tone making it sound like he would rather have his teeth filled than do any of those things.

I knew Mayra had done all the same things when she'd planned what was supposed to be a small, intimate wedding when we'd gotten married. I hadn't been interested in any decision-making back then. But I wanted to be a part of every moment when it came to this wedding. Trinity and I were partners in life, and we would start off our marriage taking on everything together—even if it sounded just as boring to me as it obviously did to my son.

"We're picking out the cake and sampling flavors."

"Changed my mind," Banks said, wiping his mouth on his napkin before dropping it on the table beside his plate. "All that sounds better than a day at Disneyland. Let me go change real quick, and we can go whenever you're ready."

Laughing, she watched him rush out of the kitchen before picking up her coffee again. "Looks like planning our wedding is turning into more of a family affair than I anticipated."

The happiness I saw shining out of her blue-gray eyes took my breath away. Pushing my plate away, I grasped her hand and tugged her out of her chair. She came willingly, wrapping her arms around my neck as she sat on my lap. I pressed my face into her sweet-smelling neck and released a contented sigh.

This was what life was all about. The peaceful moments when everything was right in the world. Having my kids safe and happy, under the same roof. The love of my life cuddled in my arms. Feeling like the luckiest man in the world because everything I never truly knew I wanted was right there for me to savor and cherish.

The sound of heels on the hardwood floor reached my ears, but I refused to lift my head as Madalyn walked into the kitchen. "I just saw Banks, and he was talking gibberish. Something about wanting chocolate cake with raspberry filling."

Trinity's fingers stroked over the back of my neck in a firm caress as she spoke to Madalyn. "I think the bakery has that, actually. I remember sampling it when Arella got married. But she went with a vanilla cake and vanilla bean icing. It was simple, beautiful, and so delicious, I had three slices before I realized it."

"Nothing wrong with simple," I said, letting my head rest on her shoulder while she continued to rub her soft fingertips over my stiff neck. "And I'm partial to vanilla."

"Since when?" she murmured low and sultry, but quiet enough for my ears only.

My dick instantly went from semi-hard to steel in my slacks in a heartbeat. I tightened my fingers at her waist and pressed her down into my hardness. I heard her sharp inhale, but her voice barely wavered when she answered whatever question my daughter asked that I hadn't heard. My entire body was one big ache. Every cell throbbed, wanting relief from the sexual tension that grew tougher to restrain with each passing day.

But Trinity was adamant that we wouldn't have sex until we were married. I respected that... My dick simply didn't understand why I was withholding the pleasure of sliding deep into our woman's tight pussy.

At first, the no sex—unless she initiated—was to show her that I was all in. It wasn't just about the sex, which had blown my mind from the moment I'd first tasted Trinity. I loved everything about this woman, and if she needed me to work for the right to touch her again, then that was what I would do. But after we'd gotten engaged, she'd decided that we needed to wait until our wedding night to have sex.

It would make consummating our marriage all the more special.

I didn't think it could get more special than giving her my last name, but if it was important to her, I would walk bent over with painful blue balls until we said our vows.

"C-catering first and then the bakery. At least we will have lunch and dessert while we're out." I felt Trinity shiver and had to bite the inside of my cheek to hold back a groan. Knowing she was just as turned on from something as simple as sitting in my lap made it harder to hold on to my promise to respect her decisions on waiting to make love again.

"I can't wait for next weekend," Madalyn said as she dropped into a chair across the table from us, not seeming the least bit annoyed that her parents were showing PDA at the breakfast table, as I imagined most teenagers would be in the same position. She'd had an entire summer to get used to it, though. "I can't wait to help you try on wedding gowns and pick out the bridesmaid dresses. Dad, when are you and Banks going to get fitted for your tuxes?"

"They have appointments next Saturday as well. The tailor's shop is just a few blocks from Paul's, so we can all go together if you want and then have a late lunch afterward. Maybe see a movie," Trinity suggested. "We need some family time."

"Mom, we just spent months cooped up on a bus together. We played video games and board games and listened to Piper, Cannon, and Asher argue and make bets on who would win." She put her elbow on the table and propped her chin on her hand. "I think we got plenty of family time all summer long."

"There's no such thing as too much family time. And I told you to always bet on Piper, but you didn't want to listen. You and your crushes on bad boys will cause you nothing but trouble," Trinity warned.

"I can't help it. Cannon's dimples are just so..." She sighed dreamily, and my head snapped up. Cannon was a decent guy, but the idea of my daughter liking him as anything other than a friend didn't sit well with me. No guy was deserving enough of my little girl, damn it. "There is just something about them that hypnotizes a girl, ya know?"

"Where Cannon Cage is concerned?" I tensed, jealousy already flooding my veins. But then Trinity snickered, and I was able to relax...somewhat. "Those dimples don't work on me. Nothing about him does. He's like a brother to me."

"Yeah, but you totally go for the older-man type. No offense, Dad. And Cannon is definitely older than me."

"Maddie, sweet, precious Maddie," Trinity said in a voice full of amusement. "You are well aware that Cannon is with Piper. I love Piper, more than I will ever love Cannon, actually. But she will open an entire can of crazy the world has yet to see from her if you so much as flirt with her boyfriend. Please, for the sake of my sanity, and your own well-being, stay the fuck away from Baby Cage."

Madalyn burst out laughing. "I'm just messing with you, Mom. He's dreamy and all, but I already have someone I'm interested in."

"What?" I barked, shifting Trinity enough that I could glare at my kid. "Who is this boy? I need his name, address, social security—"

"Jarrett," Trinity chided, causing me to clamp my mouth shut with a grunt. Shaking her head at me, she shifted her gaze back to Madalyn. "Tell me more about this boy. Wait, he is a boy, right? Not a grown man?"

"His name is Holden Renchford, and he's seventeen."

"He's too old for you," I interjected. "You're only fifteen, and who knows when he will be eighteen."

Both my girls looked at me with narrowed eyes.

"I'm about to turn sixteen," Madalyn reminded me. "And he has another six months before he's eighteen. That's less than eighteen months separating us in age. There is a two-decade age gap between you and Mom."

I couldn't really argue with that, but I sure as fuck wanted to. Things would have been easier if I could parent in the whole "do as I say, not as I do" style.

"Renchford?" Trinity repeated the boy's last name as she thankfully shifted her focus back to our daughter, making it easier for me to think when she wasn't scowling at me.

When she looked at me like that, I couldn't help breaking out in a cold sweat. Years of active duty in the marines, followed by nearly as many years working private security, and I never once had to deal with PTSD. I'd been lucky in that respect. But then my sweet angel came into my life and threw my entire world into a whirlwind that left me anxious as fuck when she wasn't happy with me.

"Isn't that the name of the family who recently moved in next door to my parents?" She made a sound in the back of her throat, as if the answer clicked in her brain before Madalyn could answer. "I think that's what Mom said. They have a few kids, but she didn't get specific."

"Yes," Madalyn said, her cheeks filling with a soft shade of pink. "They have two sons, but I've only met Holden. The other one is off at college already, Kyrie. Holden told me he's twenty and only his half brother. They don't have the same mom. Kyrie's mother died when he was a baby, and then Holden's mom came along. But Kyrie hates Holden's mom for some reason that Holden didn't get into. He also has a younger sister, who just turned fifteen. Hannah is great. She's in my dance class with Hayat and Abi. The four of us have spent the last two weeks hanging out almost every day."

"Holden and Hannah sound nice. Seems like you got to know Holden more than his sister, though." Trinity picked up her cup of coffee and drained the mug. "You and I can chat more about Mr. Renchford later. I need a new shade of polish on my toes. Let's hang out in the master bathroom tonight and have some girl talk."

"Okay. But I was going to ask, can we invite the Renchfords to the wedding?"

"We don't even know these people," I complained grumpily, picking up my fork to dig into my breakfast again.

"I have to go out to Malibu this week," Trinity said as she gathered her phone and stood. "I'll have my dad introduce me to Holden's parents and get back to you on if an invite is appropriate. But even if it's not, you could always ask this boy to be your date."

"She's not old enough to date!" I growled.

My fiancée patted me on the shoulder as she walked behind me. "I'm going to get dressed. We're leaving in twenty minutes."

"For the caterer?" I asked, looking down at the food still on my plate.

"Caterer appointment is at 1:30, Jarrett," she reminded me patiently. "First, we're checking out the three different venues we decided we liked from the email Mom sent of all the possible places with an opening on the date we picked for the wedding. You two be good. I better not hear any arguing while I'm upstairs."

"Why would we argue?" Madalyn asked, staring me down with an expression in those hazel eyes that made me twitchy. It was as if she was daring me to open my mouth, to blast her with all the things we both knew I wanted to say. She was too smart for her own good, because she knew damned well that I wouldn't do anything to risk Trinity's wrath.

I cut a huge chunk from my stack of pancakes and stuffed it into my mouth. If I was chewing, I couldn't talk and potentially get in trouble.

Problem solved.

But as I chewed, I made a mental note to email Briscoe and have him do a full background check on all members of the Renchford family.

CHAPTER 3

TRINITY

I popped my trunk, tossed the two tote bags that were so full the seams practically groaned under the strain over each shoulder, and then lifted the box out. At the same time I realized I couldn't shut the trunk without putting the box on the ground to free my hands, my phone started going off.

"For Christ's sake," I muttered. Putting the box on the ground, I shut the trunk and then sifted through one of the totes to find my phone. I'd shoved it in there before leaving the house that morning, and I hadn't given it much thought on the drive to work. As soon as my fingers finally wrapped around the damn thing, it stopped ringing. Huffing, I pulled it from the bag, spilling a few papers out.

"Shit." Bending, I grabbed everything before the wind could blow it away. As I reached for the brochure of the wedding announcements we still had to decide on, a stiletto-heeled foot stepped on it.

"Thanks," I said, my fingers grasping the paper. But the foot remained on top of it. Irritated, I glanced up and nearly fell on my ass from my crouched position when I recognized who it was.

Mayra Dawson stood over me, dressed in a black-and-white jumpsuit. Her hair looked freshly blown out, and her makeup was perfect. The sight of the woman was enough to cause my stomach to churn. I'd only ever met her once, and I'd had a killer migraine at the time. My brain might have been fuzzy back then, but it hadn't downplayed how beautiful Jarrett's ex was.

But she was supposed to be out of his life. From what little I knew about the divorce agreement, Mayra was required to keep her distance from the kids or face the consequences. With how Jarrett explained it at the time, I'd figured it was a steep financial penalty, but I'd had the strangest suspicion that it was actually something entirely different. He hadn't gone into detail, and for some reason, I hadn't pressed for more information.

What I did know was that I didn't want to deal with Mayra's bullshit any more than her ex-husband and kids did. After Madalyn explained to me exactly how bad things had gotten right before she'd moved in with her dad full time, I was ready to throw a few punches and mess up Mayra's face. She'd put her hands on my girl. It only seemed fair that I return the favor.

Slowly, I straightened, tucking my phone back into one of the totes and leaving the brochure on the ground. I could just look at all the styles online anyway; the brochure had simply been included in the packet my mom had given me when she'd put together a file to help me get started planning my wedding. She knew I preferred doing things for myself, so it was her way of helping me as much as she knew I would allow. I still included her in aspects of the planning. I wouldn't hurt her by excluding her from helping with one of the most important days of my life, but it was mostly Jarrett, the kids, and me making all the decisions.

"I'd ask why you're here, but I really don't give a fuck," I told Mayra as I bent to lift the box. "Whatever you want to say, I'm not interested in hearing. Your best bet is to turn around and keep walking back to whatever rock you crawled out from under before I forget that assault is a crime and kick your ass."

"Aw, you're sassy when you're not ready to puke all over the place." Mayra smirked at me. But then her gaze fell to my left hand, and her eyes began to blaze. The jealousy was loud and clear all over her face, but I didn't know if it was because I was with Jarrett now or because she no longer had access to his money. "Or maybe it's because you have Jarrett's ring on your finger and now you've been lured into a false sense of confidence."

I snorted. "I don't need a man to have confidence in myself. I can deal with you and your crazy just fine now that I don't have a raging migraine."

Turning, I walked toward the office building. She wasn't worth my time, and I had shit I needed to do before I met Jarrett later that afternoon to finalize the wedding invitations. I had a meeting in less than an hour, and I needed to get a little work done in my office beforehand. In the past, that space mostly went unused, and I worked from home. But I hadn't set up a room to handle business at the house yet. Until then, I would make do with the office, even if I got annoyed by all the distractions from people knocking on my door throughout the day to ask stupid questions or just to chat. It was why I'd begun working from home in the first place, so I could get some quality work done, instead of people aggravating me all day and then having to take the work I wasn't able to complete at the office home to finish.

"Don't walk away from me, you home-wrecking bitch," Mayra snarled from behind me right as I felt her hand wrap around my left elbow.

Her nails bit into my skin, digging into the flesh hard as she tried to jerk me around to face her.

All she accomplished was making me drop the box and pissing me off even more. The lid popped off, and one side of the cardboard split open. Mayra's hand remained on me, her nails burrowing deeper with each passing second until I felt blood bead. Oddly unaffected by the pain, I looked down at her grasp on my arm as if I weren't in my own body. All I felt was a weird curiosity at why the bitch with her stiletto-shaped nails and matching heels was bothering me.

And then Madalyn's tear-filled eyes flashed through my mind as she'd told me about the time her mother had taken the strap of her Louis Vuitton handbag and slapped my girl across her legs and back with it.

I pushed off the tote hanging from my right shoulder, and it hit the ground with a soft thud just as I grasped Mayra's wrist and gave it a hard squeeze. She cried out in pain and automatically released me as I twisted her hand at an awkward angle and locked it in place. Stepping into the older woman's personal space, I pressed my face closer to hers and heard her gulp as her eyes filled with the realization that she'd fucked around with the wrong person and was about to find out exactly what the consequences were.

"I don't know what you think you're doing, or even why you thought it was a good idea to fuck with me, Mayra. But I was raised to handle crazy situations at the drop of a hat. You and your brand of stupid? That's nothing compared to misbehaving rockers." I tightened my hold, causing her to whimper.

"Please let me go," she cried. It was loud enough to catch the attention of a few people on the street nearby, and it wasn't until I saw a few flashes of a camera out of the corner of my eye that I realized one of them was a paparazzi. Nothing strange about that. With our clientele, we had musicians coming and going from the building all day long. The paps were always skulking around like the vultures they were to grab a shot of someone.

But the flashing camera, then and there, was too convenient to be anything but a setup.

"Ah, so that's how this is going to go." I grinned down at her and heard her swallow hard once more, her eyes filling with anxiety as they shifted around in search of...help? To see if she was getting the attention she'd hoped to draw? It didn't matter. She'd had a decent plan, but she hadn't realized who she was trying to fuck with. "You didn't do your homework on me at all, Mayra. Did you think ambushing me and causing a scene that will land the two of us on the covers of all the gossip magazines will get you whatever it is you're after?"

"That hurts! You're going to break my wrist," she exclaimed, trying to pull free.

"This hurts?" I twisted my hold, feeling a sick pleasure when she whined. There was nothing fake about the physical pain I caused her. Good. Maybe she'd get a taste of what she'd put Madalyn through. "But I'm only defending myself." I nodded toward the building behind me. "There are high-definition security cameras at every angle that overlook the street and parking lot, as well as every entrance and exit. They will have recorded you grabbing me and then me pulling you off me. In case your small brain didn't already know this, that is called self-defense. There are scratches on my arm that are openly bleeding. All that adds up to proof you attacked me first. I'm simply protecting myself against an unhinged, potential psycho who ambushed me in the parking lot at work. Given your past relationship with my fiancé, I could even argue that you've been stalking me and finally dared to approach me with the intent of causing bodily harm. I'm not one hundred percent sure, but I think that's considered a felony in this state."

"Please," she cried louder. "My wrist. You're going to break it!"

"That's it, Mayra. Cry louder," I urged, tightening my fingers so hard my knuckles turned white. "Get the attention of the security guards just inside the building. Let someone call the cops. I would love to file a report against you. Then I can text Jarrett and tell him what his fucked-in-the-head ex did. You know, he mentioned there were consequences if you ever tried to cause trouble for him or the kids again."

All the blood drained from her face. "I-I haven't approached Madalyn or Banks. And I-I haven't contacted him. Not once. I haven't broken any of the stipulations the Russian woman spoke about."

I kept my face neutral at this new information. What Russian woman? Why did Mayra suddenly appear terrified? Did I even care enough to want to know? Locking those thoughts away for later, I lifted a brow at Mayra. "But you're here, fucking with me. Do you think Jarrett will take that as an attack on himself?"

She licked her lips nervously. "I just wanted to annoy you a little. Cause you some PR trouble so you couldn't plan your wedding as easily as you appeared to be doing."

"I'm not an idiot. I knew what you were doing," I snapped at her. "But I don't play games. You came at me, thinking you could embarrass me or hurt the people I love by attacking me. I can handle myself just fine, but if what you do causes pain for Madalyn or Banks, then I get a little twitchy."

"Why would you care so much about them? They aren't even yours."

The utter confusion in her voice only pissed me off more, and I wrenched her wrist a little harder. "That's where you're wrong. Maddie and Banks are mine. You had your chance to love and protect them, and you failed at that spectacularly. Now I get the very amazing privilege of being their mom." I lowered my head and my voice as I stared her in the eyes, making sure she understood every word that left my mouth. "You haven't seen crazy until you've seen me in momma-bear mode. And lady, you so much as look at my kids, and I will tear you apart piece by piece."

"You're not even their stepmother yet," she tried to argue, but her voice still quavered, the bravado she tried to show failing miserably.

"I will be soon, but being married to their father doesn't mean anything. They've been mine from the beginning. Now, you're going to take yourself, and whatever dumbass you hired with a camera over there, and leave. Go back to Texas or move anywhere else in the world. I don't really give a fuck as long as you never show your face to me, or them, ever again. Because if I so much as see you in a crowd, I will call you out. You will have to deal with me for real then, Mayra. And then, once I'm done with you, whatever Jarrett threatened would happen should you break the rules will fall on your head with a snap of my fingers."

"I-I'm not scared of you, little girl."

My laugh sounded manic even to my own ears. "You should be. But don't take my word for it. Fuck around, find out, and then we'll see what's left of you when I'm finished." Releasing her, I dusted off my hands, trying to get rid of the filth on them. "I might be surrounded by rock stars ninety percent of the time but test my inner gangster. Go on. I fucking dare you. Because where Madalyn and Banks are concerned, I will walk away with assault charges with zero regrets."

"Trinity?"

I stepped back from Mayra at the sound of Aunt Emmie's voice. Putting a smile on my face, I turned to face the redhead who had just stepped out of the back of her SUV. Marcus, one of her personal bodyguards, stood with his hands crossed in front of himself, assessing the situation with slightly narrowed eyes.

"Who is this?" Aunt Emmie asked, giving Mayra a slow appraisal before dismissing her.

Knowing she most likely already knew the answer to her question, I shrugged it off. "Someone who lost her way. I was just giving her directions to the airport." Bending, I picked up the tote I'd dropped. "Marcus, I hate to be a bother, but would you mind carrying this up to my office? Oh, and I dropped a wedding invitation brochure by my car. Would you grab that too, please?"

"You're never a bother, Trin," he said as he walked over to pick up the brochure and then the box. As he did, he placed his body between Mayra and me, and he stayed there, sensing an unseen threat. What he didn't understand was that I was the dangerous one. I wanted to rip her hair out, maybe scratch up her pretty face a little. The fight I'd gotten into with Shaw over the summer was nothing compared to the beating I wanted to give Mayra. "Shall we?"

"Please," I said, offering him a warm smile before glancing at Mayra. Fighting the urge to slap her around—would it have been so bad to hit her once or twice?—I winked at her. "I'm sure you can find your way now. Right?"

Her eyes shifted from me to Aunt Emmie, then to Marcus, before snapping back to my face. "Y-yeah. I'll be on the next flight to Texas tonight."

"Perfect," I said chipperly. "Bye-bye now."

Without sparing her another glance, I walked over to where Aunt Emmie was still standing, her hand clenched tightly around her phone as she stared Mayra down over my shoulder. "I think I have all the files ready for Legal concerning the next tour venues," I said, pulling my aunt's attention to me. "But I'll drop them on your desk to look over before we finalize the contracts."

"I'm confident you covered all the bases," the redhead assured me as we entered the building.

As we passed the first security guard, she paused. "There's a woman outside. Black-and-white jumpsuit. Ugly shoes. Get a clear photo of her from one of the camera feeds and then show it to all the guards. If I find out she's within a hundred yards of this building again, I'll fire everyone on duty."

"Y-yes, Mrs. Armstrong," the man rushed to assure her. "I'll take care of it personally."

Biting my tongue, I waited until we were on the elevator before commenting. "That wasn't necessary. Mayra is nothing more than an annoying fly trying to buzz around and get herself some attention."

"She can buzz the fuck back to wherever she came from," Aunt Emmie gritted out. "That cunt isn't going to bother you again, or she'll have to deal with me."

"I can handle her myself."

"I'm well aware of how capable you are, Trinity. That doesn't mean I don't worry about you. I love you, sweetheart," she said softly.

But then her green gaze got distracted, and I glanced down to where she was looking at my arm. Little lines of blood had trailed down my forearm. I was surprised the elevator didn't begin to vibrate from the sudden tension that poured off my aunt. "Marcus, once you drop the box off in Trin's office, I want you to track down the crack whore and escort her to my son-in-law's office so Jarrett Dawson can deal with his ex-wife personally. Because if he doesn't, I will."

"Aunt Emmie, it's not necessary. Jarrett doesn't need to be bothered with her attempt to intimidate me," I tried to argue, but she tilted her head and gave me the same look that could cause grown men to piss their pants. I sighed and crossed my arms over my chest. "Just let her go back to Texas. If she bothers my family again, I'll deal with her myself."

"I would have been happy to allow her to do just that, sweet Trinity," Aunt Emmie murmured, touching a fingertip to one of the scratches on my arm. It was sore and more than a little tender. Unprepared, I was unable to hide my flinch, which only caused her green eyes to flash like pyres with rage. "But then she made you bleed. That nullifies her option of living a peaceful life from here on out."

CHAPTER 4

JARRETT

Stepping off the elevator, I made a right and walked to the end of the corridor. Without bothering to knock, I opened the door, and only when I saw Trinity sitting behind her desk was I able to catch my breath.

Her head snapped up at the sudden intrusion into her personal space, but when her gaze landed on me, she began to smile.

Until she saw the wildness of my eyes, and she huffed. "I'm fine, Jarrett."

"That's not what I was told," I gritted out, walking around the desk. When I saw the bandages on her arm, I fisted my hands. Reminding myself that Anya Vitucci was already on her way to deal with Mayra, I rolled Trinity's chair back enough to pick her up.

She wrapped her legs around my waist, and I cradled the back of her head. "You should have called me as soon as you saw her."

"Why?" she argued. "I'm a grown woman. If anyone should have been worried, it was Mayra. If Aunt Emmie hadn't shown up when she did, I would have beat that bitch into next week. There was no need for you to even speak to your ex-wife."

I could hear the strain in her voice that she tried to hide, but there was no missing the way her bottom lip pouted out in displeasure. "Wait." I sat down in her chair and adjusted her on my lap so I could see her face better. "Don't tell me you're jealous I saw Mayra."

She crossed her arms over her chest. "If the roles were reversed, and I had to deal with one of my ex-boyfriends, would you—"

"I'm going to stop you right there, baby. Don't go putting hypotheticals in my head that will only cause me to murder someone." I cupped both sides of her face. "There hasn't been anything between Mayra and me for over a decade. I told you I didn't have a sex drive where she was concerned. There were only a few women before her, and only you since."

Her nose scrunched up. "I just find that really hard to believe. From day one, you were like an animal with me. We had sex at least twice a day, every day for two months. Even with us not having sex since we were in Europe, you can't stop touching me. If you start wearing flannel, I'm going to call you a lumberjack because of all the wood you sport. Hell, Jarrett, you are hard as a steel rod right now, and all I've done is sit on your lap."

I shifted her so that she wasn't pressed right into my erection, more for my sanity than discomfort. "If you gave me the green light right now, I'd already be balls deep inside you, sweet angel. But when I say that this only happens with you, I mean that it literally has only ever happened with you. Sex was boring and, therefore, pointless. It was why Mayra had to get me drunk both times she got pregnant. But with you?" I stroked the back of my hand down her cheek before tenderly grasping her throat. "All you have to do is look at me and I'm rock hard, baby. This dick belongs to you, right along with the rest of me. There is no one you should ever feel jealous of where I'm concerned. Because no one else exists for me."

With my hand still around her throat, I watched as her pupils dilated. The tip of her tongue skimmed over her bottom lip, and I could tell she was fighting with herself over holding out on sex until we were officially married. "You can say I have no reason to be jealous, but my brain doesn't understand those words. Sorry, but I'm always going to be possessive and not want anyone who has so much as fantasized about being fucked by you breathing the same air as you."

Pulling her forward, I dropped my head to brush my lips over hers. "Then you can't complain when I feel the same way about other men being around you."

Her breath fanned across my mouth as she gasped for air. "I've never complained."

"Lies," I teased. "You give me shit about Tulsa all the fucking time."

"Because he's gay!" she cried, playfully slapping at my chest.

"Doesn't matter. All my brain sees when I watch him flirt with you is someone with a dick between his legs who is making my woman laugh or smile or look at them. I can't help that it makes me homicidal."

"You are awful." But she snuggled against my chest, laying her head on my shoulder as she wrapped her arms around my neck. "Well, how did it go? Are you going to make her pay whatever penalty you decreed when you finalized the divorce for breaking the terms?"

I stroked my hand over the back of her head, combing my fingers through her long, dark hair. "My sweet girl," I murmured, mentally shaking my head at what a lucky motherfucker I was to have found her. She'd given me a second chance after everything I'd put her through and made her experience alone. She was so damn strong, yet there was an innocence to her that I prayed she never lost. "Yes, baby. Mayra will have to pay a huge price for fucking around this morning. She knew the consequences, but in her tiny brain, she thought by using you to get to me and the kids, she wasn't breaking the stipulations I'd insisted on. What she loses out on now is her own fault."

With a heavy sigh, she lifted her head. "Let's not tell the kids about this. It will only upset Maddie, and Banks gets just as growly as you do over the littlest things these days."

"This was not a little thing. Mayra basically assaulted you." I brushed my fingers over the bandages. "Maybe I should take you to the hospital. Get your wounds checked out. You might need stitches."

She rolled her eyes at me. "They're barely scratches. My mom cleaned them, put some antibiotic ointment on them, and then bandaged me up. Trust me, she's had to deal with worse scrapes than these when I was a kid. One time, we were all playing volleyball on the beach, and a piece of glass had washed up on shore and the sand was raked over it. I fell right on it and sliced my knee up so bad that my uncle Shane puked as soon as he saw me. My aunt Dallas had to clean it up and superglued the wound together before bandaging it."

"Is that what this little scar is from?" I touched her jean-clad knee, my thumb brushing over where I remembered the little white line was. I remembered every mark on her body. Even her imperfections were perfect to me.

"Yes. It was pretty painful for a day or two. These scratches are nothing."

"I don't like that she touched you. The things Maddie said Mayra did to her—"

Trinity covered my mouth with her hand. "One, Mayra can't hurt me like she did Maddie. I'm not scared of her, and I'd kick her ass before she even tried. And two, can you stop saying her name? I don't like it when you speak it."

Kissing her palm, I pulled her hand away and entwined our fingers. "What should I call her, then? That dreadful ex-wife of mine?"

"Definitely not that. I don't like you saying the word 'wife' in any capacity unless you're talking about me. Just don't talk about her at all. There. Problem solved. Subject closed." She kissed me then jumped to her feet. "I love you, but I need you to go. I have too much work to get finished before we have to meet up to finalize the wedding invitations so they can be sent out."

"You're kicking me out?" It was my turn to pout at her. "But I don't want to go back to work. Now that I've seen you, and kissed you, I won't get anything else done at the office."

She slid her arms around my waist and stood on tiptoes to brush a kiss over my lips. "How about you go pick up the kids, and by the time you get back, I should be done. Then we can do the few errands that need to be checked off the list before having dinner out."

"Or—"

"No 'or,' Mr. Dawson."

"Baby," I groaned. "You know what you do to me when you call me that."

Trinity's grin was wicked. "Go. Get our kids. I'll even leave my car in the parking lot overnight, which means you'll get to drive me into work in the morning."

"Or—"

"No 'or.'" Laughing, she pushed me toward the door. "And make sure you tell Mrs. Hoffman that she doesn't have to cook dinner tonight. Give her the rest of the day off."

"Fine. I'll be back soon. Don't work too hard while I'm gone." Bending, I stole another kiss. "I love you."

Blue-gray eyes lit up. "I love you. Be safe."

Opening the door, I reluctantly left her office. As I walked back toward the elevators, I spotted Natalie Cutter and paused when she slowed her steps. "Did you deal with the psycho-cuntface bullshit, or do I need to make a call to her daddy?"

It never failed to surprise me that Trinity's father had been more on board with our relationship than her mother was. She might not say it to my face, but she wasn't exactly subtle about her opinion of my being with her daughter. It wasn't about our age gap either. She didn't like how I'd treated Trinity, and I couldn't blame her for it. Devlin Cutter had said from day one he didn't want to know anything about our relationship. All he cared about was that I loved and protected his daughter. If she was happy, he didn't give two fucks about the past. All that mattered were the present and future where his baby girl was concerned.

Natalie had gotten most of her information about my past with Trinity from secondhand sources, the majority of which had been gossip and more of a guessing game than the actual truth. But I still couldn't fault her for how she treated me. I had put Trinity through hell. I deserved whatever her mom wanted to throw at me.

"Mayra won't be a problem for anyone ever again," I assured her. "She's out of our lives now."

"Yeah, that was what your divorce was supposed to accomplish. Yet she showed up in front of my child with the intention of harming her, while trying to embarrass her with some photographer looking for a quick buck and a juicy story." She crossed her arms over her chest and popped out her hip.

The only physical thing Trinity and her mom had in common was the color of their eyes. Every other facial feature, especially those damn dimples, were from her father. That wasn't to say Natalie wasn't a beautiful woman. She and her siblings had won the genetic lottery when it came to their appearance. As far as I knew, every one of the Stevenson clan had the same blue-gray eyes except for Trinity's cousin Violet.

When it came to personalities, I was of the opinion that Trinity took more after her mom than her dad, but not by much. The mixture of them both bottled up into the perfection that was the woman I loved more than life was explosive, to say the least.

"Natalie, I assure you, Mayra won't ever step in front of Trinity again." If she did, then the world would need to be afraid. Because she was going to be a fucking corpse when Anya got done with her this time.

Mayra had had her chance. All she'd had to do was sign the divorce papers, take the money, and leave my family alone. She hadn't been smart enough to do something so simple.

This time, there were no more chances. She'd had the opportunity to have a good life, even though she hadn't deserved it. As she was the mother of my children, I'd asked Anya not to kill Mayra when I'd first found out she had abused Madalyn. I didn't want my daughter to feel guilty for her mother's death if she, by chance, ever found out about her mother's passing. But this time, Maddie would be more pissed than Natalie if I let Mayra walk away from trying to harm Trinity.

My children were good kids, but mess with anyone they loved, and they were just as bloodthirsty as the assassin who would end the headache that was my ex-wife.

CHAPTER 5

TRINITY

I felt his hot breath on my neck, his arm around my stomach anchoring my back to his front, and his hard cock pressing into the seam of my ass. While his arm had me locked against him, his hand was already beneath my panties, his fingers spreading my lips and strumming over my pulsing clit.

"Jarrett," I whined, squirming against him, loving the way his thick cock twitched against me. A few more strokes and I would come; I could already feel it building, the frustration and relief mixing together, causing a gnawing hunger deep in my belly that hadn't been satisfied in so, so long.

Why had it been so long?

My eyes popped open as the question startled my sleepy brain completely awake, and I went stiff in Jarrett's arms. His hand instantly went still inside my panties, and after a few tense seconds, he muttered a curse. Pulling his hand away, he rolled onto his back and threw his arm over his eyes.

"Sorry. I'm sorry. I was asleep, and you were rubbing that sweet ass against me, and I didn't think."

Gulping in deep breaths in an attempt to calm my racing heart and aching body, I rolled over so that my head was pillowed on his chest. "Don't be sorry. I was half asleep too. Our bodies are taking over while our guards are down and seeking what we've been denying ourselves."

I felt him kiss the top of my head. "I swear, as soon as the officiant pronounces us husband and wife, I'm going to fuck you against the nearest flat surface."

Laughing, I scooted up and propped my head on my hand. "Maybe wait until we're alone first. I don't have many inhibitions where you're concerned, Mr. Dawson, but public sex isn't something I'm into. Especially in front of my family."

His chest rumbled with laughter even as hazel eyes turned to brown at hearing me call him "Mr. Dawson." His thumb skimmed lovingly over my cheek as he tucked a few locks of my hair behind my ear. "You are so fucking beautiful. How am I expected to do anything but look at you all day long when I'm gifted with waking up to the sight of you every morning?"

"Are you complaining?" I teased. "Because if you're not happy with the situation, I can find a different room to sleep in."

"Try it, and I'll turn that ass red, sweet angel."

"Is that a dare?"

With a growl, he rolled me beneath him, his lips already attacking my mouth. "This sassiness is only going to get me balls deep if you aren't careful," he warned. His cock flexed against my core where he was pressed into me. I could feel the dampness of his come-covered tip through his boxer briefs and my panties. Two thin layers of material that were no match for the monster between his legs if he happened to lose control and take me then and there.

But Jarrett had impeccable command over himself, or at least pretended to, as he pulled himself away from me before either of us could shift our clothes out of the way and take what we were so desperate for. Just one more week and our self-denial would be over. I would let him take me whenever and however he wanted, as long as I got to return the favor.

At times when everything inside me throbbed for relief, my insistence on no sex until after our vows seemed ridiculous. But then I remembered how crazy things had been before, when all either of us could seem to think about was getting our next fix of each other. I didn't want to risk my need for him turning into an addiction again. Not yet. Only when I was his wife would I allow myself to fulfill the ever-growing hunger that burned through me.

Standing at the foot of the bed, Jarrett raked his fingers through his short-cropped hair before jerking on a pair of sweatpants. The extra layer of clothing didn't hide the huge trunk between his legs. He would need a cold shower before he dared to leave our bedroom to have breakfast with the kids.

"What's on the agenda for the day, baby?" he asked in an attempt to distract us both.

I licked my parched lips as I watched him pull a T-shirt over his massive chest, his abdominal muscles flexing. As he watched me watch him, I knew he was doing it on purpose. "Did you forget our plans for the day already?"

He shrugged, causing the material of his shirt to strain. The glitter of amusement in his eyes told me he was all too aware of how wet he was making me and enjoying every second of it. "For some reason, my brain isn't working at full capacity this morning. Remind me of the day's activities."

"You and Banks are going golfing with my dad, brother, and nephew. I'm sure a few of my uncles and cousins will join you. Dad and Uncle Jesse love fucking around on the golf course. Uncle Jesse tortured my brother. Be prepared for Dad to do the same to you. Lucy tells me it's a rite of passage from father-in-law to son-in-law. One day, you and Dad can do the same to whomever Madalyn decides to spend her life with."

"There isn't a man alive worthy of Maddie," he grated out.

"Every father thinks that about his daughter. Remember that when you're getting hazed today."

"And what will you be doing?"

I climbed out of bed and tugged my sleep shirt down over my drenched panties. It was one of his old white T-shirts and hit me just below midthigh. The thing hung off one shoulder, flashing him to the top of my right breast. His eyes darkened, and he put more distance between us to avoid the temptation of throwing me back on the bed and fucking us both into oblivion. "My mom and aunts are giving me a bridal shower," I reminded him.

His brow furrowed as he stared at me across the bed. "What happens at a bridal shower?"

"We have brunch, they give me gifts to start my married life with, and then there is cake. At least, that was how it was for all the other showers I've been to. Why?"

"There won't be...I don't know, a guy who strips and dances around?"

I burst out laughing. "My cousins' children will all be there. Did you think my mom would hire a stripper when there will be little kids at the event? Or that she would do something like that, period? My dad would lose his mind. Much like you're doing now just thinking about the possibility."

"So it's not code for a bachelorette party?"

Snickering, I shook my head. "Of course not. Neither of us is having those kinds of parties anyway. And if Briscoe—or anyone else, for that matter—so much as suggests you have a bachelor party, you fire him, do you hear me, Dawson?"

His lips twitched as he tried to fight his amusement. "Should the need arise, I'll be sure to tell HR that is why I fired my second-in-command, sweetheart. I'm sure it won't get me sued for wrongful termination."

"Then put a bullet in his head if he suggests it," I snapped, not amused. "Because if you have a bachelor party, and I find out about it, there will be nowhere for you to hide."

He lifted his hands in a sign of surrender as he lost the fight to contain his grin. "I consider myself well warned, baby. And while we are on this very important subject, you should be aware that if anyone arranges such a party for you, and I find out there was a naked man even in the same building with you, I'll bury the motherfucker in the same hole I put David in."

I jolted at the reminder of the previous head of security from the summer tour. "Jarrett, you know I dislike it when you tease about having killed David."

"It's cute you think I'm teasing."

"Jarrett!" I shouted, only for someone to knock on our bedroom door.

Without waiting for a reply, the door opened, and Banks stuck his head inside the room. "What do I wear to play golf with PopPop and Poppy today? Maddie said I can't wear basketball shorts."

Shooting Jarrett one last annoyed glare, I crossed to the door. "A polo and shorts are fine. Have you eaten breakfast yet?"

"Mrs. Hoffman made oatmeal. I don't like playing golf, Mom. It's boring, and Dad cheats."

I snorted out a laugh. "So do your PopPop and Poppy. I'm sure watching them will be far more amusing than actually playing the game. Evan will be there to keep you company, and Cannon, Jagger, and the twins will be there too."

His eyes widened. "The twins? As in Lyric and..." He lowered his voice in awe. "Luca?"

Grinning, I nodded. "Yes. He had a Thursday night game this week and Tennessee has a bye week next weekend, so he and Violet arrived yesterday."

"Holy crap," he whispered. "I'm going to play golf with Luca Thornton."

I laughed then grimaced. "Please don't get into trouble with the twins. Apart, they aren't so bad, but together, they should come with a warning label. I've suggested to Vi and Mila more than once to slap a sticker on their backs that reads 'Caution: Chaos will ensue when these two entities are in the same room.'"

"I'm sure it won't be that bad," Banks said to reassure me.

"Remember you said that now, bud. By tonight, you'll see what I'm talking about."

CHAPTER 6

JARRETT

The venue for Trinity's bridal shower was the country club where Devlin Cutter and Jesse Thornton like to play golf most weekends. I drove the four of us to the club, where a good hundred people were already waiting for us, with more expected to arrive.

No sooner did I stop in front of the clubhouse than a valet was ready to take my keys. Banks and Madalyn jumped out and migrated to their friends or soon-to-be grandparents. I sat behind the wheel, ignoring the kid waiting for me to turn my vehicle over to his care.

Trinity hesitated with her hand on the door. "Is something wrong?"

"A week from today, you'll be my wife." I inhaled slowly as that realization hit me, and I swallowed around the knot of emotion threatening to choke me. "My kids are happy. I've never seen them so carefree and laughing this much. My world shifted the day I met you, Trinity. Maybe it was a hard road to get to this point, but I'm thankful for you every moment." Grasping the back of her head, I pulled her in for a long, lingering kiss, needing to show her how much I loved her.

The door behind her opened, and I heard deep laughter. "No sucking face, Trin. You can play Daddy and his little girl later."

Huffing, Trinity slowly pulled away. "Remember how I warned Banks about the twins earlier?" I nodded, not giving a fuck about the identical laughing hyenas behind her.

All I could see was her, the way her lips had swollen from our kiss, how she kept licking the puffy bottom one and made a little sound in her throat every time, as if she tasted me there and enjoyed it over and over again.

"Well, you're about to get a crash course in all things Lyric and Luca. May the odds be ever in your favor, babe."

She patted me on the chest with both hands, but instead of pulling away, she trailed her fingers up and around my neck as she leaned in for another kiss. When she pulled back, she was breathing heavier.

"Good luck."

The words had barely left her mouth before the leaner one of the two identical idiots who were waiting at the door reached in and grabbed her around the waist, snatching her out of my arms. "Lyric!" she squealed, kicking her feet. "Put me down!"

I quickly got out of the car, tossing the keys to the valet without looking to see if the kid even caught them. I was around the car and ready to extract Trinity from the inked-up swirly-brown-eyed asshole who had his hands on what was mine. The thicker-muscled twin, the one who played pro football, stepped into my path, and I tensed, ready to take him down to get to my woman.

"Daddy!" an adorable little voice squealed as a blond-haired little girl ran up to the Hulk look-alike.

Luca bent and gently lifted the little girl into his arms. "There's my princess," he said as he smacked kisses all over her face, making her giggles fill the air.

"Daddy, I go?" she asked hopefully.

"You're going to be with your momma today, Love Bug. Daddy has to go with Poppy."

She shook her head adamantly. "No, I go."

While father and daughter had a stare down, which I was certain the little girl was going to win, given the glazed look in the pro baller's swirling eyes, I moved around them to get to Trinity. Lyric had one arm around her waist as he carried her toward a woman several yards away.

"This is undignified," Trinity screeched. "How can I not break a one-armed hold? Jarrett, I need more self-defense lessons."

Lyric chuckled. "Yeah, your daddy needs to teach you all the lessons, babe. All the lessons."

"Ugh, stop making daddy innuendos," the dark-haired woman close to Trinity's age complained, rubbing her hand over her distended, pregnant belly. "We had this talk last night, Lyric. You said you would be good and not joke around about the age gap."

"No, you said I would be good and not make jokes about the age gap, my love." Lyric placed Trinity on her feet just as I reached them. No sooner was she on the ground than she stomped on his foot hard enough to make him shout out in pain.

"Asshole! The next time you grab me, I'm going to headbutt you in the face. And I don't care if your kids are there to see it or not." She pointed to two little boys who were playing closer to where a group of the men was standing.

"Jesus," Lyric groaned, hobbling on one foot. "I have to walk for eighteen holes, Trin! You just broke my toes."

"Meh," his wife said unsympathetically. "I gave birth your huge-headed sons with no pain medication. All too soon, I'll be doing it with these girls in my belly. You can walk around a golf course for an afternoon just fine."

Trinity stomped on his other foot. "There, now you can limp around with two hurt feet." She was about to stomp it again when she didn't get the yelp she'd gotten the first time, but I took pity on the poor idiot and picked her up, placing her on the other side of me.

Away from Lyric.

"Apologize for the daddy shit," Mila directed in a quiet yet commanding voice.

"Why, when it's true? And didn't I tell you not to curse in front of my kid?" Luca asked as he walked over to the group. He was no longer holding his daughter, and a quick glance showed that Love Bug was playing with her cousins. "But seriously, Trin, out of everyone, I didn't expect you to be the one with daddy issues. If anyone was likely to take on a sugar daddy, I would have thought it would be Shaw."

"I heard that!" Shaw yelled from nearby.

"You were supposed to," he called back.

Trinity was grim when she looked up at me. "If you want to make a run for it now, I can distract my dad, and you can grab the kids. Maybe get yourselves new identities. That way, you don't have to deal with these boneheads or risk getting infected with their idiocy. Go— it's too late for me. I've been exposed for too long to avoid contamination."

"Leaving you isn't an option, sweet angel. I'll risk an infestation for you."

"Awww," Lyric and Luca cooed at the same time. "Trin has such a sweet sugar daddy."

"Boys!" They both stood up a little straighter as their father barked at them. "Are you going to spend the entire day fucking around about sugar daddies?"

"Dad, I asked you not to curse in front of Love Bug," Luca grumbled.

"She's all the way over there." He pointed to where three of his grandchildren were playing. "I doubt she heard me, boy."

"You shouldn't curse in front of any of the children," Luca argued. "Including Trin."

"Trinity is a grown woman."

"Really?" Luca's eyes lightened with amusement. "Then why does she need to hold her sugar daddy's hand?"

A warrior-like sound escaped Trinity, and in the next moment, she was throwing herself on top of Luca, slapping him in the back of the head and punching him in the shoulders. I stood there, unsure if I should pull her off the guy or cheer her on. No one else seemed concerned for Luca's well-being. Although he howled like he was in agony, I'd seen him in action on the football field and witnessed him taking heavier hits than any of the ones Trinity dished out. I had no doubt Luca could have used his strength to untangle her from him, but that could have potentially hurt Trinity in the process. That he didn't try, told me he knew that and wouldn't harm her, even at his own expense.

And that was all I needed to know about the man to understand his character.

But the need to protect was too overwhelming, and I struggled with how to handle the situation.

"Hit him with another left, Trin!" Barrick encouraged from across the parking lot. Beside him, his daughter was bouncing up and down in excitement.

"Make sure your thumb is outside your fist, so you don't break anything, Auntie Trinny. Your thumb! Fix your thumb!" Emerson instructed, doing a little cheer-style dance.

Barrick gave his eldest a high five. "Great spot, Em. You'll make an amazing coach one day."

"I know. I'm amazing at everything, Daddy. Papa and MiMi tell me all the time." But then she got distracted and skipped over to where her brother was poking at something with a stick.

I glowered at my business partner in frustration. "Should I help Trinity...or...maybe him?"

"Does it look like she needs your help, brother?" he called with a grin. "And does it honestly look as if roid-boy needs your assistance?"

Scrubbing a hand over my close-cropped beard, I glanced back at Trinity. She'd listened to Emerson's suggestion. From where I was standing, she didn't appear to need my help, and although Luca was moaning and groaning, he could have pulled her off him at any time.

"Dad, why is Mom beating on Luca Thornton?" Banks hissed as he walked up to us.

"He said something she didn't like, son," I explained.

"She's really whaling on him. He's, like, the best defensive player in the league, and she's kicking his ass."

"Language!" Luca said, pointing straight at Banks. He just stood there, getting beat on by a considerably smaller woman, but his eyes got wild when he heard anyone say a curse word around his kid.

"Don't you scold my son!" Trinity snarled.

Fuck, but she was even sexier when she was in momma-bear mode. I wanted to snatch her off Luca's back and find a private room somewhere—anywhere—so I could taste every beautiful inch of her.

"Your son shouldn't be cursing around my daughter!" Luca countered. "And you're, like, twenty-four. He's what? Nine?"

"He's about to turn eleven," Trinity informed him. "And shut up. I don't want to hear any more of your 'daddy' bull—"

"Don't say it, Trin. I'm warning you right now!"

"And I'm warning you." Hopping off his back, she was breathing hard, but she glared from one twin to the other. "If I hear either of you saying crap about Jarrett being my sugar daddy, or my children's ages compared to mine, I will spill all your secrets."

"I don't keep secrets from Violet," Luca said with a shrug.

"Mila and I tell each other everything. She knows about everything I've ever done," Lyric said, wrapping an arm around his wife's thick waist.

"I believe you," Trinity said with an emphatic nod. "But does your dad?"

"What don't I know?" Jesse Thornton asked.

"The list is endless," she said with an evil glimmer in her pretty eyes. I had to shift my legs; the sight of all that evil inside my sweet angel was one of the hottest things I'd ever witnessed. "There was that time when Luca—"

Luca covered her mouth with his hand, and he gave his father a tight smile. "Whoa, it's hot out here. Trin must have been cooking in the heat for too long. Let's get her inside and hydrated."

Jesse gave his eldest son a skeptical brow lift, but he walked over to where Devlin Cutter was chatting with his son and several rocker legends I'd yet to be introduced to. As soon as Jesse's back was turned, Luca dropped his hand and wiped it on his shirt. "You licked me!"

"I would have bitten you, but I couldn't open my mouth wide enough."

"You would have really told him!" Luca whined. "How could you narc like that, Trin?"

"Very easily, actually," she assured him. "Be good to my family today, or I'll make sure you live to regret it. Both of you."

"Yes, ma'am," Lyric muttered, his bottom lip pouting out.

"I'll think about it," Luca said, crossing his massive arms over his chest.

"Hey, Uncle Jesse, I forgot to tell you about—" Luca's hand covered her mouth again, causing her next words to be mumbled against his palm.

"Fine. You win."

She unwrapped his hand from around her face with a grin. "Glad we could reach a mutual agreement. Now, let me introduce you to my son. Banks, this is Luca, or as I like to call him, Idiot Number One. He's going to tell you everything you'll ever want to know about football. Aren't you, Luca?"

"You like football?" Luca asked, his eyes growing wide with interest.

"It's my favorite sport," Banks said with an enthusiastic nod, wonder in his eyes as he looked up at Luca like he was a god. "I gave up baseball to save my arm for football season."

"Smart thinking. Football is a million times better than baseball. Come on, kid. Let's find ourselves a golf cart. You're with me today."

I watched the two of them walk away, and then Lyric kissed his wife and followed his twin.

Mila sighed heavily as she shifted her gaze from her husband's back to us. "I'm sorry, Trin. I really did have a talk with him last night about not being... Well, that." She motioned toward the twins.

"If Violet can't keep Luca from saying crap, I have doubts you can control what came out of Lyric's mouth," Trinity excused. "I can handle those two on my own, but if I return Lyric to you with a few bumps and bruises, don't say you weren't warned."

Laughing, Mila linked her arm through Trinity's. "That's why I love you, Trin. I swear, visiting the family down here is never boring. It reminds me of home so much that sometimes I want to buy another house so we can split our time between Creswell Springs and here."

"Yo, Dawson," my future father-in-law called out. "Are you ready to play some golf with the men?"

Trinity bit her lip. "Maybe I should have been more worried about my dad today than the twins."

Bending, I kissed her forehead. "Don't worry about me, baby. I've survived plenty of war zones. Eighteen holes of golf with your dad will be easy."

Mila snorted. "Well, at least you have his final words to you to put on his tombstone, Trin."

Trinity grimaced. "Call me if you need help with anyone—and I mean anyone, Jarrett. Look out for Dad and Uncle Jesse's cheating. The twins will hopefully be good now. But don't let them get Banks into any trouble. Or teach him bad habits. Seriously, we don't want version 2.0 of them invading our house. My brother is a safe place if you need assistance. He promised he'd help you if you need it today, because Uncle Jesse did the same thing to him before he married Lucy. He's going to have Jace, Gray, and Sin with him. They can hold their own with any of the legends. But Sixx and Bentley are playing with you guys today too, so watch out for shenanigans. You remember how those two were on the European tour. At least Ali won't be with them."

"Stop worrying. I've got this."

"That's another quote she can engrave on your tombstone," Mila said with a grim nod. "Good luck."

CHAPTER 7

TRINITY

I n that half-asleep, half-awake state, I turned from my left side to my right and reached out, wanting to pull Madalyn closer for a cuddle. We'd spent the night at my parents' house to appease my mom with the whole not-seeing-the-bride tradition. Since Maddie was my bridesmaid, we'd had a tiny slumber party with Mom in my old bedroom.

Sometime around midnight, Mom had snuck back to her room to be with Dad, and I'd passed out while Madalyn finished watching Sixteen Candles. That was the last thing I remembered, but she'd been in bed beside me. Her head on the extra pillow as she randomly ate a few kernels of popcorn, chased by a freshly baked chocolate chip cookie.

When my hand didn't encounter the teenager who was supposed to be there, I lifted my lashes enough to squint in the darkness. The bed was empty, the only sign of my stepdaughter ever being there the slight impression of her head on the pillow and what little remained of our snacks.

"Maddie?" I called sleepily, sitting up. Grabbing for my phone, I saw it was just after four. Worried, I tossed back the covers and grabbed my robe to throw over my pajamas as I left the bedroom.

Quietly, I passed my parents' room and then searched downstairs. The light was on in the kitchen, which wasn't typical at such an early hour. Checking the back door, I found it unlocked and groaned. "Damn it, Maddie."

I knew without a doubt where she was and who she was with. Whatever was going on with her and the boy next door had been moving way too fast for Jarrett's or my liking. She spent most weekends sleeping over at my parents' house with Hayat and Abi. She always claimed it was so she could spend time with Hannah too. But when she came home, the only Renchford she talked about was

Holden.

She was utterly besotted with the boy in a way I couldn't remember experiencing until... Well, Jarrett. I'd had a few boyfriends in high school, and they were semi-serious. I'd had sex with one or two of them, but nothing much about those relationships had been remotely remarkable. Honestly, I couldn't even remember what it felt like to kiss those guys, let alone go further.

But the way Madalyn acted when it came to Holden, it was too similar to how I felt for Jarrett, and I didn't like it. She was too young to let those kinds of emotions overtake her life. Not only did she seem head over heels, but there was a glitter in her eyes that scared the hell out of me.

Outside, the air was still, and everything was silent. On instinct, I walked the path from the kitchen door, around the house, and straight to the Renchfords' pool house. The slightest glimmer of light was glowing inside, and I pounded my fist against the door.

"Maddie!" I called. "I swear, if you're in there, I'm going to..." I trailed off, knowing the threat was an empty one. She and I both knew, no matter what she might or might not be doing inside the pool house with that boy, I wouldn't do anything. Not ground her. Not tell her father. Not even be disappointed. I'd snuck off with one or two boyfriends too many times to throw stones from inside my own glass house.

"Shit!" I heard a deep voice grunt, and I gripped the bridge of my nose, feeling a headache brewing. "Your mom came looking for you, baby."

"It's fine. I'll see you tomorrow?" I didn't like the uncertainty in her voice. Madalyn was too confident, and that hesitant tone set off alarm bells I didn't know how to handle.

"Yeah," he answered casually. "I'll be at your parents' wedding with my folks."

"O-okay," she muttered and opened the door moments later.

With the moon reflecting off the ocean and the soft glow from inside the pool house, I could see how disheveled she was. Her hair was tangled, and it was obvious she'd hastily put her clothes back on. Pink filled her cheeks, but there was something in her gaze that had me putting my arm around her shoulders and guiding her back to my parents' house without saying a word.

Back in the kitchen, I locked the door and then made us each a cup of comfort herbal tea. Madalyn sat at the island, fiddling with her spoon as she kept her eyes locked on the contents of her mug rather than looking at me.

"I'm not going to push," I told her when the silence became too much for me. "I just need to know if you are okay."

Her teeth sank into her bottom lip for a long moment before she nodded. "I'm good."

"Then why are you fighting tears, sweetheart?"

One shoulder lifted. "I don't know. He just seemed...different. You know. After."

"Different, how?"

Another half shrug. "He wasn't the same. Before, he was sweet, told me things that made me feel special. Then after, he was...different. Like he was a completely different guy." She swallowed hard and cupped her hands around her mug. "Maybe I'm overthinking it. It was my...first time. I thought it would be different...afterward. Like, there would be cuddling, or he'd kiss me again. Or...he'd tell me he loved me again."

Alarm bells were ringing louder in my head, but I put a smile on my face to reassure her. "Maybe he was simply nervous and didn't know how to act. Guys are strange creatures, Maddie. If it was his first time too..." I paused, disliking that we were having this conversation, but what the fuck else was I supposed to do? "Perhaps he was just embarrassed, or he didn't know what to do with the emotions he was feeling. Everyone's first time is different. They feel overwhelmed, embarrassed, even guilty."

"I don't feel guilty," she said, ducking her head. "But I did feel overwhelmed. And I'm so embarrassed right now, it hurts. Please don't tell Dad."

"This will stay between the two of us," I assured her. "But I think, to playthings safe, we should see a gynecologist soon and get you protected."

"He wore a condom," she mumbled, her face turning a deeper shade of pink.

Relief nearly made my knees weak, but I grasped the edge of the island and offered her a small smile. "Good, I'm glad he thought to protect you both. But I still think we should get you in to see the doctor. I'll set up an appointment for when your dad and I get back from our honeymoon. We'll make sure you're healthy and have everything you need to ensure that you remain that way."

Groaning, she covered her face. "Dad is going to be so weird about this."

"No, I told you, this is between the two of us. He doesn't have to know what doctor I'm taking you to unless you tell him yourself." I took her hand and turned it over so we could lock fingers. "Until we get you in to see the doctor, though, will you promise me that you won't let what happened tonight happen again? Please, Maddie. I'm not condoning you having sex at this age, but now that I know you have, I would feel so much better if you waited until we get you covered. Because it's your body. That's sacred, honey. As the woman who loves you, who will give her own life for yours, please don't play games with something so special."

Her entire face turned blood red, all the way to the tips of her ears. "I can promise that Mom. It's not like it was all that great anyway. I mean..." She huffed and folded her arms around her body. "I thought it was going to be bright lights and this amazing feeling. But really it was barely a few minutes of discomfort and feeling embarrassed. And it was more secondhand embarrassment—for his sake, and not my own. I've been naked in front of other people before. We change in front of each other all the time at dance. But he was grunting and whining for maybe a minute, and just when it didn't hurt as bad, he was just...done."

I pressed my lips together, torn between being sympathetic and trying not to laugh. "That's because you either had a stupid guy or a selfish one, Maddie. It's too early to know which type Holden is, but time will tell. Until then, please keep things G-rated instead of X."

"Like I said, it won't be a problem." She took a sip of her tea then finally met my gaze. "I'm sorry if I've ruined today."

"You couldn't ruin this day if you tried," I said as I walked around the island to hug her. "Even if the entire world exploded around us, everything will still be perfect because I get to marry your dad."

She laid her head on my shoulder and hugged me back. "I'm so glad you're my mom now. I would have seriously disowned Dad if he hadn't won you back. Banks would have too. Things are better when you're around. You make life easier."

"That's what moms are supposed to do, Maddie," I told her softly.

"Well, you're the best."

Movement drew my gaze to the door, where I saw my own mom standing there watching us. "I kind of learned from the best."

Mom's chin trembled. "I love you," she mouthed, so as not to intrude on the moment I was having with my own daughter. After a moment of watching me with Madalyn, she turned and walked back the way she'd come, but not before I saw the glitter of tears in her eyes.

After we finished our tea, we went back upstairs. The sun was already coming up, and there were a million things that would have to get done before I would be able to step into my wedding dress. Instead of jumping right into the deep end, I made Maddie take a long, hot bath to ease any discomfort she might have. And then we just lay in my old bed and talked until there was a knock on my door.

"Breakfast," Dad called. "You two girls get your butts downstairs and eat before it gets cold."

"Be right there!" Sitting up, I pushed my hair back from my face and offered Madalyn my hand. "You ready?"

"To legally make you ours?" She gave me an odd look. "I think I've been ready for this a lot longer than you."

My mind hit rewind and only stopped the moment I'd seen Jarrett Dawson for the first time. Part of me had been ready for this day since I met his hazel gaze across that café, while other parts of me had been fighting it all the way up until the very moment he'd placed an engagement ring on my finger. There had been instances of perfection and long stretches of agony. But all of it had led us to this day.

And I was going to make sure it went flawlessly.

CHAPTER 8

JARRETT

My fingers shook as I tried to knot my tie. With a curse, I pulled the damn thing free and tossed it on the little couch in the room where Banks and I were supposed to be getting ready for the wedding.

"She's going to come to her senses and decide I'm not worthy of her," I muttered as I dropped down onto the couch beside the tie, raking my fingers through my hair. "Why the fuck would she even want to marry a dumbass like me?"

"Easy there, dude," a deep, amused voice said from the doorway, causing my head to snap up in surprise.

Drake Stevenson stood there with Devlin Cutter, both of them watching me with narrowed eyes, but it was Drake who stepped forward and waved his fingers in a "gimme" sign. Grimacing, I picked up the tie and dropped it in his hand. "Up," he commanded.

Grunting, I stood, and he slipped the tie around the back of my neck before starting to fix the knot. "You're right," the rock legend said while concentrating on the task. "Trin does deserve better. You broke her heart and left her to fend for herself when you should have been beside her, helping her through the most traumatic time of her life."

The memories of my own idiocy made my stomach cramp. "She won't show up," I choked out. "She's going to wise up and—"

"She's already in her dress and waiting for you to get your shit together so we can start the ceremony," Devlin announced dryly. "Seems like you're the one pussying out, old man."

"He's younger than us," Drake reminded his brother-in-law.

"Not by much," Dev muttered, watching the other man fix my tie.

"Guess she got more from her mother than just the Stevenson eyes," the guitarist said with a hint of a grin. "If I were you, I'd appreciate that your son-in-law is closer to your generation. He's more likely to take your side when you do dumb shit."

"Why are you treating him with such kindness?" Dev complained. "He's the reason Nevi spent the summer in London, and you were so anxious about her and the boys, you ended up with a case of shingles."

Drake shuddered. "I don't know what was worse. The pain of recovering from the liver transplant or the shingles."

"You got shingles because you had chicken pox at some point in your life," I informed him. "The virus was already inside you."

"Yeah, that's true. But the stress of worrying about my daughter and grandsons triggered it. Be thankful I'm not using this damn thing to hang you outside the window right now." Drake finished with the knot and slapped a hand on my chest. "Stop thinking about the mistakes you made, dumbass. Take some advice from someone who knows all too well about fucking up. It will only eat at you until you can't appreciate the goodness you now have in your life. Accept that Trin loves you and is ready to be your wife. She's not going to make a run for it. Believe me, we already asked her if she wanted to. Even offered to drive her to the airport myself in case she wanted a little time away to consider her options."

I glared at the rocker, but he only grinned, his blue-gray eyes glittering with hilarity. "Relax. She turned me down. Trin loves you too much to walk away now. So, get your shit together, old man. Grab your boy, walk down that aisle, and get ready to have your world turned right-side up when she says I do."

Devlin dropped a hand on my shoulder and squeezed. "Listen to this old fucker."

"We're basically the same age," Drake grumbled.

"Like I said, listen to this old fucker," he chuckled. "Now that you're put together, take my new grandson, and wait for Trin at the end of the aisle. I'll bring her to you soon."

Inhaling slowly to try to ease my violently beating heart, I gave a stiff nod in hopes of controlling my emotions and walked to the door. Outside, Banks was waiting, already in his suit and looking a little green. "I thought you were gonna chicken out," he said with relief coating his voice. "That's why I sent PopPop to talk to you."

As pep talks went, Drake had been straight to the point, and I had to thank him for it. Slinging an arm around my son's shoulders, I guided him toward where everyone was waiting. Luca and Lyric stood outside the double doors. Seeing us coming, they each opened one and waited for us.

"You owe me a hundred bucks," Luca told his twin as we passed. "I told you he wouldn't pussy out."

"Yeah, yeah," Lyric muttered. "He's sweating bullets, bro. I bet he was two seconds from jumping out a window before the uncles went in there to scare him into following through."

"I still won the bet," Luca said smugly, giving Banks a fist bump. "Looking good, little bud."

Banks beamed at his new idol.

The small venue was packed with at least two hundred people, and all eyes were on us as we walked down the aisle to take our place beside the officiant. Thankfully, we'd barely stopped beside the man before the music started and the double doors opened. Madalyn walked down the aisle with a sweet smile on her face, looking like an angel in her bridesmaid dress. As my daughter took her place, I thought I noticed something different about her, but I couldn't put my finger on it.

And then the music changed, and the doors opened again. Two little girls, both in the same pretty white princess-style dresses, appeared with little baskets of flower petals. Love Bug and Grier noisily made their way down the aisle, throwing flowers on the floor, at each other, and at various guests. It was a little chaotic, but amusing, nonetheless.

When they got to the end of the aisle, Grier went scurrying off to her mother, but Love Bug walked up to Banks and frowned at him. "You hold me," she instructed. "Like Daddy."

"Um." Banks looked from her to me, his eyes startled. He looked like a deer caught in oncoming headlights.

"Hold me!" Love Bug demanded with a pout.

"You heard her, son," I said, fighting a grin. "Hold the girl."

"Fine," he muttered and bent to pick her up.

"Hi." Love Bug laid her head on his shoulder and closed her eyes.

One of the doors opened, and Luca stuck his head in. "They make it to the finish line yet..." He trailed off when he saw his daughter being held by my son. "That's going to be a problem."

"Can we move this along, please?" I heard Trinity demand. "I'm kind of waiting to get married."

Huffing, he shut the door again. The music changed once more, and my heart moved up into my throat as I waited. And waited a little longer. My hands balled into fists, and I was ready to march up the aisle to find out what the holdup was all about, when the doors swung open, and Trinity stood there looking like the most beautiful bride I'd ever set eyes on. Beside her, Devlin stood with her arm threaded through his, looking both proud and ready to cry at the same time.

My gaze automatically went back to Trinity when they took the first step down the aisle. Her hair fell in soft waves down her back, a tiara holding her veil in place, and that dress...

Fuck, I was going to have to be extra careful not to rip it to shreds when I finally got her alone later.

The closer she got, the more of her I could see through my blurry eyes. I wasn't used to seeing her in makeup, but she'd kept it natural, only highlighting those beautiful eyes and her lips. She gave me a smile that wobbled, making those deep dimples pop, and I found it hard to breathe.

When she and her dad got a few feet away, they paused, waiting for the officiant to ask who was giving her away. Devlin cleared his throat once, then two more times before he was finally able to whisper, "Her mother and I do."

Trinity pulled her eyes off me long enough to kiss and hug her father before he was placing her hand in mine. I felt his trembling fingers as he made the exchange and clasped him on the back with my free hand, the father in me understanding the difficulty of the moment for him.

Devlin stepped back and then sat beside his wife, who was openly weeping, while Trinity finally saw what Banks was doing. "Is she asleep?" she asked our son.

"Um, yeah, I think?" Banks whispered, adjusting her slight weight in his arms.

"I'll take her, bud," Luca offered, appearing off to the side.

"Nah, I got her," Banks said, holding on to Love Bug a little tighter.

Trinity and Luca shared a brief look. "That's going to be a problem," they both muttered in unison, making more than a few people snicker.

***

We'd had our first dance, cut the cake, and Trinity had already thrown the bouquet—which Violet had caught, but then had thrown at Piper like it was on fire and now her hands were blistered. Everyone had cried 'Awwwww!" until she'd tossed the flowers at Piper, who'd grabbed them and waved them in Cannon's face teasingly while calling him "jerkface." Then those same people had sighed and gone back to eating their cake.

I didn't have time to wonder what the drama was regarding Violet and her being skittish about catching the bouquet. I had other, far more pressing things to think about.

Like how the fuck I was going to get Trinity out of her dress without ripping the damn thing.

Taking her hand, I guided her out of a side door and into the main part of the hotel, trying hard not to run for the nearest elevator. My fingers shook as I held her hand. Fuck, my entire body was quaking. Something she couldn't miss as the doors opened and I guided her inside.

As soon as we were shut into the metal box, I closed my eyes and tried to do physics equations in my head. I didn't know jack shit about physics, so I would either distract myself until we could get to the bridal suite where we would spend the night before catching a flight out to the Maldives the next morning, or I'd give myself an aneurysm in the process. Either way, I'd be able to control my cock until we made it to a bed.

But then Trinity pushed me up against the elevator wall. My eyes barely opened before she was gripping the back of my head and pulling me down for a kiss that ensured I lost all control.

With a feral-sounding growl, I lifted her off her feet, deepening the kiss as her legs had just enough room to wrap around my waist, considering how tight her dress was. My hands filled with her luscious ass, and I turned us, so she was the one against the wall, dry humping my cock against her core as the elevator rose higher.

I felt the machine slow and had enough brain cells left to raise my head. Breathing raggedly, I kept hold of her ass as I carried her off the elevator and straight to the suite. I didn't remember getting the door open or dropping her onto the bed. All I remembered was tearing my tie off, followed by my jacket, shirt, and pants.

By the time I was down to only my boxer briefs, she'd thankfully unzipped herself and shimmied out of her dress, leaving her in nothing but white bikini briefs and a matching bra.

"So fucking beautiful," I rasped as I pushed her back onto the pillows and spread her legs. "I'm sorry, baby. So fucking sorry. But this first time, it's going to be real quick. I swear, the rest of the night, I'll take my time with you. Make you come as many times as you ask for. Right now, though, I can't breathe. It hurts, Trinity. I'm dying because I'm not a part of you."

She lifted her hips and helped me push her panties down her legs. "I hurt too, Jarrett. Please. Take the ache away so this agony will stop."

"Baby," I groaned, sinking balls deep in one move. The sound of how wet she was filled the room, making my spine tingle as my balls drew up. I was already hanging on by a thread. If she so much as breathed wrong, I was going to spill inside her.

"Fuck, fuck, fuck," I chanted, pressing my forehead to hers. "I thought I remembered how good you felt, but nothing could have prepared me for the reality, when I've been living on dreams alone for all these months. This pussy is addictive, sweet angel. The way you wrap around me, tighter than a goddamn fist. Jesus, you're killing me, and I want to die over and over again."

"You die before you finish me, and I'll kill you, husband."

The first spurt of come felt as if it was being dragged out of me. "Say it again," I gasped, sucking in a deep breath as I began to leak inside her.

"I'm going to come, husband," she breathed, arching her back and pressing her tits into my chest. She still had her bra on, but I didn't have enough sense to unclasp it, setting those beauties free so they could drag through my chest hair as she rubbed herself up and down me. "You feel so good inside me, husband."

The clenching of her pussy and that one magic word were enough to suck the come right out of my dick. My entire body tensed as I came, hard but quick. It left me sweating and panting, but I was still a steel rod deep inside her. "Hang on, wife. I'm about to make you scream for your husband."

"Please, please, please," she moaned. "I want to come like a good girl for you."

I wrapped my hand around her throat, squeezing just hard enough to make her writhe in pleasure beneath me. "Then come, my good girl. Come for me, Trinity." With my other hand, I reached between us and strummed her clit. "Come, wife."

EPILOGUE

NATALIE

"**Y**ou can't be serious."

I gave the woman before me a tight smile, trying my damnedest to restrain myself and not knock her teeth down her throat. From the moment the Renchfords had moved in next door, I hadn't liked Hadley. She was too fake for my tastes. Her husband was a businessman who'd made his living in finance, but he'd come from old money to begin with. Oil. Agriculture. Countless other bullshit, none of them industries he'd actually worked in. No, Peyton Renchford had never worked a full day in his entire life, unless it was to call his stockbroker and tell him what to buy and what to sell.

But in Hadley's eyes, that was the right way to make money. Whereas Devlin and I, our money was so far from right, we'd drifted left.

From that first meeting, I'd sensed what a snobby cunt she was, but Peyton wasn't too bad. He treated his children well, although he seemed a little absent, even though he was at home just as often as Hadley was herself. He let Holden and Hannah do whatever they wanted. It was his treatment of his eldest son, Kyrie, that had made me like him more than his wife. The very few times I'd seen the older boy at home, Hadley had treated Kyrie much like I imagined a wicked stepmother would. Which was probably why Kyrie stayed at college even during holidays, from what I'd seen.

I tapped my nails on the documents I'd slapped on the Renchfords' kitchen island. "Deadly serious, actually," I told her sweetly. "Holden has the option of signing away his parental rights to Madalyn's child. It's his choice. Not yours. If he wants to legally remain Avalyn's father, then that is his right. If not, I need his signature. My lawyer is right here to witness and notarize it as well."

"How many times do we have to tell you people?" Hadley snapped. "Holden isn't that little slut's baby daddy."

"The amnio says otherwise," I countered. "Your son might have hit it and quit it with every other girl at school, but my granddaughter has only ever been with your creepy little asshole of a son. And even though I dislike him nearly as much as I despise you, I am still making it clear what his rights are."

"That amnio was faked," Hadley said with disdain. "Holden wouldn't touch someone so young and...dirty."

I fisted my hands at my sides, but I inhaled slowly and counted to ten in my head, while Devlin lovingly rubbed my back. But I could feel his own anger, and it fueled mine rather than dousing it. The only thing that kept me from losing what was left of my patience was the fact that my lawyer was standing right there, watching, waiting. Ready to do his part and get the hell out of there.

And then I could slap this bitch into next week without having to worry about witnesses.

"If I wanted to fake the paternity test results, I would have picked someone a hell of a lot better than your idiot son to be the father of my great-granddaughter," Devlin bit out. "Now, do us all a favor and sit your ass down and be quiet. Holden is officially eighteen. Meaning he's an adult and doesn't need Mommy to tell him what to do."

"I want you to leave," Hadley hissed, walking to the kitchen door. "Your presence is only upsetting my family."

"Your existence is upsetting mine," I growled. "Park it, lady. I'm here for your kid, not you. But you keep running your mouth, and I'll find a reason to be here for you too."

"Mom, just be quiet," Holden instructed his mother. "Where's the pen? I'll sign now and get this shit over with."

The lawyer handed over the pen and went over all the documents Holden had to sign to relinquish his parental rights. Madalyn still had a few more months to go before she gave birth, but Trinity and Jarrett wanted this dealt with before their daughter delivered. That poor girl didn't need more stress on top of being ostracized at school because she'd made the mistake of trusting the wrong boy.

The student body looked at Holden as a god for having sex with every girl in school who would willingly open her legs for him. Meanwhile, Madalyn had sex with the little bastard once and ended up pregnant. The majority of the kids at school called her a whore and turned their backs on her. Of course, they did go to two entirely different schools, but with social media so accessible, everyone knew who Avalyn's father was.

The lawyer explained every last detail, ensuring that Holden knew what he was giving up—just as I'd promised Trinity I would have him do—before allowing Holden to sign anything. Once he scrawled his name across the last page, I snatched up the document and stared down at where the boy sat.

"Are you one hundred percent sure about this?" I asked, watching his eyes.

He didn't even blink. "A thousand percent. I don't want anything else to do with that little cocktease. She was fun for about a minute, but then she got all weird, and then she started getting fat. I don't want a kid, and I definitely don't want her."

"Trust me, motherfucker," Devlin snarled, bending so he was eye level with Holden. "Maddie lost interest in you way before you did her. I ever see you even look at my granddaughter again, and your momma will be pushing you around in a wheelchair, because I'll break your fucking legs."

"Babe." I was the one soothing as I tugged on his arm. Now that I had what I'd come for, I was considerably calmer. "We should go."

"Yes," Hadley sneered as the lawyer made his exit. "Take your stupid legal papers and go away."

I tugged my husband toward the door then turned to face mother and son once again, my smile returned. "I hope you'll forgive me. All of this has been very stressful for my family, which, of course, stresses me out, and when I get stressed, I have to be doing something continuously or I'll do something stupid. Like slash your tires or burn down your house. Or, my personal favorite, drag your creeper son into the desert and tie him to a cactus. Leave him there and let the coyotes eat him for days and days."

"Nat, you're getting a little manic again, my love."

"Right. Sorry." I waved the papers back and forth. "Now that I have these, we can all relax a little for the moment, but while I was tirelessly working away, I did a little digging and found out that Holden has been accepted into his father's alma mater. But only because Peyton donated enough money to the university to build an entirely new library."

Hadley's face flushed. "That's none of your business."

"I made it my business. Just like I made it my business to contact the chancellor at the university and let them know that your son is a predator. He may not have been eighteen when he seduced Madalyn, but she was still only fifteen when it happened. Sounds like a predator in the making to me. Especially since he likes them young. Last I heard, he was sniffing around Ali St. Charles. A bad, bad idea, by the way. Between her cousin Bentley and then Sixx..." Just imagining both of those boys ganging up on Holden was enough to give me manic laughter again. Manic laughter was fine on Halloween when I dressed up as a witch to hand out candy. Any other time, it made me seem like a supervillain, and I wasn't the villain. No, that role was solely Hadley's to play.

"Anyway, I just made the chancellor aware that he had a potential predator accepted for the fall semester, and he agreed that it would be in his female students' best interest if Holden found somewhere else to get his higher education." I winked when Hadley shrieked. "And then I made sure every Ivy League school across the country was aware of the possible dangers as well. From there, I went to every potential college that might be interested in young Holden. I can get a little hyperfocused when something keeps me from sleeping."

"You couldn't possibly have contacted every college and university in the country!"

"Of course not," I scoffed. "I left a few community colleges off my list. I'm petty, but I won't keep the boy from getting a college education. There are three or four that I thought would be a good fit for Holden. I'll email you the list later."

While Hadley screamed her rage, Devlin and I walked out the Renchfords' kitchen door and made our way across their yard and into our house. No sooner was the door shut and locked behind us than Dev grasped me by the waist and lifted me onto the island.

"That was so fucking sexy." He tangled his fingers in my hair as he jerked my head back so he could nip at my throat. "My dick got so hard at all that vindictive, petty, smoking hotness that I nearly nutted right there in front of that banshee."

My laughter was anything but manic when it left my throat. "I went one step further, babe. I had Mieke send emails to every parent of every girl Hayat told me Holden has been rumored to have hooked up with over the last seven months. She suggested to them that they get their precious daughters tested for various STIs and then linked his social medias so they could see the little scumbag who has been sowing his wild oats while our granddaughter suffers with morning sickness and the hard decision of whether to keep Avalyn or give her up for adoption."

"Luckily, Trinity and Jarrett want to adopt little Avalyn." Devlin brushed his lips over my collarbone. "Now, no more talking about our little ones. I want to focus on you for the rest of the night."

"I'm all yours, Dev," I husked, looking up at him through my lashes.

"Damned right you are."

~THE END~

Hopelessly Devoted to PIPER

BOOK 6

CHAPTER 1

PIPER

With a few spritzes of perfume, I readjusted my necklace, so the pendant was perfectly in place. A quick glance in the mirror showed my panty line was still causing an issue even though I'd changed from the bikini briefs to a thong. Smirking, because what Cannon didn't know wouldn't hurt him, I slipped off the underwear and tossed them in my hamper before smoothing the skirt of my dress over my hips once more.

After months of tirelessly planning our wedding, we were now in the home stretch. In exactly one week, Cannon and I would stand before our nearest and dearest and make unbreakable vows. I knew they were unbreakable because if he so much as thought about breaking them, I would break him.

And not in the fun way he enjoyed so much.

Our wedding planner only had a few last-minute details to put in place, but during that time, we could relax and enjoy the moment with our families before leaving for the month-long honeymoon Cannon had arranged. He said it was a surprise, and while I still wasn't the biggest fan of Baby Cage and his surprises, I was looking forward to four weeks of being alone with my new husband.

Just the idea of that word made me smile. It wasn't something I thought I would ever want. Marriage hadn't been on my list of priorities. Casual sex was fine, but long-term relationships hadn't been worth my time. The irony that my first and only one was with my childhood bully and adulthood frenemy wasn't fully lost on me. There had always been a pull between us, but we'd fought it our entire lives.

Until Cannon decided to grow a pair and fight for us.

That had been two years ago, and we'd been living together for the majority of the time since then, engaged for nearly a year. Planning our wedding while on our latest summer tour had been interesting but finding the right person to help had made things considerably easier.

Other than a couple trips back to LA for a few things, like picking out our cake and choosing the caterer—not to mention finding the right wedding dress—everything had been done through Zoom calls and emails. The pressure was still there, but our wedding planner, Francesca, had been a godsend.

At the sound of the doorbell, I grabbed my purse and phone off the bed and walked through the apartment. Cannon was already at the door, speaking to whoever was on the other side. We were having separate, small get-togethers tonight. Nothing dramatic enough to be labeled bachelor or bachelorette parties. Just a little bit of fun with our friends and a few family members to unwind and catch up with those we hadn't seen in a while, before the chaos of the wedding itself overran our time and kept us from hanging out with the people we loved.

"I thought Jagger was picking me up," Cannon said as he frowned at the two guys standing on the other side of the threshold.

"Jagger is picking you up," I reaffirmed as I walked up behind him. Putting my hand on his waist, I glanced around his wide shoulders to find Cannon and Jagger's drummer, Smith, and to my surprise, my brother, Asher.

Smith and I didn't talk that much, and the few times we had had a conversation, he kept the exchange to monosyllabic responses. I wasn't sure if he didn't like me or if he was just the quiet type, but I didn't know the drummer well enough to figure him out. As for my brother, he hated Cannon. Even when our parents had gotten on board with my relationship with my now-fiancé, Ash had remained a complete ass when it came to everything Cannon. Smith wasn't just Cannon and Jagger's drummer, but he and Cannon were friends. They occasionally went out for drinks together when we weren't on tour.

But the fact that Asher was standing there made me a little uneasy.

"Jagger is running behind," my brother excused. "He asked Smith to pick up Cannon, and he will meet us at the club."

"And you and Smith are what, besties now?" I asked, my brows lifting as I glanced from one guy to the other.

"We live in the same building, Piper," Asher reminded me. "We decided to drive to the club together. And since we were in my car when Jagger called Smith..." He trailed off with a shrug. "I'm the designated driver tonight anyway."

I wasn't surprised. Given our dad's history with addiction, and that Asher always had seemed to have an addictive personality, he avoided temptation by never drinking.

"I didn't realize you guys needed designated drivers." I shifted my gaze up to look at Cannon's face. He hadn't mentioned drinking, although I wouldn't have tried to talk him out of it. A few drinks were fine. Because of his own history and demons, he didn't typically overdo it when it came to alcohol.

"I was going to have a beer or two, sugar. But that's all." Grasping my wrist, he tugged me, so I was standing in front of him, his eyes eating up the sight of me in my dress. The front had a plunging neckline that went to my navel. The straps were thin, and it was obvious I wasn't wearing a bra. A little double-sided tape kept the material over my boobs, so I didn't accidently flash anyone a nipple during the evening. The skirt ended at midthigh, but when he twirled me around, he couldn't miss that the dress was basically backless.

Jaw clenched, he shut the door, separating us from the two guys still in the corridor. "This is what you're wearing out tonight?"

"Mm-hmm." I pulled my hand free from his grasp and fluffed my hair, unconcerned with the jealous, predatory look in his blue eyes. We'd been together for two years, and my clothes were always a sore spot for him, but I wasn't going to change any part of myself to soothe the little green-monster that resided within him. He knew it was a battle he was never going to win, but that didn't stop him from getting all growly over any of my wardrobe he didn't appreciate.

"And what club will you be going to with the girls tonight?"

I smirked up at him. "I don't believe I told you. Nor did you tell me where you were going. I think that was a requirement both Jagger and Shaw insisted on, so that no one would crash the other's party."

"Right," he grumbled. "Wouldn't want to ruin your fun."

I stroked my thumb over his left dimple. "And I wouldn't even think of crashing your party, baby."

"Who is picking you up again?"

"Trin. She and Shaw planned my party together. It was a little idea that Violet and I came up with in hopes of getting the two of them to put their animosity aside."

Cannon grimaced. "Shaw has been trying for two years to get Trin to forgive her for all that shit. Trin can hold a grudge, though. And I really can't blame her, but it's been stressful for everyone."

Admittedly, I understood Trin's reasons for blocking Shaw out. My soon-to-be sister-in-law had crossed a line when she'd taken her assumptions about Trinity's health to Jarrett Dawson instead of simply talking to Trinity about what she thought was going on. Instead, she'd gossiped about Trinity and her possible miscarriage to Aunt Dallas, and then when Aunt Natalie came to them with her own theories, they'd kept it between the three of them rather than talking to Trin about any of it. She felt betrayed by someone she'd always considered family. A betrayal that went so deep, she didn't feel like she could trust Shaw again.

Which had definitely put a strain on everyone, especially our close-knit group. Shaw was about to be my sister-in-law, and Trin was one of my dearest honorary cousins. I was torn between my loyalty to both women. I didn't want to take sides, but if they didn't settle this thing between the two of them, we would all eventually have to choose. And based on who I would pick, it would cause bigger issues. When I gave someone my loyalty, I didn't do it in half measures. If Trin couldn't forgive Shaw, I would back Trin, and that meant cutting Shaw out of my life.

Given that we were about to become in-laws, that would make family functions awkward as fuck. But I was a pro at pretending people didn't exist, even if they were standing right in front of me. Ironically, it was a trick to surviving that I'd learned from Shaw's brother and now the love of my life.

"I know, that's why Vi and I decided to try to push them to work together on this. Wish me luck that we don't end up with another catfight on our hands tonight." I pouted out my bottom lip. "Although I'm seriously sad we weren't there to see the first one. I bet it was hot."

"Stop it before I puke," he groaned. "That's my sister and a girl I consider my sister."

"Neither of them are girls now, Baby Cage," I teased. "And they are both hot as fuck."

"Pipes," he warned, his face turning green. "You know I love it when you get turned on by other women. But not this time. I'm gonna blow chunks."

"All those dimples," I sighed dreamily. I tilted my head back and winked up at him. "Do you think our kids will have dimples?"

"Our kids?" he squeaked. "Where the fuck did that come from?"

My amusement faded at his reaction, and I pulled back. "It was just a question," I muttered, adjusting my skirt a little. "You should go. Trin will be here soon, and you know how impatient Asher gets."

"Fuck Asher," he grumbled unhappily. "Where did the kid thing come from? We haven't even gotten married yet, and you're talking about kids. This is... Can't we just have a little time enjoying being married before we bring kids into the equation?"

Angrily, I walked away from him. "It was just a fucking question, Cannon. No one mentioned bringing kids into this relationship. Goddamn, you would think I'd just told you I was pregnant."

"Are you telling me that you're pregnant?" he half shouted, and I swung around to glare at him.

"No," I hissed. "I am definitely not telling you that I'm having your baby. You know what, let's just go ahead and get this out of the way since it so obviously upsets you. We are not having kids. Ever. I don't want to bring another version of you into the world. One of you as a kid was plenty for this lifetime."

I watched as the color drained from his face. "Wait, sugar. That's not what I meant. I want us to have kids. Just not... I'm not ready to share you yet. I want a year or two of us alone before we—"

"We'll have plenty of time alone," I interrupted. "Because I don't want kids with you."

I did.

So fucking bad.

But after the way he'd reacted over such an innocent question, I knew that was just a pipe dream. Maybe he thought he wanted kids later on, but I no longer wanted to think about it. It hurt too much.

He'd hurt me too much.

Not just with this little argument, but in the past. And I wasn't going to travel down any path that could potentially cause me more pain where Cannon Cage was concerned.

Kids were off the table for us.

One immature asshole was enough to deal with. Adding a baby to the mix was just a recipe for disaster.

CHAPTER 2

Cannon

I fucked up.
Again.
Shit.

She'd just been teasing me, asking if I thought our future kids would have dimples, and I'd opened my stupid mouth, said the wrong things in the wrong tone. Now she was hurt, and I knew I'd fucked up something important.

Something special.

I didn't have an excuse other than the thought of being a dad freaked me out. It wasn't that I didn't want to be one. Someday. I just didn't think I was ready yet. I needed more time. And then there was the whole sharing Piper with someone else. For two years, I'd had her all to myself. It was a dream, one I'd struggled to make come true for so damn long. Having all her attention on me wasn't something I was ready to give up.

But kids...

They would be nice. Eventually. One day, when I was calmer and less obsessed with having every spare minute of Piper's time and attention for myself.

My reaction had caused damage. I knew it the moment she'd walked away from me. I'd fucked up without meaning to, and now she was hurt and pissed.

What if having kids was a deal-breaker for her? We hadn't talked about it, and I'd thought it was because it was a nonissue. That neither of us were ready to be parents. But what if she'd just been keeping it to herself, waiting for me to pull my head out of my ass and ask when we were going to have babies?

Now she was angry, and I was positive I'd broken something I had no idea how to put back together. She hadn't tossed out any threats of canceling the wedding, but she'd been adamant when she said she didn't want kids with me.

I don't want to bring another version of you into the world. One of you as a kid was plenty for this lifetime.

I flinched as what she'd said replayed in my head. If she'd wanted to score points, she'd gotten a direct hit with each word that had left her sinful mouth. I couldn't blame her. The kid version of me had been a little shit who tormented her. Not even I wanted a clone of that asshole running around.

Yet a little girl who looked just like Piper... With her sassy personality. Her give-no-fucks confidence. That mischievous twinkle in her eyes that made my heart so full even when her devious mind was planning my demise.

I would take as many of those as Piper would give me.

But with the finality in her voice that still rang through my head over an hour later, I realized it wasn't going to ever happen unless I fixed this latest fuckup.

Picking up the beer Smith had just handed me, I tipped it back and swallowed half in one go. It tasted like shit, and I gave him a glare. "You're not allowed to pick the beer anymore."

Smith grunted in answer and tipped his own bottle to his lips while Asher played on his phone across from me. My guys' night out wasn't much fun so far. Not only was I worried about fixing things with Piper, but Jagger and the rest of the guys hadn't shown up yet. It was just Smith, who only answered in grunts and shrugs, and Asher, who couldn't be bothered to speak to me. I doubted I was much fun to them either with my mind on my little rocker, but I was getting pissed at Jagger for leaving me hanging.

He would guide me. Tell me what a fuckup I'd been, but then he'd help me figure out a way to fix this shit.

Pulling my phone from my jeans pocket, I fumbled to unlock it, blinking down as the image of Piper on the lock screen blurred before my eyes. Shaking my head, I got my phone unlocked and then called Jagger.

"Where're you?" I asked, then frowned, realizing my words were slurred. "Where...are...you?" I spoke slower, trying to make sure he understood.

"I'm at the club," my best friend said, sounding annoyed with me. "Where the fuck are you? You should have been here over an hour ago."

I shook my head to clear it and glanced around. "I'm the club..." Realizing my words weren't making sense, I glanced at the half-drunk beer in my other hand then over at Smith. He blurred, turning from one, to two, then to three of my friend and drummer in less than a second. "Shift."

"Cannon, what the fuck? You sound like you're having a stroke."

Turning my head, I looked at Asher, all three of him, and thought I caught a smirk. "Jajs, dey flucked me uff."

"They what?" he shouted. "Who? Where are you?"

I didn't think I could speak clearly enough to tell him. With my vision only getting worse by the second, I hung up and then struggled to send Jagger my location, hoping I got it to go through before the world went completely black around me. As I started to feel the void pull me under, I vowed that Smith and Asher were dead as soon as I could see again.

****

I woke up with a start, my arms swinging as I sat straight up.

The world spun around me, but I still swung my fists in a fight-or-flight reflex.

Groaning at the pounding in my head, I glanced around. I was in a bedroom with a lamp on. I didn't recognize the place, but it didn't look like a hotel room, so I was sure it was someone's home. Inhaling slowly, I tried to gather my bearings.

My shirt was off, as well as my jeans. I was under the covers, but my boxer briefs were on. Beside the bed, I saw multiple condom wrappers, but no sign of the rubbers that had been in them. I knew they weren't mine. Not only had I not needed to use condoms since being with Piper, but from the packaging, I could tell they weren't the right size. Vaguely, I remembered seeing Smith with a stash of the same brand on the tour bus in the past. Sniffing, I could smell the faint scent of perfume, but the room didn't smell like sex.

Just to be safe, I pulled down my boxers and grabbed my cock, making sure it didn't have any jizz or condom residue on it. When I saw it was clean, and I didn't catch the distinctive smell of latex or lube, I blew out a relieved breath and pulled my underwear back into place.

I felt hungover as fuck, something I hadn't been in years. Not since...that night. I didn't allow myself to drink more than one or two beers, and never anything stronger, for fear of getting drunk. I didn't want what I did that night to happen again, so I didn't put myself in a position where it could happen.

Only, apparently, I'd been played, and now I didn't know what I'd missed.

Slowly, I got out of bed and searched for my clothes. I found my shirt on the floor at the end of the bed and my jeans in the connecting bathroom. The place was tidy and obviously a guest room, but I saw nothing that could tell me whose place I was at. While I was in the bathroom, I splashed water on my face in an attempt to clear my head, but it did nothing to offer any relief to the pounding at my temples and the back of my head. My stomach was sour, but thankfully, I didn't feel like I was going to blow chunks.

What I needed was my phone. It wasn't in my pocket, and a search of the bedroom didn't uncover the device that could help me figure out just how much trouble I'd gotten into once the world had disappeared.

Fuck, I didn't even know how long ago that was. It could have been hours or days. The room I was in had closed drapes, and I stumbled over to them, trying to figure out if it was day or night, maybe even give me a clue about where the hell I'd been taken.

As I drew back a curtain, I saw the sun was coming up, but other than that, I was clueless as to where I was.

The sound of humming reached me just as the door opened. A woman with long blond hair, dressed in a robe, stood there with a huge mug of steaming coffee in one hand and a plate of dry toast in the other. "Good morning," she greeted with a smirk.

"Who the fuck are you, and how did I get here?" I demanded, thankful to hear my words weren't slurred or garbled.

Walking farther into the room, she held out the mug. "Here. Drink this to help with the headache. And this dry toast should soak up whatever is left in your stomach."

"What would be in my stomach?" I demanded, not bothering to take either dish from her. My gaze stayed locked on the woman, distrust for her rolling off me and filling the room with tension.

"Relax, big guy. I'm only here to help you."

"From where I'm standing, you appear to have helped fuck me over. I'm not drinking or eating anything but what I make for myself." I released the hold on the drapes and cautiously walked around her, never turning my back to her as I moved toward the door.

"You can leave whenever you want," she said with amusement. "I'm not holding you here against your will, Cannon Cage."

"Where's my phone?" I demanded as I backed out of the room. Once I was in the hall, I quickly found the living room. A brief glance around didn't turn up a single sign of my phone, who the chick in the robe was, or where the fuck I was.

"Smith and his friend took all your stuff with them when they dropped you off here," she informed me, taking a drink from the mug she still held. "Including your wallet."

"Motherfuckers!" I snarled, raking both hands through my hair. I'd been so focused on my lack of phone that I hadn't realized my wallet was missing. It had cash, my ID, and all my credit cards in it. Calling an Uber was out, and now, so was a taxi. I didn't have a way to call Piper or Jagger or even my sister because I just plugged their numbers into my phone and never bothered to memorize them.

Fuck. Piper was going to kill me.

Groaning, I turned on the blonde. "Tell me where I am. My fiancée is already pissed at me, and adding not coming home last night won't win me any points when I try to fix the fuckup I've already made."

Sympathy crossed her face, and she gave a small sigh. "What did you do to Smith to make him prank you like this?"

"Like what?" I shouted, only to wince as the loudness of my own voice caused my head to throb even worse.

"You're in Mexico. They dropped you here and told me to take care of you. Said they were just having a little fun with you, but the longer you stayed lost, the better I'd get paid." She shrugged. "Some harmless fun between boys is nothing, compared to earning my rent for this place on my back. Usually when Smith comes to see me, he stays for a few days. Sometimes he brings a friend or two, and I get paid really well. This time, he dropped you off with five grand and said to keep you around as long as possible."

Every muscle in my body tensed. "Smith and Asher dumped me in Mexico. At a prostitute's house." It came out as a statement, rather than a question, because for some reason, I believed her. "A house she runs tricks out of."

"Hey, I'm a classy working girl. I keep my client list high-end. They just have to cross the border a few miles to get to me." She wrinkled her nose. "I'm not exactly welcome in the States right now."

"Let me guess. You have a few outstanding warrants?" She shrugged again, and I muttered a curse. "How long did they want you to keep me lost, or around here, or whatever the fuck?"

"He said at least a week. Maybe longer. Said you would be up for a good time when you woke up and the drugs wore off. But you don't look like you're into a good time. I might live on this side of the border these days, but I follow all the entertainment news in LA. I know you're supposed to be getting married in a few days."

"A few days?" I wheezed. Fear choked me at the casual way she said, "few days," like it wasn't as far off as I assumed it was. "Saturday. My wedding is Saturday."

"Oh, that's still a good five days away." She brushed it off. "It's only Monday."

"Monday?" I whispered. "I went to the club Saturday. I've been gone for two nights?"

"Smith did say he'd spiked you twice. The first time while you were partying. The second time, right before you got here. Said he didn't want you waking up before he and his buddy could make it home."

"I'll kill them," I seethed.

"You'll have to get back home to do that, rock star."

CHAPTER 3

PIPER

My girls' night out didn't go as I'd hoped. After dealing with Cannon's shit right before he left with Asher and Smith, I'd been too lost in my own head to have much fun. My friends seemed to understand that I wasn't the best company and hadn't pushed me about it. They knew Cannon and I had the occasional argument, but in the two years we'd been together, those disputes never lasted long.

While I hadn't expected the whole baby thing to affect anything, I wasn't about to change my mind on making the decision not to have kids with him. Obviously, I still had a man child on my hands, and I wasn't going to bring a baby into that dynamic when their father was more of a toddler than they ever would be.

If I didn't love him so much, I would walk away because his tantrums were fucking exhausting.

But I did love him. And even though I was hurt and pissed, I wasn't going to let it to break us.

I got home before him. After a shower, I fell into bed and texted him to ask when he would be home. But minutes, and then an hour, passed without any response. Even when we were fighting, he always replied back right away.

Frowning, I sat up in bed and texted Jagger.

Me: Is Cannon shit-faced?

Jags: I wouldn't know.

He didn't know? What the hell did that mean? Wasn't he with Cannon?

Me: Why the fuck don't you know???

Jags: Because I haven't seen him all night. I got a weird call from him earlier in the night, but nothing since. He wasn't at the apartment when I stopped by to pick him up, so I figured he just came to the club without me. But when I got here, no one had seen him.

Alarm bells started going off in my head.

Me: Asher and Smith showed up at the apartment. They said you were running late, and you asked them to pick Cannon up.

Jags: 1. I didn't ask either of them to do shit. 2. I haven't seen them tonight either.

Tossing back the covers, I jumped out of bed and started pacing as I hit connect on Jagger's name.

As soon as I heard his voice, I was talking in a rush. "Asher and Smith picked him up. He went with them. They said you were running late."

"Piper, honey, you already told me that. And I explained that it was bullshit," Jagger's voice was calm, but I could hear something beneath. Something that made sweat break out across my entire body. "When he called me earlier, he sounded off. His words were slurred, but I just thought he was drunk."

"Cannon doesn't get drunk," I cried, my anxiety spiking higher. "You know he doesn't, Jagger. And you know why. Something is wrong. He's not answering my texts, and he always answers me, even when we've been arguing. And yes, we did have a huge disagreement before he left earlier, but that wouldn't keep him from responding. He wouldn't make me worry."

I heard Jagger blow out a heavy sigh. "You said Smith and Asher picked him up."

"Yes. It was weird. Smith, I would believe, but not my brother. There is still too much animosity between the two of them. But part of me hoped he was trying to offer an olive branch or something with the wedding so close. I thought..." Sucking in a deep breath, I shook my head. "I thought my brother was putting everything aside because he realized the wedding was going to happen whether he liked it or not, and he loves me enough to finally accept that Cannon and I are forever."

"You realize Asher is even more stubborn than you are, right? I bet even when you and Cannon have been married for twenty or thirty years, your brother will still be hostile about it."

"Ah, God," I groaned, dropping down onto the edge of the bed. "They did something to him."

"I don't doubt Asher did something, but he had Smith with him. Smith and Cannon are friends. He wouldn't let anything happen..."

The way Jagger trailed off made me tremble. "What?"

"I don't know. Just a feeling. Smith has been kind of off since Cannon proposed to you. I've heard him grumbling a time or two about the wedding plans. He was kind of an ass after Shaw, and I got married. Didn't like that I was touring with my wife and kid. Over the summer, he bitched a few times about Cannon getting pussy-whipped too."

"I really don't care why Smith would help my brother," I gritted out, my anger pushing down my nervousness. If my brother really had done something to Cannon, I was going to murder him. "I need to go. I have to call my brother."

"Shaw has his phone connected to her Find My Phone app. I'm going to see if I can locate him on the GPS."

"Let me know if you learn anything." Hanging up, I called my brother, but it only rang twice before he sent me to voice mail.

Sucking in a deep breath, I waited for the message to beep before I exploded.

"Where the fuck are you?" I shouted into my phone. "Where is Cannon? I swear to all that you hold holy, Asher Bryant, if you've done something to my fiancé, there isn't anywhere on God's green earth that you can hide from me!"

Hanging up, I called Hymn.

"Hello?" she answered sleepily.

"Is Asher at your place?" I demanded.

"No, I haven't seen him in a few days." I heard a trace of anger and sadness in her voice. "I didn't tell you at the club tonight because you seemed distracted, but we had a huge argument over the wedding next weekend, and I told him to leave. He stormed out, and I haven't spoken to him since."

"Damn, I'm sorry, Hymn." I chewed on my thumbnail as I paced the bedroom.

"What's going on? Why are you looking for him?"

I explained how Asher had picked up Cannon with Smith, but none of them had shown up at the club, and now no one could reach Cannon, and Asher wasn't answering his phone.

"I'll try calling him. Maybe Asher will pick up for me."

"Let me know if you hear from him."

After promising she would, I kept pacing. The only thing left to do was to call my parents, but it was the middle of the night. If I called them and told them what I suspected at two in the morning, a week before my wedding, they would explode. I wasn't sure they would believe me that I thought Asher had done something nefarious. It was more likely they would assume Cannon had bailed on me.

And while that wasn't off the list of possibilities, I refused to consider it as an option. Yet. My gut told me my brother had been up to no good, and that didn't bode well for Cannon's safety.

Still chewing on my thumbnail, I called Trinity instead.

"Do you know what time it is?" she hissed at me when she picked up. "I just got Avalyn to sleep. She was up all evening until I got home from your party."

Guilt and anxiety and frustration collided, and I started sobbing. Trin instantly went into fix-it mode.

"Piper! Sit down and take a few deep breaths." I dropped down onto the floor and curled my legs toward my chest. Pressing my forehead to my knees, I sucked in a few deep breaths. "When you're ready, tell me what the fuck is going on."

I tried to calm my crying, but it wouldn't stop, so I just garbled it all out through the sobs. Somehow, Trin was able to understand me. "Jarrett, I need you to trace Cannon's phone."

I sat there on the floor of my bedroom for a few minutes before she spoke again. "His phone is off, Piper. And the tracking has been disabled. But Jarrett is trying both Asher's phone and Smith's now."

"O-okay. Th-thank you."

I heard another long pause and then a curse. "They're traveling south. They've gone into Mexico. Both phones are in the same location, so Asher and Smith are together. Whether Cannon is with them or not is another story."

"We have to find him," I sobbed. "He... We... But I..."

"Piper, sweetie, just take a few more deep breaths for me. Jarrett is getting dressed now. He will find Cannon. I promise."

"Jagger," I choked out. "Take Jagger too."

"Barrick and Jagger will both go with Jarrett," she assured me. "But right now, I need you to stay calm."

"My parents will think he bailed on me. And I don't want to think about it, but maybe he did."

"Shut the fuck up!" Trin snapped. "You two have had your issues for decades. Decades, Piper. But in the past two years, that idiot has proven to me and everyone else that you are the sun he revolves around. Even if you two had the fight of all fights, he wouldn't bail on you. Pull your shit together. My husband is going to go find your man, and then we're going to sort out Asher and Smith. Until then, drink something strongly caffeinated and extra sweet. I'll be over as soon as I can."

CHAPTER 4

PIPER

T
he sun was setting Sunday night, and Trinity was still at my apartment. Shaw had shown up, minus Grier, as well as Mia. The three of them tried to keep me calm but having gone almost twenty-four hours without contact with my brother, Cannon, or even Smith, I was starting to lose my fucking mind.

Trin was on the phone with her husband, but after Asher and Smith had crossed the border into Mexico, they must have wised up and turned off their phones, because Jarrett and the guys lost track of their location after that. It was only in the past hour that my brother had turned his phone back on and, for some reason, also enabled his location once again. Oddly enough, he was in California.

While my friend spoke quietly with her husband in the corner of the kitchen, my own phone went off. Seeing it was Hymn, I immediately picked it up, hoping she had news regarding my brother.

"Hymn?" I muttered when she didn't speak.

Instead of her voice, I heard Asher's in the background.

"I fixed the problem," Asher said with a cocky confidence that set my teeth on edge.

"What are you talking about? We didn't have a problem, Ash. You had one. This obsession you have with Piper marrying Cannon is becoming too much, and I was just tired of hearing you bitch about it. They're getting married on Saturday, and there's nothing you can do about it. It's time to get over it, move on, and be happy for your sister."

"There's not going to be a wedding." He laughed heartily, making me feel physically ill. "I made sure of that."

"Fuck, Asher, what did you do?" Hymn demanded, her voice full of trepidation.

"Just dropped him off at some whore's house so he can have a little fun. Smith says Erica is so good at sucking dick, there's no way Cannon will want to come home." A deep chuckle came from the background. "Smith even snapped a few pictures with Cannon's phone. My sister will be getting the photos first thing tomorrow, and after she sees him in action with Erica, she'll be canceling the wedding."

Hymn muttered a vicious curse. "How did you get Cannon to go with you to this Erica chick's house?" she demanded. "There's no way he would just decide to go to some whorehouse. He's in love with Piper. He's loyal."

"Smith dosed his beer," my brother said so casually I nearly puked. Like dosing someone wasn't anything serious. As if he'd seen it happen a hundred times and had done nothing to stop it.

Maybe he'd even done it himself.

No, my brain screamed. My brother wouldn't do that. He wasn't that kind of guy.

But maybe I didn't know Asher as well as I'd always thought.

"Oh my God," Hymn whispered. "How did I not sense it?"

"Sense what?" Asher asked, and I could practically picture the frown on his stupid face.

"That you've turned into a monster," Hymn cried. "I don't even know you anymore. I don't want to know you anymore. Get the fuck out, Ash."

"What?" he barked. "Stop talking like that, Hymn. Of course you know me. I've loved you since the moment I met you."

"I thought I loved you too," she said in a quavering voice. "But I don't love this version of you. I can barely stand to be near you. Get out, Asher. Just being in the same room with you is making me sick."

"Hymn—"

"No!" she shouted. "Do not touch me, asshole. You let some guy drug Cannon. And then you sat here and laughed about it, like it wasn't anything unusual. Like it's not a fucking crime! How many times have you watched him do it before? How many girls have you allowed him to take advantage of?"

"I've never—"

"How many times!" she screamed.

The others around me were watching me with raised brows. Mia opened her mouth, but I lifted my hand, cutting her off, needing to hear what my brother said.

"I don't hang out with Smith," he answered, but there was an evasiveness in his tone even I could hear.

"He lives in the same apartment building as you," Hymn said in disbelief. "If you haven't seen him dose anyone, that doesn't mean you have never seen him with a drugged victim."

"I don't—"

"Do not lie to me, Asher! I can hear it in your voice."

"Fine, whatever. I saw a few unsteady chicks with him on one or two occasions."

"You knew they were drugged." Her voice was full of horror. "You knew, and you did nothing. Fuck, you're just as disgusting as he is."

"No," he rasped, finally realizing just how much he'd screwed up. "Hymn, I'm not like that."

"Why else would you ask Smith to help you cause trouble?" she demanded, the tears evident from her tone. "You knew what he did to those girls, and you decided to get him to help you stop Piper's wedding."

"Yeah, okay. I knew about the drugs he had access to. It didn't take much to convince him to help me. Smith doesn't want Cannon to get married any more than I do. He said he felt like the band was becoming too soft. Before Jagger got married, their tours were wild. Girls everywhere. Partying every night. Now there's nothing but preschool shows and tea parties and Cannon running after Piper like she will disappear if he doesn't have his hands on her every spare second of the day."

I'd heard enough. Putting my phone on speaker, I placed it quietly on the kitchen table and stood. Without a word to the others, I walked out of the room. Grabbing my set of keys to Cannon's car, I picked up my purse and left.

The drive to Hymn's apartment wasn't long. She only lived a few blocks from us. Her place was on the first floor, and I walked right up to her door, using my key to let myself in. I heard Asher's voice before I'd even stepped inside.

"Hymn, I'm not like Smith. I would never do anything to hurt a woman, especially not you. Please, baby, I'm begging you. Don't do this."

Nala was at the entrance to the living room, staying out of the way but alert and ready to act if her person needed assistance. I stroked the guide dog on the head then walked up behind my brother while he was still distracted. His entire focus was on Hymn, who was crying but holding her hands up like she was trying to fend him off.

A huge decorative wooden bowl was sitting on a table, and I picked it up. Walking up behind my brother, I lifted the heavy bowl over my head and slammed it down on his skull. He yelped in pain then went limp. His knees hit the floor first, and then he face-planted on the carpet between Hymn and me.

"What happened?" my friend cried. "Is he...dead?"

"No, but it wouldn't have been anything he didn't deserve if I had killed him," I said calmly. Scrubbing a hand over my face, I wiped away my tears. The rage was still simmering just beneath the surface. My brother and I had been close growing up, but I never would have guessed he would turn into the person he was now. This was going to destroy our parents, but I had zero sympathy for him.

Walking over to the table beside the couch, I picked up Hymn's phone from where she'd placed it facedown so I could listen in on her conversation with my brother. "Shaw? Mia? Trin?"

"We're here, Piper," Shaw answered, her voice tight.

"I made a bit of a mess. Asher probably needs medical attention." He groaned in pain and started to lift his head. Cursing under his breath, he rolled onto his back while holding a hand to his head.

Eyes still closed, he whined, "Who hit me?"

"You're lucky I didn't have a gun," I told him in a voice that was completely devoid of emotion. "Because if I'd had access to one, your brains would be all over the floor."

His body jerked at the sound of my voice, and he tried to lift his lids, but he must have had a concussion because he appeared to have difficulty keeping his eyes open. "Fuck. Piper, I can—"

"Explain?" I finished his sentence, cutting him off. "Ah, brother dear, I heard plenty of your explanation to Hymn." Walking over to him, I put my foot on his chest and leaned down so our eyes locked. "Tell me where Cannon is."

"No."

"Wrong answer." The foot on his chest went to his throat. He grasped my ankle with his hands when I put some of my weight on him. He made a gagging sound as I pressed down on his windpipe, but my brother wasn't lacking in the muscle department. He lifted my foot and then shoved me away, making me fall on my ass a few feet away.

Scrambling to my feet, I moved back to his side. When he tried to sit up, I grabbed a heavy throw pillow and slammed it against his face, making him fall back once again. "Where is Cannon?" I shouted.

"Mexico!" Asher groaned.

"Where in Mexico?"

"Hit me again, Piper. Slap me. Punch me. Call me names. I'm your brother, I'm used to your temper." He laughed, but I saw his mouth was full of blood when he grinned up at me. "But I'll never tell you where that bastard is. He doesn't deserve you."

I crouched down beside him, disappointment and disgust rolling through me at just the sight of my big brother. "You're the undeserving one, Asher. No, that's a lie. You do deserve something, and it's not the beating I so desperately want to give you. You should be in jail. Not only did you kidnap Cannon, which is a felony, by the way. But you knew about Smith drugging women for...how long?"

"I didn't know for sure," he said, swallowing hard.

"Somehow, I don't think Mom and Dad will care if you knew 'for sure.' If you even suspected, then you should have spoken up, done something. Instead, you were part of the problem, not the solution. Who knows how many lives you could have saved."

"He didn't kill them, for fuck's sake."

"You think his victims don't have trauma?" I slapped him across the face for being such an idiot. "You think they didn't wake up wondering what happened, scared, unsure of where they were? Do you think they wondered until it drove them crazy if they'd done something wrong, something that would make anyone think they deserved being drugged and taken advantage of? Are you such a bastard that you didn't give two shits if he hurt them?"

"I..."

"Here is a little lesson for you, Asher. If a woman is unable to say yes, then it's always no. And if Smith needed to drug them to get them back to his apartment, then it was definitely a no. You saw what was happening, and you did nothing. In my eyes, you're just as disgusting as he is."

"I'm not like him!" he roared, sitting up.

I slapped him with the pillow again, making him fall back so hard his head hit the floor with a loud thump. "You knew, and you asked for his help to destroy my relationship with Cannon. But you can't do anything to ruin what we have. No matter what you do, or how hard you try, he and I are forever. I will find him, and we are getting married on Saturday." Tossing the pillow on the floor beside him, I felt my heart rip apart. "But if I ever see you again, I'll fucking kill you."

CHAPTER 5

CANNON

Her name was Erica, and Smith had been one of her "clients" for about three years. They'd had an arrangement before she'd had to move to Mexico, and he'd even helped her set up her new business across the border.

For a price.

There was always a fucking price.

Erica had access to certain drugs that my drummer liked to play around with. Ex-drummer, now, because that motherfucker was dead as soon as I got my hands on him.

I got all that information from Erica for a price, one I'd have to pay as soon as I got back to the apartment and had access to my online banking account. The five grand Smith or Asher, or both of them, had paid her was nothing to how much I was willing to give her to help me get back to Piper.

Fucking hell. Piper. She was probably miles beyond pissed at me. No doubt, she either wanted to kill me or call off the wedding at this point. The idea of losing her made me sweat, and I was twitchy as I sat on the sofa in Erica's living room, waiting for her to finish the call to another one of her "clients" who she trusted to get me back across the border. I already had her offshore banking information. I'd wire the hundred thousand as soon as I opened my laptop. It was the promise I'd made, and I would keep.

And then I'd figure this shit out with Piper. I'd beg her forgiveness, sell my soul to her or the devil, or wherever the fuck she asked me to in order to keep her. No matter how long it took, I'd fix what I'd broken.

Once that miracle was complete, I would hunt down Smith's sorry ass and bury him.

I clenched my hands into fists. Asher needed to be dealt with too, but if I touched him, that would only cause more issues with Piper. I couldn't kill her brother. Not only would she leave me, but her parents would come for me. Liam was scary as fuck, but it was Gabriella I was more scared of.

After all my past fuckups, no one was going to believe me when I told them where I'd been and why. Erica had told me that the drugs she supplied to Smith didn't immediately disappear from the bloodstream, but by the time I got home, there would be nothing left. No evidence of being drugged. If I was lucky, Piper would believe me, but the chances of anyone else accepting it as the truth were slim.

Scrubbing my palms over my face, I tried not to stress over it. All I needed to worry about was Piper. Nothing else mattered. She was the only one who counted. As long as I could make this up to her, then everyone else's opinion was pointless.

A pounding on the door had my head snapping toward it. It wasn't a friendly kind of knock, but one a person on a mission used. The cops. A John. Maybe even some local cartel. Fuck, it was Mexico. I had no idea if I was in someone's territory or what. For all I knew, Erica might not have even been on the phone with a client, but some hit man.

The pounding came again. "Open the fucking door!"

At the sound of Barrick's voice, I jumped to my feet and was across the room in a few steps. Swinging it open, I saw Barrick, Jarrett Dawson, and my best friend standing on the other side. Jagger pushed past the others and gave me a back-pounding hug.

"You look like shit," he grumbled.

"Believe me, I feel worse than I look."

As he released me, I spotted Erica standing nervously in the doorway to the kitchen. "Guess I'm not getting that hundred grand now," she muttered to herself.

Barrick and Jarrett filled up the space behind me, their menacing presence overflowing the apartment. "Money is the least of your worries," Jarrett clipped. "What happens to you from here on out depends on how willing you are to assist us."

"With what?" I asked as I watched the blonde's face pale.

"She's going to help us get all the dirt the Feds will need to put Smith away for a long time," Jagger explained. "And if she doesn't help, we'll drop her at the police station and collect the bounty for skipping bail on an involuntary manslaughter charge. She allegedly overdosed a John, who just happened to be a politician."

"How was I supposed to know he had a heart condition?" she said with a huff, clenching her hands together to keep anyone from seeing how badly they trembled. "His wife just wanted me to set him up so she could get a bigger piece of the pie when she divorced him. Her dumb ass signed an airtight prenup. The only way she figured she could get it voided was with a few blackmail photos."

"I don't even give a fuck," I said. "Do what you want with her. I need to get home. Piper is going to kill me. Fuck, fuck, fuck. She's going to kill me, Jags."

"Doubtful," he said with a ghost of a smile. "Who do you think alerted us that you hadn't made it home Saturday night?"

"Yeah, but she's not going to believe any of this." I waved my hand around the room. "They took my phone, man. And Erica said Smith took pictures while I was out. I didn't fuck her, I swear. But Piper isn't going to—"

"Bro, you need to calm down. Piper has been all over this shit. Don't worry about her. Right now, the only person she's raging at is Asher, and if she could get her hands on Smith, he'd be in a hole somewhere. Pretty sure her brother would be in there with him too, from what Shaw told me earlier." He slapped me on the back again. "Come on. Let's let these two get your friend here sorted out. I have coffee and energy drinks in the vehicle. We haven't slept since Piper called me Saturday night, man. You hungry? We stopped for some tacos at a place a few miles from here. I got extra in case you needed to eat."

We sat in the back of the huge SUV, and I scarfed down four tacos before even reaching for one of the energy drinks. The grease and carbs from the food helped settle my stomach, and the caffeine pushed the headache back enough that I could think a little clearer.

"I'm going to kill Smith," I announced, crushing the empty can in my hand.

"Can't let you do that," Jagger said with an apologetic sigh. "We lost track of you after Smith and Asher crossed into Mexico. They turned off their phones and disabled their location so we couldn't track their movements, and we were just wandering around down here, searching for any signs of you or Smith and Asher for hours. Then Asher turned his phone back on and went to see Hymn. From what Shaw and Mia told us, things got really messy after that. Hymn called Piper and let her hear their conversation, and then suddenly, Piper just got up and left everyone sitting in your kitchen. Shaw said she heard Piper beat the fuck out of her brother."

For the first time since waking up that morning, I felt a smile spread across my lips. "That's my girl."

Jagger smirked. "You got yourself a real spitfire." But then he sobered. "Asher and Smith live in the same apartment building. Ash knew Smith would drug women to get them back to his place. That was one of the reasons he went to Smith for help in ruining the wedding. After Piper cracked Asher's head open and beat the shit out of him, she gave him an ultimatum. He could confess everything to their parents himself, and then make sure Smith never had the chance to victimize another woman, or she would go to the cops herself and tell them everything she knew. About both Smith and Asher."

I was stunned by this new piece of information. Piper loved her brother. She was protective of him just as he was of her. "She would have sent him to jail?"

"Dude." Jags looked at me in total disbelief. "She just found out that he'd drugged and kidnapped you to try to ruin the wedding. She didn't know if you were safe or sick or fucking dead. From what everyone said, they heard a crash and thought Piper had killed him. Literally killed him. Do you even understand why she did that?"

A lump filled my throat to the point I couldn't breathe, let alone speak, leaving me with no choice but to shrug in response.

"Because she fucking loves you, dumbass."

"But…" I swallowed hard before continuing. "We had a fight before I left the other night. She was so mad and hurt. I did that. All I do is hurt her."

"Whatever you two were arguing about, I don't think it matters. And even if it does, Piper doesn't seem to care right now. All she wants is for you to get home safe. If you need to fix something, it can wait." He grabbed my shoulder, and I met his gaze. "She loves you," he repeated. "Don't you ever fucking forget that."

CHAPTER 6

Cannon

I didn't have my keys, so I had to knock on the door. My knuckles had barely touched the surface before it swung open, and Piper was throwing herself into my arms with a sob that made my knees weak.

"You're here," she rasped, burying her face in my neck. "You're okay."

I wrapped my arms around her as I moved us into the apartment and kicked the door shut. As the lock clicked, she lifted her head. "You are okay, right?" she demanded as the tears poured down her beautiful face. "No one hurt you?"

"Sugar, the only thing that hurt was being away from you for so long." Holding her in place with one hand, I tangled the other in her hair. "I missed you so damn much, baby."

"Missed you too," she whispered. "I'm sorry. About the argument. About my brother. About not being able to find you sooner. I—"

I couldn't bear to hear her apologize for another thing. None of it was her fault, and it killed me that she thought she needed to say she was sorry. Capturing her lips, I turned so I had her pressed up against the closed door. Holding her, finally kissing her after being away from her for so many days—it had felt like a lifetime since I'd last touched her—the tension finally eased from my muscles, and I melted into her just as she did into me.

Lifting my head, I pressed a tender kiss to her forehead. "I need a shower, and then we can talk. Okay?"

"Can I...join you?" she asked hesitantly.

I tipped her chin up so I could look into her eyes. "You never have to ask me that, Pipes. The answer is always going to be 'Hell yeah, baby.' And if it's not, then you know I've been abducted by aliens and replaced by some tentacled clone."

Her soft giggle eased any lingering sickness I felt in my gut.

With my hands full of her perfect ass, I walked toward our bedroom, only to hear her cell phone going off before I could pass the bed. Biting her lip, she wiggled free, and I reluctantly released her so she could answer it.

"Hello?" I stood there waiting for her to finish the conversation so we could get clean together. But as I watched her, I could see the distress on her face. "I made my decision. If he can't live up to my demands, then I have no problem following through with my promise... Yes. Promise. Threats mean nothing, Mom... I don't care if he's my brother. And how can you even allow him to get away with any of this? Asher is a grown man, not a child. He made adult decisions that have adult consequences. I would think that you and Dad, of all people, would want him to learn from this."

Piper listened for a long moment, her face twisting with disgust and hurt before she laughed dryly. "You know what, here's another promise for you, Mom. If he doesn't do what he said he was going to do, and you support that—if you and Dad both support his pussified decision—then I promise there is no reason for either of my parents to show up at my wedding Saturday. I'll walk myself down the aisle. Make your choice. Force Asher to live up to his responsibilities or lose me. I. Don't. Fucking. Care!"

Breathing hard, she threw the phone back onto the bed and then sank to her knees beside it, pressing her face into the comforter. Her muffled, gut-wrenching sounds hurt me in places I didn't know could feel pain.

"Pipes?" I murmured her name cautiously as I crouched down beside her.

Still crying, she slowly lifted her head and met my gaze for a moment before lowering it back to the bed. "Asher doesn't want to follow through with our agreement. The Feds and the attorney general think he should be held more accountable for his actions. They offered him a deal of six months of probation and six hundred hours of community service. He doesn't want to take the deal, and my mom wants me to change my mind. If I back off, the attorney general won't follow through. But then there would be no proof of the kind of monster Smith is other than the digital evidence Mieke was able to dig up. Which wasn't legally obtained, so it can't be used against him."

Stroking my hand over her hair, I turned her head, willing her to look at me. "I don't care if Smith goes to jail. Actually, I would prefer to take care of him myself." I wanted to put my fist through his face over and over and over again. And then I would bury him in a hole somewhere in the desert. Jarrett had casually told me there were plenty of places I could bury a body where it would never be found.

"I know," she cried. "I know you would, and you deserve your pound of flesh. Deserve to even kill him. But there are so many victims, Cannon. Mieke found at least ten women on the apartment security footage who he brought back to his place. And they were stumbling around when he brought them home with him, and then the next day... Oh God, sometimes several days later, they would be spotted on the same cameras, running from the apartment. They looked scared and disoriented. While Barrick and Jarrett were looking for you, Mieke was able to do facial recognition on some of the women, and Braxton tracked them down. He took a cop buddy and got a few of them to give reports, but without Asher's testimony, it could turn into he-said, she-said bullshit because Mieke hacked the apartment security footage, so it's inadmissible."

"Jarrett and Barrick brought Erica back with them. She's going to testify against Smith about supplying him the drugs and take a plea deal for the case she was hiding in Mexico over. Her testimony against Smith will be enough. Asher doesn't have to—"

"Yes, he does!" Her fist hit the bed. "He tried to take you away from me. He got a kick out of what he did. His attempt to break us up hurt you, but it destroyed me, Cannon. My brother broke my fucking heart. And he deserves everything bad that happens to him from here out."

Dropping to my ass on the floor, I pulled her onto my lap. "I don't want any of this to hurt you more than it already has."

"They are the ones hurting me. Asher. My parents. They're treating him like a misdirected kid, not the grown-ass man he is." She pressed her forehead to my chest. "I can't accept that. I won't."

Her voice broke, and she began to sob again. The sounds destroyed me, but I was helpless to do anything but hold her. I wasn't sure how long I sat there, rubbing her back, just letting her cry. Time was meaningless as I let her get her pain out. But eventually, what seemed like hours later, her phone rang again. She tensed but curled herself against me more. Kissing the top of her head, I blindly reached over my head and fumbled around on the bed until I found her phone.

Seeing it was her mom, I answered it and put it to my ear, knowing Piper would be able to hear it too. "Hello?"

"Cannon," Gabriella greeted in surprise. "How are you doing, honey?"

"I'm currently holding my emotionally distressed fiancée. How the fuck do you think I am?" I gritted out.

She inhaled sharply. "I can hear her crying," she said with regret.

"Look, the past few days have been crazy. I didn't have the full story. Asher didn't tell us everything, and I just realized the extent of his involvement in...all of it."

"He finally told you everything?" I asked skeptically.

"No, Hymn did," she murmured. "What my son told me was a very watered-down version of the events. What with him having to get twelve staples in the back of his scalp after Piper cracked him in the head, I thought everyone was just overreacting. Her temper can be combustible at times, and I thought it was just my kids being kids. But Hymn showed up and told us everything. I'm so sorry Asher had any part in what Smith did to you."

"It was his fucking idea!" I shouted, only to feel Piper flinch. I sucked in a calming breath. Pressing a kiss to the top of her head, I closed my eyes and prayed for patience. "If you're calling, then I'm going to assume that means you're going to make Asher take the deal?"

"He's been given his options," she said, her voice growing hard. "Liam told him to either accept the deal and testify to everything he knows regarding Smith, or we will completely cut him off. As it stands, even if he does take the deal, things have changed for all of us. I can no longer trust my son's judgment. I may never fully trust him again. Liam is... He sees more of himself in our son than he ever hoped to see, and that scares him."

"I'm sorry."

I didn't know what else to say. At one point, I knew my own parents had felt the same way about me. Maybe one day, Asher would win back his parents' trust and respect. But as I knew all too well, it was a long, difficult process. I'd had to put in a lot of hard work and commitment to changing from the asshole I'd been into a better man.

"No, Cannon. Don't you apologize for any of this," she commanded. "None of this is your fault. We've stood behind your relationship with Piper, and when you asked us for our blessing, we gave it wholeheartedly. Asher was the one who had the issues. He's the one who needs to be apologizing."

"You'll excuse me if I don't accept it."

"Absolutely. It's your right not to forgive him. I just... I really need to speak to Piper. Will you try to convince her to take the phone?"

Sniffling, Piper wiped her nose on my shirt. "I'm right here, Mom. I've been listening the entire time."

"My sweet, sweet girl. I'm so sorry. Please understand that I didn't have all the facts. Asher—"

"I heard everything, Mom," she cut in. "What do you want to say?

I'm tired, and I just want to be done with anything that has to do with...him."

"Mistakes were made," Gabriella said sadly. "And I regret everything I said to you earlier. Your dad and I love you so much, Piper. We want to be there for your wedding. Please, honey, please accept my apology and forgive us for not understanding."

Leaning back, she locked her dark eyes with mine, silently asking me what I thought she should do. I pressed a kiss to her brow, letting her know I would respect whatever decision she made. More tears spilled over her lashes, and she clenched her eyes closed. "You and Dad are welcome at the wedding," she said after a long, tense pause. "But I'm not changing my mind about...him. I will never see him again, Mom. Don't ever ask, because if you or Dad do, I'll cut you both out of my life just like him."

"You can't even say his name, Piper," Gabriella whispered in a pained voice. "Or call him your brother."

"He doesn't deserve for his name to be spoken, and he forfeited being my family when he hurt Cannon."

There was a pause on the other end of the receiver before her mom blew out a heavy sigh. "You're right. I won't force the issue on you now or in the future. Do I hope that one day you can put this behind you? Yes. But I will have to learn to accept that our family will be divided from now on."

"Thank you for respecting my boundaries," Piper choked out. "I have to go now, Mom. I haven't slept in days. Now that Cannon is home, I can relax."

"Of course, sweetheart. I'll call you tomorrow." I felt the hesitation, and then, "We love you, Piper. More than anything. Please don't doubt that."

"I-I love you and Dad too," Piper rasped before hanging up.

The phone dropped from her hand to the floor, and she tucked her head under my chin. It was only natural that I wrapped my arms around her and rocked her gently. "Tell me what you need, sugar."

"You," she choked out. "I only need you."

CHAPTER 7

PIPER

As the rest of the week passed, I received daily news on what was happening with Smith...and everyone else. The Feds returned Cannon's phone and wallet back to him after finding it in Smith's apartment. With all the evidence against him, Smith decided to take a deal to avoid a long federal trial. I wasn't sure if that was his choice or if someone had encouraged him to take responsibility for his actions. It wouldn't have surprised me if Aunt Emmie had done something to make it all go away as quickly as possible..

According to Shaw, Mia, and Trinity, other people were getting their comeuppance as well. The deal Mom told me about was going forward, but this Erica person was facing jail time, right along with Smith. Not only for supplying him with the drugs, but also because of the case that had sent her into hiding across the border. However, she wasn't alone. The wife of the politician she'd been hired by was under fire as well. Because her husband died in the commission of a crime she orchestrated, she was being charged with more serious offenses than Erica. But since Erica was testifying against her—as well as Smith—she would get a much more lenient sentence.

None of it made the headlines except Erica and the politician's wife, which I was thankful for. I didn't want to cause Smith's victims more distress, and no one deserved to be in the spotlight over his crimes.

I tried not to focus on what had taken place over the previous weekend—or the many possibilities if Cannon hadn't been found. Instead, I directed all my attention to the upcoming wedding, and I refused to let my mind wander to people who no longer mattered.

Saturday morning, I arrived at the venue with my bridal party, Mom, Aunt Emmie, and Cannon's mother, as well as the wedding planner, Francesca. When we'd first started considering venues for the wedding and reception, the Observatory was at the top of my list.

Once we got the green light for it, Francesca and I were able to plan so much of the event around the theme.

All the way down to my dress and the cake.

Especially the dress.

I was nearly vibrating with excitement for Cannon to see me in it.

While everyone else got ready, I walked through the venue, double-checking all the details with Francesca to ensure they were perfect. After the disaster of the previous weekend, everything about our special day had to be nothing less than flawless or I was sure I'd lose my mind.

"Piper, you have to start getting ready," Mom announced when she found us in the Observatory. "It's going to take forever to get that dress buttoned after your hair and makeup."

Francesca touched my arm with a warm smile. "Go. I've got it from here, I promise. Plus, Cannon and the others just arrived. I need to show him everything before he begins getting ready himself."

"When you see him, tell him I miss him."

"Absolutely. Now, go." She shooed me away, and I followed Mom back to where everyone else was already dressed and perfectly made-up.

Pausing at the entrance to the room, I saw Grier and Love Bug were in their sparkly gray dresses, and I crouched down to greet them. "Hello, little flower girls."

"Daddy said we were going to look like stars," Love Bug informed me. "Are stars pretty?"

"They light up the entire sky," I assured her. "Just like you and Grier will light up the room when you walk down the aisle for me a little later."

"Do you think Banks will say I'm pretty?"

"Of course he will," Trinity said as she placed Avalyn down beside the other two. "You know what, why don't I take you to see your daddy, and we can show him and Banks how pretty you are."

"I wanna come too!" Grier announced.

"Okay. Girls, hold hands with Avalyn. We'll go together."

As they left the room, I straightened to find Violet watching them go with an amused tilt to her lips. "The only thing she talked about all week was seeing Banks. And then last night, she couldn't sleep because she was too excited to see him. Luca is torn between wanting to make her happy...and contemplating murdering the poor boy."

"Now he knows what your dad went through for all those years," Harper said as she walked in, helping my mom carry the huge garment bag that held my dress. "All I'm going to say about this subject is, whatever Luca has to go through with Love Bug and whoever she falls in love with when it comes time, he deserves one hundred percent."

"Piper, get your ass over here," Shaw instructed. "It's going to take time to get your hair right for the veil, and then we have to keep it perfect while getting you into that gigantic dress. I bet it weighs more than you do."

"It's close," Mom said with a laugh as she and Harper hung it up.

Shaw was right when she said it would take a while to do my hair. I was going with the full, heavy curls look. They had to sit just right to pull off the effect of the custom-made veil I'd had created. It was sheer, with tiny diamonds sewn into constellations that would shimmer while we spoke our vows.

Once my makeup was finished, it was time to step into my dress. Mom hadn't been kidding when she said it would take forever to get it buttoned. There were so many buttons that Mom, Aunt Emmie, and Cannon's mom had to take turns when their hands got tired. But as soon as the last one was in place, I turned to face them, and the entire room fell quiet.

"Holy shit," Mia and Shaw whispered in unison.

"That dress..." Violet eyed it with a glitter in her eyes. "Where did you find it?"

"I had it custom-made," I told her as I stroked my hands down the fitted bodice that flared into layer upon layer of tulle that had more diamond constellations throughout.

"Can you get me the information for the designer?" she asked, nibbling on her bottom lip thoughtfully.

"You want a dress like this?" Harper asked curiously.

"Maybe," her daughter said, still assessing my wedding gown contemplatively.

"In that color?" Layla asked, speaking up for the first time since they had taken my dress from the garment bag.

"Not that color, but I know I don't want another white wedding dress."

Layla laughed. "Of course it will be in white. When you marry Luca, like you were always supposed to, you'll be in a traditional gown. As my son deserves."

The tension that filled the room made me uncomfortable—not for myself, but for Violet. We all looked at Luca's mom with narrowed eyes. "She'll wear whatever fucking dress she wants," Harper said between gritted teeth. "It's her dress. You don't have any say in it."

"We'll see," Layla said with a shrug.

"The fuck we will," Harper seethed, but Dallas grabbed her around the waist and turned her to look at me once again.

"This isn't the time," her best friend hissed.

Harper inhaled deeply and slowly released it. Forcing a smile to her face, she reached for my hand. "You look beautiful. My godson is a lucky man."

Dallas let go of her and stepped forward to cup my face in her hands. "It goes without saying that I am thrilled to be gaining you as a daughter today, Piper. Welcome to our family, honey. Axton and I wish you nothing but happiness with our son."

"Thank you," I whispered, trying to control the lump that attempted to clog my throat.

When she stepped back, Mom took her place. "I know this week wasn't quite how you envisioned everything, and I'm so sorry for that. But as I look at my beautiful girl right now, nothing else in the world matters. All I care about is your happiness."

"I am happy, Mom. I never thought this day would come, or that it would be Cannon I shared it with, but once I fell in love with him, there was never anyone else I could see myself sharing my life with."

"He doesn't know how lucky he is."

I carefully shook my head, making an effort not to shift my hair in the slightest. "He knows."

"Yes, he definitely knows," Dallas murmured softly with a smile.

"He's been dreaming of this day for a lot longer than anyone realizes," Violet agreed. "Cannon has made a million mistakes along the way, but he's going to dedicate his life to making up for every single one of them, Piper."

"There's nothing for him to make up for," I assured her. "The past is firmly where it belongs. Where he and I are concerned, there is only right now and our future together."

CHAPTER 8

Cannon

Closing the ring box, I handed it to Jagger, who carefully tucked it into the inside pocket of his black tux jacket. "You lose these rings, and you're dead to me."

My best friend smirked and patted his pocket. "I'm sure I can handle this important mission."

Giving him a stiff nod, I turned back to the mirror and straightened my jacket. Behind me, Trinity appeared with a lint roller, making sure everything was perfect before stepping away. It was nearly time, and with each second that ticked away, my hands began to tremble. So close. Piper would be my wife soon. I just had to be patient for a little longer.

Jagger squeezed my shoulder. "You can do this, bro. You've come this far and not fucked anything up."

"Great pep talk, Jags," Trin said with a sigh. Standing behind me, she met my gaze in the mirror. "That girl loves you so much, she nearly killed her own brother a week ago. Get your shit together, and don't pussy out. Because if you fuck up today, there are about two hundred people in the Observatory waiting to murder you."

My lips twitched at the hardness in her tone. "You scare the hell out of me sometimes, Trin."

"Good." She winked then stepped back. "I have to go take my seat. Jarrett has Avalyn, but she won't sit still for him for long. Remember what I said."

"Are you going to hold me down while they kill me?" I called after her.

"No," she said as she opened the door. "Shaw already called dibs on that. But I'll be getting a few punches in."

As she stepped out of the room, Dad and Liam appeared in the doorway. "It's time, boys."

"Shouldn't you be with Piper?" I asked Liam, nervousness filling me once again.

"They're finishing up with her dress," he said as he crossed the threshold. "I wanted a moment of your time before the ceremony."

Gulping, I nodded and waved him over.

Liam squared his shoulders and met my gaze. "Everything that happened last week—"

"It doesn't matter—"

"It does, son," Liam spoke firmly. "I want to personally express to you how sorry I am for what Asher did. His actions nearly cost you and Piper something that not everyone is lucky enough to experience. All his anger and misguided bullshit sent him down a path that has caused everyone pain. If he had succeeded, this day might not have even taken place. For that, you have my sincere apology. My son has a lot to make up for, but I feel like it should start here, with me. I raised him. Somewhere along the way, I failed him, and in doing so, I failed Piper and even you."

"I can't accept your apology," I told him honestly, and his shoulders drooped. "I can't accept it, because I feel like you have nothing to be sorry for. We all know that I wasn't the best person growing up. I still struggle with not being a jackass most days. But I'm learning, and I'm trying. For Piper's sake, as well as my own. You did nothing wrong, Uncle Liam. Just as my parents did nothing wrong with me. I made bad choices, many of them that ruined occasions and even lives along the way. Asher made his own mistakes. He and only he will have to face the consequences. I wish I could tell you how to fix all this, but the truth is, I have no way to undo the pain he caused. If Piper walked in here right now and asked me to put it all behind us, I would. But she's hell-bent on keeping her brother as far away from our lives as possible. Should she ever change her mind, I'll willingly follow her lead. But until that happens, Asher is dead to both of us."

Liam's throat bobbed, but he nodded his understanding.

"That doesn't mean she wants to cut you and Gabriella out of our lives. You two have always been there for her, for both of your children. Between you and Gabriella, and my own parents, we have great role models for when we have our own babies. Don't beat yourself up, thinking you didn't do a good enough job. You can't control what your adult children do, sir."

"I should go," Liam rasped. "My little girl is waiting for me to walk her down the aisle. But there is one more thing I need to say."

"Sir?"

He cleared his throat roughly before locking eyes with me once more. "Welcome to our family, Cannon. I see how happy you make

Piper, and for that, I'll always be thankful. I know the fuckups you've made in the past, but you shouldn't beat yourself up more than you say I shouldn't beat myself up. The past is the past. And as long as you keep making my girl happy, it will stay there."

"Thank you," I choked out and wrapped my arms around him when he gave me a back-pounding hug. "I promise I'll always do everything within my power to make Piper happy. Always."

After he left, Dad told us it was time. The three of us walked to the Observatory, where Mom and Gabriella were waiting. Since Asher wasn't there, Jags offered Gabriella his arm, while I took Mom's. The four of us walked down the aisle, escorting the two moms to their seats before taking our place beside the officiant.

Piper had blown me away when she'd said she wanted our wedding to be at the Observatory. Even if it hadn't been a possibility, I would have worked something out with Prya to make it happen. This place was my secret sanctuary growing up. The stars had given me a peace that was all my own, something I'd only shared with my mom before bringing Piper here for one of our auctioned dates. That night would always be one of the most amazing moments of my life. Not only had the woman I loved not made light of my secret astronomy passion, but she'd given me a piece of herself that night as well.

Overhead, the stars glowed like diamonds in the sky, while around us, the lights were dimmed, and orchestra music began to play. Hymn was supposed to have been Piper's maid of honor, but after what happened with Asher, Hymn had backed out, much to Piper's disappointment. But my girl understood her friend's reasons. Hymn needed time to get her mind straight after the reality of what Asher was capable of had hit her so hard. She'd gone back to New York earlier in the week, to the apartment she and Piper used to share in the city.

Shaw had stepped up to be Piper's matron of honor, and soon my sister was walking down the aisle toward us. She looked lovely in her long, shimmery gray dress that had a sheer, cape-like train behind her. The black and white roses she carried were a smaller version of the ones I knew Piper would be carrying.

Next came the little flower girls. Love Bug and Grier made my heart melt at the sight of them in their silver dresses that glittered in the ever-dimming lights. The further lowering of the lighting made me frown, however. Francesca hadn't told me that would be happening, but I didn't want to stop the ceremony and demand to know what was going on.

Once the last black and white rose petals hit the floor, Grier ran to my dad, and Love Bug skipped over to her parents. I wasn't surprised to see that Trinity's family was beside Violet and Luca. Banks didn't get very much privacy whenever Love Bug was in the same room. It was kind of cute, maybe a little weird, but I was a bit relieved that Love Bug was so fascinated by Trinity's stepson. For a moment, I'd thought Lyric's eldest son, Ian, was going to have the same connection to Love Bug that Luca had with Violet, and that had freaked me out. Watching it firsthand with Luca and Vi was one thing, but I didn't think I could stand by and watch the same shit play out all over again in the next generation.

The lights were barely bright enough to see Piper and her dad standing at the end of the aisle when the music switched to the Wedding March. The moment my gaze landed on her in that black dress, the air froze in my lungs. "Holy fuck," I wheezed, grabbing hold of Jagger's arm when my knees threatened to give out on me at the breathtaking sight before me.

I saw Piper smirk at me, and then the lights began to fade even more. But as it turned to night inside the Observatory, plastic, battery-operated candles were lifted into the air. Piper's dress was so black that it melted into the darkness around her, but the candles caught the diamonds threaded into the material, and then they actually lit up.

It took me a moment to catch my breath before I realized that the constellation I was seeing was the Messier 50, the Heart-Shaped Cluster, that was located in the Monoceros constellation. With the mixture of blue and yellow stars, I could easily spot the cluster once I knew what I was looking at.

After first bringing Piper to the Observatory, I'd begun teaching her all about astronomy. That she'd included my passion for stars in her wedding dress brought tears to my eyes.

Once she and her dad reached us, Liam placed her hand in mine and bowed his head, whispering a prayer I couldn't hear before straightening his shoulders and meeting my gaze. "Remember what I said."

"Always, sir," I choked out.

He gave a stiff nod and stepped back. Shaw moved forward, and Piper turned her back to me, so she could pass over her bouquet. When she did, I saw the candle lights flicker over the constellation on her veil, and the reins broke on the control I held over my emotions.

Cygnus had been stitched into the sheer material with tiny diamonds. The same constellation I'd shown her the night I'd brought her to this very room and stargazed with her, after telling her I loved her for what was possibly the first time—at least aloud. Before that,

327

I'd told her I loved her at least a thousand times in my head.

When Piper turned back to take my hands, she saw that I was no longer in control, and she gave me a wobbly smile. "I love you, jerkface," she whispered.

"I love you, sugar," I rasped.

The officiant cleared his throat, and I tugged Piper closer. There, beneath the stars, with nothing but candles and her dress glowing around us, we promised to love each other forever.

EPILOGUE

DALLAS

"You're doing great, Piper," I assured my daughter-in-law as I sat at her feet, keeping my voice calm as she glared at everyone in the room. Thankfully, it was only my son, Gabriella, and the other nurses, who would take over care of the baby once my grandchild was delivered.

It took five years before Piper and Cannon decided to become parents. None of us had pushed them to start having children, and if I was being honest, I hadn't really cared if Cannon reproduced or not. I had my hands full with Shaw's girls, and I wasn't all that sure that Cannon had what it took to be a parent. He'd grown up a lot over the years, even more so once he'd married Piper, which I was eternally grateful, but Axton and I had worried if he would make a good father.

I was sure Piper had her misgivings about her husband and parenthood as well, which was why they had waited so long. But then it was taken out of their hands when Piper's birth control had failed.

Despite my misgivings, Cannon had become a completely different man during Piper's pregnancy. He'd matured more with each passing week, until I didn't even recognize the boy I'd raised—in nothing but good ways. Over the years, I'd grown bored with the kids no longer being at home and Axton more or less retired. I'd focused on my own career again and transitioned from a registered nurse to a nurse practitioner with a specialty in gynecology. Which had worked out great, because as soon as Piper found out she was pregnant, she hadn't wanted anyone but me to see to her care.

"We are almost there, honey. I promise."

"You said that an hour ago," Piper was exhausted and closed her eyes between contractions.

I rubbed her lower leg. "I know, but our girl is being stubborn and taking her sweet time coming out."

"Big surprise," she snorted "You fucking Cages."

"Aw, it's so cute that you think it's the Cage DNA making her so stubborn," I teased. "It definitely wouldn't be a mixture of Bradshaw and Moreitti bloodlines."

"Nope," Gabriella said dryly. "Not a drop of my DNA has an ounce of stubbornness in it."

The two of us locked eyes and burst out laughing. After a moment, Piper giggled too. Meanwhile, Cannon wiped at Piper's sweating brow, his fingers shaking so badly my heart squeezed with love for my son.

"Ahh—," Piper suddenly screamed as the next contraction hit hard. "Fuu—ck!"

I switched into nurse mode, and the next few minutes passed in a blur of encouraging Piper to push. Once little Danica's head was out, I commanded Piper to stop pushing.

"You're insane!" my daughter-in-law shrieked. "It hurts. It hurts. It hurts."

Ignoring her was hard, but I had more important matters to deal with. Like clearing out Danica's airway. "Push again," I urged, and Piper screamed as the baby's wide shoulders ripped her, but the moment I guided the baby out and laid her on Piper's chest, she no longer noticed the pain. While she and Cannon were distracted with meeting their screaming bundle of joy, I got to work delivering the afterbirth and then stitching up the mean tear Danica had gifted her momma.

"How is it going down there?" Gabriella asked quietly.

"She's looking good," I assured. "Our girl did a fabulous job, Nonna."

"Thanks to you," she whispered emotionally.

I glanced up after securing the last stitch. Pulling off one of my gloves, I grasped her hand. "Because of *us*," I corrected. "We did this together, Gabriella. Piper had a great support team today."

Our gazes went to our children, who were both cooing at our beautiful granddaughter. She had a head full of dark hair, but even now, we could see the dimple in at least one cheek. Cannon stroked his thumb over Danica's cheek as a tear spilled onto the top of her head.

"Hello, my beautiful little morning star," he murmured. "Mommy and Daddy are so happy you're here, Danica."

"I think..." Gabriella swallowed hard. "I think they're going to do great as parents."

"Yeah," I agreed around the lump in my throat. "I think they will be just fine."

GABRIELLA

anica hid behind Liam and Axton, looking up at her father with tear-filled blue eyes. "But I want to go to the party, Daddy!"

"There will be boys there!" Cannon growled.

"There are boys at school too, but you make me go there every day!" she shouted back. With her grandfathers acting as a shield, she was all kinds of confident in the face of her father's wrath.

"At school, there are teachers and other adults who will keep little assholes from doing things to my baby girl that will get them buried in the backyard."

"Our backyard is the Pacific Ocean," Danica said with a huff.

"Exactly," Cannon said with a predatory grin.

"You're so unfair! All my friends are going, and you won't let me go for even half an hour. I just want to hang out with my friends, and you're acting like I'm going to get pregnant! News flash, Daddy. Mom already put me on the pill, so it's not as if, even if I were having sex, I would actually get pregnant..." Her voice trailed off as both Liam and Axton slowly turned to look down at her.

Now three dominating rockers were glowering at my poor little granddaughter, and I couldn't let them torment her any longer.

"You three are being ridiculous," I told them as I pushed past my husband to put an arm around Danica's shoulders. Like her dad, she was tall. I felt like a shrimp in the room of giants. Even when Piper was there, I was still the shortest person in the room. "Danica should be allowed to go to this party."

"Brie," Liam grumbled.

"No way," Axton seconded.

"I'll kill any prick who touches her!"

"Why are you so convinced I'm into guys?" Danica huffed. "Maybe I like girls."

"You think I don't already know your sexual orientation, Danica?" Cannon asked softly. "If you were into girls, I would support you one hundred percent. No matter your preferences, I fully stand behind you. But you're not a lesbian, are you? Or bi? Or pan?"

She crossed her arms over her chest. "But if I were a lesbian or bi or pan, you would give me more room to breathe! Why would me having a girlfriend be more acceptable than me wanting to go to a party to see the boy I like?"

"Because..." He trailed off without a ready argument. He turned to his father and father-in-law. "Help?"

Liam threw his hands in the air. "She's got you by the balls there, boy. I'm out."

"Let's let her go." Axton gave in after a brief hesitation. "Just for a little while."

"Are you insane?" Cannon bellowed at his dad.

"What are you so scared of son?" Ax asked with a smirk. "That she'll meet a boy who is just like you?"

"Fuck yeah, that's what I'm scared of. It gives me night sweats."

Laughing, the older men slapped him on the back, and I gave Danica a little squeeze. "How about I help you get ready for this party?"

She watched as her grandfathers ribbed her dad then nodded. "I just want to have fun, Nonna. I'm not going to have sex or anything."

"Of course you're not, my sweet girl. There's nothing wrong with wanting to go out with your friends. Your dad is just scared."

Danica frowned as we walked upstairs to her bedroom. "What's there to be scared of?"

"When you have children, you're scared of everything, my dearest heart." I stroked my hand over her long, dark hair, my heart aching as I looked down at her. She looked so much like Piper, except for her eyes and those damned dimples. Looking at her was torture at times, especially now that she was getting older, and her personality turned more and more into my daughter.

I was putting the finishing touches on Danica's makeup when Piper appeared in the doorway. "I heard there was a lot of commotion here today."

"Nonna had my back," Danica said with a bright smile for her mom.

"Yeah, she's kick-ass like that." Piper pulled Danica into her arms, being careful not to muss her. "Have fun but be home by midnight."

"A curfew?" she whined. "That's so lame, Mom."

"You're fifteen. We can renegotiate terms and conditions as you get older." Leaning back, she gave her child the look. "Or you can change into your pajamas and come downstairs and have a movie marathon with your dad and me."

"Fine," Danica grumbled. "I'll be home by midnight."

"Great. Go on, your ride just pulled up, and I doubt you want your dad or either of your grandfathers to scare them away."

Yelping, she kissed my cheek then her mom's, before running down the stairs. I watched her go, remembering Piper at that age. It wasn't that I thought Cannon shouldn't be worried. Fuck, there were plenty of reasons for him to be scared shitless. But I trusted Danica to make the right choices. Her parents had done a great job of raising her, and she had a good head on her shoulders.

My one and only grandchild knew what she was doing.

Piper and Cannon might feel like they didn't have a clue at times, but from where I was standing, I could see what amazing parents they'd become.

~THE END~

AUTHOR NOTE

This collection had a format. Seven Stories, eight chapters, and an epilogue was supposedd to tie things into perfect Happily Ever Afters, From Mia to Violet I attempted to weave each tight tale, but Violet, being Violet, would not be silenced. She would not stick to the format, no matter how hard I tried to reel her in. So I made the decision to let her talk, and the others wanted more as well. Not wanting to rush them or lessen them in any way I've released the first seven for you, here, and have planned to expand the tales over the next year, with Violet to be the first Novella to follow this beautiful collection. Then Mia, and so on. Each will have some expansion and fill my release schedule until they and I are happy.

My duty is to you, my readers and to the characters you adore. Turn the page and see a taste of what Violet has planned for us all. Until I see you again,

HOPELESSLY DEVOTED TO

VIOLET

Violet: OMG! I have huge news.

Shaw: You finally set a wedding date!

Violet: No! Why would you think that?

Shaw: Oh, I don't know, Vi. Maybe because you have been engaged for FREAKING YEARS now. Set a date already!

Violet: It hasn't been that long since Luca proposed...

Violet: OMG, it's been flipping years!

Shaw: Yup.

Shaw: I think it's time you started making plans.

Violet: It's not that easy...

Shaw: What's not easy about it?

Shaw: You set a date. Buy a dress. Invite people.

Shaw: And you definitely have to have a traditional wedding this time, or Uncle Shane will shit a brick. No running off to Vegas like with...Remington.

Shaw: Ohhhhh.

Violet: Yeah. Oh.

Violet: Marrying Luca means letting go of the last part I have of Remi.

Shaw: But not marrying Luca is hurting LUCA.

Violet: How am I hurting Luca?!?!?!

Shaw: He's dying to make you his wife. But you're holding onto the ghost of your dead husband. Let him go, Vi. Be happy. You have a family with Luca now. Just like Remington wanted for you and Love Bug.

Violet: You're right. Okay. I'll set a date.

Violet: But that wasn't why I texted you.

Shaw: What's up?

Violet: I'm pregnant...

About The Author

Terri Anne Browning is a Wall Street Journal and USA TODAY bestselling author. She writes contemporary romance featuring rockers, bikers, and mafiosos--but mostly about the strong female characters who rule what has become known as the Rocker Universe.

Terri Anne lives in Virginia with her husband, their three demons--err, children-- a Frenchie named Ciri and a chatty as-sin bird named Raven.

Follow Terri on Social Media.

Amazon
https://amzn.to/3AigpYQ
TikTok
https://www.tiktok.com/@terriannebrowning
Facebook
https://www.facebook.com/terrianne.browning
Instagram
https://www.instagram.com/terriannebrowning/
BookBub
https://www.bookbub.com/authors/terri-anne-browning
Goodreads
https://www.goodreads.com/author/show/6906208.Terri_Anne_Browni
ng
Newsletter
https://dashboard.mailerlite.com/forms/89334/59752074343089173/sha
re

The Rocker Universe Reading Order

ALSO BY, TERRI ANNE BROWNING

Made in the USA
Las Vegas, NV
29 January 2025

17195397R00190